Praise for IN THE COMPANY OF WHALES

"Rooted in working-class realism, the novel captures the texture of Carla's daily life . . . The orcas act as a catalyst rather than a metaphor, pulling together a small, unlikely group and nudging Carla toward connection she would rather avoid . . . The steady pacing reflects the shrinking window of survival for the whales and Carla alike.
"A thoughtful, humane novel about responsibility, healing, and the nerve it takes to step in—an absolute stunner."
— The Prairies Book Review

"Judy Taylor delivers a stunning debut of one woman's transformation, hidden desires, and sacrifice to protect what she loves. Set against the quiet pull of a small coastal town and a stranded pod of whales, the novel embraces women across generations, the power of connecting to the natural world, and belief in second chances. This story will stay with you long after the final heart-stopping pages."
— Sharon Wishnow, author of The Pelican Tide

"An ultimately uplifting tale about how connections between humans and nature are forged.
"Replete with discoveries that will lend nicely to book club discussions . . . Its realistic scenarios and smooth intersections between the choices of remaining a loner or growing into new opportunities make for an evocative, compelling read."
— D. Donovan, Sr. Reviewer, Midwest Book Review

IN THE COMPANY OF WHALES

IN THE COMPANY OF WHALES

a novel

Judy M. Taylor

Loon City Press
Minneapolis, Minnesota

For Curt

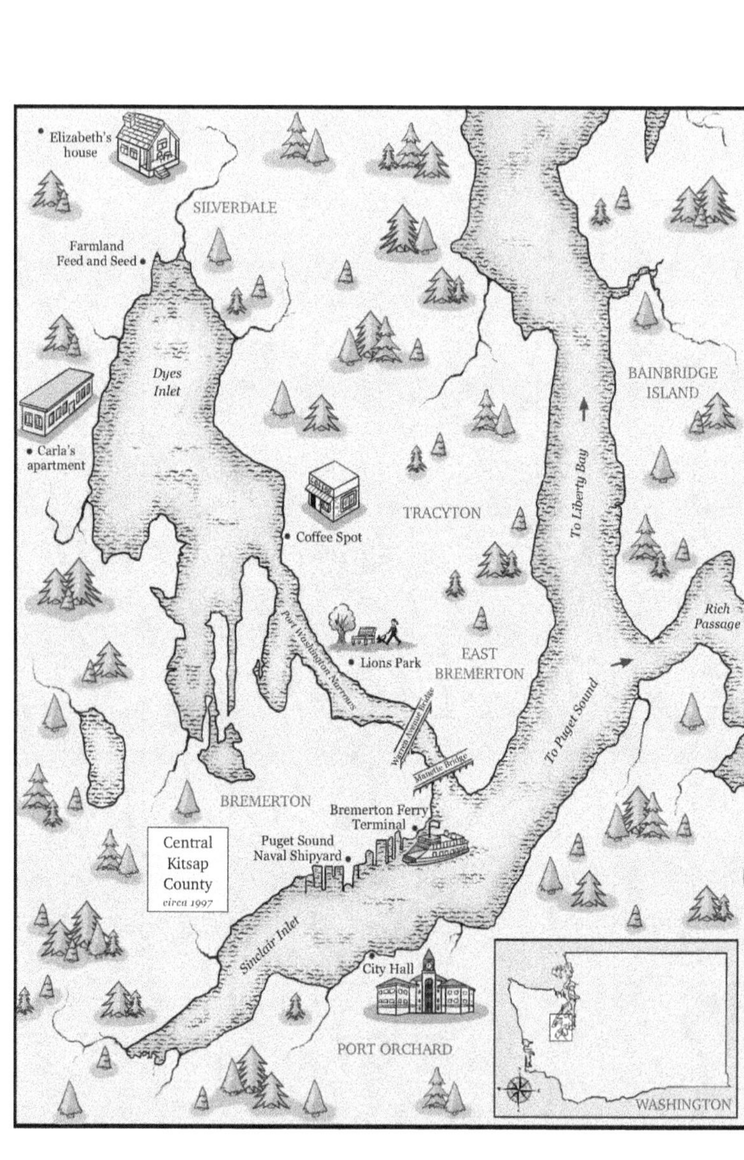

Elizabeth's house
SILVERDALE
Farmland Feed and Seed
Dyes Inlet
Carla's apartment
BAINBRIDGE ISLAND
Coffee Spot
TRACYTON
To Liberty Bay
Rich Passage
Port Washington Narrows
Lions Park
EAST BREMERTON
To Puget Sound
Warren Avenue Bridge
Manette Bridge
BREMERTON
Bremerton Ferry Terminal
Central Kitsap County
circa 1997
Puget Sound Naval Shipyard
Sinclair Inlet
City Hall
PORT ORCHARD
WASHINGTON

"Any glimpse into the life of an animal quickens our own and makes
it so much the larger and better in every way."
— John Miur

"The least movement is of importance to all nature. The entire ocean
is affected by a pebble."
— Blaise Pascal

Chapter 1

Carla drew her red felt-tip pen from behind her left ear, then paused to reposition one of the half-dozen earrings running along its upper edge. The dangly one with the silver skull was forever getting caught on things. This time it was tangled in her hair.

"Hell," she muttered and shook it free.

She spread the local newspaper on the worn lunch counter and flipped to the classified ads on the last page, but her mind was elsewhere. How the fuck did her mom get her phone number? Carla had been sound asleep and didn't hear the phone ring during the night, but the little red light on her answering machine was blinking when she got up for work. The sound of heavy traffic on the recording nearly drowned out her mom's voice, and her speech was slurred. No surprise there. Carla listened to the message twice, but all she could make out was her own name and the word *sorry*. With a shaking finger she erased the message.

After the last time, Carla persuaded her roommate to change their number and take her name off the account. But he moved out two months ago and switched the name on the account from his to hers. That must be how her mom found her. Besides not having money to pay the phone bill, now Carla had another reason to cancel it.

A muffled weather update on the radio in the kitchen slipped under the swinging door and into the quiet coffee shop. The drizzle that had started as she drove to work that morning was whipping itself into a steady downpour.

The Coffee Spot stood by itself at the end of a quiet residential street with scattered homes facing the water. The shop was a stone's throw from the shore of Dyes Inlet, and the large windows gave customers a view of the boat launch and fishing pier. Summer visitors came in for coffee or an early breakfast before a day on the water. The rest of the year, it served the locals who lived and worked in the little town of Tracyton.

Carla's secondhand Doc Martens squashed her toes as she rose on tiptoe and leaned both elbows on the counter.

"Found," she read aloud. "Black leather wallet. No ID. Baby photo. Bremerton Ferry Terminal."

Noah, the first of her early regulars, looked up, his attention divided between Carla and the fluted paper he was struggling to remove from his muffin. Under the brim of his baseball cap, his eyelids drooped. He worked the nightshift and would be heading home to bed soon. Days were short this time of year in the Pacific Northwest, and the sun wouldn't be up for another half hour. Dyes Inlet was barely visible through the streaky windows behind him.

"Seriously?" Noah bit into the muffin with a soft grunt of pleasure, set it next to his hot chocolate, and licked his lips. The jacket of his security guard uniform hung from his bony shoulders. No matter how many muffins Carla served him, the kid would never fill out his clothes.

"Right?" Toss the damn thing and get on with your life. They weren't living in fucking Mayberry. On the other hand, losing a nice wallet sucked. Nice that someone bothered to put an ad in the paper, though. Carla brushed her shaggy bangs away from her forehead. She drew a finger down the page, her short, black-polished nail scraping the paper lightly.

"Lost. Key ring. Poulsbo Cinema." She removed a pair of scissors from her apron pocket and turned back the cuffs of her heavy plaid shirt, revealing a portion of the tattoo on her forearm. She clipped both ads, her scissors making a sound like chewing, and tacked them to the crowded bulletin board next to the wall phone, muttering, "C'mon, Tony. Work your magic."

"Who's Tony?" Noah asked.

Carla ignored him. He didn't need to know about her superstitious devotion to Saint Anthony, the patron saint of lost things.

Roommate Wanted ads were next. Was she the only person in this crappy town desperate to split rent? If it didn't cost so much, she'd place an ad herself. She'd tried posting flyers at the supermarket and the library, the kind with her phone number written on little tear-off tabs at the bottom. Pathetic. Three people took her number, but not one bothered to call. If she didn't find a roommate by the end of the month, she'd have to add *get evicted* to her list of things to do. That kind of shit she didn't need. Along with her mom popping up again after all this time.

Searching in the pocket of her white baker's apron, Carla's fingers found her worry stone. She rubbed the smooth indentation with her thumb and scanned the Help Wanted ads with her pen poised and ready, always on the lookout for a better job. Nothing. At least nothing she was qualified to do. A high school diploma, a couple of years playing bass in a grunge band, and ten years working in this dive didn't amount to much. Besides, fall was the worst time of year to look for work in Kitsap County, Washington. Business was slow everywhere. It would be months before Carla saw a new face at the shop now that the summer tourists were gone. Past ten in the morning, she'd be lucky to see anyone at all.

Stewart slipped in and stopped on the doormat, clutching his thermos to his chest. He took his coffee to go but rarely said a word or came in any further than the doorway. Carla carried a steaming carafe across the cramped dining room to meet him.

Noah looked on, shaking his head. "Dude, you should find a drive-through. Carla don't need—"

"Don't listen to him. You know I don't mind." She filled his thermos and gave him a wink. His bright hamster eyes darted around, avoiding her gaze. "Besides, my coffee is better than anyone's. Am I right?" She leaned in and nudged him lightly with her elbow. He stiffened and loudly drew in his breath, recoiling from her touch.

"My bad," said Carla, stepping back. She knew how to make it up to him. "Wait here a sec."

A moment later, she returned with a small paper bag. "Just a couple cookies. See you tomorrow?"

The door opened again and Delbert lumbered in, bringing the cold damp air with him. Stewart paid for his coffee and disappeared.

"Morning, Carla." Delbert heaved his large body onto a stool at the counter and shrugged out of his jacket. He slapped his bucket hat against his thigh, sending droplets of rainwater flying, before settling it back onto his bald head. "Nasty out there."

Carla glanced at the wet floor and then toward the two large picture windows, one on either side of the door. Rain sheeted off the glass, obscuring the dark water and the opposite shore.

She refolded the newspaper. Her daily horoscope and Dear Abby would have to wait. After quickly twisting her pale shoulder-length hair into a messy bun and securing it with her pen, she set two thick white saucers on the counter in front of Delbert, placed a cup in each, and then filled the cups from the glass pot. He added sugar to his and stirred, slopping coffee over the rim and into the saucer. Carla sipped from the other and watched as drips fell onto the clean white countertop when he lifted his cup to blow off the steam. She pushed the napkin dispenser closer to him, but he missed the hint. He pulled one out and used it to dry the lenses of his giant Clark Kent glasses.

"Muffin? They're banana-nut," Carla said. Mondays were always banana-nut.

Delbert set his cup in the saucer with a loud rattle. "Where's Sylvia?" He checked his watch.

"Called in sick." What a shock. Hungover more likely.

The shop owner's daughter took the early serving shift before heading to class. She loved to drop the word *college* into every conversation, even though she was only taking courses in cosmetology at the community college, paid for by dear old daddy. And she always called the shabby coffee shop a café. Completely annoying.

Carla's job description included everything back-of-house, hidden away in the kitchen, while Sylvia, with her dimpled smile and teenage shape, waited on customers out front. It was the way Carla liked it. But when Sylvia was late or didn't show up at all, Carla stepped in, doing both jobs but getting paid for only one. At least she got tips.

Carla slid the newspaper across to Delbert. He smiled his thanks and watched as she topped off his cup and collected the two singles he set on the counter. His money smelled like stale tobacco, a smell that always reminded her of her old life with the band. Some days she wasn't sure which she missed more, the cigarettes or the music. She stepped over to the cash register, dying for a smoke.

Behind the kitchen door, drums thumped the opening riff of Alice in Chains' "Angry Chair." Carla jabbed at the register keys to the beat, jerking her head and mouthing the words. She was supposed to keep the cheap plastic radio tuned to the country station. The manager insisted on it. Since he was never around, she played her favorite punk station KNDD. If she kept the volume low enough, the customers could hardly hear it anyway.

"No, that's for you, darling," Delbert said with a wink as Carla set his change next to his saucer. With one hand she swept the coins, a dime and four pennies, into the other.

Someday she'd get her act together and do something with her life, something that mattered, far away from this dump, somewhere her mom couldn't find her. Then Carla would never have to bake another muffin or pour another cup of coffee for chump change. But first she needed to save enough cash for a fresh start. Fat chance. Crappy wages and even crappier tips, when she got them at all. And no one to split the rent with again. Leaving this job and this town was more out of reach than ever.

She pocketed her tip and pushed through the swinging door, hard enough to send it sailing. It hit the wall with a bang. In the kitchen she turned up the volume, and her voice joined Layne Staley's monotone growl. The menacing thrum of his six-string and the crash and clatter of Carla's baking pans, alive with looming catastrophe, were the perfect soundtrack for her mood.

The sun dropped to a level just below the clouds and knife-thin rays sliced through the evergreens. Carla turned west toward home. Light reflected off the wet pavement making her eyes ache. She flipped the visor down, but instead of blocking the sun, it came loose and dangled in her face.

"Dammit." She yanked it off and tossed it into the back seat. "You're a piece of crap, Dot."

The used Datsun wagon was the first thing Carla bought when she had saved enough money working at the Coffee Spot. With no roommate she could barely afford gas anymore, let alone the oil Dot guzzled and the new filter she desperately needed. Now the old girl rattled and squeaked around the north end of Dyes Inlet toward Carla's apartment on the other side. At least the heater worked. And the radio. She switched it on, and Iggy Pop's voice crackled to life.

She'd had a dog named Iggy. For a short time anyway. Iggy was Gordon's big goofball of a mutt, long dead by now. Carla's throat squeezed tight, and she coughed to push the sadness away. Gordon took everything that mattered when he split, including Iggy. On rainy days she imagined she could smell the happy stink of his wet fur.

Thoughts of Iggy took their usual path to Gordon. Memories of him had worn a deep groove in her mind, like a turntable going around and around with the needle stuck in the same place. The band, the music, the plans they made. And the love. Yes, Gordon took everything that mattered, and it all fell apart. How her life turned out since then was her own fault. She didn't blame Gordon. Not entirely.

Carla turned the volume up. The song, "I Wanna Be Your Dog," was the one that had given Gordon the idea to name his dog Iggy. She was still barking out the lyrics at the top of her voice when she pulled into the strip mall and parked near the entrance to the Shop 'n Save.

She grabbed six cans of Friskies for Grandma Moses. Hugging them to her chest in the pasta aisle, she did a quick calculation. She didn't have enough for that jumbo jar of marinara sauce to ease her growling stomach. Her apartment manager was going to pay her to clean a vacant unit next Sunday. Cash. The spaghetti could wait. She grabbed a box of off-brand instant mac and cheese.

At the checkout, while the cashier totaled her purchases, Carla looked at the neat rows of cigarettes behind the counter. Red, blue, and gold packs, 100s, menthols, lights. Packs with camels and packs with Indians.

"Anything else?" the cashier asked, following Carla's gaze to the cigarette case.

"No. That's it. Just these." Carla waved her hand toward the end of the moving conveyor belt where a can of cat food had turned on its side and rolled and rolled. "And this." Carla pulled a pack of spearmint gum from the rack. Princess Diana stared at her from the cover of *People* magazine. What happened to her was awful, but Carla had no interest in celebrity gossip. She tossed the gum onto the belt, and her gaze drifted back to the magazine rack. The front page of the *New York Times* had a photograph of Clinton. Above it the headline read: "President Plans Energy Savings In a Moderate Step on Warming." Plenty of news stories about the planet heating up lately. Global warming. She shivered in her denim jacket and pulled her knit beanie down further over her ears. A little warming would be welcome right about now.

"Five eighty-two." The cashier's voice was hard.

Carla opened her wallet and pulled out the day's tips. She handed three singles across to the cashier and spilled the jingling change from her coin purse into the woman's hands. If Carla had fifty cents to spare, she could buy a copy of the newspaper. The topic of global warming interested and terrified her, but she could read it for free at the library.

The cashier sucked her teeth as she counted the nickels and pennies so Carla would understand how annoyed she was. "That's only five-twenty."

Shit. In the pocket of her jeans Carla found the forgotten fourteen cents Delbert gave her along with a few chunks of walnuts she had snagged from the kitchen floor. Banana-nut-muffin-Monday meant a fresh supply of treats for Ghost, the albino squirrel she could sometimes coax to eat from her hand.

She dug into the bottom of her ratty canvas shoulder bag while the man behind her in line muttered something. Impatience wasn't the only reason he pushed his cart to the next checkout. Carla was used to small-minded townies sneering at her secondhand clothes, backing away when they caught sight of the large safety pin piercing her right earlobe or the Minor Threat tattoo on her forearm. Whatever.

She fished out two more nickels and a penny. Still short. There was money in her bank account, but that was for rent.

"Take one of these off." Carla retrieved the rolling can of savory salmon and handed it to the woman. Sorry Mosey. She could ask her boss for a raise, but he would never give her one. There was barely enough business to keep the lights on.

Outside, the Datsun coughed and shook when Carla turned the key in the ignition. The engine caught and chugged like a freight train, going slower and slower until it stopped. She tried again, twisting the key harder. *Moron.* As if that was going to help.

Carla pressed her forehead to the steering wheel. "Come on, Dot, you steaming heap of..." Another turn of the key and more gas, more chugging. It refused to turn over. She floored the accelerator and held it down, begging, "Come on, come on," through clenched teeth.

Flooded. *Shit.* The last time this happened was in front of the Coffee Spot after she'd locked up for the day. Noah had showed up minutes before Carla turned the sign to CLOSED at 3:00 for a slice of pie and a to-go cocoa. It was his day off, so he'd missed his usual morning stop on his way home from work. He was still in the parking lot finishing his drink when Carla got into her car.

"Open the hood for a while," he had called to her, poking his head out the window of his Jeep. "Let the extra gas evaporate. If it still doesn't start, take out the spark plugs and clean 'em. I can do it for you if you want."

"Got it. Thanks!" Carla waved him on. She waited until he pulled onto the road before getting out of her car to open the hood. Twenty minutes later she tried again, but it still wouldn't start, so she walked to the gas station up the street where she bought a socket wrench and a wire brush.

And where were these handy tools now? *Asshat.* More than a mile away. In her toolbox under the bathroom sink. A smart person would have kept them in the car.

Noah might come to help if she called from the pay phone in front of the supermarket, but she didn't have his number. Or a quarter. Besides, he would be asleep at this time of day. The only number she knew was Alex's, and he'd moved to Tacoma.

Still leaning her head on the steering wheel, Carla whispered, "Please, please, please start," and gently turned the key. The engine mocked her with its rhythmic, rapid whine. She pressed her lips into a tight line and let her breath out through her nose. *Well, shit.* She gathered her things, slammed the door shut, and headed home on foot.

Chapter 2

Tuesday, October 21, 1997

"Lost," Carla read aloud from the scrap she'd snipped from the *Sun*, Kitsap County's only daily paper. The whole newspaper was only ever eight pages long. Reading the articles and letters to the editor had taken all of twenty minutes, followed by a skim through the classifieds. No ads for roommates or new jobs were posted. Dear Abby had advice about coping with toddlers, and Carla's daily horoscope warned, "Handle money carefully and avoid unnecessary expenses." *Duh.*

She had avoided the expense of a tow truck and a repair bill by putting her limited knowledge of auto mechanics to use the day before. With a rag and a couple of tools, she dealt with her flooded engine and drove Dot home from the store before dark. Luckily the old girl started like a charm again that morning. All Carla wanted was one dull, ordinary day without car trouble or money problems.

Before she could read the rest, Sylvia swanned in, late as usual. "Hiya," she called, shaking water from her umbrella in the doorway.

All eyes were on her, a shiny object in the drab space. Her long blonde ponytail swung over the shoulder of her bubble-gum pink sweater as she pulled an apron on over her head and tied it around her tiny waist. Watching her, Carla felt tired. She was only thirty-three, but she felt ancient, from a different time. A different planet.

Carla turned toward the kitchen, glad to be free to reclaim her solitude.

"Wait," Delbert said to her. "What's lost?"

"Just one ad today." She read from the clipping in her hand: "Golden retriever mix, male. Beloved pet."

Sylvia brought a muffin to Noah's table and set it in front of him. "I had a cat. A kitten. But she ran away." She sighed dramatically and pushed out her lower lip in a pout so precious she must practice in front of a mirror.

Noah slurped mini marshmallows from his spoon. "Do you think there's some alternate universe full of lost pets?"

Carla forgave him for experiencing life as if it were a comic book. The kid was barely out of his teens.

Nothing could break Carla's heart like an animal in trouble. She pinned the ad about the missing dog onto the bulletin board and pulled off one of the other scraps of paper.

"Someone found this guy's cockatiel." Carla dropped the clipping into the trash and dusted off her palms in a well-that-problem's-solved gesture. She didn't search for the lost items she read about in the ads, but she suspected people's luck in finding their things was because of her relationship with whatever magical spirit inhabited her little plastic statue of Saint Anthony.

"How do you even know that?" asked Delbert.

She didn't want to explain how she dialed the numbers in the ads after a few weeks to ask if they found their wallets or cats or backpacks. Delbert would only tell her it was none of her business. He wasn't wrong, but Carla liked mysteries to be solved and stories to wrap up neatly. Happily ever after.

Delbert took a noisy swallow of coffee and smacked his lips. "You're obsessed with those ads."

"It's not an obsession, it's a *hobby*."

He set his cup down, raised his thick hands in resignation, and changed the subject. "You see the police blotter yesterday? Basket of dirty laundry stolen out of the back of somebody's pickup."

Carla snorted. Life in a small town. She lifted the nearly empty pot from the warming station to refill her cup before heading to the kitchen but offered it to Delbert instead. He covered his cup with his hand and gave his head a small shake, glancing in Sylvia's direction through his thick lenses.

"I got you, Delbert. Just made a fresh pot," Sylvia said, smiling and stepping between them. She giggled and leaned forward over the counter, poised to fill his cup. No tip for Carla then.

"Guess I could have one more before I clock in," Delbert said, moving his hand away. "I shouldn't, but I'll say yes just to watch you pour, honey." He drew his big palm over his cheek with a sound like sandpaper.

Carla lingered near the bulletin board. There were pans to wash, a pie to slice, and a rhubarb coffee cake in the oven. Nothing urgent. She pretended to read the scraps of paper pinned there, rearranging a few and listening to their banter. Delbert was three times Sylvia's age. And what a suck-up that girl was. Anything for a tip. She was pretty enough to be a model, with her silky hair and perfect teeth. Every day a new hairstyle, full makeup, a different outfit. Watching those two was sickening, but looking away wasn't easy.

She didn't like most people. Observing the same people in the shop day after day was like watching animals in a zoo—so predictable.

"Don't you get bored selling stamps all day?" Sylvia was saying.

"Working for the US Postal Service is a noble occupation." Delbert sat up a little taller. "But I'll admit, being a window clerk is dull compared to being a carrier. If my knee hadn't given out, I'd still have my route. So pouring coffee's a big thrill?"

"This is temporary. You get that, right? Because, like, just getting by isn't enough for me." Sylvia combed her fingers through her glossy ponytail. "I'm going to open my own beauty salon someday."

She'd been saying that since Carla met her. Even back then, as a stuck-up fourth grader, Sylvia had her whole life figured out. And now that she was in college, she made sure to rub that in Carla's face every chance she got. With daddy's help her dreams were sure to become reality. *Must be nice to have parents that give a shit. Some people are born lucky.*

"People gotta pay the bills, honey. Not everyone can afford to go to school and start their own business." Delbert turned his cup around in the saucer, frowning. "I had dreams, too, when I was your age."

So did Carla once upon a time. Dreams of a little house of her own, a dog, money in the bank. She stabbed a thumbtack into the corkboard. Even hoping for a better life was something she couldn't afford.

"My instructor says I have a gift. He says I could turn any ugly duckling into a swan. Even Carla." Sylvia giggled, and Carla turned to glare at her. "Kidding! But with a makeover—hair, makeup, clothes—you'd be *super* cute."

Carla stifled a snort. Is that who she was now? A doormat in need of a makeover? True, she dressed the same as she did a decade ago, but she didn't give a fuck. Punks were anti-fashion. That was the point.

"Anyway, I deserve better," Sylvia continued. "I mean, this job is fine for *some* people, but for someone like me with style and talent, well, doing *this* my whole life would be a waste. No offense." When Carla rolled her eyes, Sylvia bristled. "Don't you have some dishes to wash or something?"

Carla turned back to the newspaper clippings, ignoring Sylvia's dismissal. Her cheeks were hot. Did that spoiled brat think this job was Carla's chosen career? That working in this shithole wasn't a waste for anyone unlucky enough to get stuck here? The insults she could hurl at Sylvia! They threatened to fly out of her mouth. She clamped her lips together. She needed this job. It mattered. It was the only thing keeping a roof over her head. If she lashed out, Sylvia would run and tattle to daddy and her brother, Todd. Now there was a useless waste of space. Todd got the big bucks to manage the coffee shop, but he rarely showed his face. Most of what he was responsible for doing landed in Carla's lap.

A faded clipping caught her eye. How long ago had she stuck it there? Found. Two wheelchairs. Lions Park fishing pier. A gag? The ad had disturbed her when she first cut it from the paper, and it disturbed her now. She'd tried to follow up several times with no luck. If it wasn't a bad joke, something tragic must have happened. Double murder? Murder suicide? Double suicide? There was no good answer. She pulled it off and threw it away. Dark thoughts crept into the edges of her mind.

A timer sounded in the kitchen. She took a step, moving as if under water, and leaned against the swinging door. It felt heavy. Or maybe she didn't have the strength anymore. The strength to deal with Sylvia's ego or the drudgery of her job. To go on living hand to mouth, putting one foot in front of the other day after day without ever getting anywhere. The strength to cope with the terrible things people did to one another.

Alone in the warm kitchen, Carla did what she always did to chase away her inner demons. She turned her favorite Seattle radio station louder, even knowing Sylvia would make her change it. Here on the other side of Puget Sound, most people listened to the local station that played country music around the clock. They'd never even heard of grunge.

Growling out lyrics with Meat Puppets and pausing to play air guitar, Carla moved about the small space. When she shouldered the kitchen door open again a few minutes later, she carried a pumpkin pie.

"Um, Carla?" Sylvia stopped her, raising her voice over the radio. "That doesn't sound like KBAM? Is it KBAM? 'Cause Todd says—"

"I know what Todd says." Carla spoke carefully through gritted teeth. It took all her willpower not to push the pie into the girl's smug face. The last thing she needed was to get fired. Delbert watched them from his stool, smirking.

"You'll change the station, or what?" Sylvia twirled a strand of yellow hair around her finger. With her blush-pink cheeks and false eyelashes, she looked like a doll. She even smelled like a baby, some stupid baby powder perfume.

"If you'll let me past so I can put—"

"What?" Sylvia screeched, scrunching her face. "I can't hear you!"

Fucking drama queen. Carla looked past Sylvia. Noah was at the register, fiddling with his car keys. To Sylvia, she said, "Your customer is waiting."

Sylvia's voice changed to cotton candy. "Be right with you, Noah."

"You're busy. I'll just leave it here," he said, placing what he owed on the counter before dropping a handful of coins into Sylvia's tip jar.

"I'm going on break," Sylvia shouted, pressing her hands to her ears. "I've got a headache. And you'd better have that radio on KBAM when I get back." She followed Noah out into the drizzle.

Carla slid the pie into the display case, tucked Noah's money into the till, and pushed the cash drawer shut. Taking deep, slow breaths, she closed her eyes and let the music get inside her. The heavy drum riff shook something loose. She would put Princess Sylvia's station on, but she needed this a moment longer.

Carla rearranged the last three chocolate chip muffins on a glass platter. She was calmer now, whispering the lyrics to "Nearly Lost You." She didn't have a pretty voice, but it was interesting. Deep and rough, perfect for grunge. This band, the Screaming Trees, was more hard rock than grunge, but she liked their sound.

The DJ cut in, talking over Gary Lee Conner's awesome reverb at the end of the song. The next song on the playlist was one she knew well. Keeping the rhythm with her rag, Carla wiped crumbs off the counter, mostly missing her cupped hand and sending them onto the linoleum floor at her feet. She raised her eyes to the ceiling and let out a short sigh before reaching for a broom.

"Do you mind turning that shit off?" Delbert yelled. "How you can listen to that noise."

"Kurt Cobain. Nirvana," she shouted and held the broom handle up to mime screaming the next line into it like it was a microphone. "It's distortion. Heard them do this song in Olympia a few years ago. Amazing. 'No More Wars.' Benefit show."

"Commies, hippies, and druggies."

Carla gave the swinging door a hard push. She changed the station and lowered the volume, and a moment later floated back into the dining room along with the silky voice of Mel Tormé.

"Better?"

Delbert grimaced. "Not really, no."

This was the game they played. She complained about country music, and he whined about her punk rock, so she would put on the oldies station instead. The songs her mother used to sing. Carla remembered the words to every one.

Stewart came in and stomped his wet sneakers on the mat. Sylvia slipped in behind him, returning from her break, her hair and face damp with rain. She headed toward the restroom, calling, "Hiya, Stew," over her shoulder.

Singing along to "Blue Moon," Carla glided out from behind the counter, her coffeepot in one hand, a clean bar rag waving in the other, and danced slowly between the empty tables toward Stewart. He stood with his back to the windows, shoulders hunched, shifting his weight, waiting for Carla to fill his thermos and take his two dollars, the tip smaller every year as the price of the coffee increased.

Delbert swiveled around, propped his elbows behind him on the counter, and hooked the heels of his heavy work shoes on the bottom rung of his stool. He grinned and winked when she caught him watching her.

As Carla poured, Stewart stared at the dirty rainwater collecting around his feet.

"Don't worry. You can treat it like a doormat because, well"—Carla pointed at the puddle and chuckled—"it's a doormat."

One corner of Stewart's mouth twitched upward into a lopsided smile as he handed her his two crumpled bills.

Carla set the coffeepot back on the warmer and tucked the rag into her apron pocket. At the register, she flattened the damp bills by drawing them tight against the edge of the Formica countertop. She offered up the change, but Stewart shook his head.

"Thanks," she called to the drooping man who was carefully tightening the lid on his thermos. Another fourteen-cent tip. Hooray.

Sylvia bounced into the room, retying her apron over her snug pink sweater. She sashayed behind the counter. "Hey, Stew. Did Carla tell you about the dentures?"

"Yeah, some old lady lost her false teeth and put an ad in the paper," Delbert said. "Guess who found 'em?" Stewart gave a half shrug. Letting the suspense build for a moment, Delbert pulled a pack of Winstons from his shirt pocket and peered at the last remaining cigarette. He frowned and put it away again.

Carla slid her hand into the back pocket of her jeans for her gum. God. She could kill for a smoke.

"Librarian!" Delbert said and slapped his knee, wincing a little.

"Probably with the joke books. You know, like those windup chattering teeth." Sylvia giggled and sidled over to the end of the counter to collect Delbert's empty cup.

Carla unwrapped a stick of gum. She folded it into her mouth but then froze, staring in Stewart's direction. "What the hell is *that*?"

Stewart's hand flew to his upper lip where he brushed his fingertips over the new dark stubble.

"I think it's going to be a mustache," Delbert said. "Give it some time, right, Stew?"

"No, *that*." Carla pointed past Stewart to the windows behind him. She rushed close to the glass, fogging it with her warm breath. Her gaze bypassed the street below the shop, the pebbled shore, the mossy boat ramp, and the deserted pier. Through the mist in the half-light beginning to brighten the sky over the inlet, beyond the small fishing boats moored near the shore, she saw it. A black fin slicing the water.

Carla shouted, "There! See it? A shark!"

"No way," Delbert said, and he and Sylvia rushed to stand next to her. They all cupped their hands around their eyes to cut the reflections from the lighted room. Even Stewart padded over on cat feet to join them. They stayed like that for a moment, pressed against the cold window, watching the shimmering inlet.

Delbert broke the spell. "Nothing. You're losin' it, Carla." He waddled back to his stool, shaking his head. "A shark," he scoffed.

Stewart slipped out, the door closing behind him, and Sylvia went back to collect Delbert's dishes. Carla still peered through the glass. After a moment she gave the smeared window a wipe with her rag.

"There *was* something," she said under her breath.

Not a single customer came into the Coffee Spot after eleven when Sylvia left for class, but Carla kept busy. She checked the stock and ordered parchment paper, coffee filters, and napkins, something Todd should have done a week ago. She set out an old pie tin full of fresh water next to the back steps, along with some chunks of leftover banana from the day before. What the feral cats didn't eat, the raccoons would. She scanned the branches overhead for Ghost, her white squirrel, before scattering the walnut bits on the ground near the trees.

Wednesdays' muffins were blueberry. With the radio blasting, she mixed the batter and put the bowl in the fridge for morning. Baking was no thrill, but Carla was good at it, and she preferred working alone. She liked being in the kitchen with her music where no one expected her to be cheerful or chatty.

She loaded the dishwasher one last time and reset the dining room for the next day, refilling napkin holders and laying out fresh paper placemats printed with the Chinese zodiac. Mr. Wilson, the owner of the Coffee Spot, got them cheap when the chow mein place went belly-up. Between tasks Carla glanced at the inlet. She was determined to see that fin again if only to prove to herself she was right.

At three she locked the door and flipped the sign in the window from OPEN to CLOSED. After mopping the dingy linoleum from front door to back, she hung her apron on a hook in the kitchen and pulled on her slouchy gray beanie, shoving her hair under it.

The untouched pumpkin pie called to her from behind the glass of the bakery case. At least she wouldn't starve when she ran out of money for groceries. She removed a slice for herself and put the rest in the fridge. No reason to rush home to her empty apartment. Grandma Moses was the only one there. As much as Carla loved her, the cat never seemed excited to see Carla. She thought again of the lost dog. Poor thing. Maybe he was home safe by now.

When the floor was mostly dry, she carried her plate to the table by the window. Noah's table. Across the inlet, a light mist hung in the trees. She could identify them all. Towering ponderosa pines and grand firs stood on the high bluffs, and she picked out some shorter broadleaf evergreens—madrone and holly trees—hiding the few low buildings along the shoreline. The trees closest to the water's edge were reflected in its stillness. She marveled at the colors, all green but in shades from palest silver-sage to nearly black, more beautiful and varied than anything she remembered from her childhood in Milwaukee.

One of her few happy memories from that time was being taken by a foster parent to get her first library card. She borrowed illustrated books about animals and flowers, devouring the photographs and detailed drawings of foxes and dahlias, wolves and peonies. With colored pencils, she made drawings of her favorites to give to her teachers. Later, when she was a sullen teen, the library became a place to hide, her nose deep in books about venomous snakes and poisonous plants. Tracyton didn't have a public library, but the one in Bremerton had a large collection of field guides of local flora and fauna, which Carla borrowed over and over.

She chewed a forkful of pie and let her gaze wander from the trees to the water, the surface like a sheet of corrugated metal the color of an old nickel. A green fishing boat bobbed near the center, and in the distance, a cluster of sailboats glided back and forth near the mouth of the Port Washington Narrows, the channel that connected Dyes Inlet to the rest of Puget Sound. She followed the flight of a gull soaring overhead until she lost it against the white sail of a boat off Windy Point. Strangely the boats near the Narrows all had black sails. Not a popular color. She turned back for another look, but they were gone. How could so many boats disappear?

One by one, the sails popped into view again. With a gasp she jumped to her feet, nearly toppling her chair. They weren't sails at all. They were fins! Big black fins. What the hell were sharks doing in Dyes Inlet? A whole bunch of them. Would they be a flock? a pack? a school?

She stared unblinking as one of the great creatures pushed its back higher out of the water and rolled, revealing its impossibly white belly before disappearing again into the dark water of the inlet.

"Killer whales?"

Carla flew out of the shop. She ran across the empty parking lot and Katherine Street, then wobbled over the wet stones near the water. At the end of the narrow wooden pier, she stopped, her breath coming fast and hard. She gripped the railing and scanned right to left over the water. Where had they gone? The water of the inlet rippled gently. Only the green fishing boat disturbed its placid surface. Not a fish, and certainly not a killer whale. She was alone.

The cold air smelled of damp and salt with undercurrents of the low-tide stink of rotting fish. Carla shivered and wrapped her arms around herself, wishing she had taken time to grab her jacket. Gulls and Canada geese called out around her. The birds, the sound of water licking the docks' pilings, and wind moving through the trees masked the sound of distant traffic. From the end of the pier with her back to the Coffee Spot, the world was a wild place, a place where it didn't feel strange to be alone, where it didn't matter if she was broke. Her gaze circled the inlet. Carla had been seeing but not appreciating this body of water since she arrived so long ago. Looking at it now, knowing what swam under the surface, was like seeing it for the first time.

Small splashes to the north drew her attention as one slick black fin after another poked out of the water. One, two, three. She tried to count them, but they were in constant motion. Four, five. Someone in the fishing boat stood and pointed toward the gliding fins.

The whales swam closer, circling directly in front of Carla. Her mouth fell open, and she sank, landing hard on the dock. Pulling her knees to her chest she watched, amazed, as orcas rolled and dived and splashed, churning the water into foam with their flippers and huge tails. She sat, unaware of time, as the creatures played like giant children, throwing their bodies into the air with abandon.

If the single fin she had seen that morning belonged to one of these animals, these killer whales, then they had been swimming out there all day while the residents of this little town went on about their lives as if nothing had changed. Delbert weighed packages. Noah slept. Stewart drove his truck full of office supplies all around Kitsap Peninsula. Sylvia poured coffee, and Carla filled muffin tins.

But something was changing. She sensed it in the tips of her fingers and the soles of her feet. She felt a change in the air she breathed, and she heard it in the voices of the gulls. Even rooted there to the dock, Carla swam with the orcas, her body weightless and her heart joyful.

Someone was running on the pier. As if she'd startled awake from a dream, she grasped for a recollection of who and where she was. Her vision was blurred, and she swiped at eyes wet with unshed tears.

A man in a black windbreaker hurried toward her, training a pair of binoculars on the water as he jogged. Behind him people were climbing out of cars and standing on the shore, some walked toward the pier, shouting, and pointing at the water. Carla was no longer alone. She wasn't ready to share her whales with the rest of the world.

The man with the binoculars stopped a few feet from Carla but didn't acknowledge her. She sized him up. He looked to be around her age, thirty-something, judging by the tiny crinkles at the corners of his eyes as he squinted into the binoculars. His hair was dark and long, pulled back smoothly into a ponytail at the nape of his neck. Not bad. His jeans fit nicely too.

"Hey," she said, and the man jumped.

With one hand pressed to his chest to quiet his startled heart, the man lowered his binoculars and gave her a small nod. A splash directed their focus back on the inlet, where an expanding ring of ripples revealed where a creature had been.

Kids spilled out of a van near the boat ramp, and car doors slammed. A noisy, jostling crowd gathered around Ponytail and Carla, who was standing now, at the end of the pier. The whales flopped and rolled for the awed onlookers, but after a few minutes the water became still again.

"Show's over," said a woman to Carla's right. She was wearing a floppy yellow rain hat with a brim that bounced up and down as she spoke.

"They aren't gone," Ponytail said quietly. He let his binoculars hang by their strap around his neck, but he continued to stare at the water.

"How do you know?" asked Yellow Hat.

"They're feeding," Ponytail said. He pointed to a flock of seagulls circling and crying overhead. "Drawing some attention."

"I've never seen killer whales here before," a man chimed in from the back of the crowd.

"Got off course." Ponytail addressed the group, gradually increasing the volume of his voice. "They came in from Puget Sound and swam up the Narrows following a chum salmon run."

"Big fish eat the little fish. That's how the world works," Yellow Hat said.

"Actually, whales are mammals, not fish." Ponytail smiled pleasantly at the woman. He explained the difference, looking at the people on the pier one by one, making eye contact and cracking corny jokes. Christ. This guy sounded like Carla's high school biology teacher. Where do people get that kind of confidence? As he spoke, he carefully screwed a cap onto each lens of his binoculars. When he was finished, he gave Carla a quick smile before edging back through the crowd toward the shore. There was something about him that put her off. And something that pulled her in.

Chapter 3

In the coffee shop the next morning, Carla picked up a copy of the paper and rubbed her eyes to clear them. Between her worries last night about the lost dog and her excitement about the orcas, it had been hard to quiet her thoughts and fall asleep.

The front page was dominated by a huge color photograph of a small boat in Dyes Inlet surrounded by black fins. She read every word of the article below it. A smaller photo followed with the caption, "Scientists from the Center for Whale Research prepare for an orca encounter." The image showed a group standing on the deck of a boat. Carla recognized Ponytail. She blinked and moved on to the classifieds. The ad about the missing Golden retriever mix was still there and below it was a new one. Delbert stirred his coffee as she read it aloud.

"Found. Large brown dog. Male. Call Farmland Pets and Feed." She let this information tumble around in her head while she fingered the spiky earrings that pierced the upper curve of her ear, rotating them one by one. She pulled her scissors from the pocket of her apron and read the notice again. She passed that feed store on Silverdale Way every day, twice, coming and going. She looked at the first ad. Golden retriever mix. Beloved pet. Last seen Sunday near Silverdale and Lowell.

Today was going to be a lucky day. She could feel it. Carla's lips moved as she ran silently through her incantation. *Saint Anthony, grant that I may find what has been lost.* She lifted the receiver from the rotary wall phone behind the lunch counter. All she had to do was call the guy who lost his dog and tell him about the guy at the feed store who found one. Could be a match.

Carla waited, counting. Six...seven...eight rings. No answer or answering machine. What was wrong with people? If she were missing a dog, she'd scour the ads daily to see if he had turned up. And she sure as hell wouldn't miss a call until he was home. Twelve...thirteen. Not such a lucky day after all. She slammed the receiver back into its cradle.

"Sheesh," Noah yelped. He dabbed spilled cocoa from his chin and the front of his shirt with a napkin. "Scared the shit out of me. What's up with you?" He stood to leave and started toward the cash register, struggling to get the zipper of his uniform jacket to catch.

Carla wrestled the newspaper closed, smoothed the front page, and pushed it across to Delbert.

"What the heck?" His hand halted on its way to the sugar dispenser.

Noah stepped closer. "Whoa." His raised eyebrows disappeared into the curls hanging over his forehead. "Where's that at?"

"Right. Out. There." Carla pointed toward the large windows and the dark world beyond.

"There's sharks out there? For real? I thought you were crazy." Delbert pushed his hat back on his head and gave his forehead a scratch. He turned back and squinted through his smudged glasses at the headline. "Whale of a sight," he read aloud. "So...whales then?"

"Bingo," Carla said. "Here. See for yourself." She flipped the paper over to the article below the fold.

Delbert settled his glasses lower on his potato of a nose and bent close. "Listen to this. The guy who wrote this thinks he's a poet." He cleared his throat and read, his tone mocking the flowery language, "In the silvery darkness of early morning, a large black shadow passed beneath the Manette Bridge. Close behind it, more and more sleek shapes glided along Port Washington Narrows and under the Warren Avenue Bridge, making their way along the waterway until it opened out into Dyes Inlet."

"How many?" Noah asked.

Delbert skimmed the page. "Says here the last time orcas were seen in the inlet was 1962, and that time there was only a couple." He reached for his coffee, sipped it, and grimaced. "A warmup, please, Carla." She emptied the pot into his cup as he continued. "Looks like they followed the salmon up the Narrows from Puget Sound." Delbert studied the article for a moment and then looked at Noah, his mouth falling open. "They think there's at least twenty."

"For real? In this little place?" Noah walked to the rain-spattered windows, but it was still too dark to see anything. "Twenty. They must be stacked on top of each other like cordwood."

At the coffee machine with her back to the men, Carla spooned grounds into a fresh filter and wondered if it was selfish to hope the whales would stick around for a while so she could get another look. The heavy coffee tin slipped from her hand and hit the floor with a thud, scattering grounds across the linoleum. Carla froze, staring at the mess. No one spoke.

"Hiya!" Sylvia breezed into the shop. "Sorry I'm late." She stiffened, eyes darting from face to face. "Who died?"

"Mr. Coffee," Delbert said.

Following his gaze, Sylvia bounced to the counter and leaned over it. "That's gonna come out of your paycheck. Daddy won't be happy." She grabbed the broom and thrust it at Carla.

How much would that mistake cost her? Carla scowled and swept while Delbert filled Sylvia in on the whale news.

"The paper says they probably headed back the way they came, through the Narrows. It's the only way out. Came for the salmon just like tourists, and then off they went." Delbert swallowed the last of his coffee and belched loudly, then placed two singles next to his empty cup. "Or maybe they stayed for breakfast."

Noah paid Sylvia at the register and zipped his jacket to his chin. "No worries," he held his hands out, palms forward, as if quieting a restless mob. "If those whales need help, our Carla here will come to the rescue. Just like she does for every stray in the county."

"Save. The. Whales!" Delbert stood and chanted, punctuating each word with a punch to the air. "Save. The. Whales!"

He kept up his loud refrain until he and Noah had stepped out into the drizzle and the door closed behind them. Sylvia disappeared into the restroom, and the coffee shop was quiet.

Carla propped the broom in a corner. She didn't know the first thing about whales. Pets wandering off was one thing. But whales? She shrugged and whispered, "Saint Anthony, grant that I may find..." Her voice trailed off, and she looked again at the front-page photo before pushing it aside. "Wild animals can't get lost, for God's sake."

She wiped the counter, making slow circles with her rag and humming "The Stray Cat Strut."

That afternoon, Carla sat at the empty coffee shop's counter and tapped the rhythm of the guitar solo on the radio. For the hundredth time, she studied the photo on the front page. Killer whales. Why did people call them that? Were they already gone? There'd been no sign of them all day. Everything outside was still. No cars passed along the shore below the coffee shop. The pier, where she'd sat the day before, was empty. Itching with curiosity, she moved closer to the windows.

If they were still in the inlet, why weren't their fins popping up anywhere? Why weren't they playing like they did yesterday? Was something wrong? Her pulse pounded in her ears as she scanned the water once more, slowly from north to south, searching like a parent for a lost child. Like a lover. Her warm breath fogged the glass, and she wiped it with the sleeve of her flannel shirt before turning away. The whales didn't need her help, but there was a dog waiting at the feed store who did.

"Okay, Tony," she said aloud, laying the two tiny newspaper clippings on the counter side by side. "Let's get a little hocus-pocus going here."

Carla didn't believe in God or prayer and never had. Her superstitious attachment to Saint Anthony began when she was six years old. That angry little girl *did* believe in magic. She wanted desperately to make a wish and have it come true.

"What do you have there?" the social worker had asked. They were driving toward the foster home du jour after a supervised visit with her mother. Little Carla stared through the windshield at nothing, silently miserable.

Carla lifted the little plastic statue from her lap to show her. "Mommy gave me a Jesus." A rare gift. Carla set it on the dashboard where she could inspect the little man in the green bathrobe with a large gold coin around his neck.

"That's Saint Anthony. If you lose something, he'll help you find it." The prayer the woman recited was long and had lots of words Carla didn't understand, but one line stayed with her.

Now she lifted the receiver to try the dog's owner again, saying, "Saint Anthony, grant that I may find what has been lost."

As she stood listening to the phone ring and ring, Carla copied the number onto the back of her hand with a red felt-tipped pen. She'd call the number, the one for the feed store, and give them this number. Let *them* be responsible for contacting the dog's owner. She didn't need to be the middleman. Carla disconnected the call and dialed the second number, Farmland Pets and Feed. The line was busy.

Crap. For a day that had started out feeling lucky, things hadn't turned out very well. Carla wrote the feed store number under the first one. She could try again from home. She picked up the tiny ads and gave the counter a final wipe. Closing time.

In the kitchen, she hung her apron on a hook and turned off the radio. With one hand on the light switch, she ran through her mental checklist as her gaze marched around her workspace: pans scrubbed, floor mopped, maple pecan muffin batter chilling, trash out, pan of water under the steps refreshed for the animals, back door locked.

A line of cars snaked north following the curve of Dyes Inlet. Traffic was never this heavy. An accident? She could turn around and go home the other way, taking the Warren Avenue Bridge over the Narrows, but that route was longer. From the look of the traffic heading in that direction it wouldn't be any better. Carla switched radio stations hoping to find out what was going on.

Up ahead where the road crossed Barker Creek, three cars had pulled over onto the dirt shoulder. People spilled out into the road, darting between cars and running toward the water. Through the trees along the shore Carla could make out some movement below the guard rail. Whatever was happening, she wanted to see it. She parked and hurried to where a small crowd had gathered above the mouth of the creek.

From where she stood looking down from the high bluff, she counted seven whales frolicking. *Frolicking.* A word she'd probably never used before was the only word that could describe what they were doing. They burst through the surface, dove with tails in the air, rolled and splashed, churning the murky water of the estuary into a froth. The air vibrated with the slap of fins and tails.

Shouts and whoops from the onlookers around her rose and fell as if they were watching fireworks, like they were at Sea World. Carla wished they'd shut up, but nothing, not even the light rain that tap-tapped on her beanie and the shoulders of her denim jacket dampened the joy she felt at that moment. And joy had been in short supply lately. When was the last time she felt like this? She wrapped her arms tightly around herself to hold the feeling as long as she could.

A few boats moved into view, getting closer to the action. They were taking a huge risk, but she envied those people. What a thrill it would be to get so near, to see the whales' faces— their teeth, their eyes—then to feel the spray when they shot into the air, and to ride the swells, rocking and pitching over the waves created when the whales' huge bodies landed again.

These unexpected visitors were a gift. A blessing—another word she would never say aloud or even think, because until that moment she wasn't sure what it meant. Watching the orcas with their perfectly streamlined shapes, their smooth skin gleaming black on top and brilliant white underneath, Carla got it. Emotion filled her heart and spilled over, tears mixing with the raindrops on her cheeks. She lifted her chin until she was staring straight up into the sky. She closed her eyes and let the rain wash her face clean.

Looking down again at the water, she saw a single whale swimming away toward the south, its tall fin slicing the surface. The rest of the orcas turned and followed one by one. *Not yet*, she wanted to shout. *Stay a little longer.* Soon the water was still again, and the kayaks and fishing boats drifted away. The people around her fell back, returning to their cars and pulling out into the stream of vehicles, back into the ordinary world of commuting or picking up the kids from school, leaving Carla with the familiar feeling of being left behind. Her joy melted away.

Time slipped by as she stood at the guard rail, breathing the cool damp air and staring at the muddy water near the shore where the whales had been. Why did everything good have to be temporary?

Dot shuddered to life on the first try, and Carla sat waiting for a break in the traffic as rain pounded on her windshield. When she reached to turn on the wipers, she saw the red numbers on her hand. The dog.

*   *   *

Lights blazed from the windows of Farmland Pets and Feed. Carla's tires crunched onto the gravel lot, and she pulled alongside a pickup parked in front of the low building. An older couple sat in the cab while a young guy in a slicker loaded the bed with hay. She opened her window a crack.

"You guys find a dog?" she called. The man gestured to the store and continued pulling a bale over the tailgate.

Carla parked, and her soggy boots beat a rhythm across the wooden floorboards of the front porch and into the cluttered and dusty space. A heavy man stood behind the counter. She repeated her question.

"A fella picked up a stray and left it here yesterday. Said he was just passing through. I put my grandson in charge of feeding it and whatnot." He lifted his chin toward his right.

A teenage boy with a face full of pimples peered at Carla over a pallet piled with sacks of chicken feed. The kid didn't look capable of caring for a pet rock. He ducked out of sight.

"Why?" the big man asked. "You lose one?"

She opened her mouth to speak, to say why she had come, but closed it again, suddenly wary.

The boy moved closer, fiddling with a display of horse tack near the counter while he looked Carla up and down. She had seen reactions like his before. The slight scowl, eyes pinched almost shut as he took in the threadbare denim jacket, her black Dead Kennedys concert T-shirt, her ears with their collection of piercings visible below the cuff of her beanie, and her heavy black eyeliner that had smeared in the rain.

She gave him the once-over too, chewing her gum in a slow, exaggerated way. Scrawny kid in dirty overalls and a greasy baseball cap. She scowled back and fought the urge to yell *Boo!* and scare him back into whatever hole he crawled out of. No need. The kid took a step back and knocked over a rack of cat toys.

"Clay!" the man shouted. He rolled his eyes and gazed at the low ceiling, muttering, "God help me." To Clay he said, "I'll take care of that mess. You'll just screw it up. Take this girl out back and show her the stray."

Without a word Clay shuffled away. Carla followed him out the back door and into the rain.

The dog was behind the store, locked in a cage meant for a couple of rabbits or chickens. How could anyone leave an animal out in this weather, trapped in a cage? The heat of her anger rose from belly to cheeks. The dog growled and bared his teeth as Clay came closer, but when Carla squatted next to the cage, he whined and wriggled, shaking the rusty wire pen. The top was too low for him to stand, so he army-crawled until his body pressed against the side.

"Hey, boy. Whatcha doing in there?" Carla stooped and put her fingers through the bars, scratching his wet fur. His tail twitched to life. Something about Carla drew animals to her. It had always been that way. She was drawn to them, too, especially the ones in trouble.

Carla stood and looked squarely into the boy's ugly face. She avoided situations that required her to stand up to people, but this was different. This wasn't about her. "Let him out."

Clay released a complicated latch. The dog sprang out and took off before Carla could grab him. In the waning light he raced toward the parking lot in front of the building. Toward the busy road. *Shit.* Now that he was free, he was on the run. Carla panicked. She might just have lost the dog again, someone else's dog. She started after him, but a second later, he reappeared, galloping around the other side of the store with his ears pinned back and his tongue flapping comically in the corner of his grinning mouth. He jumped and bowed at Carla's feet and was off again for another lap.

"Good boy," she said, when she finally captured him. She wrapped her arms around his soggy neck and held him close, humming low and shushing him until he quieted. "Thanks," she called after Clay, who was already halfway to the door. "Thanks for nothing, jackhole," she said under her breath. The dog gave a hard shake, and Carla said, "Come on, boy. Let's go home."

Once the engine was running, Carla turned the heat to full blast. The dog settled himself on the back seat, circling a few times and leaving muddy pawprints everywhere, panting hard after his wild run.

"You're making a mess." She smiled. A wet dog was the nicest thing to happen to old Dot for a while.

The dog's tail thumped a response, and he rested his chin on his front paws, studying Carla. First one eyebrow, then the other rose and fell the way Iggy's used to move when he wanted to soften her heart. It always worked. Carla reached back between the seats and let him sniff her hand. She rubbed his ears. His coat was shorter than other retrievers she had seen, and his face was mostly black. He had the golden eyebrows and wide muzzle of a Rottweiler but the furry ears of a retriever.

"Are you the right dog?"

He cocked his head at her question. It hadn't occurred to her until that minute that this might not be the lost dog in the ad after all. All she'd wanted to do was give somebody the dog owner's phone number. Now she had a dog in her car. Whatever happened next didn't matter.

There was no way she could have driven away and left him at the feed store with those assholes.

"What do I do now?"

Her wild impulses usually ended this way. Carla sat in the car outside the feed store considering her options, accompanied by the whir of the heater, the rattle of the engine, and the ping of rain on the hood. The windows fogged up, and a strong smell of wet fur and dog breath pervaded the car.

The dog pound was out, obviously. She could bring him home, take care of him until she reached his owner. Simple. How long could that take? A day? Two, tops. But keeping him in her apartment overnight was going to be complicated. Grandma Moses, Alex's cat, wouldn't be happy about sharing her space. Carla didn't have dog food or a leash. The backyard was fenced, but she would have to be careful not to be seen in the yard by her neighbors. The landlord had a no-dogs policy, and some nosy jerk would rat her out. If she couldn't reach the dog's owner tonight, then the poor dog would be alone all day while she was at work.

Shit. I didn't think this through. She turned on the wipers and the radio and pulled onto Silverdale Way.

"Should I call in sick tomorrow?" She glanced at the dog in the rearview mirror. He raised his head at the sound of her voice.

Mr. Wilson paid her for any unused sick days at the end of the year, so taking a day off was a sacrifice she couldn't afford even with the extra thirty bucks she would make Sunday for cleaning the empty unit in her building. No, the dog would be fine on his own, right? At least he'd be better off than he was at the feed store. She'd come home to check on him during her break. It would take longer than she was allowed, but Sylvia could cover for her. Carla had done it for her often enough. A solid plan.

Cheered by the dog's presence, she sang along with the radio until she was home. She parked on the dead-end street in front of the single-story apartment building, designed with zero imagination and built with the cheapest materials. The cinder-block walls made it look more like a prison or a bomb shelter than a place to live. Perfectly symmetrical and perfectly hideous, the building held identical apartments laid out like an egg carton, six facing the street and six facing the alley behind. The dog, alert now that the engine had stopped, stood and shook himself.

"This is home." Carla turned to look at him. He scratched behind one ear, making satisfied grunts. "Stay here a minute. I need to deal with Grandma Moses."

Inside, coiled on the couch, was the sleek Siamese who'd been left behind temporarily, along with Alex's furniture, his bike, and some boxes. Carla picked her up and carried her toward the bedroom, humming and nuzzling the fur behind her ear. Her plan was to settle her in the bedroom and close the door, but the cat had other ideas. She melted out of Carla's grasp like quicksilver and streaked under the couch, where she stayed out of reach, glowering at Carla with her round blue eyes.

"Hide if you want, silly. I was trying to do you a favor." She went back to the car.

Holding tightly to the scruff of his neck, she led the big dog into the entryway of the building. She stopped to get her mail, and he sat at her feet without being told. "Good boy." She kissed the top of his damp head.

"Mosey," she sang softly, cracking open the door to her apartment. "I have a surprise for you."

An angry, hissing yowl was followed by a loud crash. Carla opened the door wide, but the dog didn't move. A small spindly table was on its side, and next to it were the shattered remains of a ceramic bowl, still shivering on the kitchen floor. The bowl, a nasty neon yellow thing shaped like a daisy, couldn't have met a more fitting end. Alex's mom once tried her hand at painting pottery and gave the bowl to Alex. Goofy gift for a guy, which might explain why he hadn't taken it when he moved out.

Alex got a new job at a pulp mill in Tacoma and moved closer more than a month ago. He'd called recently and told her when he'd be back for the rest of his stuff, but she didn't remember which day and hadn't bothered to write it down. He'd promised the same a couple of times and stood her up.

Carla invited the dog inside. She grabbed a bath towel and rubbed his fur. The towel came away filthy, and his coat stood out in ridiculous chunky tufts. He followed her back into the kitchen and watched her collect the pieces of the daisy dish into a plastic bag in case Alex wanted to glue them together. Unlikely. And impossible.

Next she filled her biggest saucepan with water and set it on the floor, smiling at the way the dog stuck his whole head into it to drink. Alex had left a couple of his nasty hot dogs in the freezer, so she thawed them in the microwave. The smell made her gag. She hadn't eaten meat since she was old enough to understand where it came from.

Offering small pieces one by one, like treats in exchange for tricks, she tested him on all the commands she knew: sit, stay, paw, speak, down, roll over. He obeyed each one. When the last bite was swallowed, he licked her fingers.

"Somebody somewhere is staring at your dish of uneaten dog food and wondering where the hell you are."

Grandma Moses poked her head out around the corner, and the dog lunged toward her, barking. The sound was too big for the tiny kitchen. It bounced off the hard surfaces, amplified and reverberating.

"Shhh. It's okay, boy." Kneeling, Carla ran her hands over his ears and neck until the cat retreated and his barking stopped. His muscles were tense, and so were hers as she listened for sounds through the thin walls. *God, I hope Weird Wallace didn't hear that.*

The dog shivered and yawned. Cold and sleepy or anxious? In her deep, growly voice, she sang to him until he relaxed and slid down to lie panting on the vinyl floor. A door slammed somewhere in the building, startling both Carla and the dog, who let out a soft woof. She held her breath, senses alert, waiting. Her door buzzer sounded. *Shit.* But it was the security door, so not Weird Wallace. He would have knocked.

"Stay," she said, holding her hand like a stop sign. "You're not here, okay?"

"Hey." Alex brushed past when she let him into the building and headed down the hall. "I'm here for my stuff."

His long stringy hair fell over his eyes, and in the doorway, he tossed his head to flick it back. "Christ! When did you get a dog?"

"It's temporary."

"What is it with you and stray animals?"

Carla didn't feel like going down that road again. "So you finally showed up?"

"Holton's here with his truck. I'm putting a bunch of it in storage for now."

"One of those self-storage places? That'll add up fast."

"Nah, Holton's garage. He says I can leave the furniture and my kayak and other stuff that won't fit in my car until he has a free weekend and can drive it all down for me."

Alex's cousin Horny Holton was good for something after all. Every time he came to pick Alex up, which had been often—for bowling league, pool tournaments, dart competitions—he'd tried to hit on her.

"Your cat is hiding under the sofa, by the way." Carla kneeled to peek underneath. "Be good, Mosey. Hope to see you again someday."

She stretched out her hand and rubbed a finger up and down between her eyes until she purred. Secretly, she'd hoped that Alex's new place would have a no-pets policy and Grandma Moses could stay with her.

Brushing dust and cat hair from her knees, Carla picked up the plastic bag containing the remains of the broken bowl. Bits of ceramic tinkled musically. "Here. Sorry." With a wry smile, she said, "Maybe your mom can make you a new one."

Alex glanced into the bag and handed it back. "Mom's into scrap-booking now. Trash it."

The buzzer sounded again, and Alex left to open the security door for Holton.

"See you around," Carla called after him and walked into the bedroom with the big dog at her heels. She closed the door, leaned on it, and slid down to sit on the floor. The dog settled next to her and pushed his snout under her hand until she rubbed his head. She listened to the guys talking and bumping around in the living room as they carried things out into the hall. No need to watch him haul everything away. Alex had been a decent roommate. Plus, she didn't need another encounter with Holton.

Carla stood and retrieved her bass from her closet. The strings sounded like rubber bands when she plucked them. Playing without an amp was one of the sad realities of living in a crappy apartment with paper-thin walls. Almost as sad as not owning an amp anymore. She'd sold hers—a good one that Gordon had given her—to buy a bus ticket to Milwaukee six years ago after an overdose landed her mom in the hospital and then jail. That trip was the last time Carla saw her.

She pressed Play on her mini boombox. *My Brain Hurts*, her current favorite CD, was already in the player. She shuffled the tracks and turned it as loud as she dared, letting little bounces begin to travel through her body, unleashed by the first notes of the distorted electric guitar riff. The drums and fast-driving bass kicked in. She joined in with hers and let the music toss her around the room until she was jumping up and down, whipping her hair from side to side, releasing the wild energy fed by the music, freeing her mind and untangling her emotions. She added her voice to Ben Weasel's and whisper-screamed the lyrics of "What We Hate."

The last song on the album faded out, and Carla dropped to the floor, panting, her legs splayed in front of her.

"What's your opinion of Screeching Weasel?" she asked the dog. He flopped onto his side and presented his belly. "Not a fan then?"

She leaned into her instrument, singing soft and low. The dog curled up behind her and pressed hard against her back while she played. His weight was comforting. The warmth of his body seeped through Carla's shirt and into her bones. She paused her fingers and twisted to look at him, admiring the way he pulled himself into a tight, protective circle. The rhythm of his breathing was slow and regular, and her own synced with his. She put her bass aside and wrapped her body around his, burying her nose in his musky fur.

Alex was gone. Carla came out and stood in the empty space. With his couch and end tables gone, the room looked smaller. And shabbier. Indentations on the shag carpet showed where the furniture had pressed for so long, and plenty of dirt and cat fur that had mostly been hidden was now exposed. The vacuum cleaner was Alex's too.

"Help me out, Tony. Don't be a dick."

Carla stood in stocking feet in her kitchen that evening holding Saint Anthony. The original statue—six inches tall and painted in gaudy colors—had been lost, which was ironic. She probably left it behind at a foster home when she had to leave unexpectedly. This was an identical one she found in a thrift store when she first arrived in Seattle with Gordon.

Some of her charms only worked with physical contact. Like the worry stone she always kept in her pocket or the rabbit's foot she had when she was little, which was a fake, of course. The thought of some poor bunny amputee would have made her cry. She didn't need to hold Saint Anthony for the magic to work—conjuring his image while repeating the memorized line worked fine—but she liked having him nearby.

She set the statue down and picked up the phone, squinting at the faded red numbers on the back of her hand. Which was the feed store, and which was the dog owner? The last digit of one number was impossible to read. Carla dialed the wrong number twice before remembering the newspaper clippings she had stuffed into her jeans pocket, but dialing the right number only got the familiar unanswered ring tone. She hung up, but as soon as she let go, it rang.

"Is that you babe?" A shaking female voice threaded into Carla's ear like a thin wire.

Shit. "Mom," Carla answered flatly, jaw tense.

"I'm so happy I reached you. How long has it been? A couple three years, I think, right?"

"I've asked you not to contact me. I'm hanging up."

"Wait! I just want to know if you're okay, Cargo." Carla hated that pet name, like she was a burden.

"Right. You never call unless you want something." Carla massaged her temple.

"That's not true, honey. You know I love you. Mothers need to talk to their kids. And kids are not supposed to change their phone numbers and cut their moms out of their lives!" Her pitch rose to a squawk.

What if that kid had a mother who dropped out of the picture when being a parent got in the way of what she wanted to do? A mother too fucked up to care about her own daughter, her only child.

"What is it this time? Need me to bail you out of jail again?" Carla stomped into the empty living room and began pacing. Couldn't Alex have left a single fucking chair?

The last time she'd seen her mom was when Carla cleaned out her savings for the Greyhound to Wisconsin. She'd barely had enough to pay her mom's fines and get her out of the lockup.

"I thought you'd be proud of me. I'm clean! Isn't that great? I got out of rehab yesterday. There's some things I want to talk to you about. Can I come see you? Maybe you could spare a few bucks, sweetie? A loan. I'll pay you back as soon—"

"I'm hanging up." Carla lowered the receiver, her mother's pleading voice fading to a tinny whine, and ended the call.

No. Just, no. Carla refused to be sucked in again. How many times had she scraped together some cash to send her mom after believing the promises that it would be the last time, that she would pay her back, that this time would be different? Who would want their mom living on the streets, panhandling and shooting up in an alley somewhere? But things were finally stable in Carla's life, or at least they had been until Alex left. If she gave her mom money this time it would cost her dearly. Already there wasn't enough to pay the rent. She couldn't let her mother ruin everything again. Things weren't perfect, but Carla had a car, and that car got her to her job every day, and that job paid enough to live on. Almost.

For the first eleven years of her life Carla was bounced from one foster family to another with no money or possessions of her own. She was shuttled between people who said they didn't know how to reach such an angry child. More than once, she overheard foster parents begging to have her placed somewhere else and social workers tossing around terms like *reactive attachment disorder* as casually as a mechanic points out what's wrong with your car. Having begun her life as the daughter of a homeless drug addict, Carla's life had always been a mess. Until she met Gordon, that is.

Standing in the middle of the living room with the dog staring at her, head cocked, from the doorway, Carla rolled her head like a ball on a stick and shook her hands to fling away the feelings still clinging to her after the phone call. She picked up her bass, settled the strap onto her shoulder, and played. What came out was the last song she played with Gordon and the Gutter Rats—a few weeks before he left, before he loaded a duffel bag full of clothes, his guitar and amps, his Patti Smith poster, and sweet Iggy into his van. He left her sitting cross-legged in the middle of their bed. She was still sitting there hours later when the sun sank below the horizon, pulling all the light from the room. Unanswered questions had buzzed in her head like flies. How did she miss the signs that he was unhappy? What had she done wrong?

She waited all night in the sound of his absence until the buzzing in her mind faded and she lost the feeling in her legs. She waited for him to change his mind and come back. By morning all hope evaporated, and in its place was a fist of pain under her collarbone. She stood on her numb and shaky legs in the shower until the heartache turned to anger, and the anger turned to resolve. Carla made getting over Gordon an act of defiance. It was an act of survival.

Now she laid the bass carefully back into its velvet-lined case. She could sell it, the only thing she owned that was worth anything. She might get a hundred bucks, maybe more. But then she would lose this connection to Gordon. He was the one who taught her to play and gave her his favorite bass. He said she was a natural. What good was his gift to her now? Playing in a band was more his dream than hers anyway. She snapped the latches closed.

Carla bent to kiss the top of the dog's head and said, "C'mon. Let's get some fresh air before bed. We can check the dumpster for something to use as a chair."

Chapter 4

Thursday, October 23, 1997

By the time she climbed into the Datsun the next morning, Carla was running late.

As soon as she got up, she tried calling the dog's owner. Five was early for most people, but she had nothing to lose. Sitting on the floor examining the back of her hand, she waited for someone to pick up. Both phone numbers had disappeared. Good thing she saved the ads. There was no need to keep the feed store's number anymore, but she would need to continue calling the other one a while longer. She turned her hand over and saw pink crescent-shaped indentations in the fleshy part of her palm. Back to her old habit of clenching her fists in her sleep.

The dog's needs took extra time too. Carla fed him two cans of the Friskies she forgot to give Alex. He licked the plate clean while she refilled his water. She stood in the dark backyard waiting for him to sniff around for the ideal place to relieve himself. Poor guy wouldn't get another opportunity for hours, and she couldn't risk losing her security deposit if he peed on the carpet.

Carla turned the key in the ignition.

"What now, Dot?" Instead of its usual cough before coming to life there was nothing, no sound at all. No whining and chugging like a flooded engine, something she knew how to fix herself. The battery? On the third try she heard a single metallic *clunk*. She smelled something hot, like melting rubber, and even in the dark she could see curls of gray smoke rising from under the hood on the passenger side. She turned the key again. *Clunk.*

There wasn't enough in her bank account for a tow truck or a car repair. Or even a taxi. If she didn't show up for work, she could be out of a job. Rent was due in less than two weeks, and she still had no one to split it with. Tears gathered in the corners of her eyes, threatening to fall. She stopped them by tipping her head back and letting out a cry of rage.

Her weird neighbor Wallace appeared at her window, startling her. His bulky form was a dark shadow against the streetlight behind him. An enormous man, whose job had something to do with computers, he often worked at night. Most of his spare time he spent alone playing video games in his apartment. Carla knew this because of the *pew-pew* sounds of lasers or light sabers or whatever coming through her bedroom wall. She rolled her window down a crack.

"Car trouble?" he asked.

"My battery is dead."

"I have jumper cables. You want me to jump you?"

He pulled his car around, nose to nose with Carla's along the curb, opened both hoods, and fiddled with the cables.

"All set. Give it a try."

Carla turned the key once more. *Clunk. Shit.*

He came over to her window again and leaned down to speak. "I don't think a dead battery is your problem. I would venture to guess you have something more serious going on. Sounds to me like your engine is seized."

"That's bad, right?"

The big man nodded his head so vigorously his jowls quivered with the effort. "It happens when there's no oil. You're looking at a whole new engine, which"—he looked left and right, appraising the car—"would cost more than this old gal is worth."

Oil. One more essential thing she couldn't afford. Before Alex moved out, Carla changed the oil herself every six months.

"Thanks anyway." Carla cranked the window up.

"Wait—" His face was so close to hers that she could smell his breath. "You need a ride somewhere?"

God, no. "I'll catch the bus."

Ten minutes later she was boarding the bus headed toward Bremerton. Even this early in the morning the bus was full. People in navy uniforms heading to the shipyard, others in suits and ties who were on their way to the ferry terminal and their office jobs in Seattle. A few eyed Carla in her Doc Martens and black fishnet tights as she clomped up the aisle, trying to keep her balance on the lurching bus.

She took a seat next to a plump blonde woman in a forest-green pantsuit and felt her shift away. Hoping for maximum annoyance, Carla chewed her gum a little louder as she settled in with the timetable and route map she'd grabbed from behind the driver's seat. She could be without a car for a while.

It turned out this route was her only option. She would have to transfer in Bremerton and then walk what looked like a half mile or more from the stop closest to the Coffee Spot. To make matters worse, this one was a commuter bus, so it only ran a couple of times in the morning and a couple in the evening. Not only would she be stuck in Tracyton until the first bus left around four—more than an hour after she closed for the day—but there was no way to get home on her break to let the dog out. *Fuck.* She pushed the paper into her pocket.

Wallowing in self-pity, Carla's mind landed on the call from her mom the night before. In the past when Carla gave her money, her mom disappeared for a few months or even years. If Carla refused to give her a handout, she would continue calling until she wore Carla down. This time was different, though, because Carla had nothing to spare.

The solution to all her problems was money. Having too little meant it was never far from her thoughts. People who had plenty didn't get it, how it felt to live so close to the edge all the time. They looked down their noses at her, like that guy across the aisle rummaging in his briefcase and scowling at her. Like Pantsuit Blondie over here clutching her purse for dear life, ready to clobber Carla if she tried to take it from her, the weight of her fat wallet making it a weapon. But having *enough* would shield Carla from whatever the world threw at her. There was safety in it, and safety was what she craved.

Why couldn't she get a job working in a nice office, answering phones or typing or whatever? She could learn to do that. How hard could it be? She rubbed her worry stone deep in her jacket pocket. But without those skills, no one would hire her to do anything except bake muffins and serve coffee. It was all she knew how to do. That and play bass, but there was no money in that. Not for her, anyway.

Carla dropped her eyes and examined a hole in her tights, picking at a loose thread with her short black fingernail. The song in her head at that moment was "Thrift Store Girl," and she hummed a line. Pantsuit gave her a dirty look.

Carla glanced across at Briefcase Guy. He was holding a copy of the *Sun* and reading the front page. He opened it with a sharp snap, giving Carla a good look at the headline. She looked away to stare out the window at the inlet, crossing her arms tightly over her chest to hold in her worst fears. Was it possible? It had only been three days. The words printed boldly on the paper said: "Visiting Whales Might Be Distressed."

Chapter 5

Friday, October 24, 1997

Not having a car complicated things. That and the dog. For the second day in a row, Carla took the bus to the coffee shop, but this time she wasn't late, and the dog situation was under control. Breaking her own rule, she had knocked on Weird Wallace's door after work the day before and asked for help.

"I'd need to drop him off before the ass-crack of dawn."

"Not a problem. I get home from the shipyard around then." That explained why he looked like an unmade bed at five in the evening. She'd woken him up. His soft face lifted into a smile as he said, "I'd be happy to have his company."

Now she owed him, which made her uncomfortable. If she didn't reach the owner by Monday, she would have to come up with a better idea.

The shop door opened. "Hiya," Sylvia said. She blew through the dining room into the kitchen and out again, tying an apron around her waist with hardly a glance at Carla. Still pissed that she had to open by herself the day before, most likely. Shit happens.

Sylvia had chosen the preppy look this morning. She wore loafers with no socks and tight jeans rolled up a few inches to show off her delicate ankles. Her striped rugby shirt in pastel colors and her hair piled on top of her head in a perfect bun transformed her into a lollipop.

On her way to the kitchen, Carla paused to watch two women seat themselves near the windows. Well dressed, so not from around here. One had tight gray curls, a string of pearls, and a belted navy-blue dress, and the other, a brunette in a red blazer, had the older woman's high forehead and large round eyes.

Sylvia pranced over to greet them. "What can I get you?"

Red Blazer asked to see a menu. Carla stopped, her hand on the swinging door. A menu? She found one, a laminated card, wedged between the cash register and the bakery case. It was sticky so she gave it a wipe with her bar rag, and then hung back for a moment, curious. It had been ages since anyone new came in.

With a pair of reading glasses perched on her beaky nose, Pearls studied the short menu.

"Hot tea for me, with milk, please. Not cream. And I'd love to try one of your apple spice muffins."

"Sorry." Sylvia cocked her hip and gave an exaggerated shrug. "Apple spice isn't available anymore, but we have apple-rhubarb coffee cake. It's pretty popular. Today's muffin is bran."

"What a shame." Pearls smiled politely and put her glasses into her purse. "Just the tea for me. Cake for breakfast seems decadent."

"We could share a piece, Mom. Then it's only half decadent!" Her mother didn't object, so Red turned to Sylvia, "Tea for me as well, please, and a slice of that cake with two forks."

In the kitchen Carla lifted the cake pan from the cooling rack and set it on the cutting board. A red-letter day. Two more customers than usual. They looked like they might be decent tippers, but that would only benefit Sylvia. Carla cut a thick slice and heard the knife crunch through the sugary topping.

She carried the plate through to the dining room. Sylvia was filling two tiny steel teapots with boiling water behind the counter, so Carla brought the cake to the table. Sylvia giggled at something Delbert said.

"You're just a little ray of sunshine." Delbert's eyebrows danced above the heavy frames of his glasses. The girl giggled again and crossed the room with the tea tray she had prepared.

"Old goat. She's young enough to be your granddaughter," Carla muttered as she paused to wipe the spilled milk Sylvia had left on the counter.

"And you, my dear, are a big black rain cloud." Delbert stood to leave, pulling his face into a frown as he handed three singles to Carla. "Be sure to give the change—all of it—to Little Miss Sunshine over there."

At the register, Carla counted out the entire tip in pennies and made a show of letting them slide noisily from her hand into the tip jar.

A group of four stepped in after Delbert left and looked around before choosing a table. Two moms with kids in strollers followed. Soon every seat was taken, more people stood waiting near the door, and still more gathered outside. Not a single familiar face among them. The coffee shop hummed with voices, creating a kind of melody with the clink and rattle of cheap stoneware and spoons that drowned out the country music playing on the radio.

By noon the tip jar was full, and the pockets of Carla's apron jingled cheerfully as she moved between the tables refilling cups. She'd come out of the kitchen to lend a hand and already earned more than the boss could dock her pay for the wasted tin of coffee.

"Sorry. We're out of muffins," she said, standing near a two-top with four people squeezed around it.

"What kind of pie do you have, then?" one of the women asked, sliding her thin arms out of a brand-new Eddie Bauer fleece jacket. Seattle people. Carla could spot them in a hot second.

"Pumpkin."

Sylvia passed behind Carla carrying a bus pan full of dirty dishes. "Nope," she said over her shoulder on her way to the kitchen. "Pie's gone too. I just served the last slice." She rested her load on the end of the counter with a clatter, tilting her head at Carla. "What the heck is going on? I've never seen so many people in the café."

Carla blew out a short breath. *Café, my ass.*

"We're here for the whales," Mrs. Eddie Bauer said for the whole room to hear.

So that was it. Carla's heart sank a couple of notches. Now that news of the orcas had spread beyond her little town, she would have to share her whales with a mob of city people too.

Carla brushed past Sylvia and through the swinging door to the kitchen. "Christ," she said aloud, glancing at the bare work surfaces. If she couldn't feed them, they'd go elsewhere, and she might be out of a job.

Sylvia bumped the door open with her hip and barely made it to the dishwasher with the heavy bus pan. "I can't believe I skipped class for this. I'm missing blowout techniques today!" She set the dishes down with a grunt. "And I ruined my manicure. Look." Two splayed hands appeared under Carla's nose.

Carla ignored her and slid a day-old pound cake from the refrigerator. She placed a slice on a small plate, spooned some crushed strawberries over it, and added a dollop of Cool-Whip on top.

"Here. See if her majesty will take this instead of pie." Carla held out the plate. Sylvia snatched it and flounced back into the dining room.

The quickest thing to make was biscuits. There were plenty of strawberries and a bucket of whipped cream. That added up to strawberry shortcake around here. She set the oven to four hundred degrees, rolled up her sleeves, and got to work measuring flour, baking powder, and salt as fast as she could, sifting it all together into a huge bowl. With her pastry blender, she cut in shortening with all her might, her irritability growing. The overcrowded dining room was getting to her. All those city people, demanding this and that. And how about that Sylvia—what an attitude!

Milk was next. Carla changed the radio station. She needed the right music to steady her nerves. She dug both hands deep into the bowl and mixed in the liquid. A voice from the speaker said light rain was expected in the afternoon and announced the next track on the playlist, "Punk Rock Girl." As the drums and the bass drove the fast beat of her favorite Dead Milkmen song, Carla dumped the whole sticky mess from the bowl onto the flour-dusted countertop, and her rolling pin kept time with the percussion.

Sylvia pushed her head through the swinging door and called, "Change the station!" over the music. "And the whales showed up, if you want to see." She disappeared again.

Wiping her hands on a bar rag Carla joined the crowd pressed against the picture windows. Sure enough, two orcas swam and splashed in the inlet right outside the shop. Sounds of awe and wonder rose from the group.

"Looks like they're having fun," said the man with Mrs. Eddie Bauer.

Carla couldn't help smiling as the whales circled in a game of chase, sleek fins and flippers and tails shining black against the gray water. There was a collective *oooh* when one whale threw himself out of the waves with a mighty thrust, giving everyone a good look at his perfect white underside before he landed with a splash so big the spray doused the end of the pier where several people stood. Shaking water from their arms and hands, a woman and two children ran for shore laughing.

"I'm so glad we found this place," Mrs. Bauer gushed.

Mr. Bauer said, "Definitely worth the drive. It's the perfect whale-watching spot."

It was, but Carla had mixed feelings. The whales were beautiful, but they'd disrupted her routines, and she found herself wishing they would move on so things could get back to normal, back to boring and predictable. Back to easy and safe. She slipped her hand into the pocket of her apron and measured the thickness of the wad of bills there. But back to broke too. It would be a good thing for her bank account if the whales and the crowds stayed a little longer. She squared her shoulders. This hungry mob was nothing she couldn't handle.

Everyone on the pier had stepped back to avoid another shower. Except for one man. He stood perfectly still, looking out over the inlet through a pair of binoculars, his jeans soaked, droplets of water shimmering on his jacket and his dark ponytail.

The steady flow of hungry whale watchers kept Carla in the kitchen and Sylvia hopping in the dining room. Carla helped clear plates and ring up customers. Each time Carla emerged from the kitchen, she stole a quick glance at the inlet. Her timing was off though, always looking just before or just after the whales made an appearance. The crowd along the shore below the coffee shop grew throughout the day, swarming near the boat ramp and out onto the pier. People gathered on the opposite shore, too, and boats of all sizes drifted in and out of view.

After the last customer left, Sylvia split her tips with Carla and even thanked her for helping out before heading home. There was at least an hour of cleanup and prep work ahead, but Carla needed a break and to see the orcas. She grabbed her beanie and jacket and locked the door behind her.

All three Seattle television stations had vans parked along the road, and crews were setting up to film the whales for the evening news. A cameraman was attracting some attention himself, and people were trying to get into his shots, waving like idiots.

On the pier, Carla claimed a spot with a good view of Rocky Point to the south, where the inlet funneled into Port Washington Narrows, the way out of Dyes Inlet—the only way out. Not a whale in sight. A couple of kids squeezed between the adults toward the front. One stepped hard on Carla's foot. Her feet were already sore from the insanity in the coffee shop, and even through the sturdy leather of her Doc Martens, she felt his full weight. She fought the urge to shove the kid into the water.

The whales had been swimming back and forth through the deep center of the inlet all day, but now it was still. An empty stage. The audience waited, tension building, for the stars of the show to appear. Motorboats, rowboats, canoes, kayaks. Carla counted eleven boats going nowhere. Occasionally someone would dip a paddle or an oar into the water to direct their aimless floating. A slight hump rose in the water, a swelling that grew as a whale below the surface pushed upward. The voices around her became louder and more excited, anticipating the sight of a whale or even the tip of a fin. But the stage remained empty, the surface leveled off, and the audience settled again.

The official count was nineteen, and the newspaper said they were all part of the same family, the same pod, the reporter called it. Carla found it hard to imagine so many whales, traveling together, young and old, male and female. Thinking of the size and grace of these great visitors, knowing they were right out there, swimming out of sight deep in the inlet, made Carla shiver. She pulled her denim jacket tighter and tucked her hands into the pockets.

All at once, the crowd let out a collective gasp, and Carla looked over hats and shoulders as a tall fin emerged close to the pier. Then the whale exploded out of the water, throwing itself into the air with such force that the shock, like a bomb, struck Carla in the chest, knocking the air out of her lungs. The whale paused at the top of his arching dive, showing off, proud of himself for drawing such a crowd. With his gleaming black eye shining like a polished stone and rolling in its socket, the whale took in the sights—trees, clouds, seagulls, human faces—before crashing back into the water. The force of its landing made the wooden pier tremble on its pilings.

Drenched with salt water, people in the front headed for dry land, leaving room for Carla at the end of the pier. A couple of soaked kayakers paddled madly toward shore over the expanding rings where the whale had been. A thrill, judging from their whoops and loud laughter. Alex had let her try his kayak a couple of times, showing her how to grip the paddle and how to keep her balance. The last place she wanted to be was out there in a small boat with whales everywhere.

Following the kayaks and gaining on them were three people in an inflatable boat with a motor. The driver steered with one hand and frantically waved with the other, yelling something Carla couldn't hear. He picked up a bullhorn.

"Stay back! Please, stay back!" he warned over and over. The kayakers slowed their pace, and people on the pier took a step back. No one was sure who the man was speaking to.

The inflatable pulled alongside the pier, and Carla saw *Soundwatch* painted in white on the blue rubber. The mob moved back to give them room, and the driver jumped out. Ponytail. His hands wound a stiff rope around the wooden post closest to him.

"Need a hand?" Carla called. He didn't, of course, but if he had, she would have been of little use to him. She knew nothing about boats but figured if she could strike up a conversation, she could ask about the whales. She had a growing list of questions in her head.

His back was to her. There was a sureness to his movements that she respected. Here was a man who knew what he was doing. He straightened and looked at Carla with eyes exactly the same color as the pale gray sky behind him. It was as if she was seeing right through him.

"I got it. Thanks, though." Ponytail smiled, and her face warmed. She stepped back into the crowd.

"What a bunch of fools," yelled a man. "Did you see how close they were getting?"

"They deserve whatever they get," said a woman in a leather jacket. She folded her arms across her chest and raised her chin, ready for a fight. "Nobody would need to chase away those kayakers if one of them got hurt. I think they'd get the message loud and clear." To Ponytail she said, "Nice of you to tell them to back off, though."

"Well, it's part of our job. Me and my team." Ponytail gave a nod to the man and woman climbing from the boat to the pier. He addressed the whole group in a louder voice. "We don't want anyone to get hurt, but at the moment we're more concerned about the orcas. If any of you have boats, please leave them at home, and pass that advice along to people you know. At least until we know for sure they aren't causing undue stress for the whales."

He pointed to a large vessel coming out of Ostrich Bay on the other side of Rocky Point. "Those guys have been patrolling out here all day, enforcing the law, telling people to stay at least two hundred yards away."

Carla squinted, trying to make out the insignia on the side of the hull.

"Who are they?" Leather Jacket asked.

"The Feds," Ponytail said. People on the pier stopped talking. "National Marine Fisheries Service. It isn't only dangerous to get close to these animals, it's a federal crime. You folks have the right idea. Anywhere along the shoreline you can get a good view. No one needs to get any closer. These whales are nervous."

"How can you tell?" the loud man behind Carla asked.

"Saw a few swimming in small circles and some high-speed swimming. Both are signs of distress. And there's been a bit of spy-hopping." Ponytail stood straight with his feet apart and hands clasped behind his back, binoculars hanging around his neck. He spoke with authority, like someone used to speaking in public.

One of the kids raised his hand like he was in school and asked, "What's sky-hopping."

"*Spy*-hopping. They are peeking out to spy on us. They pop their heads out like they're standing straight up on their tails and look around. Could be they're just curious about being in a strange place, like you'd be." Ponytail gave the boy a warm smile, one that said he was genuinely happy to answer the kid's question. "Hey, do you know where spies sleep?" The boy shook his head. "Undercover!"

A few people groaned. His female colleague gave a loud whistle and called out, "Want us to bring the truck down to the ramp and pull the RIB out?"

Ponytail tossed her a set of keys.

"What's your role in all this? You seem like you know a thing or two," a voice called from the back.

"Concerned citizen like you. But also a marine biologist. Been studying these Southern Resident orcas for several years and giving whale talks at schools, educating young people about how important these animals are to the ecosystem."

"The what?" said the boy.

"The environment. Everything we do affects animal habitats too." Ponytail checked his binoculars and adjusted the strap. "Too early to get alarmed, but if people love these whales as much as they say they do, they should want them to be safe." He paused and scanned the water. "Don't get me wrong, the number of people coming out to see them up close is great."

"Any idea how long they'll stay?" someone asked.

"Yeah," a round woman said, her stringy hair mostly hidden under a baseball cap. "I'm as thrilled as the next guy that they're here, but the traffic is unreal!"

"They can stay as long as they like, as far as I'm concerned," the man chimed in. "I run the Quik Mart up on Stampede Boulevard, and I'm loving the extra business."

Ponytail pressed his lips together, then said, "Well, today is day four. That's three days more than we expected. If they stay much longer, I'm afraid they could be stuck."

He answered a few more questions and stepped back into the boat, as the word *stuck* rolled around in Carla's head.

"Are you going back out?" she asked, one hand on the post and one foot on the side of the boat as if she were about to climb in.

Carla studied his movements as he looped two cameras around his neck where the binoculars were already hanging, and then he worked his arms through the straps of a heavily loaded backpack. "Not today. We're packing it in." A pickup with a trailer backed onto the ramp. "But we'll be here in the morning as soon as the sun is up."

Carla scanned the inlet. Only a handful of boats were left. The whales, too, had spread out and settled down. A few thin shafts of light pierced through the low clouds as the sun sank in the west.

Ponytail picked up the bullhorn and checked once more for anything he might have left behind in the boat. He climbed out and stood a foot or two from Carla, smiling. His teeth were large and even.

"I could help," Carla said, pointing at the bullhorn. This was how she got herself into trouble, by jumping into things before thinking them through. The stray dog waiting for her at Weird Wallace's was evidence of her impulse control problems.

"You really want to?"

She'd never been more certain of anything. Carla nodded, embarrassed as she realized she was leaning forward like a wide-eyed kid.

Ponytail removed his backpack again and set it on the dock at his feet. He unzipped it and pulled out a sheaf of bright yellow paper. He held it out. "Hand these out anywhere people are watching the whales. Would be great if you'd ask around at local businesses, too, see if they'd stick them in their windows."

Carla took the flyers and read the large print on the top sheet that announced a meeting at the bowling alley for anyone who wanted to volunteer to help protect the whales.

"So, passing these out. Is it a paying gig?" A girl could hope.

"Strictly volunteer." He reached to take the papers back. "Not a problem. I'll ask someone else."

Carla swung the posters behind her back. "Like hell you will." Reading again, Carla said, "Hey, this meeting is Saturday, as in tomorrow night. Pretty short notice."

"Passed out more than a hundred yesterday. As long as a few people come, it'll be fine." With a small hop, he settled the backpack onto his shoulders again and looked into her face. Those eyes!

Walking backward toward the coffee shop, she said, "I got a question for you. Why do some people call them killer whales? Are they that dangerous? Do they kill people or is killer, like, a good thing. You know. Killer haircut. Killer band. Killer whale."

"Tell you tomorrow at the bowling alley. You're coming, right?"

Far enough away to pretend she hadn't heard, Carla turned and picked up her pace, stuffing one copy of the flyer into her pocket.

Even if she had time to go to the meeting, it was crazy to think she could make time for volunteering. That was for retired people and rich do-gooders who didn't have to work for a living. Still, she couldn't ignore the whales. Instead of being an observer, she could be part of something important.

Chapter 6

Saturday, October 25, 1997

Over the thunder of bowling balls and crash of tumbling pins, Ponytail introduced himself to the dozen or so people who showed up for the meeting. They sat at tables in the back room of the bar inside All-Star Lanes. Some might be there because of Carla's efforts the day before.

After agreeing to help pass out the notices, she had taken the bus to the Silverdale Marina. She walked onto the long dock, handing out Ponytail's yellow flyers to everyone she saw. She had already given some away at the bus stop and on the bus. Most people were nice about it, taking a flyer and saying thanks. A few were jerks, but whatever. Carla didn't mind taking a bit of abuse if it meant getting volunteers to help the whales. At home, she slipped the last of the papers into the mailboxes in the entry of her apartment building.

Ponytail's name was Nathan Decoteau. The spelling on his name badge didn't match how he said it, almost like Dakota. He started in on his spiel about his work at the Center for Whale Research. Carla only half listened since she had heard most of it already.

In the seedy bar beyond the doorway, three tired-looking men, mostly keeping to themselves, were seated on stools facing a counter. They looked like nighttime versions of the regulars at the coffee shop. Even the same shitty music was playing. But these guys were winding down with alcohol at the end of the day rather than amping up with caffeine at the start. Why don't people have a beer or a cup of coffee at home? It would certainly be cheaper.

Beyond the bar, people in the bowling alley were having a good time. Most of the lanes were in use. The stink of stale beer and cigarette butts almost overpowered the smell of floor polish and disinfectant. The room was too warm. Carla slipped her jacket off but left her beanie pulled down over her eyebrows. Nathan's authoritative voice brought her attention back to the meeting.

"So, what we especially need," he was saying, "is people with boats. People to help get information out to other boaters, the ones racing around in the inlet every day trying to get close to the whales."

Sounding hopeful, Nathan told them that once everyone understood how important it was to keep the whales safe, things would improve. Even the most stubborn offenders would be encouraged to stay back, he said, when they heard about the steep fines they could face from the Feds or the Washington Department of Fish and Wildlife for failing to follow the rules.

A tiny woman stood up. "I heard there's lots of killer whales left. Why do they need protection? I mean, people still hunt them, right?"

"Sadly, yes," Nathan said. "In Norway, Japan, Greenland, and Iceland where some subspecies of transient orcas are thriving. They're apex predators, meaning they have no natural enemies. Except for humans. But the orcas that live here—called Southern Residents—are declining in number, the L pod in particular. The ones in Dyes Inlet are members of this pod. We need to do what we can to protect them while they're here."

At the end of the short meeting, Nathan stood near the exit and handed each participant a bundle of brochures held together with a rubber band. Carla hung back, busying herself by collecting empty cups and cans from the tables while Nathan made small talk with the volunteers. Did he really think any of this would make a difference? Handing out flyers and brochures wasn't what she had in mind when she said she wanted to help the whales. This was bullshit. She wanted to do something real, something important.

"Looks like you're aiming to be Volunteer of the Year." Nathan dragged the garbage can closer. The room was empty now.

"*Pfff.*"

"No, really. In my business, an eager volunteer is like gold."

She studied his expression. His smile was a practiced one, but not flirtatious. "If you're going out there tomorrow, can I come?"

"I was out today, and it was crazy." Nathan dumped an ashtray into the garbage, saying he'd been with the other scientists from the research center and they noticed the whales were behaving strangely, more active than normal. "Probably because there were so many people out there. Counted more than a hundred and twenty boats. Broke a record. Thousands of people are here from all over the place."

He continued talking as they walked slowly out of the bowling alley and into the cool, wet night. They stopped in the parking lot under a cone of light from one of the tall security lampposts, making the darkness around them even blacker. Carla wished old Dot were parked there waiting for her and dreaded the walk to the bus stop, which seemed longer now that it was dark.

"Around five o'clock," Nathan was saying, "we couldn't believe it. The whales made a run toward the Narrows. Great, I thought. They're on their way out at last. But then this crowd of boats, dozens of them, start chasing after. They were getting too close. Boats are supposed to stay—"

"Two hundred yards away from whales. See? I was paying attention."

Nathan's laugh echoed off the wall of the building. Carla liked this less teacher-y Nathan.

"You were! And you're correct." His voice became serious again. "But those cowboys were way too close. Then, while we're watching all this unfold and yelling at the top of our lungs for them to back off, I see a couple of boats get ahead of the whales and cut them off!"

"Assholes." Carla shuffled her feet on the pavement to keep warm. She didn't understand people, especially when it came to their cluelessness about animals. "But what if the whales come up to the boats? I mean, if you're out there staying in one spot and the whales come close to you?"

"Then I count myself lucky."

It was quiet for a moment. Wispy clouds formed in front of Nathan's face each time he exhaled. He stood near her like they were old friends, comfortable and natural. Old friends didn't exist in Carla's world.

"Back to my original question," she continued. "Can I come with you and your team? I mean, are volunteers allowed?"

"I'll be on my own tomorrow trying to get photos and some sound recordings of the orcas. Can you operate a two-stroke outboard?"

Carla cocked an eyebrow.

"My Boston Whaler," he said.

"Nope."

"Do you know how to use a 35mm camera?"

She shook her head.

"How about a hydrophone?"

"A what?"

Nathan chuckled. "Okay, how about a bullhorn?"

"I'm sure I could figure it out. I'm not a complete idiot."

"I bet you have lots of hidden talents." Carla's cheeks warmed.

"You really care about the orcas, I can tell," he said. "Not everyone who's interested is willing to go the extra mile. In this case, I'd say your passion more than makes up for not knowing how to drive a boat or take pictures. If you're serious, be at the Tracyton boat launch at seven-thirty."

"Cool." Carla tried to keep the excitement out of her voice.

"You know where that is?"

"Duh. I met you there, remember? It's right by the Coffee Spot. Where I work." She walked out of the circle of light and toward the street.

"What's your name?" Nathan called after her.

"Carla," she yelled over her shoulder.

"You need a ride somewhere?" But Carla kept walking, giving a dismissive wave.

She didn't remember until she reached the bus stop that she was supposed to clean that vacant apartment in the morning. She could reschedule. And a dog to think of. *Shit.* She could ask Weird Wallace again. He was grateful for the day-old baked goods she'd brought him from the coffee shop.

She really should stop calling him weird.

Chapter 7

Sunday, October 26, 1997

"You can see some whales over there." Nathan pointed toward the north end of the inlet. He'd killed the motor, but Carla had to grip the edge of her seat to keep from bouncing off as the boat—and her stomach—heaved and dropped.

He held out his binoculars. "Look for the one with the biggest dorsal fin, Carla." He spoke loudly over the steady rain pinging against the metal body of the boat. Ever since she told him her name, he seemed hell-bent on using it every chance he got. It was jarring, but she liked the way her name sounded when he pronounced it in two distinct syllables: Car La. "That'll be L-57, but we call him Faith."

And now it seemed he was about to introduce her to all nineteen whales, one by one. If each had a number and a name, this was going to be a long day. The life vest was bulky and smelled bad, and Nathan had given her a plastic rain poncho that flapped and twisted in the wind. She'd been sitting with the bullhorn across her lap for hours feeling uncomfortable and useless. The cold, windy weather kept most boats off the water, and the few that had braved the high waves were keeping their distance from the whales. What was the point of being here?

The worst part was that by choosing to waste her time on the inlet, she lost out on making thirty bucks. Going with Nathan to see the whales seemed like a no-brainer last night, but when she called Gary to ask if she could clean the vacant apartment in the evening instead, he gave her shit.

"No dice," the manager had said. "My buddy's cleaning the carpet in the afternoon. All the other cleaning has to get done first. It's tomorrow morning or the deal is off."

The choice wasn't one Carla wanted to make. The cash would mean she could buy some proper dog food. Still no sign of his owner. The cans of Friskies were almost gone. She'd been counting on the extra money, but this might be her one and only chance to do something she gave a fuck about.

"Don't you have someone who could fill in for me, just this once?" The hand of bad luck was reaching down to yank that money away.

"Yeah. *I'm* the someone. Well, there goes my Sunday." He slammed the phone down.

What was she thinking? Turning down paying work so she could go in some dude's boat? Now Gary might not call her the next time he needed an apartment cleaned or a minor repair done. He managed a couple of buildings so the gigs were pretty regular. Crap.

Sighing, Carla set the bullhorn in the bottom of Nathan's boat—a Boston Whaler, he'd said—and took the binoculars from him. At least she might learn something. She pushed her hood back for a better view, letting the rain soak her beanie, and stood. It had been a while since her kayaking lessons from Alex, and the only other boat she'd ever been on was a ferry, basically a floating parking lot.

"Better sit down," Nathan said, and she did.

She peered into the eyepieces as he explained that each whale's dorsal fin was unique. He said if you knew what to look for, they were like human fingerprints. Carla spotted a trio of fins. "Those sticking up—those are dorsal fins? I don't know how you can tell them apart. They all look the same. Black and pointy, sort of...fin-shaped."

Nathan laughed lightly. "Fin-shaped. Right." He came around to the bow and sat next to her on the small seat, resting his forearm on her shoulder to point into the distance. "Look there, Carla."

She almost pulled away, but a delicious shudder ran through her under the weight of his arm, a small touch that might break her heart. He leaned down to eye level, his cheek only a few inches from hers. He smelled of wind and salt.

"See one fin that looks taller than the rest? That's Faith. Males' dorsals are taller and less curved than the females." His heat seeped through her damp clothes, and an electric surge flooded her belly. She tamped it down and focused on the whales, moving the binoculars a little to the left to point her gaze where he directed. She said she could see the taller fin, but she couldn't.

Nathan lowered his arm and moved back around to the steering wheel, the helm, he called it, and she instantly missed his warmth. The wind whipped a strand of hair across her mouth. She lowered the binoculars and tucked the loose hair under her beanie.

"Where are your buddies? And that other boat you were in?"

"In the Narrows." He nodded toward the south. "Figured since I'd have a volunteer with me, I'd use my own boat." He paused and his shoulders dropped. "Truth is, my boss and I've had a difference of opinion."

"About?" She handed him the binoculars, strap dangling.

"Long story. Let's say we have different ideas about what we should do in this situation. He only wants to observe. I'm observing, too, but I think we should be prepared to act." He looped the strap over his head. "Pod's been here for almost a week, and I'm seriously worried about their well-being. Nobody on the team objected to my calling for volunteers, but they said I was wasting my time. They're probably right. I'm afraid educating people won't make much of an impact at this point."

A whale swam toward them, and Nathan raised his camera. The huge fin rose silently out of the water, as tall as a man and coming closer. Carla's heart knocked against her ribs.

"See that notch, like from a bite, near the tip of her fin?" He took a couple of pictures before it slipped below the surface. "That's L-47. Marina."

Besides males having taller dorsal fins and females more curved ones, he told her, there were other ways to distinguish one orca from another.

"Scratches, nicks, and notches help in identifying them. And did you see that grayish-white area behind the dorsal fin? That's a saddle patch. Each has a slightly different shape and pattern."

Another whale surfaced to exhale, a fine mist spraying from its blowhole. Even through the rain, droplets found Carla's delighted face.

"Look! That saddle patch has kind of a chevron design. Like a sergeant's stripes. Can you see it? I don't think that one's in the catalog." He was animated, talking fast and clicking the camera shutter.

"There's a catalog?" She snickered. "Like mail order?"

The Sears *Wish Book* was delivered each September to every foster home she had lived in. The kids browsed page by page, circling the toys they wanted for Christmas. Carla never dared to imagine gifts the way the other kids did, the *real* kids in the *real* family.

Nathan threw his head back and laughed. He told her a Canadian scientist was the first to discover that individual orcas could be identified by their markings. He created a record that included photographs and descriptions.

"My boss worked alongside him back in the seventies. Guy by the name of Michael Bigg. His research is the basis for everything we know about killer whales."

"Hey, you never answered my question. Why *killer*? Do they kill people?"

"In the wild, never. Story I heard is ancient sailors saw them hunting whales and called them whale killers. But these whales here, Southern Residents, only eat fish. Anyway," he said, wiping rain off his forehead, "part of my job at the center is to update the catalog, removing the ones we know are dead and adding any new calves."

"I could help with that." Always on the lookout for a way to make a little extra cash. "I'm not much good with a camera, but I could help with the other. Paperwork is something I can handle. I do a lot of that shit at work. Inventory, ordering, bookkeeping."

"A person with a nose for numbers and an eye for detail." Nathan nodded his approval. "I've been spending so much time out here checking on the whales that I've fallen behind on the catalog. Once they're gone, I'll get back to it."

"Whatever."

"If they stick around and I can't keep up, it'd be great if you want to help."

"How much would you pay me?" Carla crossed her fingers under her poncho, aware of how silly it was to think this gave her power. But other people didn't have to worry about survival the way she did. They had people to fall back on if their roommate left and their car broke down or if a job or a romance didn't work out. They had safety nets. All she had was superstitions.

"Can't make any promises. We're a nonprofit, so most of our funding comes from grants."

Carla gave a quick nod. She didn't want to show her ignorance by asking what grants were. She had a vague idea but didn't know who handed them out or why.

"If you're serious, I'll look into a way to compensate you."

All afternoon, the whales swam from one end of the inlet to the other. Each time they passed, heading south toward the Port Washington Narrows, Carla held her breath. Maybe this time they'd keep going, back to wherever they belonged. Sometimes they got close to the mouth of the inlet, but always they turned back.

"Get ready. Here they come again!" Nathan shouted. He raised his camera. He'd been taking photos of the whales and of any boats following too close. Later he could record their registration numbers and file complaints.

Carla switched the megaphone on and lifted it to her mouth, prepared to tell anyone off who was foolish enough to take up the chase. A cluster of fins passed Nathan's boat and sure enough, one idiot raced after them.

"Hey!" Carla yelled into the mouthpiece. The ridiculous sound of her amplified voice made her laugh. The weird electronic blast was nothing like the mic she used when she sang with the Gutter Rats. She adjusted the volume and tried again. "Hey, you! Stay back!"

"There needs to be more law enforcement!" Nathan said, angrily swiping a finger across his wet camera lens. "Those jerks are taking full advantage of the fact that no one's policing out here today."

Carla scanned the inlet. "What about the Feds? Those guys who were out here before."

"National Marine Fisheries." He shrugged. "No idea. And we called the Coast Guard requesting a patrol, but they didn't have any vessels available. Supposed to be a Washington Fish and Wildlife boat out here somewhere, but I haven't seen it."

"Can't the police do anything?"

"The sheriff? They had an officer out here yesterday when all hell was breaking loose, when those cowboys were herding the whales into the Narrows, but he did nothing. When I told him what those guys were doing was against the law, he said his duty was to keep the boaters safe, not the whales."

There was a commotion in the Narrows, and Carla turned in time to see a huge tail rise out of the water and come down onto the surface with a loud slap. Even as far away as they were, she could hear it. A couple of bright yellow kayaks paddling too close were tossed around on the waves the whale created. Another tail appeared and slapped the water three times before more tails lifted and slapped like the others. Could they be signaling to the pod that it was time to go? One last big show to say goodbye? Carla pushed her hands into her pockets and wrapped her cold fingers around her worry stone.

Chapter 8

Monday, October 27, 1997

Getting to work on the early bus had its advantages. With the CLOSED sign in the window, Carla blasted the radio, the best way to jump-start her day. Two dozen banana-nut muffins were already cooling alongside some cookies that needed icing. Scones and biscuits were in the oven, pastry for pies was chilling, and the fillings were next. Cherry and apple, plus pumpkin, the featured flavor for October. If the whales were still in the inlet—and as far as she knew, they were—then hordes of whale watchers would be back in the coffee shop today. This was the calm before the storm.

The sputter and gurgle of the old coffee machine layered its own soundtrack over the final notes of "Wasted Life." Stiff Little Fingers had a new album out, but Carla liked this old stuff better. Steam carried the aroma of the fresh brew to her brain as she waited for the water to trickle through.

The dog was on her mind. She was doing her best, but it wasn't good enough. No matter what time of day she tried calling the number from the ad, nobody ever picked up. Until he was back where he belonged, he was her responsibility, but Weird Wallace—Wallace—said he was happy to have the dog stay with him again. But what if she never found the owner?

Before seven, Carla switched the radio station and turned it low so she could barely hear Garth Brooks's country twang. She flipped the sign in the window and unlocked the door. A moment later, her boss strode in. And he wasn't alone.

"This is Libby. Libby, Carla." A short and sweet introduction. The woman smiled at her as Mr. Wilson brushed past. He showed Libby around the empty restaurant, pointing out the coffee maker and the cash register. Carla retreated to the safety of the kitchen. The only reason she could think of for her boss to be familiarizing this woman with the inner workings of the shop was that he had finally decided to fire his lazy son and hire a real manager. *Shit.* There went Carla's hopes to step into that role herself. It had been a long shot anyway.

Todd had finished business school six months ago, and his dad had put him in charge of running the shop. Not one to get his hands dirty, Todd delegated most of the inventory, receipts, and ordering to Carla. She could run the place blindfolded. She'd been watching how it's done since before Todd could tie his own shoes. *He still can't.* Carla smirked.

Through the small window in the kitchen door, she spied on the two as they moved through the room, in and out of her view. The woman was slim and wore a long soft skirt in red and gold with a white peasant blouse tucked in. At last, they came over to sit at the counter where Carla could get a better look. Libby was older than Carla by at least twenty years. She was one of those people it was hard to pin a number on. Her straight hair, cut short and spikey, looked like something in a 1960s fashion magazine. Like Liza Minnelli if she had been a dishwater blonde.

The shop door opened, and Noah stepped in. Carla left the kitchen and greeted him, brought him his hot chocolate, and delivered a banana-nut muffin. Nothing else needed to be done in the dining room, but she went around pushing in chairs and squaring up napkin holders and placemats. She was listening in on the boss's conversation, sure the other shoe was about to drop, the shoe that would squash her dreams of a promotion.

She didn't have to wait long. Mr. Wilson waved Carla over. She bit down hard, tightening her jaw. This was it. Carla didn't even try to smile.

"Libby's starting work here today," Mr. Wilson said, smoothing his mustache with thumb and forefinger. "I gave her the grand tour out here, but I'll leave it you to show her the ropes in the kitchen."

The kitchen. Was Carla being replaced? Fired?

"Two coffees, please." Her boss rapped on the counter with his hairy knuckles.

The cups in their saucers rattled in Carla's trembling hands as she placed one in front of each of them. She picked up the decanter of coffee and tipped it toward Libby's cup before the woman placed her hand over it to stop her.

"Sorry. Do you have decaf?"

Carla turned again and grabbed the seldom-used carafe with the orange handle, the one reserved for decaffeinated coffee. It was empty. *Shit.* Nobody ever asked for decaf at the Coffee Spot, except for last Friday when the whale-watching crowds went through half a dozen pots. On a normal morning, Carla would have made one pot anyway, just in case. But this didn't feel like a normal morning. Libby's arrival rattled her. "It'll just be a minute."

"Don't fuss," Libby said, but that was exactly what she was making Carla do. She had a pleasant voice, though; one that seemed to have a smile behind it.

Carla poured regular into her boss's cup and turned her back to measure ground decaf into a paper filter, being extra careful to hold tightly to the heavy tin.

"Ricky told me about the mob scene here Friday," Libby said.

It took Carla a second to figure out who she was talking about. The fact that Libby was using the boss's first name threw her. She felt excluded. She hadn't even known he was called Ricky, but it made sense for someone named Richard. Carla never called him anything but Mr. Wilson.

"Those whales sure draw a crowd," her boss said. "It turns out this place is a prime spot for whale-watching. Sylvia said you two were run off your feet on Friday. I figured you could use an extra pair of hands, just while the whales are here, so I persuaded Libby to come out of retirement for a spell."

So, Libby was there to help Carla, not take her place. She exhaled her relief and started the decaf brewing.

Mr. Wilson sipped his coffee. "Speaking of whales, I'd like you to open on the weekend, or weekends, until they're gone. You know, to benefit from the extra business."

Another greedy bastard looking for a way to turn whales into dollars. It was bad enough that people like him took advantage of people like Carla. Now he wanted to make a quick buck off wildlife.

"No need to open this early, though," he continued. "They're tourists, not working stiffs, after all. Can you open at nine? Be here at eight? You could knock off at about noon once the kitchen is ship-shape since Sylvia and Libby will be here too. I'll pay you time and a half. How does that sound?"

Carla did a quick calculation. Rent was due in a week. The extra pay on top of last Friday's tips would bring her closer to her goal.

"Good," she said. A little financial gain for the community—and for herself—might not be such a terrible thing after all.

Delbert arrived, and spotting Carla with the owner, he sat at the opposite end of the counter. Carla poured a cup of coffee, set it in front of him, and returned to the conversation.

Mr. Wilson was telling Libby that before the whales arrived, Carla could run the place single-handedly. To Carla he said, "Libby'll come in the same time as you during the week to help get things in the ovens. But I think Libby and Sylvia can handle the front of house from now on."

Crap. Say goodbye to tips.

"I've been a server pretty much all my life, but I never was much good at baking," said Libby, "but I'm a quick study with a good teacher." She patted Carla's hand.

"That way you can focus on the rest." The boss gave Carla a sly smile.

"The rest?" she asked, afraid to hear the answer.

"I'd like you to take over as manager. Temporarily."

Carla took a step back and banged her elbow hard on the cabinet behind her. She rubbed her elbow for a moment until the pain eased, waiting for her brain to catch up with her ears.

"You've got your work cut out for you, hon. Managing *and* baking. What kinds of things do you make?"

The shock hadn't worn off yet, and Carla stood with her mouth hanging open.

"Nothing fancy," Mr. Wilson answered. "Good home cooking like your momma used to make. Phenomenal."

"I second that!" Delbert called from his stool, raising his cup in a salute.

Phenomenal? Carla didn't take compliments well. She didn't trust them. Praise was like love, temporary and controlled by the person giving it. And what did he mean by nothing fancy? She almost tossed out a sarcastic remark but held back. Normally she didn't give two rips about what other people thought of her, but this Libby—there was something about her Carla immediately liked. She had a cool-grandma vibe. Something that made Carla want to be liked in return.

With a hiss, the coffee maker finished its brew cycle. Carla filled Libby's cup, and the woman stirred in four pink packets of Sweet'N Low. Libby winked at her when she saw Carla noticing.

"I like my coffee like I like my men. Strong and sweet." In a stage whisper aimed at Carla, she said, "And decaffeinated. I don't wanna be up all night, if you get my drift."

Mr. Wilson glanced at his watch, gulped the last of his coffee, and stood. "By the way, Carla, you'll need to do the end-of-the-month inventory after closing today. Your first managerial task. Todd didn't, uh, didn't get around to it."

"And the pay, for managing?"

"Same as I was paying Todd." Mr. Wilson wiped his mustache with a napkin.

Carla had no idea how much that was, but she was certain it was more than what she was currently making. Of course, Todd never set foot in the kitchen if he could help it, and as a manager, he was the hands-off type. As in he rarely showed his face. She wanted to ask where Todd was in all this, but it wasn't her business. Besides she had a more immediate problem.

"When? I mean when will I get paid?"

"On the fifteenth and thirtieth, same as usual. You'll see the increase after you've worked two full weeks as manager, if I haven't found a permanent replacement for Todd before then. So not until the middle of November." He buttoned his coat.

"Could I get an advance? My rent is due next week." Carla had asked her landlord for an extension, but he was being a hard-ass as usual.

Mr. Wilson said he'd think about it.

After he left, Libby slid gracefully off the stool and smoothed her skirt. She said, "Have you got an extra apron? I can handle things out here if you want to get back to your phenomenal baking." She smiled a genuine smile. "Something smells amazing."

Carla found a clean, folded apron under the counter and tossed it. Libby caught it easily, then cinched the ties of the apron snugly around her waist before clearing away the dishes where she and the boss had been sitting.

Carla glanced at Delbert. "You can refill him and see if he wants a muffin."

"Please and thank you," said Delbert from the other end of the counter.

"What's in the oven?" With a bar rag in one hand, Libby gave the counter a wipe while pouring Delbert's coffee with the other.

"Cookies. Black-and-whites." Carla had first seen them in an episode of *Seinfeld* a few years ago, but this was the first time she'd attempted to make them. "I thought, with the killer whales out there and everything, they might sell."

"Genius!" Libby said, and she laughed, her face pink and shining. "Let me know if I can help in the back. I don't imagine it will get busy with whale watchers for a while yet."

They both glanced at the windows. The still water of the inlet shimmered in the first weak rays of dawn.

The earliest whale watchers of the day, an elderly couple, were diving into their slices of pumpkin-raisin loaf. Noah and Stewart had come and gone. Sylvia was waiting on Delbert, the only other customer in the shop, and Libby was arranging freshly baked scones on a platter like a pro. Carla took advantage of the quiet moment to dial the number she knew by heart. To cover all her bases, she rubbed the worry stone in her pocket while whispering the magic words to Saint Anthony.

"Yes?" said a voice on the other end.

"Hi! Hello. Are you—Did you—" Carla had gotten so used to hearing nothing but a ring tone that she wasn't prepared to speak to anyone. She took a breath and started again. "Did you lose a dog?"

A few minutes later Carla hung up the phone and wrote something on the back of her hand with a felt-tip pen.

"What was all that about?" Delbert asked.

Sylvia leaned in to refill his cup. "Yeah. I heard you say something about a dog."

"What dog?" Delbert said. "The one from the ad?"

"Don't you have somewhere to be? That mail won't deliver itself," Carla snapped.

The circumstances of how she came to be in possession of the dog still bothered her, no matter how certain she was that he was better off with her than the people at the feed store. She hadn't exactly lied to that nasty Clay, but she let him believe something that wasn't true, which amounted to the same thing. Every preacher and Sunday school teacher she met as a foster kid hammered that message home. An omission of truth is the same as lying, and lying is a sin. Kids didn't need church or the Bible to know they shouldn't lie, but the whole sinners-will-burn-in-hell part made them feel guilty and afraid. It was hard to shake off that feeling even now.

"Not yet." Delbert stirred his coffee and gave the rim of his cup a tap with his spoon. "I'm not a carrier anymore since my knee surgery, remember? Window clerks are eight to four."

Carla tried to return to the kitchen, but Sylvia stepped in front of her, blocking her way.

"I didn't know you had a dog." Sylvia cocked her head to one side, causing her long bangs to fall across her face like an Afghan hound. She blinked them free from her false eyelashes.

"God, you guys are so fucking nosy."

Carla shouldered past Sylvia and pushed the kitchen door so hard that it swung all the way back and hit the wall behind it with a bang. It was the next best thing to slamming a door, the most satisfying way to blow off steam. But where was this steam coming from? She should be happy for a change. On track to earn more money, on track to pay her rent on time, a surprise promotion. And the best news? The dog would soon be back with his owner. One less mouth to feed.

She lifted some sticky baking trays out of the big stainless-steel sink and hurled them in again with a tremendous crash. She gripped the edge of the sink, the muscles in her neck and shoulders rigid. After a moment she added liquid detergent and twisted the ancient handle to start the flow of water, trailing her fingers back and forth under the warm stream. As the basin filled, she inhaled the chemical citrus scent and watched the bubbly foam rise.

The dog was going home. Someone loved him and missed him. This fact *should* make it easier to say goodbye, but it didn't. After five days of hearing the phone on the other end ring and ring, Carla let herself believe that she would never reach the owner, that she could keep him for herself. But it wasn't meant to be. Her disappointment was selfish, but it was real.

Water from the tap splashed over Carla's hands as she chewed on her thoughts. The water, growing hotter by the second, finally made her pull them away. She turned off the taps and dried her hands on a clean bar rag. Then she reached up to the shelf that held the radio and found her station. Music made everything easier to bear. She sang along with Bad Religion as she carefully spread icing on her black-and-white cookies, concentrating on making the two halves perfectly symmetrical and neat. Her back was to the swinging door, so it wasn't until Libby tapped her on the shoulder, startling her, that Carla realized she was there.

"What the actual fuck?" Carla scowled at the ruined cookie in her hand. "Look what you made me do." She tossed it onto the worktop.

"So sorry, hon," Libby said. "I said your name a couple times, but I guess you didn't hear." She switched the radio off. Carla moved to turn it on again, but Libby put a hand gently on Carla's shoulder, which she shrugged off.

"You want to talk about it?" Libby asked, drawing her eyebrows together.

"Talk about what?" Carla turned the radio on and lowered the volume.

"Whatever's eatin' you. I know it's none of my business, but maybe you need to vent a little?"

"I got nothing to vent." Carla turned to the sink and scrubbed furiously at one of the baking trays.

"I was never a good student," Libby said, "but I can read people."

"Well, quit trying to read me." Carla put the dripping tray on the drainboard.

"I get it, hon." Libby picked up a towel and began to dry the clean tray. "People tell me I come on a bit too strong. But if you ever want to talk, I'm a good listener."

Carla glared at her but said nothing. She went back to icing cookies, which was more difficult now because her fingers were warm and damp.

"You're a Scorpio, right?" Libby went right on talking. "They're tough on the outside, hiding their feelings from other people. I'm guessing you have a birthday next month." Carla didn't respond, so Libby continued. "Not a believer in the zodiac?"

"That stuff's bullshit." Carla wouldn't meet Libby's eyes. She read her daily horoscope in the *Sun.*

"Is it, though?" Libby said. "Take me for example. I'm a Gemini, known for being social butterflies. I can talk anybody's ear off, given half a chance. I see you as the opposite. Someone who keeps everything inside, doesn't like feeling vulnerable." She was quiet for a moment. "Oh! Capricorn. Some of them don't believe in astrology, but that's because they are secretive and astrology spills everybody's secrets." She gave a little laugh.

When Carla didn't respond, Libby continued. "My guess is that you bit Sylvia's head off out there because there's bigger problems in your life than people asking too many questions about your dog. Whatever's going on, it's not about the dog, is it?"

"Nope. It's about the dog."

"So, tell me about your dog, then."

Carla was happy to change the subject. "He's not mine. He belongs to an old lady." She looked at her hand where she had written the owner's name and address. The ink was smeared now but still legible. "Elizabeth Hartman. The lady, not the dog. His name is Gizmo."

She gave a quick summary of the events of the past few days, carefully spreading the thin icing on each perfect cookie as she talked.

"It was someone else, a cleaner or a housekeeper, who answered the phone. She said the owner's been in the hospital, which is why I couldn't reach her." Carla finished the last cookie and put the icing bowl into the sink to soak.

The woman on the phone had spoken with a heavy accent, but Carla got the gist of the situation. The dog had disappeared from Elizabeth's fenced yard about a week ago. She searched but couldn't find him, so she put an ad in the newspaper. The day her ad appeared in the *Sun* she fell and ended up in the hospital with a broken hip.

"How awful." A crease appeared between Libby's eyebrows. "Are you sure it's her dog?"

"Yeah. Pretty sure he'll be sleeping in his own bed soon enough." Carla didn't say anything about how she was going to get the dog back to his home without a car. She was still working that out. "The lady's coming home tonight, the cleaner said, so I'm bringing the dog back before work in the morning." Carla's voice cracked with emotion. She pointed to the writing on her hand, "I have her address."

"Aw, hon. That'll be tough, I can tell. But you're doing the right thing." Libby looked into Carla's face, her eyes soft and her tone softer. "You're attached to him."

"You don't know anything about me," Carla snapped. "He's just a damn stray dog!"

Libby held her palms toward Carla in a calming gesture. "You're right. I don't know you, but I'd like to."

"Then you need to know I don't like people sticking their noses into my life." Carla lifted a rack of clean cups and flatware from the dishwasher. "I don't need a friend, and I don't want to *open up*. I don't want to *share*. I don't want to *talk about my feelings*. Okay?"

Libby took the heavy rack from Carla's hands and studied her face for a moment. "I'm good at reading people, remember?" she said with a wink and went back into the dining room.

Chapter 9

Tuesday, October 28, 1997

The dog's whining grew louder and more urgent when the taxi stopped in front of a rusty mailbox. Carla had been dreading this moment. Libby was right about one thing. She was hopelessly attached to the dog, whose name she now knew was Gizmo.

"You said 4262, right? Gustafson Road?" the driver asked.

Carla checked the faded address written on her hand and peered through the darkness at the numbers painted on the mailbox. They matched. An overgrown gravel driveway led down a slope and into dense woods. She could barely see the house.

Taking Gizmo home in a cab was the only solution Carla could think of. Her car was undrivable. Getting a ride from someone was out because who would she ask, anyway? The bus was out because pets weren't allowed. Besides, according to her route map, there was no bus that went anywhere close to Gustafson Road. Walking was out too because the old lady's place was at least five miles from Carla's apartment.

Luckily, she found this cut-rate taxi company that was willing to let Gizmo ride along. She couldn't afford to pay for it, so she would show up with the dog and ask Elizabeth to pay for a round trip. Considering all Carla had done, the old lady owed her that much.

"Are you sure this is the place?" the driver asked. She had told him briefly about the situation.

"How should I know? Pull in." Carla wasn't about to get out of the cab until she was sure she had the right house.

A couple hundred yards further on, a big house, wide and low, came into view in the headlights. The soft gray of its weathered shake siding was the perfect camouflage among the trunks of soaring pines and cedars. A thick carpet of brilliant green moss had taken hold on the roof. Ancient ivy crept over the brick foundation and up the chimney to the eaves. Unruly rhododendrons as tall as trees ran along the high wooden fence on the side of the house. The driveway continued past the fence, probably to a garage in the back. Three concrete steps led to an open porch. The front window was large and covered by heavy drapes. No light showed through anywhere.

Gizmo panted and squirmed, stepping on Carla's lap with his huge paws and pressing his muzzle against the window where he left a slobbery smear. Carla scratched his ears, preparing herself to let go of the dog who had become part of her life in six short days. She leaned in for one last long hug. Humming softly, she kissed his neck. A light came on over the front door, a harsh flood light with no welcome in it.

"Looks like someone's expecting you after all. The fare's twelve-fifty." He flipped on the dome light.

"Right, yeah. About that—" Carla sighed. "The lady who lives here is going to pay. And I need a ride back, like I told you on the phone." The distance from Elizabeth's place to the coffee shop was about the same as back to her apartment. It would save time—and bus fare—to have the driver take her directly to work. "I'll be right out with the money. Wait here."

"Believe me, I ain't goin' nowhere until I get paid. Twenty-five plus wait time."

She picked up the nearly full bag of kibble, the biggest package she could afford. Gizmo needed proper food more than she did, so she'd splurged on it. As she stuffed the bag into her big canvas purse, she chewed on her lip. If it was the wrong address or this wasn't Elizabeth's dog, who would pay the cabbie? *Shit.* She had her tips in her wallet, but she needed every penny.

As soon as he was free, Gizmo leaped from the lighted taxi into the darkness and galloped like a racehorse toward the big house. The front door was wide open now and a wedge of light fell over the steps like the lady was rolling out the red carpet. The dog disappeared inside before Carla was even on her feet.

"How much?" called a scratchy voice from the shadows of the doorway. It must have been obvious that Carla was not a person with money for taxis.

The voice came from an elderly woman in a wheelchair, her knees covered with a colorful shawl, and a pair of enormous glasses sitting high on her nose. It would be so easy to ask for more than the fare. A little extra because she could and because she needed money so badly.

"Twenty-five, if I don't keep him waiting." Carla started up the steps, noticing the ornate but rusty wrought-iron railing.

"Here," the woman snapped, holding up three tens in a shaking claw. "The rest is a tip, for the driver, not you."

Carla took the bills and looked past the old woman for a peek inside. She wanted to say goodbye to Gizmo, but he had run to the back of the house, probably to find his food dish. She remembered the bag she was holding and gave it to the woman. "Well, bye."

"What's your name?"

"Carla."

The dog appeared at Elizabeth's elbow with his tongue hanging out. He stepped forward and leaned against Carla's leg for a moment.

She rubbed his head, and her vision blurred. Gizmo returned to sit beside his owner.

Practically curling over on herself, the woman gazed at him and stroked the fur at his neck. Without raising her head, she whispered, "Thank you."

Carla wasn't sure if the woman was thanking her for looking after her dog or thanking Gizmo for coming home and for just being a dog. Emotion pricked the back of Carla's throat. She turned and walked toward the taxi.

"Wait!" came the scratchy voice again.

Carla came back to the bottom of the steps.

"This is for you. For your trouble." Elizabeth produced a pale-blue envelope from under the blanket. "Take it." She waited, her owl eyes huge behind thick lenses.

The paper was thick, expensive, but the contents were thin. A check or a single bill. Was it a five? A ten? More? Carla shoved it into her jacket pocket. "He was no trouble. But thanks."

Elizabeth cleared her throat and turned her face away. "I'm not one to ask for help, but under the circumstances—" she sighed and looked down at her wheelchair. "I'm not sure how I'll manage now. Come in for a little while until Gizmo settles in."

No way was she going into this old lady's house. The place was probably full of furniture with plastic slipcovers and fake flowers everywhere. Besides, it was almost six, and Carla was due at the Coffee Spot in half an hour. "What about the taxi? He charges by the minute to wait." In the pockets of her jacket, Carla gripped the cab fare with one hand and the blue envelope with the other.

"Yes. Of course. Go on." The woman rolled herself back away from the open door and pushed it closed with a bang.

Sitting on the floor of the living room that evening, Carla tuned her bass and tried some scales. Her fingers were cold and stubborn. She leaned back and for a moment expected to feel Gizmo's warm body behind her. The emptiness now that he was gone felt enormous. Nothing could take her mind off the loss of him. Except maybe the two crisp twenties she had pulled from Elizabeth's envelope as she rode to work in the back of the cab.

She paused her finger exercises to blow on her hands. Her heart wasn't in it today. She laid the instrument back in its case and stretched out flat on the grubby carpet, listening to the silence. She looked at the ceiling and at the cobwebs in the corners before she closed her eyes against the ugliness. Quiet pressed on her ears. Stillness was a weight holding her down. No Alex. No Moses. No Gizmo. Just Carla, alone in her dump of an apartment that she couldn't afford, with the bass she didn't feel like playing.

Wasn't Elizabeth lonely, living by herself so far from town? No, she had a dog. What about Nathan? What's his story? If he had a wife and kids, he would have mentioned them. Or not. It wasn't like they were friends. They'd only spent a few hours together. Carla liked being around him but couldn't read his body language. People were good at hiding their feelings. With animals she could tell how they felt about her by noticing the tension in their bodies, the angle of their ears, the sounds they made. Nathan wasn't interested in her. Why would he be?

No point in dwelling on things she couldn't control. And the truth was there wasn't much she *could* control. Carla learned early in life how to push away unpleasant thoughts. But the longer she lay there and the closer she came to sleep, the more her feelings inched lower, each tiny dip pulling her to yet another deeper sadness.

She missed Gizmo, and the way he zoomed around when she got home from work. No human was ever that excited to see her. Iggy had done the same thing, so happy to see her and Gordon when they dragged themselves in after a gig.

Oh, Gordon. In the rare moments when Carla allowed herself to sink into memories of him, her chest ached until the tears flowed as they did now, flooding her ears and trickling through her hair to the carpet. Those tears held years of longing, years of pain and regret. A decade of simmering anger. When she was honest with herself, she still blamed him for everything. For how desperate and truly alone she had been the night he left. For her eviction when she couldn't pay the rent, and for the weeks she spent living on the streets of Seattle, without even Iggy for company and protection.

One cold night she slept on the floor of the ferry terminal because the shelters were full. Snow swirled outside, and she woke in the morning to a woman's round face peering at her with an expression of worry pinching thick eyebrows together. "You okay, hon? What's your name? I'm Val."

Val paid for a one-way ferry ticket across Puget Sound and walked with Carla to a shelter in Bremerton where there was room for her. She stayed there until she got the job at the Coffee Spot and answered Alex's ad for a roommate. Carla never saw the woman again and only knew her first name, but she always hoped that one day Val might come in for a cup of coffee so Carla could thank her properly.

Fear of being homeless again was real. If she couldn't come up with the rent, Carla would have to move out. Maybe not this month, or the next, but the day was bound to come. She had nowhere to go. Her security deposit would go right into her landlord's pocket because that's how it was. Her thrift store mattress and the kitchen table Alex left behind would end up in the dumpster. What would she have left? Some clothes in a duffel bag, a little blue suitcase full of useless trinkets, a few CDs and a cheap little player, and her bass. Exactly what she had carried with her when she stepped off the ferry in Bremerton and followed Val to begin the next part of her life.

At least she still had her job. But with no car and nowhere to live, that wouldn't last long either.

"Done feeling sorry for yourself?" Carla said aloud. She sat up and slowly unfurled her fingers, trying to rub away the little crescent moons in her palms. She wiped her eyes roughly with the sleeve of her shirt, smearing her heavy black eyeliner. "You've survived worse."

Taking stock seemed like the place to start. She retrieved her canvas shoulder bag from the kitchen table and pawed through the contents for her checkbook and wallet. Coins jingled in the bottom from her tips the day before, so she dumped everything out. From the mess of tissues and scraps of paper, she rescued the last stick of gum. Chewing fast, she organized the change into one-dollar stacks.

Carla bent over the table and scribbled the amounts onto the back of Elizabeth's blue envelope, checking her math twice to be sure she had made no mistakes. To the final number she added her usual two-week pay she would collect on the thirtieth.

"Yes!" she shouted, punching the air over her head. But her triumph was short-lived. Once she subtracted what she owed her landlord, she would have $4.87 left in her bank account to last until her next paycheck. She wouldn't even be able to afford bus fare. Over one hurdle only to crash into a brick wall.

Scooping everything back into her bag, Carla paused to open the crumpled yellow flyer about the volunteer meeting. She smoothed the paper out against the edge of the table and read it again. An idea was taking shape. A way to climb over that brick wall.

Carla needed a temporary solution to her financial troubles. A bit of fast money. It took a few minutes to organize her thoughts and make a list of options. She dismissed her first couple of ideas, but when her glance landed on the blue envelope, she hit on something promising.

"Who's calling?" came the scratchy voice.

"It's Carla." She stood in her kitchen picking at a loose corner of the Formica countertop. Her nails were in bad shape anyway. She was down to the last of her polish and eyeliner.

"Who?"

"Carla. I brought your dog—"

"What? Just a moment while I get my hearing aid." Elizabeth put the phone down with a loud clunk.

Minutes passed. The lady must have wandered off for good. Faint music from a television or a radio played in the background. Carla remembered the wheelchair and summoned all her patience. She hummed along with the melody and tapped her foot to the beat while she waited.

One by one she had crossed her money-making schemes off her list. Helping Nathan protect the whales was never going to be a paying gig. Gary might give her another chance at cleaning empty apartments after he got over his sulk, but she couldn't bank on it. Thinking about cleaning and housekeeping brought Elizabeth to mind. Her housekeeper answered the phone yesterday. Paying someone to clean your house couldn't be cheap. The lady must be loaded. Carla held the empty envelope thinking of how easily the lady had parted with forty dollars, and another thirty for Carla's cab fare. Too bad she already had someone to clean for her. But there was something else she might pay Carla to do.

"Hello?" the woman said, startling Carla. "Is someone there?"

"Oh. Yes. It's Carla. I brought your dog home this morning."

"My what?"

"Your dog!" she shouted into the receiver. The old girl was further gone than Carla thought.

"Oh." A pause. "What do you want?"

This question rarely entered Carla's mind anymore. Her desires weren't for things, but for the absence of things. Not to be broke. Not to be homeless. Not to be harassed by her mom.

"What do you want?" the old woman snapped again, louder this time. Carla flinched. She hated people barking at her, but she'd learned to pretend it didn't sting. Making this call was what she had to do to survive, so she stood a little straighter and barreled ahead.

"Before I left your house today, you asked if I could stay and help you. That you didn't think you could manage the dog by yourself. The taxi was waiting and everything, so I left." Carla tugged on one of her earrings. "But I have an idea."

Her fidgety fingers resumed picking at the countertop as she laid out her plan. She would take a cab to Elizabeth's after work every day until the lady was back on her feet. Carla would walk Gizmo and take a cab home again. For a fee, of course.

"And I'd be only taking care of the dog." Carla had no interest in being Elizabeth's nurse, wiping her ass or whatever else might be necessary in that department.

"I've hired a private health aide to take care of me. I would no more ask you to take care of me than I would ask her to take care of the dog." There was a pause while Elizabeth considered the idea. "How much?"

Carla had given this number careful thought. It was a lot to ask for, but the lady clearly had money—big house on a couple of acres, a maid, and now a private nurse. Between bus fare and groceries, Carla figured she could survive on about six bucks a day until payday in mid-November. Six times sixteen days. She'd need almost a hundred dollars. Carla had no idea how long Elizabeth might need help with Gizmo, but she hoped to get at least a week out of the deal.

"Twenty dollars a day plus cab fare?" Carla didn't mean to lift her voice at the end, making it sound like she was open to negotiation. She pushed her thumbnail under the Formica. "Five days minimum."

"Highway robbery!" Elizabeth screeched.

A piece of the thin counter material the size of a quarter snapped off and flew into the air landing at Carla's feet. She picked it up and tried to fit it back into place with trembling fingers. There was silence on Elizabeth's end of the line for a moment. The old lady was right. Carla opened her mouth to ask for less, when Gizmo barked.

"Hush, Gizzy," Elizabeth said. He whined softly, and then the woman said, "I hate to admit it, but you're right. I do need help. I had difficulty getting Gizmo out into the yard to do his business today. How long did you say until your car is repaired? If you drove, I wouldn't have to pay for your taxi."

"My car is toast. And there's no bus up your way."

"Well, use mine then. It's been sitting in the garage since I broke my hip. The gas tank is full, which should be more than enough to get you here and home again for a week. Does that arrangement suit you?"

"You would trust me with your car?" This was more than Carla could believe.

"More importantly, I am trusting you with my most prized possession. My dog. Gizmo is a good judge of character, and he likes you. I'll pay you twenty dollars a day to walk him for an hour each evening. I'll pay for your cab here tomorrow, and you can take the car after your walk."

With a little persuasion, Elizabeth agreed to let Carla drive her car to and from the coffee shop if she paid for the extra gas. And best of all, she would get to spend more time with Gizmo. His goofy face flashed in her mind making her smile. By the time she hung up, it was settled.

Next to the phone was the bundle of brochures from the volunteer meeting. She studied the photo of the orca midair, thinking of the day she spent with Nathan on his boat. The two of them in that moment when he rested his arm on her shoulder to point out a fin in the distance. The way the heat from his body warmed hers. The memory sent a tiny jolt into the middle of her chest that made her blink.

Carla found a bottle of glue in a kitchen drawer and dabbed some onto the corner of the counter. Humming to herself, she slid the broken piece into place and held it with her thumb, whisper-screaming "Rise Above" while the glue set.

Chapter 10

Wednesday, October 29, 1997

Carla rode toward Elizabeth's house in the back seat of the taxi, mesmerized by the strobe effect as tree trunks, silhouetted against the violet evening sky, whipped past. Their black branches stretched across the road, as if to join hands with the trees on the opposite side. She settled back and closed her eyes, letting her thoughts go where they wanted. They landed on Sunday, the day she'd spent with Nathan. With the whales.

She had done something useful for a change. Shouting through a megaphone a couple of times wasn't exactly saving the world or even saving the whales, but it was something. Nathan told her she had been a big help. A lie, but a nice one.

Elizabeth opened the door to her knock, and Gizmo practically toppled Carla with a tail that wagged all the way to his shoulders. His owner spoke quietly, and he sat on the gleaming floor next to her wheelchair. Carla removed her boots and set them by the door. Was this lady's house always so clean?

"I know this isn't part of our agreement, but unfortunately Gizmo has had an accident in the living room." Elizabeth had a roll of paper towels and a bottle of some kind of cleaning spray in her lap.

Carla stroked Gizmo's head, and he pushed his snout against her forearm. She straightened and sniffed. The smell was terrible even in the hallway.

"My housekeeper doesn't come until Friday. I can't possibly leave it. Poor baby." Elizabeth gazed at Gizmo and ran her thin fingers lightly over his ears. "You haven't done that since you were a puppy. I guess I didn't get you out quickly enough this morning." To Carla she said, "It takes me so long now to do simple things." She held out the cleaning supplies, her magnified eyes watery.

Carla took the paper towels. The heavy spray bottle shook in the old woman's raised hand. It crossed Carla's mind that she could demand more money to do this and any other unpleasant tasks that came along. Elizabeth was loaded. And desperate.

"You've got her over a barrel, Cargo," her mother's voice chirped in her head. *"This gig's a cash cow!"*

If anyone knew how to take advantage of a situation and make money from it, it was her mother. Some kids grew up trying to be like their parents, but others—like Carla—wanted to be nothing like them.

She took the bottle from Elizabeth's hand and stepped into the living room. A stone fireplace with a high mantel dominated one wall. No fire, no logs, no ash. Spotless. Classical music floated from speakers on either side of the fireplace, and modern, expensive-looking furniture was arranged like a magazine picture. Carla cracked open the large front window for some fresh air, knelt on the soft oriental rug, and got busy.

She couldn't bring herself to ask for more money for this chore, but maybe there was more to be earned another way. Carla worked out the details of her new plan as she scooped up the mess, saturated the spot on the rug, and blotted up the wetness.

In the kitchen with her wheelchair pulled up to the table, Elizabeth poured tea. Two mugs sat on a small tray along with a miniature pitcher of milk, a tiny bowl containing sugar cubes, and a plate of pale cookies. Despite what she had just dealt with, Carla's empty stomach growled.

"Get yourself cleaned up and carry that into the living room," Elizabeth barked over her shoulder with a nod toward the tea tray as she wheeled herself slowly through the doorway. Gizmo followed her out.

Carla did as she was told and returned to the living room with the tray. When the old woman flapped a bony hand toward a coffee table, Carla set the tray down on it.

"Sit down. Drink your tea before you take Gizmo out."

Carla took a mug and sat. Man, this lady was bossy. If it weren't for the fact that she was now her employer, Carla might have told her off. But as cranky as Elizabeth was, something about her felt familiar. Her tone was direct like Joan's, the foster mother Carla remembered most clearly, the only foster parent who understood her. Carla had almost been happy living with Joan's family and might have stayed until she was eighteen if Carla's mother hadn't won legal custody after proving to the court that she could handle raising her eleven-year-old daughter.

The living room was cool now with the window open, and Carla's socks were damp, so the warm mug felt good in her hands. She leaned back, shivering a little as she took her first sip.

"I was thinking, E," Carla said, her voice trembling slightly. She hated the way she sounded, nervous and timid. "Is it okay if I call you that?"

Elizabeth looked up from stirring her tea. "If you must."

Carla lifted her chin and cleared her throat. "I was thinking, if you want, I could come twice a day. Seems like Gizmo could use at least a short walk in the morning so he doesn't end up pooping in the house again. I have to be at the coffee shop at six-thirty on weekdays, so it would be early."

Elizabeth leaned forward to set her mug back on the tray without drinking, wincing with the effort. She settled into her wheelchair again delicately, as if her body were a basket of eggs. With lips tightly pinched, she closed her eyes. There was a long pause, so long that Carla was afraid she might have fallen asleep. Even Gizmo was concerned. He'd been lying on the rug near the coffee table, his gaze fixed on the plate of cookies, but now he stood and padded over to Elizabeth and rested his chin on her thigh, eyebrows dancing.

The room was quiet except for the soft violin music and the ticking of a clock somewhere nearby. Carla squirmed in her chair. She wanted to get Gizmo out for his walk so she could head home for a hot shower and bowl of instant ramen.

With her eyes still closed, Elizabeth said at last, "That would be a lot of driving for you. More of your time and more of my gas."

Carla couldn't let this opportunity slip away. She inched forward. "I guess, but I don't mind. Really."

Elizabeth stroked Gizmo's head slowly from his snout to his ears, again and again while Carla waited. After a moment the hand stopped moving. The old woman's chin rested on her chest. This time Carla was sure she had dozed off.

The clock ticked off the seconds. Following the sound, Carla spotted the clock, an old-fashioned one, on the mantel. The painting on the wall behind it was not what Carla expected an old lady to like. Instead of a stuffy portrait or a boring landscape, it was modern, abstract, and done in bright colors. The more Carla stared at it, the more it looked like nude figures dancing.

On the end table between Carla's chair and Elizabeth's wheelchair were some framed photographs, and one in a small gold frame caught her eye. Carla picked it up and saw a young man leaning against a car with his arms crossed. The picture was black-and-white, faded almost to brown, and the car was one of those old-fashioned ones with bulging fenders and wood side panels. He wore a uniform. The focus wasn't sharp, but the serious expression on the boy's face couldn't disguise his pride in that car, his confidence in his future.

Carla glanced back at the woman napping in the wheelchair. Did they have an agreement about the morning walk or not? Elizabeth's eyes fluttered open. Carla quickly put the picture back on the table. She shouldn't have touched it.

"It's my impression," Elizabeth said as if she were picking up the thread of some other conversation, "that you and I are alike."

Carla scoffed and disguised it with a cough. No need to be rude.

"For instance, I'm guessing you're alone in the world, judging from the fact that you had no one to drive you and Gizmo here yesterday. No family or husband?" The old woman pursed her thin lips. Her clipped tone and stern expression made Carla feel like she was being scolded. Why did everyone think she needed a man? Did she look helpless or something? When Carla didn't respond, Elizabeth said. "I thought as much."

"Generally speaking," she continued, "I'm not the sort of person who worries about living by myself. I've done it most of my life, since my parents died anyway. I've always felt safe here in my childhood home, but I admit that since my recent injury, I've had trouble sleeping. Pain is part of it and worry, I think. Fear. The knowledge that I'm more vulnerable than ever before. Therefore," she said crisply, "I would like to propose a mutually beneficial plan." She looked Carla squarely in the face. When she spoke again, her tone was softer.

"I'm afraid we got off on the wrong foot yesterday. I'm somewhat of a misanthrope, I suppose. But that's no excuse for being unpleasant. Something about being helpless brings out the worst in me. I do apologize." The woman's lips lifted into a smile. "If I promise to behave, would you consider staying here until I am up and around, until I'm myself again? I would feel better if someone were here with me. At night."

Carla stiffened. The lady was out of her mind, giving a stranger the keys to her car and asking her to move in, to live in her house like…what? One of those companions in the old-fashioned novels she had to read in high school where a young woman is hired to keep an old one company? The whole situation was too weird. "No way." Carla stood to leave, but E had more to say.

"For an additional fee, of course. I'd pay you one hundred dollars a day."

Carla sat again. The idea was nuts, but the extra money was tempting. Very.

"You could more easily manage a walk with Gizmo in the mornings before you leave for work at the—what did you say it was? A coffee shop?"

"Sorry. But I…"

The woman's shoulders sagged, and the corners of her tiny mouth pulled down. So what? What did Carla care? She didn't owe this lady anything.

"But what if there was a fire or I had another fall? Gizmo is smart, but he can't dial a phone to call for help."

"Why would you even trust me?" The lady had clearly lost her marbles. "How do you know I'm not a thief or an ax murderer? I mean, look at me!" Carla jumped to her feet and waved her hand at her shabby clothes.

"Don't be ridiculous." Elizabeth frowned, squinting at Carla. "I don't care what you look like. You are no threat to me. Gizmo would protect me with his life from anyone attempting to do me harm."

"What about your nurse? Couldn't she stay overnight?"

"I asked. She turned me down flat. She doesn't like dogs, and the feeling is mutual. I have to shut Gizmo away when she's here. But he trusts you, so I know you are trustworthy. I value his opinion of people because he's never been wrong. He has never let me down."

"He let you down by running off," Carla mumbled.

"Speak up!" Elizabeth adjusted her hearing aid.

"Why did he run away then?"

No one spoke for a long moment. The only sounds besides the clock and the violins came in through the open window. Crows arguing in the pines.

"Shut that window," Elizabeth snapped.

Carla flinched but got up and closed it. Daylight was almost gone, but she could make out a large rabbit at the edge of the lawn. In the woods beyond, there would be deer, foxes, owls, and bats coming out of their dens and nests to graze and hunt in their own safe, familiar territory. Why would any animal venture far from home? What drew pets away from the comfort of their beds, perches, and food dishes? Why were there orcas in the inlet? Curiosity or some inborn longing for freedom that lured them to places where they didn't belong?

A soft sound behind her made Carla turn. Elizabeth was carefully lifting a record from the turntable. She slipped it into its paper sleeve and then the cardboard jacket. "If you don't want to stay overnight, it's fine. Suit yourself."

When the album was tucked away on a shelf with the rest of her large collection and there was no more to be said, Elizabeth wheeled her chair through the doorway and disappeared around the corner.

Carla returned from walking Gizmo to find the house dark and quiet. In the empty living room, she turned on a small lamp. Its light made the space snug and warm. The tray with the mugs of cold tea and uneaten cookies was still on the low table. She sat and helped herself to a cookie and then another, suddenly ravenous and weary. The sleek leather sofa was comfortable. Gizmo sat at her stocking feet and placed a heavy paw on her knee. Carla rubbed her thumb up and down between his eyes in time to the ticking clock. She looked around the room at the fireplace, the paintings, the oriental rug soft under her feet. Maybe it had been a mistake to dismiss E's idea.

"What should I do, Gizzy?" He cocked his head and gazed at her with those intelligent, persuasive eyes. "It's good money. Easy work." His tail thumped.

She hoped she didn't blow it by pissing the old lady off. Not only had she refused E's offer, but she hadn't been exactly polite about it. Carla replayed the conversation in her mind, trying to understand how she had managed to get under E's skin so badly. Bringing up the fact that her dog ran away set the old lady off.

"I guess I hit a nerve, eh Gizmo?"

She stood and crossed the room toward the spotless kitchen with Gizmo at her heels. She found and refilled his water bowl. As she leaned against the counter watching him slurp and splatter until the bowl was dry, Carla weighed her options.

The most pressing problem was that if she was going to get home tonight, she needed car keys. And there was still the question of whether she was expected in the morning. She hated to bother E, but it wasn't even eight o'clock. She listened, hoping for some sign that E wasn't sleeping. The house was silent. Carla would either have to sleep on the couch or call a cab she couldn't pay for. Good thing the sofa was comfortable. She headed back to the living room and spotted a pale blue envelope with her name on it propped against the mantel clock. The note inside read:

Keys on hook by back door: car, house, + remote for garage door opener. I will be asleep when you arrive in the a.m. but will see you tomorrow evening. 10 days - $40 per day, for 2 walks. I hope that is acceptable.

More than fair. She'd be four hundred dollars richer! Feeling kindly toward the old lady now and sorry she had upset her, Carla picked up the tea tray and carried it into the kitchen. She had to get the keys anyway, so she might as well be helpful.

As she lifted the key ring from its hook, Carla's eye was drawn to a small photograph on the wall above it. It was the same as the one in the oval frame, the one with the young man. Exactly the same. Why two? Who was this guy? Carla peered closer. It was a sailor's uniform, and the man was handsome in an old-fashioned way, smiling crookedly as if he was trying hard not to show how pleased he was with himself. It was the confident smile of someone who had his life all figured out.

She had a similar photo of Gordon, taken by his mom on the day the band left for Seattle to follow his dreams. Carla's only dream was to get out of Wisconsin any way she could. The details of the picture were stamped in her memory. Gordon, leaning against the rusty old van in his Ramones T-shirt and tight jeans as his shoulder-length hair lifted in the breeze. His grin had the confidence Carla saw in E's sailor's smile.

Soon after Gordon left, Carla threw away everything that reminded her of him. The photo turned up much later inside a CD case, and she'd kept it—she didn't know why—adding it to the odds and ends she saved in her child-size blue suitcase.

Carla opened the back door. The moment she stepped out onto the small landing overlooking the sprawling fenced yard, a single floodlight mounted near the roofline of the house came on. It cast its light over everything within twenty yards of the house. The garage was in shadow outside the tall wooden fence and the woods beyond were darker still.

She stood motionless for a moment, listening to the sounds of night animals moving through the brush. A bat swooped into view under the light where moths fluttered in crazy circles. Chittering raccoons drew her attention to the low branches of a cedar in the corner of the yard. A pair of eyes caught the light, and then the yard was plunged into darkness again. Carla turned to lock the door behind her, triggering the floodlights once more. She looked at the keys in her hand. So much trust. So much responsibility. Exhaling a long breath, she started down the wooden steps, which were steep and slick with moss. She held the handrail until she reached the brick walkway. As soon as she did, more lights came on. At least her walk to the garage would be brightly lit.

Chapter 11

Thursday, October 30, 1997

"You look beat, hon," Libby said after Carla locked the shop door behind the last customer. "Let me clean up so you can take care of the register and be on your way."

"I got this. You should go." Carla turned a chair over and put it on top of a table. The floors were dirtier than usual from the heavy foot traffic all day. Plus, her day had started earlier than usual, walking Gizmo in the cold. She was due back at E's in a couple of hours. This pace was going to be tough to keep up every day.

She reached for another chair, but Libby stopped her hand. "Take five. We can get some air, and then I'll help you with all this. It's Kevin's bowling night."

Carla pulled away and continued stacking chairs on tables. Libby's light steps moved across the dining room and into the kitchen with a swish of the swinging door. Carla was spent. That was a fact, but she had no intention of confessing it to anyone.

A moment later Libby appeared holding a mop and a bucket. "Want me to do this now or after we take a break?" Libby smiled like someone who knew how to get what she wanted.

"Fine." Carla exhaled letting her shoulders sag. The truth was she was glad Libby was there. "I'll take a break."

The two went out the back door and sat on the wooden steps. The air was cool and damp, but the steps were mostly dry. Carla scanned the branches for a flash of Ghost's white fur amid the green of the alders bordering the rear of the coffee shop. If the squirrel was around, he was keeping out of sight. A crow landed near the pan of water Carla always left out. He cocked his head and looked at Libby, sizing her up—safe or dangerous?

"Mind if I smoke?" Libby said loudly. The startled crow flew off and perched on the powerline above them. Libby pulled out a pack of cigarettes and offered one to Carla, who refused with a quick shake of her head. She wanted one desperately but was afraid one would lead to more. The habit was an expense she couldn't afford. She'd chewed her last stick of gum too.

Carla pushed both clenched fists into her large apron pocket. Her knuckles pressed against the handful of walnuts she had saved for Ghost from the morning's baking. The pecans were there too from last Thursday's maple-pecan muffins. Had she seen him last week?

"So, what's your story, hon?" Libby lit her cigarette and snuck a look at Carla's bare left hand. "Boyfriend?"

Why was that always the first question? As if being in a relationship was expected. As if being tied to someone day in and day out was something great.

Libby searched Carla's impassive face for a response. "Nobody? You must get lonely." She took a drag and tapped the ash onto the step below.

If she'd been someone who shared every thought, Carla would have said what was true: everyone is lonely. It was the first feeling she could name, riding in the back seat of yet another social worker's car to yet another home where no one loved her. Talking about her emotions, even feeling them, wasn't safe. Loneliness was deep in her bones, but it sprang to the surface, bright and sharp, at the lightest touch—an accidental brush of someone's hand against hers—reminding her it was still there.

But she wasn't one of those people, so instead, she said, "You got kids?" Carla didn't want to hear this woman's life story, but if she got Libby talking, she would be off the hook to answer more questions. She could sit and listen. Or not listen. Whatever.

"It's just me and Kevin now. The two sons are married and live back East, and our daughter is at UW." Libby took another drag on the cigarette and blew the smoke away from Carla, but the breeze pushed it back. It smelled so good. "Maggie's smart but plays it cool, like you. You remind me of her a little. I told her she should study business. She's got the brains for it. She *says* she's studying hospitality. I'm like, you need a degree for that? Hell, I learned everything I know on the job."

The crow on the wire swayed as he squawked three times, eyeing the water dish. He was staying nearby, curious but cautious.

"I know what you're thinking," Libby continued. "You see a middle-aged woman working in a hole-in-the-wall, and you're thinking she should have a better job at some posh place by now. But you see, that's where you'd be wrong. I *did* have that job. I was the hostess at Reiner's downtown Seattle. And before that I was waiting tables in the Space Needle."

Carla stopped listening. Damn, the woman could talk! A Steller's jay shrieked from the dense foliage. Carla followed the sound, hoping for a glimpse, but its blue feathers kept it hidden in the shadows of the Douglas fir.

"I'm kidding, hon." Libby was still talking. "I'm not after your job. I gave up this line of work last year on account of my back. My doctor says it's—whatchamacallit—*osteo-sporosis*. Kevin's retired from the navy with a good pension, so I'm not in it for the money. No, Ricky called and asked if I'd help him out, because of the whale watchers and all. We go way back." Libby examined her cigarette.

Carla still wasn't used to hearing her boss referred to by his first name. "Way back, like, high school?"

Tracyton was that kind of town. People were born here and stayed here. Everybody knew everybody's business. Except for outsiders like Carla.

"Hell, no. Kindergarten!" Libby ran her free hand through her short hair, leaving it sticking up on one side. She didn't seem to notice or care.

Libby smoked for a while without talking, and Carla looked for the screaming jay. She'd spent hours flipping through bird books from the Bremerton library. She appreciated the logic of the classification system and quickly learned the identifying features of each kind of bird. She did the same with every native plant and mammal on the peninsula. She could even name most of the insects and reptiles. Then the orcas arrived. She didn't know anything about the creatures that lived in Puget Sound. A stop at the library before heading to E's tonight might turn up something useful, something that would help her understand why the whales were in the inlet and why they were staying so long.

Like all kids who loved animals, Carla wanted to be a veterinarian. Teachers always told her she was a good student and should go to college. And who would pay for that? No one. On her eighteenth birthday, she was off the foster-care rolls. The State of Wisconsin said goodbye and good luck. Veterinary school was another dead dream.

The jay had gone quiet or flown off. Carla unfurled her hands and stared at the marks made by her fingernails. Libby was studying them too.

Carla tucked her hands under her thighs. "Don't tell me you read palms."

"Not palms, but I started playing around with tarot. I love all that woo-woo stuff. Can I practice on you sometime?"

"*Pfff.* That hocus-pocus shit?"

Carla's practical side knew tarot was nonsense, but the other side, the one stuck in her childhood hope that magic was real, believed in good-luck charms, horoscopes, tea leaves, all of it. The small pale-blue suitcase on a shelf in her closet was full of evidence. It held a wild assortment of things that at one time or another she believed had magical power. Four-leaf clovers pressed in waxed paper, a Saint Christopher medal on a key ring, the bigger half of a wishbone, her lucky penny, feathers, some polished stones.

"I'll bring my cards in tomorrow. It'll be fun!" Libby said, bumping Carla gently with her shoulder. Carla's skin prickled, and she swallowed the lump that grew in her throat.

The smell of burning tobacco was suddenly too much for her. "Is the offer for a cigarette still on the table? I think I changed my mind."

Libby's laugh was contagious. She threw her head back and her mouth opened unselfconsciously to reveal imperfect teeth. Carla laughed with her and gratefully accepted a cigarette and a light.

"I'm going to get started on the floor. You sit tight and enjoy that." Libby nodded toward the cigarette Carla held between her fingers. She smoothed her skirt, opened the kitchen door, and was gone.

Carla drew deeply on the cigarette, and the nicotine hit her bloodstream. She had tuned out a good chunk of what Libby said, but she was warm and funny and interested in Carla. Libby was okay. It had been a long time since Carla had a friend. A human friend.

Carla put her cigarette out against the sole of her boot and dropped the butt into the dumpster by the back door. Human relationships were dangerous, and the riskiest were the ones that felt safe. Smoking out here with Libby felt safe, which was why it couldn't happen again.

Standing at her kitchen table that evening, Carla leaned on her elbows to read the newspaper under the dim ceiling light. Her legs and back complained, but she didn't have anything to sit on. Alex had been nice enough to leave his wobbly table for her, but it wasn't much good without the chairs.

She used to have time at work to read the *Sun* cover to cover. The Coffee Spot had been so busy today that she never found time to look at the front page. She'd tucked the last dog-eared copy of the paper into her bag as soon as she and Libby had finished closing. They had worked side by side, one not saying a word and the other talking nonstop.

"So, my older son, the one in Indiana? He told me his wife's old boyfriend has been stalking her. My son wants her to carry mace in her purse because she's so scared of the guy. Mandy—that's my daughter-in-law—says he's being paranoid, but if anyone's paranoid, it's Mandy! The girl jumps if you say boo."

On and on Libby had chattered like a magpie until Carla's head ached. The quiet walk with Gizmo in the woods after work had been exactly what she needed. She'd felt nervous about how things would go after refusing E's offer to pay for overnight stays, but the lady was cool with it. Or cold. Hard to tell.

Today's paper was full of stories related to the orcas. Front page news about whose responsibility it was to issue citations to boaters who got too close. Articles in the business section about the increasing trade in local hotels, restaurants, and harbor tours. Traffic reports about blocked lanes and fender benders at some of the best whale-viewing spots. A letter to the editor begging everyone to leave their dogs at home because their barking could scare the whales. Another letter advised people watching the whales from canoes and kayaks to tie up together and continually tap on the hulls of their boats to avoid startling the whales, and in the next letter a guy advised against making noise of any kind because curious whales will come closer to check out what's making the sound.

In his boat last Sunday, Nathan had expressed his opinions about all these topics, but he had a favorite.

"Those cowboys aren't following the rules," he'd said, pointing to a group of about a dozen motorboats. They'd been out for hours in the rain, and Nathan's frustration was bubbling up.

"If it's against the law to get so close, why don't the cops arrest these asshats? Or give them tickets?" Carla asked.

"I'll tell you why," he'd shouted. He took a breath and started again, but she could see he was struggling to keep his temper. "Nobody's in charge. All kinds of law enforcement at our disposal." He counted them off on his fingers. "National Marine Fisheries Service, Washington Department of Fish and Wildlife, the Kitsap County Sheriff's Department. The damn Coast Guard, for crying out loud, if they ever show up. And each one seems to think it's someone else's job to issue citations."

Carla hoped she'd see him again, but now that Mr. Wilson expected her to work weekends, finding the time would be difficult. Thanks to Libby, her workload was manageable at least.

Turning to the last section of the paper, Carla skimmed the classifieds. People offering waterfront access and all-day parking for a fee, trying to make a buck off a pod of whales. So much greed. She couldn't bear to read about lost pets today, and there was still no one looking for a roommate.

She rubbed her temples for a moment and then flipped to the entertainment section to see which bands were playing. Carla was so far removed from all that now, and she hadn't been to a concert in ages, but the habit lingered.

She read an article about a band she liked, Eddie and the Trash Pandas. They played old-school rock and roll, but for a bunch of local guys, they were pretty good. A couple of ads for upcoming shows at the bottom of the page barely registered, since there was no way she could afford tickets.

A moment later, she did a double take, then slapped her hand flat over the corner of the paper and held it there, hiding what she had already seen. She straightened and stared at the wall while her heart hammered in her chest. Closing her eyes, she took a couple of deep breaths to steady herself. After a moment, with a dismissive sniff to prove to herself that she didn't care, she lifted the edge of her hand and peeked underneath it before quickly covering the ad again. It couldn't be Gordon's band, could it? They broke up years ago. Must be a different group with the same name. She slid her hand away to reveal a grainy photo of three guys she didn't recognize. Underneath it said:

One show only
The Chemical People
Halloween Night at The Weathered Wall
1921 Fifth Avenue

In smaller print were the words that caught her attention in the first place: *Also appearing: Gutter Rats—Belinda Hanley and Gordon Invaar.*

Fuck. It was him. She balled up the newspaper, stuffed it in the trash, and walked into the living room for her bass. She snapped open the latches and stared down at it.

"I'm not going to see him," she said aloud. "He dumped me, remember? I have a little pride."

Gordon dropped her when she became inconvenient for him the same way her mother had. She'd survived both. She'd figured out how to take care of herself when no one else would and was stronger for it. A refrain she repeated to herself often.

Carla had forgiven Gordon. Mostly. Maybe it had something to do with the fact that Gordon didn't owe her anything. He had never promised her anything. And he couldn't have predicted what kind of impact his leaving would have on her. But her mother? That was a different story. Carla would never forgive her mom for abandoning her—twice. The first time her mom was a kid herself when she walked away from her infant, and Carla had learned to let that go. But the second time? No. Her mom knew what she was doing. She knew the consequences but chose drugs over her teenage daughter.

Carla lifted her bass out of the case, settled cross-legged in the middle of the carpet, and began to tune the strings. She played a few chords. The fingers of her left hand wandered up the fingerboard, forming a G chord while the pick in her right played a single riff. She let her imagination take her back to the bar in Ballard where she played with the Gutter Rats for the last time. She stopped and laid her bass across her lap. She squeezed her eyes shut. *Don't think about Gordon. Push him out of your thoughts.*

What would be the harm in saying hello? She didn't even need to go to the show. She could scrape together enough money for the ferry and wait outside the Weathered Wall at the end of the night, catch Gordon to say hi, to see if any sparks were left between them. He would be pumped and in a good mood after the gig. Why wouldn't he be glad to see an old friend who had come a long way to say hi? If it didn't work out, she would get back on the ferry and be no worse off than she was right now. And if it *did* work out?

Stop. Just stop. Change the channel. Joan, the only foster mom who cared a rat's ass about Carla, had taught her the trick to help her chase away nightmares.

"Flip your pillow to the other side. It's like changing TV channels," Joan said. "Try thinking about something happy."

It was so simple then. Carla would turn her pillow over and fall asleep again, dreaming of birds and foxes, wildflowers and crab-apple trees. All the things she loved.

Try thinking about the whales in the inlet.

She had so many questions about the whales. The newspaper didn't reveal anything Nathan hadn't told her already. She wanted to know what could be done to help them. If she knew more, maybe she could understand what was happening. Feeling so powerless, so stupid, was maddening. She'd meant to stop at the library after work but forgot. She could ask Nathan. He knew a lot, and he said he was working on a rescue plan just in case. If she saw him again—and she would, wouldn't she? —she could ask him. She had to do something.

Carla pictured the whales performing. The inlet was their stage, and the cheering crowds on the shore and in their boats were their audience. Putting on a show without lights or music. Music. Gordon's concert. Damn. She was right back where she shouldn't be.

How would the night go? She'd stand outside the club, waiting for him to come out. He would sweep her into a hug, lifting her feet from the ground the way he used to. He would tell her he was sorry he ever left her. After, a motel room near the Weathered Wall, a bed with rumpled sheets, sweaty and soft, Gordon sleeping on his back with his long golden hair fanned out over the white pillowcase. His belly and his chest, rising and falling rhythmically under a tangle of pale fur, and his smooth, closed eyelids on either side of his wide, straight nose. Her lion. She would curl against his body, safe.

He would beg her to join the band again and travel with him to his next gig. And the one after that. She would follow him, give up the life—pitiful as it was—that she had built for herself to be part of his. She was wasting her talents. Sylvia, with her beauty-shop dreams, had the right idea after all. Carla deserved better, too. This was her chance, her one and only chance to see Gordon again and to know once and for all if he still loved her. And if she still loved him.

Carla jumped to her feet and marched to the kitchen. She pulled the *Sun* out of the trash and spread it out on the table, smoothing the creases she had made when she crumpled it into a ball. She found the ad and read it again. Twice. Seeing his name in print set her heart racing. She would cut out the ad and stick it on her fridge under a magnet. She couldn't lose him again.

Focused on finding her scissors in the mess of her kitchen drawer and on the possibility of seeing Gordon, Carla didn't notice the blinking light on her answering machine right away. She gasped. Gordon was so present in her mind that for one tiny fraction of a second, she expected his voice when she pressed Play.

"Honey, it's Mom," the shaky voice on the recording said. "Can you pick up? Please?"

Shit. Carla dropped the scissors.

There was a pause and a muffled PA announcement in the background. A hospital? Not again.

"Well, okay. I get it," her mom said. "You don't want to talk to me. I can't blame you. But I came all this way to see you, to show you I've changed. I got a ride from a guy I know as far as Vegas. Then I hitched the rest of the way. Could I stay at your place for a couple of days? You still live there, right? Near Bremerton?" A loud blast of a ferry whistle and her mother stopped talking into the phone. She was hollering at someone in the terminal, asking which boat was leaving. She came back on the line, saying, "Gotta go. My ferry's loading. I'll wait for you when I get off. Please, Carla, come pick me up. I'm begging you."

The recording ended with a click, and the red light blinked off.

What the hell? Her mother must have left Milwaukee right after their conversation last week. Carla checked the time stamp. The call came in at ten fifteen that morning so if her mom took the ten-thirty ferry across from Seattle, she'd been waiting in the Bremerton terminal all day.

So what? She wasn't Carla's responsibility. The temptation to pretend she hadn't listened to the message was strong, to get on with her life as if this had never happened. Soon enough the phone company would close her account anyway because she hadn't paid the bill. Her mom wouldn't be able to reach her again. The last thing she needed was this hassle. Helping her mother always backfired.

Back when she was in high school, Carla was the one who went looking for her mother whenever she went on a binge or a bender. Terrified of losing her and scared the police would find her first, Carla searched her mom's favorite haunts and dragged her home.

After Carla and Gordon moved into their tiny studio apartment in Seattle, Carla called her mom to give her their new address and phone number. She was out of jail and living in some kind of transitional housing outside Milwaukee, working at a dumpy motel as a housekeeper. She told Carla she needed money for a security deposit on a studio apartment she'd found. Carla and Gordon were barely scraping by, but Carla sent her a couple hundred bucks she couldn't spare. Then she was back in rehab after blowing Carla's money on heroin.

She never did get that place of her own. She got fired from the motel job for stealing towels and was back living on the street. It was almost six years ago that Carla took time off from the Coffee Spot, drained her savings, and traveled by Greyhound all the way to Wisconsin to bail her mother out of jail and pay her fines. Only a couple of months later, her mother violated her parole and was back in jail. That was when Carla asked Alex to change their number and take her name off the account.

Twenty minutes later Carla was pulling Elizabeth's Volvo into a parking space in front of the Drift Inn, a seedy bar near the terminal. She had stuffed all her cash, forty-three dollars and change, into her purse before leaving home, prepared to hand it over to her mother and demand that she get back on the ferry and leave her alone, for good this time.

No matter how she wished for that kind of resolve, she would end up letting her crash at her apartment until she got her hands on some heroin and disappeared after trashing the place. Or wound up arrested again. Or in the ER. Or worse, dead in some alley or squalid motel.

But would it be worse if her mom died of an overdose? Carla ran toward the ferry dock, taking long, angry strides. Wasn't it only a matter of time anyway? Sooner would surely be better than later. Put them both out of their misery.

Once inside the terminal she stopped to scan the passenger waiting area. This scene had played out so many times Carla could hardly separate one instance from another. Bus stations, dive bars, stairwells, police stations, hospital waiting rooms. Her mother would be drunk, high, unconscious, or manic. Needing money, a meal, a ride, a drink, a fix. Carla had rescued her again and again, and she was about to do it again.

A long blast from the ferry in the slip outside the window startled Carla. Three short blasts followed, before the huge boat moved slowly away from shore on its way back across the water to Seattle. Would her mother have gotten back on? Given up on finding Carla? Unlikely. Carla was her meal ticket. Her ATM.

In the waiting area were rows of plastic chairs arranged back-to-back, half facing Carla and the rest facing the water. Most were unoccupied. She studied the faces of the people she could see and the backs of those she couldn't. When none looked like her mother, she scanned the room a second time. The terminal was an open space. There was no place to hide. She crossed to the restrooms. Empty. Maybe her mom never got on the boat in the first place and was still on the Seattle side, staggering around Pioneer Square, turning tricks in exchange for a hit.

Carla's heart pounded under her flannel shirt as she walked along each row of seats slowly, taking the time to be sure. Her mother's appearance had probably changed since Carla last saw her. Then, her hair was shoulder length and bleached blonde with dark roots showing, and she had put on some weight. No telling what she looked like now. A lot can happen to a person in six years, especially to someone living rough.

A bone-thin guy staggered to his feet and stepped in front of Carla, blocking her path. His filthy clothes reeked. "Hey, you selling?"

"What the hell. Get away from me, asshole." Carla pushed past him. "I don't deal. Jesus fucking Christ."

At the end of the last row, she stopped and squeezed her hands into fists. Goddammit. Her mother was not in the building. Carla ran through all the possible explanations. She passed out in the Seattle terminal next to the pay phones. Good. She changed her mind and was hitchhiking back to Milwaukee. Even better, but unlikely. She was wandering around Bremerton at this moment causing trouble, and when she got bored or hungry, she would call again. *Shit, shit, shit.*

Chapter 12

Friday, October 31, 1997

Libby held a deck of cards. "Come on," she said to Carla. "I need practice."

Delbert and Noah were in their usual spots, the bakery case was stocked, and there were racks of freshly iced cookies and scones cooling in the kitchen. The whale-watching mob wouldn't start pouring in for a while yet.

Carla yawned and set the coffeepot on the warmer. She didn't have energy to refuse Libby. It had been a sleepless night. Upset about her mother and anticipating the next desperate phone call sure to come, she had stared at her bedroom ceiling until time to get up and go to E's. Stumbling along the road in the dark with Gizmo, she argued with herself about whether going to Seattle to reconnect with Gordon was a good idea. Wind whipped through the trees, showering her with wet leaves. Would Nathan be on the inlet in this weather? If the whales were out there, he would be too.

"What do I have to do?"

"Cut the deck as many times as you want and stop when it feels right." Libby settled on a stool and placed the cards on the counter.

Carla split the deck in half and placed the bottom half on top. The cards were stiff and slippery in her hands, brand new. Libby admitted it was only her second reading for someone other than herself. Carla paused, hand poised over the cards. Delbert watched them with detached interest, chewing his breakfast. Sleepy Noah stared into his cocoa.

"What does *right* feel like?"

"You'll know."

Carla cut the deck again, waited, and did it four more times. "Ready. I guess."

Libby rested both hands on top of the cards. "What question do you need answered?"

Carla told her she didn't have one, which was a lie. Her mind was a tangle of questions, but none she wanted to say out loud. She shouldn't have to speak. Wasn't that how this worked? Like praying or making a wish. Spirits can read your mind.

"No problem. I'll do an open reading." Libby lifted the cards as if they were sacred. "Name a person or tell me something about your current situation."

A person. Her mother. Gordon. Nathan? Current situation. Money trouble, always money trouble. She didn't want Libby's pity. Keep it impersonal. After a moment she said, "I'm worried about the whales."

"Let's start with that. So, the most basic reading is a three-card spread. I don't actually know any of the others yet." Libby laughed and turned over three cards one at a time, laying them in a row. Carla leaned over to examine the artwork.

Libby closed her eyes and sat very still.

"Are you in a trance or something now? Channeling the spirit of my dead grandmother?" A grandmother she had never met and would never know, still alive somewhere in Milwaukee. Carla suppressed a laugh.

Libby opened her eyes, and her cheeks colored a little. "No, I'm trying to remember what each card means. I'm pretty sure I know this one." She tapped the card in the center that depicted a bright full moon and within it a crescent moon. "Would you mind if I use my cheat sheet?"

Delbert chuckled from his stool and took a loud slurp from his coffee.

Libby removed a folded piece of paper from the small black velvet bag that had held the deck of cards. She studied it. Returning her attention to the cards, she said, "This kind of spread represents your past, present, and future." She touched each one from her left to right. "I'll start with the present." Her finger returned to the one in the middle.

She explained that a deck of tarot cards contained two subsets. One of them had twenty-two cards that tell the story of the fool's journey. She said they revealed major turning points in a person's life. "This is one of those. The Moon card. It symbolizes uncertainty, and it appears when you project your fears from your past onto your future." Carla crossed her arms over her chest. She felt exposed. "This path in the distance," Libby traced it with her finger, "is your way forward. It winds between two towers, showing some indecision. But I'll come back to the Moon card later. There might be more to say after we look at the others."

"What about these?" Carla pointed to two animals in the foreground.

"A dog and a wolf, both howling at the moon. They represent your tame and wild natures."

Noah wandered over and stood behind Libby. She looked at the card on her left, and her face tensed. "The Five of Cups is a sad card, but it's better to have it in the past like this, rather than in the present or future." In the foreground was a standing figure in a black cape with his head in his hands. "Remember I said there are two parts to the deck? The second set is numbered and has four suits like regular playing cards, but instead of hearts, diamonds, and all that, it has wands, swords, pentacles, and cups. Cups represent the emotional aspects of our lives," Libby read aloud from her cheat sheet. "It says here this one represents regret, abandonment, loss, loneliness, and heartbreak."

"Bummer," Noah said.

"Not entirely. Because these things happened in Carla's past, this card means things haven't turned out the way she expected."

"That's an understatement," Carla muttered.

"The castle in the background represents home and safety. The man in the cloak is separated from it by a river. But there's hope." Libby tapped a finger on a bridge in the distance and read from her paper again. "Bridges symbolize breakthroughs, crossing over from one emotional state to another. So, on this side of the bridge, the man is in despair. But if he crosses over into his future, there are good things waiting for him on the other side. Trouble is, he can't see it."

Libby moved her finger to the golden cups on the ground near the man's feet. Three of them were on their sides in front of him, empty, but behind him the other two were upright and full.

"He can't see the bridge because he's so busy looking at what he lost," Libby said. "And he's emotional. If he could stop living in the past, he would see the bridge as a way out. My interpretation of what it means for you, especially in relation to the Moon," she touched the center card again, "is that you suffered some kind of trauma in the past and you're letting it overshadow everything good in your life. You've pushed that painful memory down, but the feelings are hard to control, and they reappear. Maybe something happening now is bringing those emotions up again, and you don't know what to do with them. You said you've been worried about the whales, so the fact that they appeared in the inlet at this point in your life has maybe stirred something up."

Carla leaned her hip against the edge of the counter. All this was hitting too close to home. "Bullshit. Sorry. I mean, I don't believe any of this. Thanks, but we're done here." She turned and placed both palms flat against the kitchen door and gave it a mighty push. "Some of us have work to do."

"But there's one more card!" Libby called after her as the door swung shut.

The DJ on Carla's radio station had promised songs with Halloween themes, and "I Don't Wanna Go Down to the Basement" played as she scrubbed her hands at the sink. Who did Libby think she was, anyway? Acting like some sort of psychic. More like a psycho. Carla moved to the racks of sugar cookies decorated with skulls and black cats in honor of the season. She touched the orange icing. Almost set. Sliced loaves of fragrant pumpkin-raisin loaf and a couple of pumpkin chiffon pies were already in the bakery case out front, and now the scones—pumpkin with dried cranberries—were cool enough to handle. She arranged them on a platter.

Stupid cards. Did people seriously believe that shit? Just like the horoscopes in the newspaper with predictions that could be made to fit anyone's life because the wording was vague on purpose. *Everyone* had some kind of trauma in the past, didn't they? There was nothing unique about that. And everyone has moments where they can't decide what to do.

With her hands full, Carla backed up to the door and used her hip to open it, struggling to keep the pyramid of scones balanced. The dining room was quiet except for the muffled voice of Mike Ness singing "Mommy's Little Monster" on the kitchen radio. Noah and Delbert were gone and Sylvia—late again—hadn't arrived. Libby still sat at the counter with the three cards in front of her. Her face brightened when Carla emerged from the kitchen.

"Nope," Carla said. "You can put that shit away."

The expression on Libby's face! She wanted more than anything to explain the last card. Carla set the platter down, came around to the other side of the counter, and dropped onto the stool next to her. "Oh, fine. Let's get this over with."

The image on the final card was upside down. When Carla had first seen it next to the others, she wanted to turn it around to face the same way as the rest. She got a good look at it, though, from the opposite side of the counter when it was the only card with the picture facing her. The picture of a couple dancing under a canopy of flowers was beautiful. But when Libby first dealt the cards, slowly turning them over and laying them straight and even on the counter, she made no move to turn the card around the right way.

"This card, your future card—" Libby began.

"Hold on. You're not going to tell me how I'm going to die, are you?"

As she'd been bounced from one foster family to another, Carla had attended services and Sunday school in houses of worship of every denomination. In every one of them, one message was consistent and stayed with her still: God had a plan for her. It had been a relief as a child that not only did God know who she was, but he had figured out her life for her in advance. Her fate was written and sealed the day she was born. She didn't want Libby to spoil the surprise.

"I mean, if I don't have control over what happens to me, why would I want to know what's coming?" Carla said.

"Tarot doesn't show you what *will* happen in the future. The cards show you what's possible."

Carla sighed and leaned her elbow on the counter. "Fine. Let's hear what's possible."

"This card, your future card, is the Four of Wands. These poles are the wands." Libby tapped them one by one. "The other cards are upright as you can see, but this one is reversed." Libby paused. She didn't belong in the fortune-telling business if she was the kind of person who didn't deliver bad news well. "Upright, this is a happy card, but even reversed it's not all bad. In fact, I see this as a good sign for you." She was trying hard to put a positive spin on this. "Not so much on its own, but when you consider all three cards together."

Libby explained that the Four of Wands card appeared in the reversed position when someone was having trouble financially or socially, when things in their life were unstable. This card clearly had Carla's name on it. If someone read her cards every day of her life, this one would always turn up. Reversed.

Libby continued, "It could also be a warning that a ceremony or celebration could be cancelled or that this is a bad time to try to mend fences in your family."

Carla swallowed. Behind her attempt to find her mother the night before was the familiar hope that this time things would be different between them. If she believed what Libby was telling her, now wasn't the time for a reunion with dear old mom. Did this apply to Gordon too? She was still wrestling with the idea of showing up at the Weathered Wall.

"Or rekindle an old flame," Libby said, right on cue. Now Carla was sure seeing him was a stupid idea. And not because some card predicted a bad ending. Memories of Gordon, of the good times and even of their breakup, made her feel loved. He *had* loved her once. He hurt her once, too, but existing only as a memory now, he couldn't hurt her again. She was safe with the Gordon who lived in her mind, but she would lose that safety if she saw him. He *could* hurt her again. Carla's mind jumped around, but Libby was still talking. She tried to pay attention.

"Remember what I said about this bridge?" Libby pointed to the background on the Five of Cups. "You're going to have a break-through, I can feel it. The Moon means you're indecisive, you're afraid of what might be on the other side of the bridge. So, whatever conflicts lie ahead for you, you *will* overcome them. That's not the cards talking. That's me."

Libby gathered the cards and squared the deck. She slipped them into the velvet bag without saying another word.

"But wait," Carla said, suddenly at a loss once the bag was cinched closed. "What does any of this have to do with the whales?"

"Your concern for the whales must have a deeper meaning. You'll figure it out. Want my advice?" Carla nodded. "You have more control over your life than you think, more than you want. Let go of the past and those old fears. Look at your full cups instead of just your empty ones. Look at all that's good in your life." Libby rested her warm hand on Carla's forearm and left it there.

"What's on for Halloween?" Libby asked. The two were sitting on the steps behind the shop at the end of the day. The rain had stopped, but they'd put a layer of cardboard down to keep from getting wet. These short afternoon breaks together were becoming a regular thing, if two days in a row counted as regular. Carla accepted a cigarette and waited for Libby to light her own.

"No plans." No money. Yesterday was payday, but the money was as good as spent already. Would there ever come a day when money wasn't all Carla could think about? One thing was certain, though. She wasn't going to Seattle to hear Gordon's band, and money wasn't the only reason. A round-trip ticket on the ferry didn't cost much with no car. The tarot reading that morning had rattled her. The upside-down card and Libby's explanation of its meaning was the reason. Not a good time to rekindle an old flame, she'd said.

Other strikes against seeing Gordon? He might not recognize her after all this time, or he might pretend he didn't. He might say hello, ask how she's doing, and leave. Carla couldn't take another rejection. Something else nagged at her but she couldn't put her finger on it.

Libby passed her the matches. The wind made it hard to light up, but at last the rush of nicotine hit her bloodstream. She exhaled, watching a large spider lower itself on invisible thread from the handrail, fighting the breeze. It landed safely on the step.

"No parties?" Libby blew smoke upward with her lips forming an O, trying unsuccessfully to make smoke rings. "We got a ton of kids in our neighborhood. Kevin and I dress up and hand out candy. This year we're gonna be *Men in Black* agents. I love that movie. You'd be more than welcome, if hanging out with a couple of old-timers sounds like fun." Libby nudged her lightly. Carla leaned away. "Be a nice change from clubs and bars."

Carla had been using Elizabeth's flashy red Volvo since Sunday night. Even if Carla had a party to go to, taking the old lady's car wouldn't be right. Her own dead car still sat in front of her apartment building mocking her. Each time she saw old Dot, she was reminded of one more thing in her life that had failed.

A mechanic confirmed on the phone what Wallace had said—the engine was seized. A scrapyard would take it for parts, but the guy said the value of her old heap was less than the cost of towing. She couldn't even afford to get rid of it.

"What makes you think I'm the club type?" The last time she was in a bar was for the volunteer meeting at the bowling alley. The only time she ever went out now was to hear a band she liked and only when she had the money.

"Ricky told me you used to be a singer in a band. And you're young, you're cute. You dress really cool, like that band my daughter likes. Bikini Kill. You know them?"

The spider wandered up Carla's calf, climbing deftly over the threads of her fishnets. She hadn't changed her look since moving to Seattle with Gordon. They'd shopped together at thrift stores where he chose things for her, transforming her from an ordinary teenager into a copy of his idol, Joan Jett. Jeans with a wide belt, black faux-leather jacket, and Converse high tops. The Doc Martens came later, and the denim jacket replaced the black one somebody swiped at the homeless shelter. Everything she owned was secondhand and ratty. These days she looked less like an anti-fashion punk icon and more like a...what? That creeper at the ferry terminal thought she was a drug dealer. Is that what people saw when they looked at her?

"Not a singer exactly. I'm a vocalist. My mom was a singer." She stopped. *Shit. Quit renting space in my head, Mom.*

"So that's where you get your talent then. Is your dad musical too?"

Talking about her mom made Carla uncomfortable, but talking about her dad was never going to happen. Mainly because she knew nothing about him, not even his name, but also because the pain of having an absent father cut deep.

After a while, Libby took the hint that the conversation was over and went inside. So much for her plan to relax. The wind died down, and Carla made a perfect smoke ring. She watched it rise and expand until it disappeared before stubbing out the cigarette under the heel of her boot.

The spider made it to her knee, and she studied it. It could be a wolf spider, which could deliver a nasty bite. She caught a glimpse of its underside. The yellow markings of a harmless hobo spider. She put her hand in its path and waited for it to crawl into her palm. She carried it to the bottom step and lowered it gently into a patch of weeds.

Gizmo hurried along the road in the dark toward home. His thick fur was beaded with rainwater, and the stiff wind pinned his ears back. At the other end of the leash, Carla struggled to keep up. She hadn't eaten much all day, and her energy was low. All she had to look forward to for dinner was instant noodles. The same dinner as yesterday. And the day before.

They had the road to themselves, so they walked down the middle. The people who drove this way lived in the houses scattered in the woods, and they were settled in for the night. This far from town there were no kids out trick-or-treating. The rain smacked Carla's face and made a racket on the hood of Nathan's cheap plastic poncho.

She had hoped a long walk with the dog would clear her head and settle her fried nerves, but her thoughts ricocheted between her mother and Gordon, two people whose sudden reappearance had caused so much turmoil. Both required her to focus, to draw a map for the way ahead, and to get her emotions under control.

The tarot-card reading that morning had set Carla's thoughts whirling. Those three cards appeared by pure chance. The same cards could have been drawn for anyone. So, why was she still thinking about them?

The card representing her past had been on the nose with its abandonment and heartbreak. Libby said the Moon card, Carla's present, showed indecision. That card made sense now because wasn't that exactly what she was doing, wavering about her next moves? With most choices, Carla was too impulsive, making quick decisions and dealing with the fallout later. So why was this situation different? That last card was causing trouble. She shouldn't have let Libby explain that one, the upside-down card, the one that meant it was a bad time to fix her broken relationships. The decisions were more difficult now because of this new information.

When it came to her mom, the past had trained Carla for the present and future. She'd felt safe in Joan's house, and her foster mom was kind to her, but Carla longed for her mother and what she imagined a real family was. The day her mother came for her, Carla pulled her in with both hands, hungry for her love. In their little bungalow in Milwaukee, Carla had all the normal things: friends, homework, acne. She did all the normal things: complain about school, learn to drive, argue with her mother.

Once out of foster care, the reality of her previous life became visible for the first time. Until then Carla didn't know what she was missing. She'd had no baseline because she had never known what it was like to be loved the way a mother loves her child. The adults in her life had taken care of her needs, but no one had loved her. Not a soul. The realization was heartbreaking.

In the beginning her mother would sing with the car radio in her beautiful voice as she drove Carla to school. Jazz standards and Motown, rock and gospel, she could do it all. Whenever "Ain't No Mountain High Enough" played, Carla joined in and let the lyrics give her the reassurance she so desperately needed. And before she got out of the car, her mother would kiss the palm of her daughter's hand and tell her she loved her. She told Carla that if she needed a reminder during the day, she could press that hand against her cheek to feel the love.

Gizmo's leash was slack as he waited for her to continue their walk. She opened her free hand to the rain, studied her palm for a moment in the fading light, and began to raise it toward her cheek before she stopped herself and pushed her hand into her pocket. The magic was gone.

Gizmo sniffed a clump of Scotch broom in the shallow ditch next to the road. Carla touched his back, and he flinched as if he had forgotten she was there. "I've learned my lesson," she said to him. "Let people in and they'll hurt you. Every damn time." She shivered on the empty road.

The years of hating her mother for tearing their fragile life into shreds. The years of trying and failing to cut her mother out of her life. And what about Gordon? She'd let him in too. He had witnessed her life implode that day in the school auditorium and stuck by her in the dark weeks and months that followed. But in the end, he took the chance that a better life was possible without her. He had real talent, and she was holding him back. Maybe it paid off. She hoped it did. She wanted him to be happy, but she also wanted him to hurt a little. To think about her sometimes, and to miss her. Could she let him go, once and for all? Could she cut her mom loose for good? Just because Libby told her she had control over her life didn't mean it was true.

Carla followed Gizmo back to Elizabeth's driveway, through the gate into the backyard, and up the mossy steps to the door. As she turned the key in the lock, she pulled her face into a blank mask. No one belonged in her world but herself. Not her mother, not Gordon, not Libby, not Nathan. She shook the water from the plastic poncho before stepping inside. Not E, either.

"Take off your shoes." Elizabeth's thin voice greeted Carla from somewhere in the house. "And wipe Gizmo. Clean rags are in the basket behind the door."

Carla sneered and mouthed, "Yes, your highness." To the dog, she said, "Sit. Good boy."

Gizmo followed her movements with his intelligent gaze as she hung her dripping poncho on a hook, untied and pulled off her boots, and picked up a rag. He lifted his front paw for her to wipe without being asked. When his feet were reasonably clean, she used a second rag to rub his back, belly, and legs. Finally, she dried his head and kissed him between the ears.

"Where do you want the dirty rags?" Carla called.

"Laundry chute. The little door in the hallway."

Carla found it and shook her head in disbelief as she dropped the cloths in. She poked her head through and peered after them. In the dim light she could make out a heaping basket positioned directly below to catch the laundry. *How cool is that shit?*

"Tea?" The voice came from the living room.

Carla came to stand in the doorway. Classical piano music played softly from the stereo, and the room was warm and inviting. Gizmo was already curled on the rug at E's feet. "I should get home. Thanks anyway."

"If you're hungry, there are some sandwiches in the refrigerator. I asked my housekeeper to make them for you." Elizabeth cracked a small smile. "I hope you like egg salad."

Carla's stomach growled. How long had it been since anyone made her a sandwich? "Um, yeah. I love egg salad."

"Help yourself. Bring it in here and keep me company."

Half an hour later, feeling warm and well fed in Elizabeth's fancy car, Carla pulled out onto Gustafson Road. Holding the old lady at arm's length was hard when she was being nice for a change. Carla reached for the radio and saw the dash clock. It was 8:25. Her stomach flopped when she realized Gordon's band was on stage at that moment in the Weathered Wall. She had missed her chance.

Blasting the music to push down her emotions Carla drove toward home. It was fine to pretend she had forgotten about Gordon's gig, that she had been too busy and distracted to think about it. But the truth was no matter how hard she'd tried, Carla hadn't been able to put him out of her mind, checking the clock all day at work, doing a quick calculation. Thirteen hours until Gordon's show. Nine hours. Five hours.

All this time, since the day Gordon left, Carla had pinned her fading musical hopes on the possibility of resuming her life with him, picking up where they had left off. Wasn't that why she still practiced her bass? The romance hadn't survived, but couldn't she go see him for the chance to get back in his band?

At the intersection of Old Frontier and Anderson Hill Road, she idled at the red light. A right turn would take her home. A left would take her to Bremerton. If she hurried, she could make the 9:00 ferry and catch Gordon after the show. Her pulse pounded along with the bass on the radio.

An image of the tiny newspaper ad formed in her mind. A few words came into view, words that hadn't registered until now. The Gutter Rats were *opening* for another band. They weren't the headliners. So not such a big success after all. Carla chewed on the inside of cheek. Left or right? She had to choose before the light changed.

There was something else. Only two names were listed, Gordon's and one other. The original band had four people, and they were the headliners at a few dive bars around Seattle in the eighties. Not the greatest places, but they had drawn decent crowds. A smaller band opening for someone else? Not a good sign.

What was the other name with Gordon's in the ad? Bradley or Brandon. Carla pressed her foot on the brake pedal, concentrating. She squeezed her eyes closed to conjure the bit of paper stuck to her fridge. Blake?

Belinda.

Fuck! The light turned green, and Carla stepped on the gas.

Chapter 13

Saturday, November 1, 1997

At noon, Carla stood at the shop window overlooking the inlet. *I'm such a fool.* She pressed her forehead against the cool glass, fighting to hold back her furious tears. She needed to keep it together. The Coffee Spot was packed with customers.

Belinda. The other name in the ad was Belinda. Carla bumped her head on the window to the beat of the song playing in her mind, "Story of My Life." Gordon's bandmate was a woman. A girlfriend. A lover. Of course she was.

Nathan's Boston Whaler came into view. A week ago, Carla could hardly tell one kind of boat from another. At least the new weekend shift was short. It would be a relief to head for the water. He pulled up alongside the pier below the shop and tied off, his movements sure and practiced.

Carrying a full bus pan, Libby stopped behind Carla and looked over her shoulder. Nathan looked up, spotted Carla, and waved with his whole arm.

"Who's that fine specimen?"

A guy I know? A friend? Buttoning her jacket, she said, "See you tomorrow."

Libby followed her to the door. "Why so secretive?"

"Nathan. Okay?" Carla suppressed a smile. "His name is Nathan."

A few minutes later, she was seated in the bow of his boat. They were heading south toward the Narrows, traveling faster than usual. Carla's beanie was useless in the cutting wind. At the mouth of the inlet, he killed the motor, and they drifted among the other boats. The orcas were swimming in a tight circle, their fins slicing the water like hot knives through butter.

Nathan stood at the helm and raised his binoculars. He watched the whales, and Carla watched him. Something was off. Last week he talked more. Today he barely said hello. Had she done or said something last weekend to piss him off?

"Lucky I ran into to you, Carla," he said at last, still peering through the binoculars. "I need another pair of eyes."

Luck had little to do with it. She would have stood on the pier all afternoon, like a dumb kid with a crush, hoping he might pass by.

He handed her the binoculars, his face serious. "Tell me how many whales you see."

She did her best to count the moving fins, trying to remember what he'd taught her about how to tell one from another. Male dorsal fins were taller and less curved than female. She concentrated and counted and then counted again. It felt important to get this right.

"I see eight females." She counted again. "Maybe nine. Some smaller ones, plus some babies. Two big males."

"Right. Cetus is there with a couple of calves," he pointed and took the binoculars again. "And Hugo..." Nathan scanned the water. "There he is. But the third male is missing. Haven't seen Faith since Thursday morning."

"Don't lose Faith!" Carla's attempt at humor fell flat. Nathan's jaw muscles flexed as he continued to search. Not even a twitch of a smile. This wasn't a laughing matter. None of it was. Since their arrival, the daily news was full of articles about the precarious orca situation in the inlet, concerns about their dwindling food supply and the danger to whales and boaters alike with so many people on the water. Everyone had an opinion about why they were staying so long. And now Faith was MIA.

"Do you think he left on his own?" she asked.

"Orcas rarely wander from the pod."

"Maybe he's sick, and the others kicked him out?"

"Unlikely."

He squatted near her feet, his back against the helm. He laced his fingers together, nails short and skin the color of warm caramel. Carla wanted to touch them. She pushed her hands deeper into her pockets.

"Some species," he continued, "chickens for example, will turn on a weak or injured member of the flock and kill it, while a crow will defend its injured parent or offspring and even mourn when they die. Orcas are more like crows in that way, caring for the sick, bringing them food and protecting them. Faith has an interesting story. Never injured as far as I know, but always a bit of a loner. His mother died a couple years ago, and ever since, two other whales, a mother and daughter, have hardly left his side. They're inseparable. It's like Canuck and Lulu sense his loneliness and want to, I don't know"—his voice cracked—"help him be less alone."

Emotions clawed up from her belly. Carla turned her face away. She didn't want him to see the way she had to screw it up and pinch it to keep back the tears. Was he talking about himself, about his own loneliness? Or hers? Did he see her as just another damaged creature?

Nathan raised his binoculars again and was quiet for a moment. "I've been watching those two females the last couple of days, and Faith is nowhere. I'm afraid he may be dead."

Dead? If one could die, they all could. She shivered and tried to keep her shaking legs still. There was a ringing in her ears. It was too much. They'll all die! *Change the channel,* Joan's voice chimed in her head. *Think about something happy. Don't cry.*

A whale swam toward the boat, getting too close, moving too fast. Carla froze. Nathan spotted it, too, gliding just under the surface. In seconds it reached the boat, the short dorsal fin fully exposed. A little calf! Carla held her breath. That night at the bowling alley she had asked Nathan what he'd do if a whale came closer than two hundred feet. His words came back to her. *Count myself lucky,* he'd said.

The little whale circled the boat, splashing with its tail, showing its tender belly. It was so close that Carla could have reached over the side and touched its glistening body. Nathan sat next to her on the small seat, his thigh pressed against hers. Too many emotions mixed and swelled, and her body struggled to contain them all. The playful calf. The missing whale. The pain of letting Gordon go. The warmth of Nathan's touch.

On the third pass, the whale lifted its little face out of the water, opened its smiling mouth, and showed two neat rows of baby teeth, shattering Carla's self-control. A single sob escaped. Nathan grinned and nudged her shoulder. "Awesome, right? Never gets old, this job."

He moved to the stern and opened a heavy case. "Good news is that high tide will be at around three a. m. tomorrow. Should give them the best chance of swimming out."

He lifted some equipment out of the case. "Can you hold this?" She reached and took a coiled cable from his hand. "I appreciate you coming out here with me again."

"*Pfff.* I'm just taking up space."

"No, I mean it. I get tunnel vision when I'm working on a project. Can't see the forest for the trees. Having you along, seeing what these orcas mean to you, reminds me why I went into this field in the first place. Instead of seeing through my biologist eyes, I see them through yours." He looked steadily at her.

Carla lifted the cable in her hands and broke their gaze. "What's this for?"

He unwound one end and used a wrench to attach something to it. The other end was connected to a black box at his feet.

"Hydrophone." He began lowering something into the water. "Let go now. Kind of feed it out little by little."

He pulled a pair of headphones over his ears, pushed the jack into the black box, and adjusted some dials and gauges. Carla studied his expression as it changed from a frown of deep concentration to a look of delight. He motioned her over.

Her life vest gave her little peace of mind as she cautiously worked her way to the stern. The iron gray water was ruffled with white-caps. She had never learned to swim, and the thought of dogpaddling around in that icy water made her shudder.

He lifted the headphones off and made room on the seat next to him. "You ever hear a whale?"

She shook her head. He moved to fit the headphones to Carla's head and waited while she folded a deeper cuff in the woolen fabric of her beanie to expose her ears. He eyed the silver earrings that ran along the edges. Not repulsed or even curious, but in a practical way, as if wondering whether they might damage the headphones.

He leaned in, facing her squarely, and placed the headband on her head, adjusting its position over her hat. He fiddled with it to make it secure, checking the right side, the left side, and the right again. His fingers grazed her jawline, and her skin prickled. This man was having some kind of effect on her. In his touch there was something she couldn't name. He smelled of salt and rain. She saw tiny creases in his full lips, and his breath was warm on her cheek. She almost pulled back, her pulse drumming in her ears. *You don't need to help me,* she almost said, but she stayed quiet.

Nathan dropped his hands but kept his eyes on hers. She pressed the cushioned pads tight against her ears with her hands, watching his expression. She tried to focus on listening through the headphones to the watery sounds, but her attention was not on the whales.

And then she heard it. A single high-pitched squawk like a bird, but steady and as long as an exhaled breath. Another voice joined the first, a bit louder, closer. A chittering run of chirps, and a slow, deep bellow like an elephant. A short howl followed by what sounded like the yawn of a dog. A car alarm, a belch, a cow mooing. Someone laughing, someone crying for help. A whoop of joy.

Carla's mouth dropped open, and she let out her own whoop. She pulled the headphones off and stared at Nathan. "Which one is the whale?"

His smile widened. "All of them."

"Whoa." She put the headphones on again. She closed her eyes and imagined the whales gliding through the water, fat and sleek. Singing together through this adventure or this crisis, whichever it was to them. Now the voices sounded like mourners. Could the whales be calling for Faith? Their sad songs resonated though her body, vibrating in her belly, her chest. She was sure animals felt grief. Maybe not the way humans did, but grief all the same.

Faith may be gone, but there could be no more deaths. Not Canuck or Lulu. Not Cetus. Not Hugo. She couldn't turn her back on these friends and go on with her life, just hoping and wishing they would swim to freedom. She couldn't bake pies and mop floors all day while they were out here fighting for their lives. For as long as they stayed, and as long as Nathan would let her on his boat, Carla wanted to be out here too. But that was impossible. She'd lose her job.

Carla pushed the headphones back until they curved around her neck. "How does a person get a job like this?"

"Marine biologist? It starts with school. Lots and lots of school."

"In that case, I'm fucked."

To earn that kind of money, she needed a better job. To get a better job, she needed to go to college. No wonder throwaways like her never got ahead.

"Not necessarily." Nathan told her about some jobs at the research center that didn't require as much education or training. Administrative jobs, laboratory work, and community outreach. "We have a boater education program called Soundwatch my boss started about twenty years ago. Operates in the summer months. And we always need volunteers."

Carla rolled her eyes. She needed paid work. "So...these volunteers drive around in a boat yelling at people, like we've been doing out here. Yelling at people who bother whales and handing out brochures?"

"Yes, basically. Education and outreach. It's what I do."

"Education. Like a teacher? I thought you said you were a biologist."

He explained he was both. "Been observing this pod for years, their family structure, migration habits. I take what I've learned to schools and communities. That day the whales arrived, when I first saw you out on the pier, I was on my way back from a whale talk at an elementary school in Seattle."

"Little kids? What good does that do?"

"A lot, I hope. Or else the next generation will see the extinction of more animals in their lifetime than we have in ours. By studying the largest animals in the ocean food chain, we can measure the effects of shipping traffic, water pollution, and changes in the climate. Global warming." His face darkened, and the sadness in his voice couldn't be missed. "If killer whales are behaving in unusual ways, something is wrong in their world. Something wrong in their world means there is something wrong in ours."

His words frightened her. She didn't want to hear any more. She lifted the headphones, but he stopped her, his hand warm on her cold one.

"We are all connected, you know?" he said. His eyes locked onto hers, those silver-gray eyes. Those lips, relaxed and full and inviting. Carla was sure he could hear the pounding of her heart under her life vest. She let go of the headphones and took his face with both hands, pulling his mouth to hers.

"Any chance staying overnight is still on the table?" Carla raised her voice over the orchestra music blaring from the stereo. The question hung in the air that evening while Elizabeth adjusted her hearing aid. The wheelchair was folded and parked against the living room wall, and a walker stood next to Elizabeth's chair. Gizmo lay panting between them, still winded from his long walk. Carla tugged on a strand of hair, wishing she could start the day over and make better choices.

Her first big mistake was kissing Nathan. What the hell. A little impulse control! Her body had gone ahead without her, reaching for him without consulting with her brain. The poor guy looked like she'd shit in his hat. He fell all over himself apologizing for sending the wrong signals, for not mentioning earlier that he had a girlfriend. After that everything was too fucking awkward, so she asked him to drop her off at the boat ramp.

Carla's second mistake was agreeing to help her mother.

The piece of music ended with a series of terrifying cymbal crashes, making Carla jump.

"There. It's working now," Elizabeth said. "Turn that music down."

Carla did and then repeated her question. For once her motivation had nothing to do with money. Mr. Wilson had relented and given Carla a small advance on her manager's salary. So, no wolf at the door this month.

"Has something changed?" Elizabeth's voice was softer than usual. "I had the impression you weren't interested in my proposition."

Carla inhaled deeply and let the breath out slowly. "I have a situation, E," she began.

Cold, wet, and embarrassed after her afternoon with Nathan, Carla had stopped at her apartment for a hot shower. The phone was ringing when she turned off the water. She grabbed a towel and hurried to pick it up.

"Hi, Cargo! I'm so glad I caught you." Caught was exactly how Carla felt the second she heard her mother's voice. "I waited at the ferry terminal all day on Thursday, but you didn't come." She went on to say she got a bed at St. Vincent's the first night but not the second.

"Last night I hitched a ride to Denny's. The only place I knew would be open all night. The waitress reminded me of you, and I told her that. We talked a little while since the place was dead. I mean, by then it was like two in the morning. She let me stay in my booth with a bottomless cup of coffee."

Carla rubbed a towel over her wet hair. "Get to the point."

"When the breakfast people started coming in, she said it was time to move on. I pulled out my wallet to pay, and she must have seen it was my last two bucks because, guess what? When she brought my change, it was a five-dollar bill. Plus a quarter for the pay phone."

Was she charming or a master manipulator? Carla was staggered by her mother's ability to cast a spell over people. The story was typical. Carla had seen it a hundred times during the good years when they lived together. Her mom would lie, cry, rage, flirt—whatever it took—to get out of paying for things. She stiffed cab drivers and made-up sob stories at the movie theater about lost tickets. Once she even pushed Carla through the gates at a flea market and pretended to chase after her child to avoid paying their admission.

Time to head to E's. "What do you want, Mom?"

"It's asking a lot, I know, but if I could crash at your place for a couple of days…" her voice trailed off.

Carla had rehearsed the answers to the questions she knew her mom would ask. No, I can't give you any money. No, you can't stay with me. But the words refused to form in her mouth.

"I'm a hundred and seventy-three days clean and sober, Cargo. I know I still have a long way to go, but I'm not going to fail this time. I've been going to meetings every day, and I'm back on the twelve steps. I just finished number eight, the one where you write down the wrongs you've done to others. The next one is making amends. Starting with you, honey, because you are the one I hurt the most."

They had been down this road before. Twice. Carla had a right to be wary of her mother's claims of sobriety and desire to make amends. Their final phone conversation before she disappeared the last time began with the same pronouncements and ended in a tantrum brought on by Carla's refusal to send her any more money. She called Carla selfish, unfeeling, cold. Her jabs hit home because she was a pro at finding her daughter's weak spots and twisting the knife deep. The last words her mother had said she'd spit out like a bad taste: "Who could ever love someone like you?" Carla carried the question like a sack of stones, its weight a reminder of why she was alone.

"If I can't get a bed at the shelter tonight," her mother's voice brought Carla back to the present, "and if I can't stay with you, I don't know where to go. And, babe," she rushed on, "I have something for you. I brought it all the way from Wisconsin."

"I don't want it," Carla said through clenched teeth.

"It's important, though. I could meet you somewhere. We could talk." Her mother's voice, which had once been so beautiful, was now a hoarse croak. "It's been such a long time. My fault. But there are things I need to tell you, honey."

As far as Carla was concerned, they had nothing to say to each other. "I'm hanging up."

"Wait!" her mother cried.

"If it's so fucking important, tell me now. On the phone."

Her mother insisted they needed to meet in person, if only so she could give Carla what she brought. The call ended a few minutes later after Carla agreed to try to work something out. Now she was kicking herself.

"A situation." Elizabeth prompted. "What kind of situation?"

"So, my mom's in town," Carla said, trying to sound casual. "There's what you might call a bit of history between us. She needs a place to stay for a couple of days, but I don't think we can live under the same roof. We'd kill each other. Literally kill each other."

"I see." Elizabeth frowned, deepening the creases that framed her thin lips like parentheses.

"Besides, my apartment isn't set up for more than one person at the moment." No shit. A mattress on the floor, no furniture. Possibly a step above the shelter where her mother had spent the night, but a small one. St. Vincent de Paul was a shelter Carla knew well.

"Of course, the offer stands." Elizabeth picked a bit of dog fur from the blanket covering her knees. "My nurse only visits in the mornings now, so the evenings feel long."

"Thanks," said Carla. She wouldn't admit it, but she had been feeling the same. Ever since the day she brought Gizmo to E's in the taxi, her apartment felt so empty. "She's only staying one night—two max. I don't want to get under your feet."

Elizabeth waved Carla's words away. "Even Wendy who comes to clean twice a week used to feel like an intrusion. I was grateful for the clean house but even more grateful to be left alone when she was finished. Now, I find myself inventing extra tasks for her to keep her here longer." She sighed. "Getting soft and sentimental in my old age."

"Me, too, I guess."

Elizabeth cocked an eyebrow. "So, there's a chink in your armor after all."

Carla chuckled. Gizmo sat up and put his chin on Carla's lap. "Only big enough for dogs and whales."

"Whales?"

"The orcas in the inlet."

"Of course. I read about them in the paper. Are you involved somehow?"

"I'm helping a guy keep them safe while they're here." She should have used past tense. Nathan would steer clear of her now that she'd made an ass of herself. The memory of his face so close to hers, his breath on her cheek, her lips on his. Something swooped and fluttered low in her belly.

"I thought something was different about you," Elizabeth said, eyes dancing. "You have a purpose and a young man. What's his name?"

Carla's face was hot. "Nathan. He works on San Juan Island doing some kind of whale research. He's not my young man or whatever."

Elizabeth gave a knowing nod and changed the subject. "I'm sorry to hear of your difficult relationship with your mother. Do you care to elaborate?"

Carla shook her head and stroked Gizmo's ears. For years no one cared enough to ask about her life, and it never felt safe to open up when someone did. Her own mother ridiculed her when she came home from school in tenth grade, gushing about a boy named Gordon.

She laughed when Carla confided in her about her dream of being in a band with him, telling Carla she had no musical talent.

But Libby's interest and now E's touched her, making Carla feel less alone.

"Never mind." Elizabeth patted Carla's hand. "I didn't mean to pry."

"Somehow, she always manages to find me," Carla blurted. "Calling me for a handout. This time she decided to come in person. She's a drug addict, E. Makes my life a living hell. I was in foster care from the day I was born until I was eleven. I was so angry, so jealous of her drugs because she loved them more than me. But she got herself clean and the state gave me back to her. It was great. I forgave her." Hot, angry tears stung Carla's eyes. "I forgave her."

"She fell back into her old ways at some point? How very sad, Carla. You've suffered so much."

Carla pressed her fingers against her eyes for a moment. They came away smeared with eyeliner which she wiped onto her jeans. "I didn't mean to go off like that."

"You're a fine person, Carla, and you hide it well," Elizabeth said. "All things considered, it's good of you to put a roof over her head."

"Temporarily," said Carla, louder than she meant to.

One hundred seventy-three days clean and sober. It wouldn't last. It never did.

On the steps of the house across the street from Carla's apartment building, a forgotten jack-o-lantern with its shriveled face grimaced from the shadows. E's car idled quietly under a streetlight at the curb. A leaf the size of a dinner plate landed with a *splat* on the windshield from the maple tree above. The ride to Carla's place that evening had been a silent one. Her mother was curled on the back seat, too exhausted to talk. A filthy backpack, her only luggage, was her pillow. Carla's own canvas tote bag with her overnight things to take to E's was in the trunk.

Carla swiveled in the driver's seat to hand a key ring to her mom. "Don't lose these."

"But...wait," her mom stammered. "Why are you... Aren't you coming in?"

"I'm staying with a friend." Carla gave the keys a shake. Alex's old keys, her spare set. "Take these."

Her mother sat up and opened her mouth to speak, but Carla cut her off.

"Go in through that main door"—she pointed to double glass doors—"and turn left. It's number three. The silver key gets you in the building, and the other one's for my apartment." Carla's neck was getting stiff from twisting around, and she wanted to get away.

"I thought we'd be together for a couple of days, babe, so we could talk." Her mom looked at the dangling keys but made no move to take them. "It's why I came. To say I'm sorry for everything. To make amends."

Carla thought of the upside-down tarot card and how Libby said it meant this wasn't a good time to mend fences with family. The idea that her mother had traveled across the country to tell her something, to give her something important, made Carla's head ache. Whatever it was, Carla wasn't ready. "Not tonight."

The words were meant to end the conversation, to get her mom to go inside, but they were giving her mother false hope, planting the idea that Carla might be open to hearing her out sometime in the future, possibly the near future. She wasn't.

"Tomorrow?" Her mom waited, but when Carla didn't answer, she took the keys saying, "Thanks, Cargo." She stared at the keys in her hand but made no move to get out of the car.

Carla put both hands on the steering wheel and squeezed. "Any time."

"Really? You mean that, honey?"

"I mean"—Carla let out a short, exasperated sigh—"you can get out of the car any time. I have to be somewhere."

Looking in the rearview mirror, Carla saw her mother struggling to get her skinny arms through the straps of her backpack. Once it was on, she zipped her threadbare jacket and pulled up the hood.

"Give the keys to the guy in number four across the hall when you leave. I told him I had someone staying for a couple of days." Carla hadn't wanted to ask Wallace for another favor after he helped so much with the dog, but it was safer than having her mom put the keys under the doormat outside.

"Can't I just give them to *you*? When you come back?" Her mother's whine rose in pitch.

"There's a towel in the bathroom you can use. And no long distance calls on my phone."

"Why are you always so cold to me? I'm your mother, for God's sake." She cinched the straps of the backpack tighter, a warrior preparing for battle. "I gave birth to you!" There was that shrill, frantic tone again. "I mean, if it wasn't for me, you wouldn't even be here."

Carla pushed her bangs off her forehead. The skin underneath was damp. She rolled the window down a crack, letting the cool night air spill into the car. This was how it always started. In a moment, her mother would launch into the story. Carla had never figured out how to stop her from telling it or which parts to believe.

Some of the details changed with each telling. One version had her mom running away from a home for unwed mothers because they were going to "steal" her baby. In another she ran away from a back-alley abortionist. Sometimes she runs away from home. Sometimes her parents kick her out. But no matter what, her mother managed to paint herself as a saint.

"It's late," said Carla. Her mom's eyes were brimming. She could magically produce tears on cue and was working up to a full-on pity party. "Can't we do this some other—"

"I saved your life, you know." Her mom crossed her arms over her chest and glared at her.

Here we go again. Carla turned the engine off and leaned her forehead against the steering wheel. Her mother was like a boulder rolling downhill, picking up speed and destroying everything in its path, oblivious to the pain she was causing.

"They were going to kill you!" her mother screeched.

So, the abortionist this time.

"But I got away. I couldn't go home because my parents would have made me give you up." Her mother manufactured a dramatic sob. "My baby girl."

This was more than a sore spot. Her mother's resistance to surrendering her was the reason Carla spent her childhood in foster care instead of being adopted. By holding onto her fantasy of being Carla's mommy, her mother had betrayed her, sentenced her to a revolving door of social workers and supervised visits.

"I wandered around the streets of Milwaukee, dodging cops, getting handouts. People got more generous once I started showing, so I played it up wearing a tight T-shirt and caressing my belly. I made pretty good money."

The pride in her mother's voice was unbelievable.

"When I went into labor, someone took me to the ER. The doctor said I was an unfit mother. I admit I'd gotten in with the wrong crowd while I was on the streets, but I was hardly using any drugs back then."

This was new information, but so many things her mother told Carla over the years were untrue. "You took drugs while you were pregnant?"

"Well, I don't remember, but they *said* I had heroin in my system."

The boulder came to the bottom of the hill and stopped. The picture came clear for the first time. Babies born to alcoholics and drug addicts went through withdrawal, fighting for their lives from the moment they were born. Sometimes they had difficulty in school. Behavior issues. Social issues. *Am I damaged?*

The distant cry of a screech owl came through the open window. Carla rolled it all the way down and leaned out, afraid she might be sick. She took a few deep shaky breaths, and the nausea passed.

Her mother was still talking. "And those people at the hospital treated me like dirt. Everyone did. They took you away from me and sent me to rehab. I was so scared and alone."

For a few minutes, her mother cried softly. Carla should feel something for her. Pity, compassion, empathy...anything. But she was numb. She turned the key in the ignition, and the engine came to life. "I need to go," she said.

"Wait. Wait. There's something I have to say." Her mom sniffed and cleared her throat. "I never told you this. This next part. I never told anyone."

"Why tell me at all? Let it go already."

"I can't. My sponsor says I need to come clean about everything with you or I'll never be free of my addictions. I've tried to erase it from my mind, but it's still there, like it happened yesterday. And I still feel the same way I did then. I..." her voice dropped to a hoarse whisper "I'm...ashamed."

Was this what her mom had said she needed to talk about, or was it going to be another piece of fiction? Carla waited, her chest tight.

"I was in rehab after you were born. I'd been there for about a week when they said someone was going to bring you in so I could see you. Hold you."

Carla had never heard this story before. She wasn't sure she wanted to hear it, but her mother plainly needed to tell it as her thin body trembled, and the air around her vibrated with urgency.

"In the visitors' room there were lots of kids—babies, older ones too. I guess there were a lot of moms in that place with me. I saw a lady holding a baby wrapped in a yellow blanket, the crocheted kind, homemade. 'Pretty blanket,' I said to her, and I got closer so I could see the baby. It had that puckered face newborns have and a mop of white hair. She had a pink headband on, but that hair was sticking up all over." A smile flickered across her face. She began combing her fingers through her own filthy hair, untangling it and smoothing it down. "'She's real cute,' I told the woman, and I walked away."

There was a pause, and Carla waited, the air from the vents growing warmer as the engine warmed up. She welcomed the comfort it offered.

"The lady came over and sat next to me. She asked if I was Leanne. When I said yes, she laid the baby in my arms." A beat. "She said, 'This is your daughter. This is Carla.'" Tears flowed, dripping off her mother's nose and chin. "I was so ashamed. How could I not recognize my own child?" The last word was swallowed by sobs.

Carla slowly came around to a new thought. She got out of the car and joined her mom in the back seat. She took her mom's frail body into her arms and held her. This woman who had given birth to her had been treated as a throwaway by her own parents and by society, left to figure life out on her own. She'd played the cards she'd been dealt. This woman, Carla's mother, was just like her.

Chapter 14

Sunday, November 2, 1997

Carla scrubbed at the stinking grease and burnt sugar on the bottom of the big oven. On her knees with her head inside, she worked with fierce energy. Working late and alone gave her time to think. About her mother. About Nathan. She had plenty to keep both mind and body busy.

The boss liked her idea of adding lunch items to the weekday menu. Starting tomorrow, she would offer a rotating quiche-of-the-day and a green salad. She'd spent the afternoon cleaning out the fridge to make room for the fresh ingredients that were delivered. The oven was the last chore on her list.

"For the Punx" played on KNDD, but Carla wasn't singing along. Her mind was on the conversation the night before. Instead of leaving her mom at her apartment and driving off to sleep at E's as planned, Carla and her mother talked all night, more allies than enemies.

Carla had lived through the nightmare of her mom's arrests, her accidents, injuries, and overdoses. She'd witnessed her recoveries and the turning over of so many new leaves. Carla's childhood wish—on the first star she saw every night, on every penny thrown into a fountain—was for a real home with her real mom. And her real dad, someone Carla could only conjure in her imagination, someone her mother refused to talk about or even name until last night.

Sitting back on her heels, Carla took off the rubber gloves. She allowed herself to rest and clear her lungs of the fumes from the cleaning chemicals. The stories her mother told were always suspect, but the one she told last night was different. Carla tried to reconstruct it.

The year is 1960. Leanne Peterson takes her fourth bow on the stage of the Central High School auditorium. On their feet, the audience whistles and applauds. The first freshman to be cast in the lead role of Oklahoma! *Leanne has stolen the show.*

In the front row, her parents beam, and behind them, cheering loudest of all, is a young man. He is proud of the part he has played in making this moment happen, his part in guiding her to use her beautiful voice to its potential.

Backstage, he waits in the shadows until she is alone to congratulate her. The roses he has brought for her are crushed between their bodies, their sweet fragrance swirling around them as they kiss.

The school year ends, but the private singing lessons continue. Tuesdays he comes to her house. Her parents are at work. He shares more than music on those long, warm afternoons.

In September, he is offered a teaching position in another city. Leanne's sophomore year begins with heartache, soon followed by morning sickness.

"I loved him," her mother confessed through her tears as the darkness closed around them in Carla's bedroom. They sat side by side on the mattress and leaned against the wall. "I wanted to protect him, but I ended up hurting you. He was an adult—my teacher!—and I was a kid. He would have gone to jail if I told anyone. My parents were furious that I wouldn't say who the father was.

"But the truth is," she continued, "Mom and Dad looked after me. They didn't send me away. Dad said they would arrange for me to give my baby to a nice young couple who would raise it as their own. I could finish high school like nothing ever happened. I could go to college to study music. That was the plan they laid out for me. I liked the sound of it, you know? But I changed my mind. I was selfish and stupid. I didn't want to give up my baby, so I ran away from home. I had a romantic idea that I would find your father, and we would hide someplace and be a family. I took a bus to Madison, but I didn't know the name of the school that hired him. I made it back to Milwaukee, but I was afraid to go home. I knew my parents wanted me to give the baby away. I ran out of money, and then I ran out of hope."

"No abortionist, then?" Carla's stomach churned. She couldn't keep track of which parts of the story were true and which were lies.

Her mother shook her head. "I made him up so you'd think I saved your life. So you'd think I had done at least one good thing." She used the hem of her shirt to wipe her face. "I'm sorry, Cargo, but—"

"Where was my father in all this?" Carla didn't want any more excuses. "Who is he? Didn't he ever want to see me? Didn't he care at all about us—about me?" Her throat tightened around those last words.

She stared at her mother with all the hurt and anger and resentment she had ever felt, then grabbed her by the shoulders, giving her a shake. "Does he even know I exist?"

The air crackled between them, and for a moment the only sound was their breathing. The silence was broken by a whisper, like air leaking out of a puncture deep inside her mother's chest. "No, babe."

Her mom pulled away and rummaged in her backpack. She handed Carla a crumpled envelope addressed to Leanne Peterson in neat cursive writing. The postmark on the envelope said 1962, Madison, Wisconsin. No return address. Inside was a yellowed sheet of stationery folded into thirds with only a few lines, a love note. He'd always love her, always remember her. It was signed "Ted." A name at last. Something else was in the envelope, a newspaper clipping, new and crisp. It was an obituary bearing the name Theodore Miller, a handsome face smiling out of the small photograph. The date was October 6, 1997.

Carla pulled the gloves back on and picked up the wire brush, staring at it through eyes blurred with tears. The best thing to come from her mother's confession and the secrets she revealed was that Carla understood why her mother was the person she was, why her life had turned to shit. Why it had been so hard for her to be any kind of mother.

She had held the clipping and read the long tribute to her father so many times that pieces of it came to her as she knelt in front of the oven—award-winning performer, beloved teacher, devoted husband and father—floating like ribbons, like scraps of paper turned to ash.

Carla resumed her cleaning, but the brush in her hand had become a weapon. Scraping furiously, teeth clenched, she tried to erase the story of missed opportunities, to rub out the lost chances for a family. How different things could have been! For her mother and for herself. Carla threw the brush as hard as she could into the back of the oven where it made a satisfying crash. Two lives ruined.

"Get a grip," Carla said aloud.

She turned up the radio and blasted the Smoking Popes until her thoughts were obliterated.

"Hey!" A voice behind her called.

"Christ!" Still on her knees, she twisted around to face Todd. He stood in the doorway with a stupid smirk on his face, swinging his key ring around his index finger like a spoiled kid showing off his new car. "You scared the shit out of me. What are you doing here?" she yelled over the music.

"Just rolled into town."

"I heard you moved to Portland."

Todd turned the radio off. "That didn't work out."

So, Pee-wee's big adventure was over.

"You can relax now." Todd leaned against the counter and crossed one foot over the other. "Well, after you finish what you're doing there. Don't let me interrupt you."

"What the hell are you talking about?" Carla got to her feet.

"You can go back to whatever you did here before. Baking or whatever." He looked around the room like he wasn't sure what a kitchen was for. "I'm sure Dad'll want me to manage again. I was heading there to surprise the folks when I saw the lights on back here. No doubt he'll kill the fatted calf. Prodigal son and all." He jingled his keys and gave her an arrogant smile.

Still wearing her apron, Carla burst out the back door of the Coffee Spot. At the bottom of the steps, she hurled her jacket, beanie, and bag to the ground and stared at them. Sparks of rage blazed before her eyes.

Throwing her rubber gloves in Todd's face and telling him to rot in hell wasn't the smartest thing she'd ever done, but it felt so good. It took balls for Todd to waltz in and announce he was taking over. The boss said the position was temporary, but shit. It had only been a week. Could Todd do that? Pull the rug out with no notice? This fight wasn't over.

The sparks slowed, blinking and fading like fireflies. Tomorrow she'd call Mr. Wilson. Would he fire her? Maybe he'd take her side. She should be terrified. The possibility of eviction had been looming for months, and now her job was in jeopardy.

Everything was getting away from her, like a plate falling off a table. Carla's small achievements and successes always came at a price. Or they didn't last. As if someone, somewhere, could see she was finally gaining ground and reached into her life to snatch it all away.

But for the first time she could remember, she had people she could turn to if everything went south. Her mother couldn't offer money or a place to live, but there was a new relationship to build on and a chance for some normalcy. E might let Carla stay longer if she were suddenly homeless. She could run errands for her, do yard work in exchange for room and board until she got a new job and her own place. And Libby was someone she could trust, someone who could advise her and give her things to laugh about, share a cigarette with.

And Nathan. What about him? That kiss yesterday. She had been so distracted by all that happened with her mom, she'd hardly had time to consider what it meant. A tiny tremor ran through her now, imagining his lips against hers. Can a real relationship be built on lust? Or gratitude or feeling safe? Maybe. But not with him. Remembering how quickly he pulled away, how exposed and stupid she felt, she had the sensation of sinking, as if the plug had been pulled from the bathtub drain.

Carla gathered her things. She brushed off the wet leaves and dirt and put them on. The sleeves of her denim jacket were cold against her bare arms, and her beanie was damp on one side. Shivering, she fished in her bag for E's car keys as she walked toward the unlit parking lot. Instead of stopping at the car, she crossed the street. The soles of her boots pressed into the damp sand at the water's edge.

The familiar evening gloom closed in, the smell of salt water, the *lick lick lick* of the tide creeping in over smooth pebbles on the shore. The inlet was smooth and still, mirroring the gunmetal sky and the faint outline of the Olympic Mountains to the west. No one was on the pier at that hour, and the boat ramp was deserted. A motor hummed in the distance, growing louder and a boat came around Windy Point. Nathan? She froze. She couldn't face him.

No. This boat was much larger. It passed, heading south toward the Narrows.

Relief was immediately replaced by disappointment. Avoiding Nathan meant cutting herself off from the whales too. The wonder of hearing them singing to one another, the intensity of her feelings when they swam close to the boat. The ache of wanting someone and just for a moment imagining that he wanted her too.

Carla stepped into the entryway of her apartment building and checked her mailbox. All junk except Alex's *Outside* magazine and a letter from the phone company with "Past Due—Final Notice" in red across the envelope. Crap. Saw that coming.

Wallace appeared in his doorway.

"I've been meaning to ask you, is everything okay?" he asked. "With your car. Did you get it fixed?"

"It's totaled. I'll get someone to haul it away. Eventually." She held up a hand and rubbed her thumb against the tips of her fingers, the universal sign for money.

"Ah. Right." He nodded, sending ripples down his fat neck. "Have you thought of donating it? A charity would pick it for free."

He told her how it worked and said he knew a guy who worked with Kars4Kids. "I'll give him a call tomorrow if you want and set it up. You could do it yourself, of course, but it seems you have your hands full." He tipped his chins toward her door and mouthed, "House-guest."

"I got it, but thanks for the info. And thanks again for helping out with the dog." Carla slipped her key into the lock.

"Don't mention it. He was no trouble at all, but I thoroughly enjoyed the muffins. Do you mind if I ask where you got them? I was thinking I'd buy some more. I'm a bit of a muffin snob," he raised his nose to prove it, "but those were delicious."

Still weird, but in a nice way. "Coffee Spot." She pushed the door open. She could have said she worked there, but he didn't need to know that. And maybe she didn't work there anymore. She swallowed.

"Have a nice—" She closed the door before he finished.

The apartment was dark and quiet. Carla flipped the light switch. "Mom?" she called. Nothing. She squashed the sprout of panic. "You here?"

The bathroom was empty. The bedroom door was shut. *Shit.* Not again. Taking long strides toward the door, Carla flung it open, expecting the worst: another OD. Her mother wasn't there.

Carla sank onto the mattress, and her heart resumed its normal rhythm. No paramedics would be needed tonight after all. Mom was restless, went out for a while. With no money, she couldn't get into too much trouble.

But something didn't feel right. Carla's focus jumped around the room. Her CD player on the floor with an overflowing ashtray perched on top. A grimy bath towel hanging from the closet doorknob. An empty coffee mug on the windowsill. What was the source of her uneasiness?

The truth was staring her in the face. The strangeness wasn't what was *in* the room but what was missing. The filthy backpack was gone.

Carla jumped to her feet and pulled the closet door wide. The rod was empty except for a tangled clump of wire hangers. *Bitch stole my clothes!* Her winter coat was gone. And her only decent belt. *Shit. Christ on a stick.* More hangers on the floor underneath and a half-empty box of black trash bags her mother must have used to haul everything away. Carla's gaze darted around. Something else was missing. Her legs stopped working, and she dropped to her knees.

"Fuck no!" Carla punched the floor and the walls and the floor again with both fists as she screamed, "Fuck! Fuck! Fuck! Holy mother of scum-sucking fuck!"

Chapter 15

Monday, November 3, 1997

Morning light filtered through lace curtains. Carla's head throbbed. Her fists were clenched so tightly it hurt to unfurl her fingers. She had meant to head home after Gizmo's evening walk, but Elizabeth insisted she stay the night. She hadn't misread Carla's dark mood when she stormed in, stinking of the Marlboro Lights she'd bought in a moment of weakness.

"Good for the nerves," Elizabeth had said, frowning, when Carla and Gizmo came through the back door into the kitchen. She set a steaming mug on the table. "Chamomile."

Carla dropped onto a chair and wrapped her cold hands around the mug. Time outside with the dog had helped her find a shred of calm. Instead of doing their usual three-mile loop on paved roads, Carla had let Gizmo lead her to the trail through the woods that surrounded Elizabeth's house. They picked their way along the overgrown path. Decades of fallen pine needles made a spongy and fragrant mat under their feet. Fern fronds, heavy with rainwater, brushed against Carla's jeans as soft as feathers. In a clearing she had stopped for a cigarette, tipping her head to follow the smoke as it drifted toward the soaring evergreen branches and the moonless sky. Gizmo leaned hard against her thigh, and she tapped a second cigarette out of the pack but reconsidered and pushed it back in. If she smoked only one a day, she could make this pack last three weeks. No telling how the next few days would go.

"Eat." In the warm kitchen, Elizabeth maneuvered her walker from the counter to the table with a plate of cheese and crackers. Wincing, she lowered herself onto the hard wooden chair. "Then tell me what's on your mind."

Carla had meant to keep it to herself, but she unloaded the story of her mother the thief.

"Not just my clothes, but my bass guitar!"

Elizabeth puffed up and shook her head, indignant on Carla's behalf.

"She'll hock it or sell it, get enough money for a solid high, and show up on my doorstep looking for forgiveness and something else to steal." Carla stuffed her mouth with dry saltines and cheese that tasted like sweaty feet. She washed it all down with gulps of weak grassy tea. It didn't matter if she liked it. Beggars can't be choosers. She was used to never getting what she wanted but being grateful anyway.

"How awful!" Elizabeth said, and refilled Carla's cup.

Where was the you-brought-this-on-yourself lecture? Where was the blame for trusting someone unworthy of trust? It never came, so Carla kept talking. Now and then, Elizabeth patted her hand or nodded encouragement.

By the time Carla crawled into bed in Elizabeth's frilly yellow guest room, she had confessed to kissing and being rejected by Nathan, telling off her manager, and not knowing how to feel about losing the father she never knew.

Now she sat on the edge of the bed in her underpants and T-shirt with her heart thudding against her ribs and filling her ears with its sound. Quiet voices from the bedroom across the hall startled her. She parted the window curtains. A car was in the driveway. Must be the nurse who came every morning to help with bathing and physical therapy. Carla pulled on her jeans and socks and found a jar of instant coffee in the kitchen. She made a cup while Gizmo ate his breakfast.

At least she didn't have to go to work today. She rarely lied, but after spilling her guts to Elizabeth the night before, she called Mr. Wilson and said she had the flu. The truth was that she *had* felt sick when she dialed the phone. She was sick of falling for her mom's bullshit. Sick of being jerked around at the coffee shop. Sick of people walking all over her like she was a well-used doormat. Sick of breaking her balls for peanuts. Sick of being expected to kiss Todd's ass because he was the owner's son. This was no virus, but it *was* a matter of life and death. If she saw Todd's face again, she would kill him.

Head cleared by the caffeine, Carla found the Yellow Pages in a kitchen drawer. Five pawn shops in Bremerton, none in Silverdale or Tracyton. Three dealers advertised musical instruments, and she wrote their addresses on her hand. The closest was on the other side of the Warren Avenue Bridge. The other two were near the ferry terminal. She would go in person, being careful not to spill the whole damn sob story about her candy-apple-red Gibson Victory bass they may have acquired in the last twenty-four hours. She wasn't stupid. Desperation gave off a scent, and desperate people paid more. If—fat chance—she found it, she could negotiate a deal on the spot, offering a down payment big enough to hold it until she figured out how to come up with the rest.

Over the sound of water rushing through the pipes came women's voices talking in the bathroom. The nurse was filling the tub. Carla left a note for Elizabeth on the kitchen table. *Heading out to track down my bass. Wish me luck. Haha.*

It didn't take long to confirm that the instrument hadn't surfaced. Even Saint Anthony let her down. Disgusted, Carla drove back across Port Washington Narrows, glancing toward the mouth of Dyes Inlet in the distance. Nathan had told her he'd recently seen the whales swimming a little way into the Narrows, that limbo between being stuck and being free. Practice runs maybe. From the high bridge, she might have been able to spot a fin in the water below if she wasn't busy driving E's car at forty miles per hour.

She needed to see the whales, to get back out there and feel useful, to help Nathan. It was the only thing she could think of to keep from spiraling into the abyss of depression. But that kiss had ruined everything.

Carla pulled over near Lions Park at the edge of the channel. Half a dozen people stood on the fishing pier, and others huddled under picnic shelters nearby. She walked closer. Colorful umbrellas dotted the opposite shore and boats crowded the channel. The wet weather hadn't dampened their excitement, even though no whales were in sight. Voices carried over the water as people in the nearest boats called to one another, their scraps of conversation and laughter contrasting sharply with Carla's black frame of mind. She planted her feet on the shore and scanned the length of the channel for fins or tails, letting the wind carry away her long list of reasons to be miserable.

A shout from someone on the water broke into her thoughts. Weaving between the boats was a lone fin, tall and straight. A hush fell. Canoes, kayaks, sailboats, and fishing boats parted, giving the orca room to pass. Whether any of them were two hundred feet back she couldn't tell, but no one interfered with its progress.

More whales joined the first. They passed, backs exposed, exhaling loudly and sending a fine mist into the air. Carla tried to see notches and nicks on their fins or patterns on their saddle patches, but they were too far away. One rolled, slapping its pectoral fin on the surface. Another dove, bringing its tail flukes down with a splash. Carla gave up trying to identify them and lost herself in the marvel. She would never get tired of watching these wild creatures.

A motor roared and a speedboat suddenly tore down the middle of the Narrows. The orcas dove and dodged, scattering in all directions.

"Stop!" Carla yelled with hands cupped around her mouth, frantic. "Stay back!" A few heads turned in her direction. The driver of the boat couldn't hear her over his roaring engine, and in seconds he was gone. A bullhorn would have been handy. Where was Nathan? And the other official boats? Why isn't anyone doing anything? Carla scanned the Narrows in both directions. The whales had disappeared under the waves. If she hadn't blown it with Nathan, she could be with him now, chasing after that asshole in the speedboat. People like that had to be stopped before they killed or injured an orca. What she needed was a boat.

Chapter 16

Tuesday, November 4, 1997

Carla paddled clumsily into the middle of the inlet. Determined to prevent another near miss like the day before in the Narrows, she had called Alex and asked to borrow his kayak. It was still in his cousin's garage, and Horny Holton met her at the Silverdale Marina where he wrestled the red plastic boat and all the gear from his Jeep to the edge of the water.

"I'll swing by after work to pick everything up," Holton said. "We could grab a beer."

She'd rather swallow broken glass. Carla ignored him as she slipped her arms into the too-big yellow life jacket and cinched the strap snugly around her waist. Alex had the physique of a twelve-year-old, so it was hard to imagine it wouldn't be swimming on him too.

"See you around five?" Holton said, rocking back and forth on his heels like a kid.

Carla settled into the kayak and pushed off. "Thanks," she called.

The rain had stopped, but the wind blew in strong gusts. It took a while to get the hang of paddling and steering without Alex there to remind her what to do. By the time she got close to the center of the inlet, she was exhausted. Her arms and back muscles burned. She laid her paddle across the cockpit and floated among the boats full of people waiting to see the whales. Nathan was nowhere in sight.

Calling in sick this time had been less an act of defiance and more because she had a reason to be somewhere else. With or without Nathan, she wanted more than anything to find Faith. Her plan was simple. Borrow the boat, paddle around, spot the missing whale. Turned out simple didn't mean easy. Or quick.

In the early afternoon a group of orcas passed close to Carla's kayak. She identified one as Ankh, the matriarch, by her large irregular saddle patch. Ankh broke away and headed south toward the Narrows. The other whales followed and so did a few small boats.

"Stay back!" Carla yelled. Without the bullhorn her small voice was blown around by the wind. "Don't chase the whales!"

Paddling furiously after them Carla closed in on the last boat, a canoe carrying two men and trailing behind the others. She tried again. "Keep away from the whales! Please stay back."

The men pulled up their paddles and watched her approach until she was close enough to see their smirking faces.

"Hey," said the one in the stern to his friend. "That little girl thinks we give a shit."

"You're breaking the law," Carla shouted.

The men laughed and resumed paddling.

"You are endangering them!" she yelled at the top of her voice, but they continued to chase the whales.

Two more boats joined the chase using their motors to speed past her. Their wake nearly swamped the kayak and slowed her progress. She fell further behind, but she pressed on, grunting with effort, the kayak rocking from side to side each time she dug her paddle into the water and pulled with all her strength. Every muscle in Carla's body strained, and her breathing quickened. Despite the cold, a trickle of sweat rolled down between her breasts. The life jacket was hot, and she had tightened the straps so much that she now couldn't fill her lungs. It chafed under her arms, so she unbuckled it and kept on, paddling more freely. The wind cooled her damp skin and whipped up waves that tossed the kayak around like a toy. Anger and frustration surged like a rush of adrenaline.

With every stroke she fought all that was wrong with the world. The stupidity of those people in their boats. The manager job, taken away without so much as an apology. Missing her chance to see Gordon. Her manipulative mother. Her bass. Screwing up everything with Nathan.

Carla jabbed her paddle in and pulled as hard as she could, teeth clenched. The sea spray stung her face as she pulled again and again against the water and wind. Her grunting became wailing, so loud she alarmed herself.

She spotted a tour boat approaching from the opposite direction and prepared to navigate over its huge wake by turning to take it head-on as Alex had taught her. The nose of the kayak tipped up and down as the waves broke under her, and she paddled like crazy. And then the kayak flipped and dumped her out like a stone from a shoe.

The shock of the frigid water made her gasp the moment she pushed her head into the air. Her rapid, panicked breathing left her lightheaded. She tried to call out for help, but her mouth and nose kept filling up with icy, salty water. No other boats were near. Panting and spitting, Carla treaded water, moving slowly toward the bobbing kayak, its red underside visible but staying out of reach, taunting her, laughing at her like the men in the canoe. Arms and legs flailing, she couldn't close the distance.

At last, she stopped fighting and let the waves carry her. It took all her will to keep her head up, but still she swallowed and inhaled water, choking and gasping for breath. Cold pricked her skin like thousands of tiny needles making the muscles in her legs and arms cramp. It was impossible to keep treading water, and soon she could no longer feel her fingers or feet.

Sensing movement, Carla twisted left and right praying for a boat, a savior. A fin tip poked though the surface and grew taller and taller. Too close! Carla struggled to back away, kicking and crying out as an orca's back appeared, like the hull of an overturned boat. It lifted its head, and the yellow of her life jacket reflected in its eye. Diving again, it slapped the water with huge tail flukes, the sound deafening. Water foamed and heaved all around Carla, washing over her and pulling her in deep.

She squeezed her eyes shut and braced for the end. Whale food. The mouth clamping down, teeth ripping her skin, jaw crushing the last breath from her. *Why did I think going for a swim was a good idea? Why am I wearing clothes? Where is the shallow end of this pool?* A buzzing sound in her ears and the fast thumping of her heart became music. Carla tried to recognize the song. The buzzing got louder. Her left arm slipped from her unfastened life jacket, and she sank.

The buzzing in Carla's head became a rumbling drone, getting louder until it shook the air around her and stopped. Someone grabbed the collar of her denim jacket, pulling her roughly up and over the side of a boat where she lay gasping like a fish. A pair of hands turned her onto her belly. Carla coughed and gagged, choking on seawater until she vomited.

"Take it easy. You're safe," said a woman's voice above her.

Carla tried to sit up, but a man wearing a uniform told her to lie still and tucked a blanket around her body.

"Is that your kayak?" the woman, also wearing a uniform, asked. *Oh God. It's not mine. Alex.* Carla lifted her head and tried to answer, but her throat was raw. She couldn't feel her lips. Her teeth chattered so violently she was afraid they would chip.

"Don't worry," the man said. "We'll come back and tow it to shore later."

The motor came to life again, and the boat swung around. The rough wool blanket scratched the skin of her neck and chin. It smelled of gasoline.

"A few more minutes and you'd have been in big trouble." The woman squatted near Carla's head. She had a silver badge pinned to her brown jacket.

Trouble? Was she being arrested? "Cops," Carla tried to say through numb lips, but no sound came out of her mouth. She tried again, her glance moving from the badge to the woman's eyes and back again.

"I'm Officer Sundgaard." The woman patted her badge. "Fish and Wildlife. People call me Sunny. Lucky my partner spotted your capsized vessel. He's Officer Mooney. What's your name?"

Carla's head swam. Everything was muddled. Her jaw locked and she couldn't speak. She shook uncontrollably. Sunny wrapped a second layer around her, a crackling silver emergency blanket, and then produced a stocking cap and pulled it gently over Carla's wet hair. *Where's my beanie?*

The man drove the boat steadily on, gradually increasing their speed. Sunny moved away for a moment and returned with a first-aid kit. Carla studied the two officers in their brown uniforms but couldn't make sense of them, who they were and why they were there.

Moving efficiently, Sunny took Carla's pulse and temperature. "You'll be okay. We'll get you to shore and into some dry clothes. Do you remember what happened? How you landed in the water?"

Carla tried to concentrate, but her thoughts danced away like the shredded remnants of a dream. "I-I—" she stammered.

Darkness closed in and Carla was spinning away. The woman yelled over the sound of the motor, "Tim, did you radio ahead for an ambulance?"

"Yes. Is she conscious?"

"Barely. But she's shivering, so that's a good sign." To Carla, she said, "Stay with me."

And Carla tried. As they flew over the water, her mind organized itself, putting events in order. The laughter of the men in the canoe. The tour boat with its huge wake. The whale coming closer and closer. And now she was safe.

By the time the boat pulled into a slip at the Silverdale Marina, Carla was more embarrassed than anything. At the end of the pier, an ambulance waited with lights flashing. She shrugged off the blanket and sat up insisting she was fine, but her speech was slurred, her eyes wouldn't focus, and the world swam around her. She needed to get home. Where had she left her car anyway? Wait. She didn't have a car anymore, did she? How did she get to the inlet? *What's wrong with me?* Panic squeezed her throat, and she struggled to fill her lungs.

"Lie down." Sunny took Carla's shoulders firmly and lowered her back to the bottom of the boat. "We'll get you checked out at the ER. Hypothermia is serious business." To the man she said, "EMTs are here, Mooney. They're bringing a stretcher."

"I'll walk." Carla tensed her legs and tried to stand, but they shook wildly and wouldn't hold her weight.

"Is there someone we can call for you?" Sunny asked. "Someone who could meet you at the hospital?"

Faces floated through Carla's mind, dissolving and reforming. One by one she named them. Mom. Libby. Nathan. E. The only phone number she knew was Elizabeth's. She had dialed it so many times it was permanently in her memory. But E couldn't come.

"No." Carla had never felt so alone in all her life.

Before he signed her discharge papers that evening, the ER doctor insisted that Carla arrange to stay with a friend or family member for at least twenty-four hours in case of complications from hypothermia. That would have to be Elizabeth. Their phone conversation was brief. Carla downplayed her accident, but Elizabeth was horrified anyway.

"Thanks for letting me crash at your place again. I hate to ask, but could you spring for a cab? I'll pay you back."

The doctor shook his head and interrupted. "No taxi. You'll need a responsible adult to sign you out."

Forty minutes after the call, a nurse parted the curtains around Carla's corner of the busy ER. Nathan rushed in, drops of sweat glistened on his forehead and upper lip. Elizabeth had promised to track him down, but until Carla saw him standing there, his face pale in the fluorescent light, she hadn't believed it was possible.

"What happened?" He sat next to the bed.

"How did you get here so fast? I thought you'd be on your boat." Carla pulled the sheet up to cover the flimsy cotton hospital gown, her still-damp hair hanging in stiff, salty clumps.

"A colleague radioed me from the office. Got a call from someone who said you almost drowned?"

Carla gave him the short version, mostly pieced together bits from what she overheard the EMTs telling the admitting nurse at the hospital.

"I was there, too, in the inlet. Why didn't you just come with me? Flag me down at the boat launch by the coffee shop?" He gently tucked her hair behind her ear before she pulled away.

She didn't want to answer directly. What would she say anyway? That she'd been avoiding him, too embarrassed to look him in the eye after that awkward, unwelcome kiss? That she called in sick and could hardly hang around waiting for him outside the coffee shop?

"Plenty of people are out there in kayaks," she said.

"You'd do more good in a bigger boat. With a bullhorn. With me. I need your help."

"*Pfff.*"

"You don't give yourself enough credit, Carla. Like I told you, an eager volunteer is like gold. Besides," he said, smiling, "I enjoy your company."

She sniffed the ends of her hair and grimaced.

"Eau de Seawater?" He laughed. "Let's get you home."

Nathan sat in the waiting room while Carla changed into the new clothes he brought to the hospital in a plastic K-mart shopping bag: a gray sweatsuit, a three-pack of underpants, and a pair of slippers. Nothing was her size, but they were dry and warm, and she was grateful.

In the truck, Nathan tried to make small talk, but he stopped after Carla's one-word answers made it clear she wasn't interested in conversation. He asked if she wanted him to raise the heat. She did. Carla gave him Elizabeth's address and asked if he needed directions. He didn't. While he focused on the road ahead of them, she stared out the side window into the darkness, hot air blowing over her feet and face.

The details of the accident came back to Carla in fragments, out of order and fuzzy. The sensation of being lifted out of the inlet like a soggy rag doll, the orca close enough to touch, the shock of hitting the icy water, the big tour boat barreling toward her, the way she shook under the smelly blanket tucked around her by the Fish and Wildlife officers as her confusion faded.

The rest was in sharp focus. Two EMTs helped her onto the stretcher and wheeled her from the dock. In the ambulance they removed her sodden clothes and wrapped her shivering body in heated blankets. An ER nurse gave her warm broth and checked her temperature every fifteen minutes. Everyone was efficient and competent, doing their jobs, that's all. But looking after her wasn't Nathan's job. She stole a glance at him. He was leaning forward slightly with his slender fingers curled around the steering wheel. In profile, his serious expression was softer.

When Elizabeth opened the door, he registered surprise. He probably assumed Carla's friend was the same age. Elizabeth invited him in for a hot drink, and he accepted, but she excused herself first to usher Carla down the hall to the bathroom. Fresh towels and a faded terrycloth bathrobe were waiting for her. She felt silly, all this fuss, but it was nice.

A few minutes later, Carla crawled into bed under crisp sheets and a soft yellow blanket. Her head ached, but she was warming slowly, and her muscles began to relax. A lamp next to the bed glowed. The rest of the room was in shadow, but she let her gaze slide from corner to corner. How quickly the old-fashioned furniture and lacy curtains had become familiar, as if she'd lived here all her life when it was only her second night in this room.

Nathan called out a cheerful goodnight and the front door closed.

Elizabeth appeared in the bedroom doorway. "What were you thinking? You might have drowned." The lenses of her large, round glasses caught the light. "Foolish, foolish girl." Her tone was stern. With Gizmo at her heels, she pushed her walker in over the braided rug and stopped next to the bed.

"Let me be." Carla closed her eyes. She had done a good job of berating herself already. All she wanted was to be left alone. It had been stupid, going out there. She *was* foolish.

"Well, never mind. Go to sleep." Elizabeth's voice was gentle now.

Carla adjusted the pillow under her wet head. Her shampooed hair still smelled faintly fishy. Gizmo sniffed at it, his warm musky breath tickling her ear, reminding her of her responsibility.

"I need to walk Gizmo." The dog's ears perked up. Carla pushed the covers back and waited for Elizabeth to move her walker out of the way. She didn't budge.

"He's perfectly fine. I can manage letting him out into the backyard."

"Let me at least check that the gate is shut. You don't want him running off again."

"Lie down." Elizabeth pulled the blanket back in place with her gnarled fingers. "You know, I still don't understand why Gizzy didn't come back the last time. He's run off before but was always back by dinnertime. I feared the worst, that he'd been hit by a car." She pressed her lips together.

"He didn't come home because he couldn't, E. Somebody locked him in a cage."

"No!" Elizabeth pressed her hand to her breast. "You never told me that. Why didn't you tell me before?"

"You didn't ask."

Carla pictured herself walking up to E's door that first time. The taxi waiting in the driveway, the way the old woman looked—shriveled and weak in her wheelchair—and the demanding tone in her voice. Carla squirmed now at the memory of E's sharp *What do you want?* when Carla called to offer dog-walking services, and her indignant *Highway robbery!* when Carla told her the fee. Nothing about that old lady had inspired Carla to volunteer the story of how she rescued

Gizmo. But this was a different woman. She treated Carla like a friend. Like a daughter.

"Well, I'm asking now." Elizabeth leaned over her walker.

Carla told her about seeing the two ads in the paper, for a lost dog and a found one, and how she tried to connect the two. Her voice cracked as she described finding Gizmo at the feed store.

"I couldn't leave him there. I tried your number for a week. I had to ask my neighbor to take care of him when I went to work."

"I'm truly in your debt, Carla. I had no idea the lengths you went to for me...for us." Elizabeth patted Gizmo's head. Then she stroked Carla's arm, her fingers warm and soothing. "Thank you."

They were quiet for a moment. "Get some rest. Your handsome friend said he'll call your boss to tell him about your accident. In the morning, he'll fetch my car from the marina," Elizabeth tried to hide her smile when she said, "and he'll return it when he comes to walk Gizzy."

"Walking Gizmo is *my* job. He doesn't know Nathan, and you said he doesn't like strangers."

"True, but I also said he's a good judge of character. Gizmo knows a gentle soul when he meets one." Elizabeth fussed with the covers, folding the sheet into a cuff over the top edge of the blanket below Carla's chin. She smoothed it, drawing her hand along the cuff. When her hand was still, she added, "And so do I."

Carla closed her eyes, and a moment later she heard the wheels of Elizabeth's walker rolling across the rug. The bedroom door closed softly, and Carla was alone.

Until she heard it said aloud Carla hadn't thought of Nathan that way, as a gentle soul. Thinking of him now, she saw it, but his was also a soul full of passion for his work. There was a quiet inner strength about him, a confidence Carla lacked. His commitment to the safety of the orcas in the inlet was so fierce he had put it ahead of keeping peace with his colleagues and even his boss. *There* was something they had in common, putting the whales above everything else.

Gratitude, helplessness, shame, hope. Everything mixed and swelled and stretched Carla's chest until she was afraid her body would split open. A woman she barely knew was looking after her so tenderly, and she hadn't done anything to deserve it. She hadn't earned it.

Chapter 17

Tires crunching on Elizabeth's gravel driveway woke Carla. She'd been up before sunrise but after baking a cinnamon-apple coffee cake to thank Elizabeth for everything, she fell asleep on the sofa.

"It looks like your young man is here," Elizabeth said from her chair near the living room window. The doorbell rang as she reached for her walker.

"I'll go." Carla stood too quickly, dizziness almost dropping her back onto the couch.

Gizmo was already at the door when Carla pulled it open.

"You look better." Nathan's arms were loaded with three-ring binders, muscles flexing under his light jacket. He chuckled and said, "Can't get over you in that sweatsuit."

"Yeah, my clothes are in the washer." She ran a hand over her hair, feeling naked without her beanie. "But it's all about the slippers anyway." Carla looked down at her feet. "Not just pink, but sparkly."

"The more ridiculous the better."

She stood back and held the door open for him to come in. He sniffed the air. "Something smells fantastic. Apple pie?"

"Close."

On the mat he stooped to remove his shoes, and Gizmo gave him a sloppy kiss. He laughed and wiped his wet cheek on his sleeve.

"Hope you don't mind me barging in for a couple of minutes before I walk the dog, Ms. Hartman," he said through the doorway to the living room. "Just dropping these off." He dipped his head toward his load.

"Not at all." Elizabeth's face was bright. "It's good to see you. Thanks again for bringing my car back and for looking after Gizmo." The dog settled at her feet, and she brushed her hand lightly over the top of his head.

"Glad to help." To Carla he said, "Thought you might be bored, so I brought you a project. Whale catalogs. Only if you feel like it. No pressure."

"Come on. Let's work in the kitchen." Carla walked away and Nathan followed. "Coffee?" she asked automatically.

"Sure. Thanks. Got a buddy coming at ten to take me back to my truck at the marina. I have a meeting with my boss and a guy from the feds to figure out our next move. Reporter from the *Sun* is coming to do an interview after." Nathan put the binders on the table and opened the one on the top of the stack. He bent over it and flipped a few pages, peering closely at the photographs. "Still interested in helping with this, right?"

"Yup." Carla almost asked if he had found a way to pay her, but it didn't matter. She set a mug on the table along with a slice of cake.

"Can't tell you how much I appreciate this." He slipped off his backpack and set it on the floor with a thump. "This one on top," he began, drumming his fingers lightly on the open binder, "is the Southern Residents—J, K, and L pods. Brought the others in case you can't identify one and need to look further." He was excited and speaking fast. "But I'm getting ahead of myself. Sit and I'll walk you through my process."

Nathan emptied a large manila envelope of loose photographs onto the table and explained the task. He wanted her to look at the new photos he he'd taken of the whales in Dyes Inlet and compare them to the whales pictured in the catalog, looking for any that matched. Once a match was found, she was to write the number of the whale shown in the catalog on the back of the new photo.

"Start with our orcas, the L25 sub-pod. We've got positive IDs on more than half of the nineteen." He handed her a sheet of paper. Names, numbers, ages, and genders were neatly handwritten in black ink. She studied the page. Some of the names were familiar: Ankh, Canuck, Lulu.

"I'm pretty sure of the rest of the adults," he continued, "but the juveniles can be difficult to identify. I need your sharp eyes to confirm these." He turned the paper over to show her a second list on the back.

"Every year I go through all the pictures taken by me or the researchers at the center. Sometimes ordinary people send me photos of whales spotted in the area. In a normal year it's impossible to find and photograph an entire pod or sub-pod because their movements are unpredictable. So, having nineteen whales in a small space like Dyes Inlet gives us a unique opportunity to study them up close and to see who's died and who's had babies and so on. There's at least one new calf under a year old. He'll need a number."

Nathan paused and searched the pockets of his backpack until he produced a small, zippered case and removed a magnifying glass from it. He showed Carla where to look for scars, notches, and other markings, as well as variations on the dorsal fins and the saddle patches.

"It's slow and tedious, but—" Nathan sat up suddenly, both hands flying to the top of his head. "Almost forgot to tell you! I saw Faith yesterday!"

Carla cheered and high-fived him to keep herself from throwing her arms around him. But then she did it anyway, jumping from her chair and hugging him from behind. She slid back into her seat, snatching the magnifying glass and bending over a photo to hide her embarrassment at being so impulsive. Again. With the glass held close to her eye, she stole a sideways glance at Nathan. He was beaming, crinkling the corners of his eyes.

"I followed Canuck and Lulu around all morning, then POP! I saw three. Faith is back!" As he talked, he picked up a stack of pictures and set them in a row one by one, dealing them out like cards. Carla's thoughts jumped back to the tarot reading and the card with the man crying over his spilled cups. Libby said the bridge in the background meant she might have a breakthrough if she could let go of the past. Not that she believed in it, but ever since Carla flipped the kayak, something in her had shifted. Not a breakthrough, but she was unsettled.

Nathan raised the fork and took a bite of cake.

Which cards would show up if Libby read his cards? He had his shit together already. Carla might be at a crossroads, but Nathan wasn't.

"Delicious," Nathan said with his mouth full. "Wow. Seriously amazing." He took another bite. "You make this at the coffee shop? Your customers will be glad to have you back."

She dreaded returning to her job, but she didn't have a choice. Tomorrow would be her last sick day, and then back to the grind. Nathan chewed quietly for a moment, and she peered at the pictures.

"Is this a match?" she asked, pushing the catalog closer to him. He reached for the magnifying glass.

"Close, but no. Look at the pattern of scratches here at the base." He slid the book back across the table.

Gizmo wandered in and sat by the back door, ready for his walk.

"I'd better get him out." Nathan zipped the pockets of his backpack closed and checked his watch. "Can't be late for the meeting. I need the feds on my side today. I won't get the boss's go-ahead to work on a plan to get the orcas out if the feds don't go along with it. This is day sixteen, Carla." There was that small flutter under her breastbone. "None of us at the center thought they would stay this long. It's too long. They've been showing signs of distress."

"Meaning?"

His eyebrows crumpled together, and Carla met his steady gaze. The sobering precariousness of the whales' situation showed in his eyes. Those gray eyes. The soft lashes.

"Swimming in tight circles, high-speed swimming, spy-hopping, dehydration." He counted them off on his fingers.

She tried to focus on what he was saying. Her attention was not on his words, but on the lips forming them. The way they moved, pulling up and down, creasing and smoothing. A warmth flooded her belly, spreading upward into her chest, and a smile threatened to betray her thoughts.

He stood and slipped his arms into the straps of the backpack, breaking eye contact.

"Why won't they leave?" she asked.

"If we knew that, our problem would be solved."

Chapter 18

Thursday, November 6, 1997

Squinting at photos of dorsal fins for hours the day before and again that morning made Carla's head ache. The fins were all starting to look alike, and beads of sweat formed on her upper lip. Elizabeth had turned up the heat, convinced that Carla must still be chilled from her unplanned swim in Dyes Inlet. She only succeeded in making her uncomfortably warm. Carla needed to get outside.

"Gizmo needs his walk." Carla stood and stretched.

"Not until this evening." Elizabeth didn't look up from the newspaper. "Doctor's orders. No strenuous activity for forty-eight hours. Besides, Nathan was here and took him out before you were up."

Carla had slept deeply during the night and dreamed that the whales swam out into Puget Sound while she urged them on from somewhere above. Her dream-self had a bird's-eye view of their sleek bodies gliding through the water single file, as if she were watching from a cloud or a hot-air balloon. Or a bridge. The dream left her restless and afraid that she had already missed their departure.

At noon Carla made grilled cheese sandwiches, and they shared a can of ginger ale which Elizabeth confessed was her only vice. Carla cleared away their plates, wrapped the remaining cheese in foil, and opened the fridge to put it away. An excuse to get out for a while stared her in the face.

"Sheesh. You could use some groceries, E. You're out of milk," said Carla, lifting the carton and swishing the last drops around inside. "Low on eggs, too, it looks like. How about I pick up a few things at the store?"

Elizabeth reluctantly agreed, making Carla promise not to overdo it. "You might get some more ginger ale too," she said and pulled a twenty-dollar bill out of an old blue cookie tin next to the stove.

Feeling almost normal again in her own clothes, minus the lost beanie, Carla drove straight toward the inlet, passing two grocery stores on the way. Whales first, bass second, food last. She switched on the car stereo, and Mick Jagger's voice filled the car. Not her station. She reached for the dial but stopped and let it play. The last person to drive Elizabeth's car was Nathan when he brought it back from the marina. She smiled and inhaled, picking up a trace of his scent. Clean. Minty. She raised the volume and added her voice to the Rolling Stones.

Traffic was heavy for a Thursday afternoon, but at least it was moving. The road followed the eastern shore at a distance, giving her brief glimpses of the water between the trees and houses. No sign of the whales, but plenty of hopeful watchers in boats.

Approaching the intersection where she would have turned if she were going to the Coffee Spot, Carla felt a small tug. Libby was on her mind. And Noah, Delbert, Stewart. Even Sylvia. Who was doing the baking in her absence? Did they miss her? Mr. Wilson knew about her accident, but did the others know?

Four days was longer than she'd ever been away from work. The big surprise was that she was looking forward to tomorrow, to seeing everyone and getting back into the kitchen, back to her routines and her radio station. Four days was also the longest she'd gone without music—her music. Elizabeth had classical on in the house most of the time, but it didn't do anything for Carla. It didn't shake her loose. She missed hearing the rhythm of the drums and the pulse of the bass. If she never found her bass, would she be able to afford another someday? Would she play again?

The choir sang the long, monotonous chorus at the end of "You Can't Always Get What You Want." Ironically appropriate. Carla smirked and switched the station. The traffic light turned green as "25 Cent Giraffes" blasted from the speakers. Smiling, she glanced down the road toward the coffee shop as she passed.

The Narrows came into view. Here the road hugged the shoreline. Boats of all types and sizes crowded the channel and moving among them—the whales! Carla felt a lift in her chest, followed by a sinking feeling. Her dream, seeing the whales from above as they left the inlet for good, had left her with a sense of unease, a strange kind of nostalgia. She was longing for the whales while they were still there under her nose.

Traffic slowed to a crawl as drivers rubbernecked, watching one orca after another breach and crash back into the water. The Warren Avenue Bridge just ahead would be the best place to see the whole length of the channel, like the view in her dream. Driving over wouldn't work. She wouldn't be able to take her eyes off the road for a good look. She would walk to the middle on the pedestrian walkway instead.

With sudden urgency, she parked the Volvo in the empty community theater parking lot below the massive bridge. Concrete steps led to Warren Avenue overhead, where the road began its slow incline to cross the channel. Her gaze traveled up the long flight of stairs and then along the railing that ran the length of the bridge. From that angle, trees on the near shore blocked her view of all but the first hundred feet of the bridge, and she couldn't see the water at all. The middle of the span, somewhere out there, could have been a hundred miles from where Carla stood. An endless walk on legs still shaky from her recent accident.

Hoping for a different solution, Carla walked under the elevated roadway and followed it toward the water. Traffic rumbled above. Even the ground under her feet trembled. The road rose higher as she neared the channel, and the land sloped downward, getting steeper as she walked over bare dirt littered with trash. Her dream had been bright and peaceful, nothing like this shadowy, noisy, lonesome spot. A tall chain-link fence stopped her progress. She entwined her fingers through the cold wire, breathing hard from the exertion, and took in the view.

To her right and left, the last yellow and gold leaves clung to vine maples and black cottonwoods. In front of her, the ground dropped away. Over the tops of trees growing along the shore thirty feet below, white sails drifted by, stark against the dark water. Colorful canoes and kayaks clustered in groups of four or five. Bigger boats motored in lazy circles. Carla's eyes tracked the movement of the whales. Their dorsal fins pierced the surface as they paced up and down the Narrows, but each time they got close to the bridge they turned back.

Nathan must be somewhere in the mix, hoping as she was that the pod would continue down the channel and find their way back where they belonged. She had learned from him that Puget Sound was part of the L pod's regular hunting grounds in the fall, and every year in December they headed out into the Pacific Ocean. He knew each individual in this sub-pod by name. Moonlight and Faith. Ankh and Nugget. He knew who was related to who. Grandmothers, mothers, daughters, sons.

At first the whales had all looked alike, but as Carla worked through Nathan's catalog, peering through the magnifying glass in search of subtle differences in the shapes of saddle patches and the notches and scars on fins, she was becoming an expert. Each individual whale had its own story. The more she knew about them the more she worried they would never get out. Nathan had pointed out that the whales were exhaling with more force than normal, a sign of stress and agitation. Time was running out. Her friends were in trouble.

Carla lit a cigarette and looked up at the underside of the bridge. It was solid concrete. How could something so heavy stay up there? She counted seven pairs of massive pillars like a troop of giants, arms over their heads, carrying their load as they marched the quarter mile across the channel. Libby said that a bridge was a way to reach something better—like the castle on her tarot card—but on the other side of this bridge was just more of the same.

A heavy truck thundered onto the bridge, and the ground under Carla's feet trembled. What if the vibrations were scaring the whales? If it *was* the traffic noise keeping the whales in the inlet, the solution was to make the traffic stop. But how?

Near the library's front entrance, at a table covered with stacks of books and magazines, Carla thumbed the pages of one volume and paused to examine an illustration of an orca.

"Where did I see..." she muttered, and her voice trailed off. She closed the book and reached for another. "No, maybe it was in here."

The hour she spent under the bridge had left Carla more puzzled than ever about why the whales wouldn't swim past it. Hoping to find some answers, she took a detour to the Bremerton Public Library. She had little hope of discovering anything Nathan and the other biologists didn't know about whale behavior, but she had to do something.

The librarian helped her find some information about whale rescues, but there wasn't much, a couple of short articles in magazines.

"Here's a story in the *Daily Sitka Sentinel* you should see," he told her, handing her a small cardboard box. She should know his name by now after all the times he'd helped her find books on local wildlife. Only two librarians worked afternoons: Adelle, the round woman whose ever-present corduroy pants turned her into a human cricket, and this guy with his collection of sweater vests. *Marvin, was it? Marlin?* Carla considered his neat white collar showing above the brown sweater. The long nose and small, glistening eyes. Minus the shiny green head, he looked like a mallard duck. *Melvin?*

She turned her attention and her confusion from the man to the box. Inside was a reel of film. "A movie. What am I supposed to do with this?"

Mallard shifted into high gear, practically crackling with excitement. "Follow me!" He led her to the reference section where he showed her how to use the microfilm reader.

After some fumbling Carla found the article. October 1994. Nine orcas ended up in a place called Barnes Lake, Alaska. The reporter said Barnes Lake wasn't a freshwater lake but a tidal saltwater lagoon. In some ways, the situation was like what was happening in Dyes Inlet. Both groups of whales entered small bodies of water through narrow channels and appeared unable to leave. The good news was that eight of the nine Alaska whales survived. Imagining an article in the *Sun* saying that all but one member of the pod in the inlet survived made Carla's heart hammer in her chest. That one dead whale could have been Faith. She closed her eyes and mouthed, "Thank you, Saint Anthony."

She continued reading. The Barnes Lake orcas were starving after six weeks, more than twice as long as Carla's whales had been in the inlet so far. Somewhat reassuring. A group of volunteers from the small community had successfully combined two rescue methods Nathan talked about: herding and making noise. Other ways whales had been moved in the past were by using nets or by luring them with food or recorded sounds of related whales. Herding them with boats was the riskiest.

"Look at those cowboys," Nathan said the first day he took her out in his boat. They were watching a group of boaters chase the whales, ignoring the warnings Carla shouted through the bullhorn. "Herding them like that is stressing them out!" Not only was it bad for the whales, he told her, but it could be dangerous for the people in boats.

"If the whales panic, they might dive and come up under the boats. A little boat is no match for a six-ton whale the size of a bus," he'd said.

As for the second method—making noise to move them out—Nathan had opinions about that too. He told Carla the racket from all the motorboats was confusing the whales, and adding more noise intentionally would do more harm than good.

Carla continued reading. The people in Barnes Lake combined the two methods, driving their boats slowly closer while hammering on metal pipes they lowered into the water. The whales acted like the noise was a threat and moved away from the line of boats and the sound they were making, until they were safely out of the lake. The same method had been used several times before as a deterrent, to keep whales away from an oil spill, for example.

The news article referred to the pipes as "oikomi," which sent Carla to the encyclopedia, where she read that the Japanese word *oikomi* referred to a traditional—and cruel—method of catching and killing dolphins. There was a photograph. She snapped the volume shut and shoved it back onto the shelf.

Something else that caught Carla's attention was that the whales in Barnes Lake seemed to be avoiding a big kelp bed near the mouth of the channel, which scientists called a psychological barrier. The kelp, like the Warren Avenue Bridge, wasn't really an obstacle, but the whales were afraid of passing through it.

The noise, the vibrations, or even the hulking shadow of the bridge on the water could be creating one of those psychological barriers. But what if there was something about the bridge itself? Maybe there was something about *this* bridge that made the whales afraid to pass under it.

"Hey," she said, approaching the circulation desk. "Do you have any books on bridges?"

Mallard's face lit up. "We may. Let's check the catalog, shall we?" He motioned to the chest of small wooden drawers in the middle of the room. Carla knew how to use the card catalog and the Library of Congress classification system, but Mallard always found what she needed faster than she could, and it gave him such joy. No need to deprive him.

Carla stood back while the man expertly flicked through the cards in one of the tiny files, jotting down numbers on a scrap of paper.

"This is a departure for you. New interest?" He closed the drawer and pulled open another. "Usually, we're hunting in QK or QL."

It was true. Carla rarely strayed from botany and zoology. "You could say that."

By the third drawer Carla's attention drifted, her thoughts jumping from topic to topic. Fatigue was setting in, and the day was far from over. Tired or not, she was determined to walk Gizmo when she got back to Elizabeth's. And there was a pile of unsorted whale photos waiting for her on the kitchen table. She hoped she could keep her eyes open for an hour or two after dinner to look through them. Dinner. Her stomach growled. The housekeeper stocked the freezer with meals, but they were mostly meat. Last time Carla ate meat was Easter ham when she was eight, before her foster father ruined the meal by asking if she wanted another slice of pig. A can of vegetable soup would do for tonight. She could pick one up with the other things on E's list. She also needed to check the pawn shops again for her bass.

They were open late. A couple of quick stops on her way home. Funny how quickly she started calling it that. Home.

"This title"—the librarian was saying, pointing to the slip of paper in his plump hand—"is in Juvenile Nonfiction. Depending on what you're looking for it might be a good place to start. The basics of bridge design. These other four are in Technology against that wall. Any books marked TG will be related to the engineering aspects of bridges, so once you're there, you might find others that interest you."

Carla pulled as many materials from the shelves as she could find on bridge construction and design. She skimmed the table of contents of one called *A Span of Bridges: An Illustrated History* and turned to the chapter on tension. The language was technical and foreign.

"I found the maps you asked for earlier." Mallard's voice startled her. "Nautical map of Puget Sound and street map of the Kitsap Peninsula." He set the folded paper maps on the table next to her. "Also, I found a current book on bridge design. Someone just returned it." He handed it to her and looked over her shoulder at the open book she was reading. "The one you have there is out of date."

"Thanks for all this," Carla said. And she meant it.

"I'm still on the lookout for books about orcas, if you're interested." He hesitated for a beat. "There's a new bird book. Should I bring it over?"

Carla shook her head. "Next time."

He padded back to his desk over the thin industrial carpet. Carla unfolded the large map of the Kitsap Peninsula. She stood and carried it to a second table nearby where there was room to spread it out. Her index finger hovered for a moment as she oriented herself. The finger came down on Puget Sound to the east, and she traced the whales' route around the southern tip of Bainbridge Island, through Rich Passage toward Sinclair Inlet. At the mouth of the strait dividing Bremerton, the Port Washington Narrows, she paused.

"The whales came in this way," she whispered. She drew her finger slowly up the channel, circled the shoreline of Dyes Inlet, and stopped again at the Narrows. "You came in," she said to no one. "Why won't you go out?"

The pod had arrived during the night, before the Tuesday morning commuters began to spread over the main roads. It would have been mostly dark and quiet at the shipyard in Bremerton. Under the bridges, the hungry whales, intent on eating as much salmon as they could, would have been oblivious to everything except following the fish into the inlet.

Once people started pouring into Kitsap County to see the whales, the towns and neighborhoods around the inlet and along the Narrows came alive with thousands of whale watchers. Boats with all their noisy occupants filled the inlet and cars crowded the roads, going back and forth over the two bridges day and night. It made sense that all the chaos could be affecting the whales in a way the peaceful waterways they found on their arrival did not.

Their supply of salmon must be running low, too, so it was time for the whales to leave. The whales knew it, trying again and again to return to the Sound. But something stopped them in their tracks at the same place every time. The Warren Avenue Bridge.

Carla refolded the map and returned to the table piled with books where she scribbled some notes and continued reading about trusses, cantilevers, compression, force, cables, abutments, and girders. There was so much to learn. Most of what she read went right over her head, but she managed to learn more about bridge design than she thought she would ever need to know. It could all be for nothing. A wild goose chase.

Mallard's voice over the PA system broke into her thoughts. "The library will be closing in ten minutes. Please bring all materials to be checked out to the circulation desk at this time."

Carla's head snapped up. What? But the library stayed open until eight on Thursday nights. She checked her watch. Almost eight. *Fuck.* Elizabeth must be wondering where she was, and she still needed to stop at the pawn shops and get groceries. She grabbed her jacket and purse from the back of her chair and scooped up the materials she'd spread all over the table.

"Is there a phone I can use?" she asked Mallard, eyeing the one on his desk.

He was busy checking out a teetering stack of romance novels for an elderly woman.

"Pay phone near the restrooms," he said without looking up.

Carla dumped her books and maps onto the counter and shoved her hand deep into her purse. Hunting for coins for the phone was pointless, all drama. Carla had no loose change, no money at all except the twenty Elizabeth had given her for groceries. Romance Lady saved her, pressing a quarter into Carla's hand with a kind smile.

Elizabeth answered the phone on the first ring. She chewed Carla out for making her worry but was relieved she was all right. In a strange way, the scolding was nice. Someone cared.

After the supermarket she checked the pawn shops. Nothing. It had been four days since her mom helped herself to the contents of Carla's closet, so the chances of her bass surfacing now were slim. If her mom hopped on the ferry to try her luck selling it in Seattle, it was truly gone. *Bitch.* Driving toward Elizabeth's, Carla silently cursed her mother to the rhythm of the wipers. *Fucking bitch. Fucking bitch.*

Under the heavy canopy of cedars and Douglas firs, the road was dark. No streetlights. No moon. Only her headlights cut through the blackness ahead. Carla was grateful when the motion detector lights came on in E's driveway. Home.

A dog was barking. It sounded like Gizmo, but the pitch was too high. She hurried to the gate and jiggled the rusty latch, the handles of the heavy grocery bag biting into her wrist. The barking grew more frantic. Gizmo! Why was he outside?

"Hey, buddy," she called to him through the fence, trying to keep the rising panic out of her voice. "It's okay. You're okay."

The catch came free at last. More lights came on the second she shoved the gate open.

"Whatcha doing, boy?" Carla rubbed his neck and ears with her free hand, but he pulled away and ran toward the house, setting off another motion detector and a flood light came on. Elizabeth lay on the brick path at the bottom of the steps.

"Fuck! E!" Carla dropped the groceries and sprinted to her. She pushed the toppled walker away and fell to her knees. Elizabeth was on her side, eyes closed, and she was still. Carla called her name a few times and patted her cheek. No response. No blood anywhere, so that was something. Gizmo sniffed and licked Elizabeth's face, and her eyes fluttered open for a moment before closing again, and she groaned softly. Thank God. Not dead.

"Don't move. I'll get help."

Carla ran through the light drizzle toward the wide-open door, nearly losing her footing on the slick steps. In the brightly lit kitchen, she grabbed the wall phone and dialed 911. She gave the house number, relieved that she remembered it. "Sixty-two forty-two Gustafson Road."

"She's probably in shock. Keep her warm and don't try to move her," the dispatcher said. "And don't leave her alone. Can you stay on the line with me?"

The phone on the kitchen wall was the old kind. The cord only reached as far as the door. "No."

"Okay. Don't hang up. I'll stay on the line until the ambulance gets there in case you need to report any change in her condition," the calm voice said. "It's important that she stay awake. Can you do that?"

Carla answered that she would do her best. She dropped the handset onto the counter and ran to the bedroom. She grabbed a heavy blanket and returned to the backyard. Elizabeth's slacks and blouse and hair were soaked with rain, her glasses and one of her shoes had fallen off. After tucking the blanket in all around Elizabeth's body as gently as she could with her shaking hands, Carla sat cross-legged on the path near her head. The bricks were wet, and the rainwater soaked through her jeans, but it hardly registered.

"Stay with me, E. Help is coming." Carla reached under the edge of the blanket and found Elizabeth's cold fingers. She squeezed them gently and drew her thumb back and forth across the back of her hand trying to warm it. Elizabeth twitched and let out a high-pitched whimper, like a tiny kitten.

"I'm here. It's me. Carla." She thought of scenes like this she'd seen on TV. "What's your name? Who's the president?"

"Elizabeth. Elizabeth Hartman." Her voice was weak, Carla leaned in closer. Gizmo whined and pawed at the blanket. "Gizzy, down."

Good. She was making sense, so it wasn't a head injury. Carla had no idea if that was true, but it was plausible. Gizmo was now lying alongside Elizabeth, pressed close, but he was tense and alert.

"What happened? How did you end up here?" Carla asked.

"Clinton," she whispered. "President Clinton." A pause. "Slipped. On the steps."

"Are you hurt?" Carla shivered, her jaw tense with cold and with fear.

"Help me up." Elizabeth raised her head and tried to push herself up on her elbow but winced and lay down again. Carla told her she mustn't move in case anything was broken. The hip. Or something else.

Elizabeth closed her eyes again, and Carla strained to listen for the sound of an approaching siren. What was taking so long?

"Stay awake." Keep her talking. That's what she had to do. "How long have you lived here?" It didn't matter, but Carla couldn't think of anything else to say. "It's a nice house."

Elizabeth perked up a little. In a slow, quiet voice she told Carla she had lived in the house all her life. She talked in short spurts about her life and the dogs she had raised. No husband, no children, no siblings.

"Who's the man in the photograph then? I thought he was your husband. The sailor with the old car." Carla's ass was numb. She shifted her weight and put her cold hands into her pockets. At least the rain had stopped.

Elizabeth smiled a little. "*New* car. It was new then." The old woman's words slid with great effort from vowel to vowel.

Carla lay on the path facing her with the dog between them and tucked her soft canvas bag under E's head. Carla touched her shoulder. "Does this hurt?"

E gave her head a small shake, and Carla began to gently stroke her shoulder and upper arm, rubbing it a little to get her circulation going to warm her.

"Engaged. Never married. Arnold was the only man for me. I've been alone a long time."

The handsome man in the photo, slim and proud with one foot resting on the front bumper, melted into an image of Gordon, leaning against his van. "I'm alone too."

"Why?"

"Just the way things turned out, I guess. But it's better this way, being independent like you." Carla looked at the big house. Being alone and rich was better than being alone and broke.

"Nonsense." E let out a short laugh but winced and stopped. "Don't end up like me. Mourning him—" she faltered and lay quiet for a moment. "Mourning Arnold and the life we could have had together became a habit." She closed her eyes again. In a voice barely above a whisper, E said, "I forgot how to be happy."

The happiest day of Carla's life, the day her wish was granted, had been her eleventh birthday. Her mother came to see her for their monthly supervised visit, dressed in new clothes, her long hair gleaming. She handed Carla a large box, a real gift, the only one she'd ever received from her mom. Carla pulled away the colorful wrapping paper. Inside was a suitcase, bright blue. There was a ribbon around the handle and a tag with her name in neat cursive writing. Carla opened it and inhaled the scent of newness, of possibility, of hope. She touched the pink satin lining with the tips of her fingers.

The social worker beamed when she said, "Go ahead, Leanne. Tell your daughter the good news."

Tears rolled down her mother's cheeks, and her smile nearly cut her face in two when she said, "Cargo, baby, let's go pack your things. I'm going to take you home with me." Carla could still hear her mother's voice, shouting with joy. "Forever!"

"You're crying." E's quavering voice brought her back.

Carla sniffed and forced a smile. She took E's hand again. It was warmer now, and when she squeezed it, E squeezed back. "Tell me about Arnold. How did you meet?" Change the subject. Her emotions were too close to the surface.

E was quiet. After a moment her eyes closed. Maybe she was remembering the moment Arnold appeared in her life or deciding how much to tell. Her hand in Carla's was still, and she said quietly, "I'm so tired."

"Wake up, E!" Carla patted the old woman's cheek until her eyelids parted a little. "Stay with me. Come on. Please."

How much longer could they continue this way, lying on the cold ground waiting for help? Carla lifted her head a little, listening.

"I'm not supposed to leave you, but I need to find out what's taking so long. Promise not to move? I'll be right back." Carla got to her feet and so did the dog, ears up. "Sit." Gizmo obeyed. "Stay."

In the kitchen Carla lifted the receiver from the counter. The dispatcher was still there, and he assured her help was coming but they were having trouble locating the house. Could she give the address again? Carla repeated the number. There was a pause on the other end of the line while the dispatcher spoke to someone on the radio. Carla waited, fidgeting with a pile of unopened mail on the counter. *Shit.*

"Hello? Hello?" *Idiot.* Carla called into the phone until the dispatcher came back on. "Hey, I gave you the wrong address. It's not 6242. I had it mixed up. It's 4262."

"Got it." The dispatcher spoke to the person on the radio again and came back to Carla. "They'll be there in two minutes."

She ran back outside. Gizmo was standing now, trembling, and licking E's pale face. Carla called her name, but there wasn't even a flicker of response. Carla knelt to feel for a pulse in her wrist. Thank God. Still alive.

"E!" Carla shouted. "Stay with me."

A siren wailed faintly in the distance and then, "Carla," came E's voice in a croaking whisper.

Lying face-to-face again Carla said, "I'm here."

"Talk to me." Her words slurred. "Your mother. What did she do that hurt you so badly?"

The only thing that mattered at that moment, more than Carla's need to keep the walls around her past, was keeping her friend awake and alive, and talking to her might help her stay conscious. But before she could strip away all the layers to reveal the betrayal that fueled her pain, the ambulance pulled into the driveway. Carla ran to open the gate and let the paramedics in. She stood apart as they rolled E gently onto her back and checked her heart and her airways, speaking to her loudly.

A short woman addressed Carla. "How long has she been unconscious?"

"No, she's awake!" Carla stepped closer, peering into E's face. "Or...she was a minute ago. I mean...she was talking." Carla faltered and took a step back. And another. Carla's one job was to keep her awake, and she had failed.

"Got her ID and insurance card? We don't need it to admit her, but it would help in treating her," the woman said, and Carla hurried inside. When she came out again with E's purse, they were strapping her onto a stretcher.

"Can I ride along?" Carla's voice, high and loud, betrayed her fear.

"Are you next of kin or legal guardian?" The short woman took E's purse from Carla and put it on the stretcher.

"A friend."

"Once she's stable you can see her. Best wait until morning."

At the gate Carla took Gizmo by the collar. The paramedics wheeled out of the yard where the open rear doors of the ambulance spilled light onto the gravel driveway.

Chapter 19

Friday, November 7, 1997

Carla turned her worry stone over and over in her hand. The sky through the living room window had changed to the deep violet of approaching dawn. She was cold and stiff. The rug, throw pillow, and crocheted afghan made an inadequate bed, but together they had allowed her to stay close to Gizmo through the long night as he paced, head held low. Back door to front door to back door, whining like a child trying not to cry, while the hands on the mantelpiece clock circled its face.

Now he padded over and with a sigh slumped against Carla's side. He smelled of mud and grass and dog. He stared at the door, waiting for E to come through it. His heart was breaking, and Carla's broke for him. And for herself.

"E's going to be fine. I promise," she said with more certainty than she felt, and rubbed her hands over his ears, burying her fingers in his ruff.

Carla's head pounded. Coffee was mandatory. In the kitchen she measured out Gizmo's breakfast, refreshed his water, filled the kettle for herself, and scooped two heaping spoonfuls of instant coffee into the biggest mug she could find.

The ceiling light did the job of pushing darkness into the corners, but the warm glow was missing. Small, comforting sounds—the gas flame licking drops of water from the side of the kettle, the hum of the refrigerator's motor, the *slurp-slurp* of Gizmo's tongue in his water bowl—did little to soothe her.

A desk calendar was open on the counter. The left-hand page was a photograph of Mount Rainier, and the right displayed the current week. It was blank except for today, Friday. Written neatly in blue ink were the words, *Pay Carla*. Rotten timing. She was counting on that money. Next to the calendar was the blue cookie tin. Carla gave it a shake. Empty. The twenty for the groceries must have been the last.

Gizmo's lapping changed to a soft metallic ringing as he licked up the last of the water. He sat by the back door and stared at Carla.

"Hold up, buddy."

She'd left a message the night before for Mr. Wilson saying she couldn't come in this morning after all. It was probably chaos at the coffee shop without her, but she had bigger problems. She needed to make two more calls. Carla found the phone number for the home health nurse and told her not to come until further notice. The second call was to Harrison Hospital. E was in surgery and would be transferred to intensive care for observation afterward. Only the next of kin was allowed to visit her there.

She hung up the phone and stood staring at it for a moment, not seeing it. Next of kin? If the nurses wouldn't let her into the ICU, then who would visit? Who would hold E's hand, comfort her? Fatigue and worry made Carla's head swim. And there was something else. A shadow slipping around the edges of her thoughts like a tiny fish, a tattered fragment about the events last night. Carla shook her head and broke her gaze. The kettle was whistling.

Coffee mug in hand, she opened the door. Gizmo bounded down the mossy steps, triggering the flood lights that bathed the shadowy yard in a harsh glow. Carla paused to shove her bare feet into her boots and her arms into the sleeves of her jacket. She transferred her cigarettes and lighter from her purse to her pocket and made her way down the steps, feet skating on the slick surface.

The ruined groceries were scattered on the walkway. Gizmo sniffed at the milk pooled around the split carton. The eggs were smashed, and an animal—raccoon probably—had chewed through the plastic cheese wrapper. All trash now except the can of soup. What a waste. Carla gathered it into the grocery bag. She set the toppled walker on its wheels and stooped for the giant glasses E always wore. The sturdy frames and thick lenses were intact. In the grass next to the path was a shoe, small and empty. Carla wiped it clean against her jeans. E would need her things when she came home. If she came home.

Carla drank her coffee in scalding gulps and waited to feel better. Some crows assembled in a tall cedar tree behind the garage for some gossip or an argument. A murder of crows. A charm of humming-birds. A pod of whales. Not all animals grouped together. Crocodiles and bears preferred their own company. Great white sharks were soli-tary creatures too. Most young animals left their mothers once they could fend for themselves, but orcas often stayed with their mothers their whole lives. The nineteen whales in the inlet were a family, a com-munity, hunting and traveling together, looking out for one another.

Gizmo nudged her hand, and Carla stroked him, thinking of how he stayed at E's side after she fell. She was his family, his pack. Poor dog. At least he wasn't alone now. He had Carla. It was lucky she arrived when she did and called 911 before it was too late. E could have died lying out there in the cold all night without even a coat on. And who would have taken care of Gizmo? There weren't any neighbors close enough to notice him raising the alarm, so he'd still be barking in the backyard if she hadn't shown up. Things could have been worse. Much worse.

Carla set her empty mug on the bottom step, shook a cigarette from the pack and lit it, her mind playing over the events of the day before like a movie, one of those movies that starts at the end of the story where the main character is alone with a dog, smoking, and scene by scene, the story goes backward in time, unfolding the events that led to that moment. The ambulance driving away. The paramedics loading E onto the stretcher. Carla lying on the path with her, talking to her to keep her awake. Calling 911. Coming through the back gate from the garage and finding E in a heap at the bottom of the steps with Gizmo licking her hands and face under the floodlight.

Carla took a final drag and smiled at the dog. Yes, it was lucky Carla got there in time to save E's life. She put her cigarette out and followed Gizmo into the house, remembering to wipe his paws and remove her boots. Her stomach rumbled. She put the kettle on for a second cup of coffee and searched the cupboards until she found a box of cereal. She stuffed a few handfuls into her mouth and chewed. It was dry and tasteless.

In a couple of hours, she would call the hospital again. She needed to know if E was all right. She probably messed up the mending hipbone and maybe sprained a wrist or an ankle. It was a risky for old people to live alone. They could fall, cause a fire, lock themselves out. Or choke. Carla swallowed the pasty mass in her mouth and coughed, spraying the counter with crumbs.

That accident should never have happened. What kind of stupid person tries to manage a big dog when they can barely walk? Anyway, E didn't need to step out onto the wet landing or go down those nasty steps. All she needed to do was open the door and let the dog out. She wouldn't be in the hospital right now if she had used her head and waited for Carla. She took a gulp of coffee to clear the crumbs from her throat. Wasn't that why she hired Carla in the first place?

And there it was. That tiny fish, that niggling scrap of a thought, swam into focus from the margins of her sleep-deprived brain and right into her net. E *had* waited for Carla to take Gizmo out. While Carla lost herself in her research at the library and then drove all over town, checking pawn shops and deliberating over whole milk or nonfat, E waited and waited. And waited.

Carla doubled over the sink as a wave of nausea threatened to empty her stomach.

"I did this," she said aloud. She was no savior, no saint. The movie going in reverse wasn't telling a story that began when Carla walked through the gate and saved E's life. It began when she left to buy milk and forgot that someone needed her. Carla was the tipping domino that set the events in motion. E counted on her, and Carla let her down.

Which was exactly why it was easier to stay out of other people's lives and keep people out of hers. Carla filled her mug with cool water from the tap. Who needs the hassle of looking after someone else? Or letting someone close enough to look after her? Eventually everyone will disappoint you or abandon you. Or break your heart. And she would do the same to everyone she cared about.

A happy bark from the front hallway broke into her thoughts. The doorbell chimed a second later. Carla held Gizmo's collar and opened the door. Nathan stood on the porch smiling, lit from behind where weak sunlight had washed away the last traces of night from the sky.

"Got your kayak," he said, nodding toward his truck in the driveway. "Thought I'd see how you're doing."

Carla glanced at Alex's red plastic boat sticking out over the tailgate but said nothing. What had Holton thought when she didn't show up at the marina?

"Stopped at the coffee shop first, figuring you'd be back at work, but they said you called in sick again. What's up?"

The tears would start if she tried to speak or if he touched her. The concern in his voice alone made her throat tighten.

"Can I play with the dog at least?" Gizmo's whole body wagged as he strained against Carla's grip.

This isn't a good time, she wanted to say. She needed to figure out what to do. How could she face E? She would never forgive her, never trust her again. Carla couldn't stay at her house anymore, drive her car, or look after her dog. Everything good snatched away.

"Wipe your feet." Carla stood back to let him in and then led Nathan through the quiet house to the kitchen.

"Where's your friend today?"

"Not here." Carla opened the back door, and the dog skittered down the steps. She and Nathan followed. "And she isn't my friend. She's my employer." As soon as the words were out of her mouth, Carla regretted them. They sounded so cold.

"What? I thought you worked at the coffee shop." Gizmo appeared with a shaggy tennis ball in his mouth. He dropped it at Nathan's feet, grinning.

"I do this too. I'm just helping out." *Yeah, I was a big help and now E's in the hospital.*

Carla changed the subject. "I worked on the catalog, if you're wondering."

"Great. Find any matches?"

"A couple."

They walked around to the side of the house and sat on a low brick wall bordering a neglected tangle of rosebushes. Gizmo was back with the ball. Nathan threw it for him again and wiped dog slobber from his palm onto his jeans. The dog ran after it, laser focused and legs flying. Had he already forgotten about E, shifting his affection to whoever held the ball?

"I'll be out with the whales later, if you want to come." Nathan was close enough that Carla could see crow's feet around his eyes.

She opened her mouth to tell him what she'd learned at the library about the whale rescue at Barnes Lake, but an image of E sprawled on the walkway flashed in her mind, and she closed it again. *My fault. My fault.* If she talked about it, the floodgates would open.

"Maybe Monday after work then?"

"I'm sure you can manage without me." Carla stuffed her fists into the pockets of her jacket.

"You're right."

"Gee, thanks."

"I didn't mean it like that. I *can* manage, but it's a lot for one person."

"You have people." *You have a girlfriend.* She curled her fingers around the pack of cigarettes in her pocket. *Don't say it out loud. Don't.*

"True, but you and I are a good team, Carla." Her heart turned to pudding, hearing her name in his voice.

"What about your girlfriend?" *Idiot.* "Is she a scientist too?"

"Real estate." Nathan frowned. "Has no interest in orcas. Complains about how much time I spend working."

They were quiet for a while. Carla wanted to know why he would be in a relationship with someone like that. Instead, she asked, "Why are you here?"

"Like I said, came to see if you're okay. Bring your kayak."

"I'm fine, as you can see. So..." She gestured toward the gate.

Gizmo was back. Nathan picked up the ball and stood, tossing it into the air and catching it neatly. The dog's body was tense, watching the ball go up and down. "Last one, buddy," he said and let it fly. Gizmo was off like a shot.

Nathan reached to put his hand on her shoulder, but Carla pulled back. *If you touch me, I'll shatter.*

He let his hand drop and looked at her for a moment. "Sure you're okay?"

All Carla could manage was a nod. They walked together toward the gate.

"If you change your mind about coming with me—" Nathan lifted the latch and pulled the gate open. Gizmo galloped back and sailed straight through it.

Nathan froze. "Shit."

"Gizmo!" Carla ran after the dog. "Come!" she hollered, but the dog kept running. Her feet skidded on the gravel driveway and then the loose soil and stones of the two-track lane leading uphill to Gustafson Road. Panic rose in her throat as she chased after him, calling his name. He disappeared over the crest of the hill. At the edge of the paved road she paused, looking left and right. All was quiet.

"Gizmo! Come!" she yelled, her voice evaporating into the trees lining both sides of the street. Nathan caught up with her.

"You're a fucking idiot!" Carla needed a place to pin her anger.

"We'll find him. You take the road toward Old Frontier," he called over his shoulder as he ran in the opposite direction.

Ignoring him, Carla crossed the road and crashed straight into the woods. Her feet pounded the damp earth under the cedars. When the undergrowth thickened, her pace slowed as she dodged low branches that whipped her arms and face, salal and wild blackberry tore at her knees and ankles.

"Gizmo!" she cried. "Here, boy." Her words caught in her throat, tight with the effort of running and with emotion. She couldn't lose him, she just couldn't. E would go out of her mind.

She stumbled on, making slow progress. Her legs began to shake. Gasping, she sucked air into her lungs, unable to fill them or find the breath to call out. She was drowning in the woods.

In a small clearing she stopped, breathing hard, alert for any sound that might come from a big dog. A snort, a tail swishing against low-growing plants, a whine or a growl. Only gulls and crows and a rustle overhead. A squirrel scrambling through the limbs. The scraps of morning sky visible through the branches were bright but below was as dim as dusk. She scanned the ground at her feet, hoping for a sign. A tuft of fur. A pawprint. The fallen needles made a soft bed under her boots, begging her to sit down. Her throat was raw and her tongue thick with thirst.

Nearby was a young salal bush, its leathery leaves shiny and dark. Animals had eaten most of the berries but a few dangled within reach. She twisted one free and popped it into her mouth. Sweet, but no longer juicy. The shrub supported others behind it. Salal always grew best that way, in tight groups to shade and protect the weaker ones from wind and driving rain. People tore them from their gardens like weeds, but Carla liked their wild, untidy shapes and the clusters of dull blue-black berries—secretly sweet, unappreciated, misunderstood.

Exhausted and hopeless, she dropped to her knees. Her breathing gradually returned to normal. There was a low spot a few feet away, muddy and mostly clear of debris. She stood for a better view. A fresh pawprint. Could be a dog, but bigger than Gizmo would make. A few steps on, there was another clearer print. A bear? They were spotted sometimes on the edge of town. A twig snapped. *Don't panic.* Carla reversed slowly, placing one foot behind the other and using her hands to guide her between the saplings and the trunks of trees.

Sweat prickled under her arms and on her upper lip despite the chill in the air. Fear rose from her belly to her throat, choking her. She turned and ran, pushing away branches, tripping over roots, a strangled cry escaping from her chest. She fell, and fell again, hardly noticing the scratches on her hands and the mud on her knees, tearing through the undergrowth until she was back on the road.

In the open Carla ran faster, arms pumping, boots slapping the asphalt. She glanced over her shoulder. Nothing was chasing her. The bear was a figment of her imagination, but still she ran. From what? *Get a grip.*

"Carla!" Nathan's voice halted her feet.

She ran back to the lane leading to E's. Nathan stood at the bottom of the hill in front of the gate holding Gizmo by the collar. The tennis ball was still in his mouth. Gravel flying behind her heels, Carla ran down the driveway. She fell to her knees and threw her arms around the dog's neck. He was panting hard. And so was she.

"Good boy." Carla buried her face in his fur. Relief and gratitude flooded her heart. After a moment she looked at Nathan. "Thank you."

"Sorry I let him out in the first place."

They led the dog into the yard, secured the gate, and dropped onto the low wall again. Gizmo coaxed them to resume the game, offering the ball to Nathan who threw it for him.

"I'm...I shouldn't have..." Carla faltered. She was no good at apologizing. At least her mother taught her how *not* to do it. Every apology Carla got from her was full of rationalizations. They always began with 'I'm sorry, Cargo, but...'

I'm sorry, Cargo, but I was drunk.

I'm sorry, Cargo, but I was high.

I'm sorry, Cargo, but you made me mad.

Nathan said, "I should've been more careful with the gate."

Carla shook her head and began wiping mud from the toes of her boots with her hands. He knew Carla was sorry for yelling at him, didn't he? No need to say the words out loud. She wasn't in some Twelve-Step program like her mom, needing to make amends for everything she ever did or said.

Nathan pulled a tissue from his pocket and wiped the dirt off her fingers. His hands were sun-browned and rough, but his touch was gentle, the side of his thigh warm against hers. A strand of hair came loose from the elastic holding his ponytail and fluttered across his cheek. Those pale eyes, those lips. *Don't kiss him.*

Gizmo was back. He gave up the chase and stretched out on the grass nearby, gnawing on the ball.

Carla took the tissue and finished cleaning her hands. "I'm sorry. For losing my shit and for calling you an idiot."

"I believe you said *fucking* idiot."

"Sorry for calling you a *fucking* idiot then."

"Apology accepted."

"Gizmo's a runner," Carla said. "I should've warned you he's got a bit of a wild streak."

"So I'm not the first fucking idiot to let him out?"

"It's how we met. Me and Gizmo. And E."

Carla told him the story of how she ended up working for E.

"It was only supposed to be a short-term gig. A week, max." Carla told him about E's fall, leaving out her part in causing it. As she talked, she picked at her chipped nail polish. The day she brought Gizmo home in the taxi, she thought it was goodbye. Now she would have to say goodbye for real, after E fired her and kicked her out. She swallowed hard.

"Sorry to hear it. Give her my best."

"They said I can't see her until she's out of intensive care."

"Guess you'll be taking care of Gizmo full time for a while."

Hearing his name, the dog raised his head. This responsibility could go on for a while and with it better pay than she'd ever made, but only if E forgot what happened before she fell. As soon as she figured out that the fall was Carla's fault, she'd find someone else to look after her dog.

"That's good for both of you, right? You keep the job a while longer, and she has someone she trusts with her dog."

Trusted. Past tense. Carla's stomach clenched.

Nathan checked his watch and stood, brushing the seat of his jeans. "I should get going. If you're free tomorrow, I'd love your company." He laid his palm softly on top of Carla's head and kept it there a moment. The warmth and weight of his hand seeped in, his affection a confusing impossible possibility.

Chapter 20

Saturday, November 8, 1997

On the passenger seat was a small bag containing a few things from the house for E. Flowers would have been nice, but even a cheap bunch of daisies from the supermarket wasn't in Carla's budget. The only money she had on her was the change from E's twenty. Pretty thoughtless to buy a gift with the lady's own money.

The plan was to drop off the bag at the hospital, find out if E was okay, and leave. She was still in the ICU, and anyway Carla couldn't face her yet. Maybe not ever. As soon as E remembered why she fell that night—because Carla, someone she was paying to take care of her dog, didn't show up for work—she would hire someone else. It was only a matter of time. Carla would be back in her shitty apartment and back to her shitty job.

She drove past the turn for the Coffee Spot, but at the next intersection doubled back and pulled into the parking lot.

It wasn't eight yet, and the CLOSED sign was still in the window. Weekend hours. Libby would be on her own inside. Good. A few whale watchers stood along the shore with their backs to the coffee shop, but there was no traffic on the street. In the quiet, Carla walked around to the back of the little building. A rustle of leaves and a flash of white drew Carla's attention to the scraggly trees. Ghost!

She felt around in her pockets and found a few broken walnut pieces. The squirrel raced down around the trunk of a red alder as if it was a spiral staircase. Carla stooped and held out her hand, making soft coaxing sounds with her tongue. Ghost peeked out of the ferns and then approached, stopping every few feet to check for danger. Fear and uncertainty. That's what the Moon card meant in Libby's tarot reading. The wolf and the dog howling at the moon. Wild and tame, like Ghost.

Carla held still until the squirrel reached her and sat, nose twitching. With tiny paws, he snatched a crumb from her palm and nibbled, then another, watching Carla with ruby eyes that caught the light and flashed like sequins. His claws tickled and her heart swelled.

The kitchen door banged open, and with a flick of his tail Ghost bounded back to the safety of the trees. Libby appeared in the doorway carrying two huge garbage bags, country music spilling out behind her.

"Hey!" Libby shouted, rushing down and dropping the bags at her feet. She pulled Carla into a warm hug. "I've been worried about you."

The two wrestled the trash into the dumpster and sat on the bottom step. Carla pulled out her pack of Marlboro Lights. "Here," she said, and offered it to Libby. "I figured I'd stop by to repay my debt. Take a couple. I owe you."

Libby let out a loud laugh. "You didn't need to come all the way here for that!" She took one and handed the pack to Carla. "You look freakin' adorable by the way. Your eyes are so pretty without all that eyeliner. And where's the hat?"

"At the bottom of the inlet." Carla brushed her hand over her hair. As soon as she had money—if she ever did—she'd hit the thrift stores for a new one.

"I heard you had quite a week. First you get the flu, then you practically drown?" Libby shook her head. "Seriously though, are you okay, hon? I thought you were supposed to be back today."

Carla shrugged. "Something came up."

"It's been nuts without you, not gonna lie. Todd's been here every day, if you can believe it. I tried to fill your shoes with the baking but failed miserably. Ricky started buying muffins at some wholesale place, but they're not exactly flying off the shelves here."

They lit up and smoked in silence for a while. Carla blew a series of smoke rings.

"What's going on? Spill it!" Libby smacked Carla's leg. Her grin faded, and she looked closely at Carla. "Ah. Sorry. You're hurting. Wanna talk?"

Carla *did* want to talk. That was the reason she came, even though she hadn't known it until that moment. "I don't know where to start."

"At the beginning."

Carla snorted. "The beginning? Okay, but do you mind if I skip the whole miserable childhood thing?"

"Fine with me. I haven't got all day anyway," Libby said, pretending to look at her watch.

Carla stubbed out her cigarette and lit another. It was a two-cigarette day.

"For one thing, Mr. Wils—Ricky threatened to fire me if I'm not back on Monday."

"Easy. Come back on Monday. Next problem?" Libby accepted a second cigarette.

"It's not that simple. The lady with the dog is in the hospital again. I'm on my way there now. She fell down the stairs and needs me to stay at her house. For the dog. I can't leave him alone all day every day. And with Todd back, I can't afford to work here anymore. I can't live on what I earn baking. That's why I started moonlighting, walking E's dog. But what'll happen if she goes to a nursing home or dies?"

"Aren't you helping that guy with the whales too? How much is he paying you?"

Carla felt her face coloring. "Nothing. I'm a volunteer."

A sly smile bloomed on Libby's face. "I get it. You're not in it for the money. He's a hottie." A wink.

"*Pfff.* That's another thing. I thought there was something there, but I struck out with him big time." Carla buried her fingers in her hair and squeezed her fists tight. "My whole life I've been a bad luck magnet."

"It's easy to say it's bad luck when crap happens. People blame God or the devil or the planets and stars when things don't turn out the way they want. Remember when I said you have more control over your life than you think, maybe more than you want? This is what I was talking about."

"I don't have control. I don't even know how anyone gets control."

"You don't *get* control. No one gives it to you. You *take* control."

Carla was quiet for a moment, letting that sink in.

"The hard thing is—" Libby paused. She cupped Carla's chin and turned her face so they were eye to eye. "The really hard thing is to see that the choices you make *matter*. They impact your life and other people's too."

Carla pulled away.

"Please don't shut me out," Libby said. "The way I see it, whenever things get difficult, you run from the people who care about you, and then you're surprised to find you're alone."

Carla didn't like seeing herself through someone else's eyes this way. What she saw was ugly. To avoid the painful act of coming clean with E, Carla was willing to leave an old woman alone in the hospital, to cut and run when she needed her most. What kind of a person does that? And Carla needed E too. She needed the faith E had in her. Restoring that faith was suddenly the most important thing in the world.

—ele—

"Ms. Hartman was transferred from ICU to a private room this morning." A man in scrubs stood facing Carla at the second-floor nurses' station. "We have her on pain management, and she's responding well to treatment."

The muscles in Carla's neck relaxed. "So I can see her?"

"A short visit is fine."

Overhead lights in the hallway glared off the polished floor. The odor of disinfectant, the rattle of wheeled carts, and the squeak of rubber-soled shoes were familiar to Carla since this was the second time in a week she'd been at Harrison Hospital, but last time she was the patient.

She stopped at the door and checked the label below the room number: Ms. Elizabeth Hartman. Carla peeked through the small window in the door. E was propped on pillows. Her eyes were closed. What if she was sleeping? Carla was about to leave when E moved her head, squinted in her direction, and motioned her in.

"Who's there?" E said, her voice wobbling.

"It's me. Carla." She stepped into the room. "I bet you've been missing these." She produced E's big glasses from the bag she'd brought, gently slid them into place, and settled them on the bridge of her nose.

"You're a sight for sore eyes."

"So are you. You're looking good," Carla said, although she wasn't. E was pale, her thin skin stretched tight over her bones. There was a restlessness about her, as if she were planning to spring out of bed.

"This thing isn't working." She handed Carla the call button and let her hand drop onto the blanket.

Trying not to look at the bruising around E's eyes and the gauze bandage on one side of her head, Carla concentrated instead on the call button. She pressed it firmly, and a little amber light came on. "It's okay now."

"What?" E waved at the table next to her bed. "My hearing aid please, and my glasses."

Carla handed her the tiny device and reminded her that she already had her glasses on.

"Deaf, blind, and forgetful." E frowned and fiddled with the hearing aid for a moment. She picked up the call button again. "This thing isn't working."

The forgetfulness was new. "Can I do something, get you anything?"

"I need my pills." E's face was strained, her eyes huge behind the thick lenses. "The pain is unbearable."

"Your hip?" Carla pulled a chair over. The confession could wait for another time. It would be a mistake to bring up a heavy topic now.

E gave a brief rundown of her injuries: hip, shoulder, head. Her fractured hip had been re-set, her dislocated shoulder would heal, and her head injury didn't need stitches.

A tiny, dark-haired nurse breezed in and turned off the call light.

"I need my pills," E said again. She rubbed at her hands and fingers, making a papery sound.

The nurse checked her watch. "Not for another thirty minutes, Miss Liz. Are your hands bothering you?" She held and examined first one and then the other, turning each over and checking the nails.

"A little numb is all."

"How's the dizziness?"

She shook her gray curls and scowled. "My brain is all scrambled."

"It's normal with concussion. It should pass in a day or two. Doctor Montrose will be by to see you." The nurse straightened E's pillows and checked her IV. "I'll ask him if we can increase your pain meds to make you more comfortable."

Concussion was serious. Definitely not a good time for her big apology. The nurse breezed out again.

Carla said, "I have your shoe." She pulled it from the bag and set it on the floor under the bed. Why had she brought it? E wouldn't be on her feet anytime soon. "And something to cheer you up." She produced a small, framed picture. "I hope it's okay. This is the one from your nightstand at home. You sure have a lot of copies."

E reached for it, long fingers curved like a bird's delicate foot. Carla placed it in her hand. E laid it face down on her chest and was quiet for a moment. "My Arnold. Thank you," she said and patted the bed, indicating that Carla should sit closer.

Carla perched on the edge of the mattress. She wanted to know more about this man—Arnold—but E didn't look like she was up to the third degree. "Must be a pretty special guy."

"He was." She folded her hands over the little frame, holding it tight against her heart.

A silent minute passed. Carla stood. "I guess I should go."

"Stay. Please. The truth is"—E scowled—"I'm lonely."

Loneliness was exactly what Carla had felt during the few hours she had spent in the ER after dumping herself into the inlet. Here in this busy hospital with nurses and doctors in and out of her room, patients and visitors passing in the hallway, she had been more alone than she was in her empty apartment. She felt that loneliness in the Coffee Spot, on a crowded city bus, or in the grocery store. Being alone around other people was like holding a magnifying glass up to examine her separateness.

Carla sat on the bed again.

"He had a lovely smile," E said, peering at the photo. "So young and strong and handsome he was. So was I, I guess."

Carla tried to picture what E looked like all those years ago with a forties hairdo and nylons with the seams up the back. "What happened to him?" she asked.

"He was on the USS Arizona in Pearl Harbor when the Japanese attacked." E set the little frame on the table next to her bed but continued to gaze at it.

Carla tried to remember what she had learned in school about World War II. She was pretty sure the Arizona was one of the ships that sank, carrying hundreds of men with it.

"I had other suitors after that," E continued. "Other boys who saw they might have a chance with me after Arnold..." Her voice trailed off. She smiled coyly. "I was quite the looker back then. Anyway, I was sweet on one of them for a couple of years. Jimmy, his name was."

"Why didn't you marry him, have a bunch of kids?" Carla pictured how different this room would be if she had. E and Jimmy, their children and grandchildren, filling the space with their voices and laughter.

"I've thought about that a lot. Lately, especially. I think I just couldn't let go of Arnold. I couldn't let go of the past, or of the future we planned together. My heart broke when he died. I was afraid of having it broken again. I stopped living life."

"But you didn't. You have it all. You're happy—" Carla stopped. Maybe she had seen only what she wanted to see. A big house with paintings on the walls and a fancy clock on the mantel, a nice car, a sweet dog.

"I'm content. There's a difference," E said quietly. She tried to change her position in bed and winced. "I need my pills. Call the nurse, Carla. She said she'd be back. Where is she?"

All this talk about the past was too much. Carla wanted it to be a distraction, to help pass the time. Instead, E was becoming more agitated. Her hands plucked at the blanket, and she was taking short, quick breaths. Carla pressed the call button again, offered a drink of water, and stroked E's cool arm. After a moment, E motioned Carla away and closed her eyes.

Until the nurse arrived with whatever magic pill she had promised, there was nothing Carla could do. But to leave now, when things got tough, was cowardly. She hated hospitals. They made her think of her mother's overdoses. Better not go down memory lane.

E was quiet now, waiting for relief from her pain with her eyes pinched shut and her face twitching. Carla picked up the folded newspaper from the bedside table and read the headline: "Dining on a Scarce Resource." Under it was a photograph of the inlet and a pair of dorsal fins. The picture wasn't clear enough for Carla to identify which ones they were. She skimmed the front-page article about the dwindling salmon in Puget Sound since the arrival of the whales, but she was glad they weren't being blamed for the shortage. Further down the page her eye fell on a familiar face. Nathan. Her cheeks warmed. The reporter had interviewed, photographed, and quoted him in the article. Nathan talked about how the unusually low numbers of salmon in the Sound might explain why the pod of orcas ended up in Dyes Inlet, where salmon were plentiful this year.

Smart guy. Nice to look at. Too bad about the girlfriend. Carla sighed and peered at his face in the photo, the lines at the corners of his eyes, his lips relaxed and full.

The nurse returned. She gave E a tiny paper cup with pills, refilled her water glass, and held the straw to her lips. There was some discussion about the timing and frequency of the medication, so Carla resumed reading.

The room was quiet after the nurse left. Minutes passed, and Carla assumed the meds were kicking in. The front-page article continued to hold her attention with some interesting facts, namely about how much orcas eat. Nathan told the reporter that based on the estimated total weight of nineteen whales—126,000 pounds—and the assumption that orcas eat about five percent of their body weight every day, they needed 6,300 pounds of salmon total, or about 700 fish daily to keep the pod alive.

"Carla?" E said.

She looked up from the paper.

"How's Gizmo?"

"He misses you. But he's fine." No need to upset her with the story of how she nearly lost him. "I've been staying at your place. I hope you don't mind."

E assured her it was what she would have asked Carla to do if she'd been able to.

"I have to go to work Monday, E." Carla had given this next part a lot of thought. "Instead of leaving Gizmo alone all day, I was thinking of asking my neighbor to help out." She hadn't discussed this with Wallace yet. "Gizmo stayed with him a couple times before I tracked you down. They get along great. But only if it's okay with you."

"Is he trustworthy? Kind?"

Carla nodded, not just to reassure E, but because yes, he really was those things. With Carla's endorsement, she agreed to the arrangement. When the matter was settled, E glanced at the newspaper in Carla's hand. "Finish your story."

Carla put it aside. "I'm done, actually."

"Keep the paper. I'm not allowed to read. The concussion." E touched the bandage on the side of her head. "No, I meant finish *your* story. I can't remember much about the night I fell. When was that?"

Her wispy eyebrows pulled together. "Anyway," she flapped her hands as if shooing a fly, "You were telling me about your mother."

"*Pfff.* Why dredge all that up? I was only yakking to keep you awake." Carla folded the newspaper and pushed one end of it into her purse. She hadn't checked the lost and found ads since she walked out of the Coffee Spot a week ago, and she was pretty sure more lost pets were needing Saint Anthony's help. "Are you feeling better now?"

E's drowsy smile answered the question. Her words slurred a little when she said, "I'm grateful for what you did."

Carla shook her head. If there was ever anyone less worthy of gratitude it was Carla.

"I wouldn't be here if it weren't for you," E said.

Well, she had that right. "About that…" Carla's unfinished sentence hung in the air between them. At last, she said, "I'm sorry."

"For what?"

"This—" Carla tipped her head toward E's frail body "This happened because of me, because I was late to walk Gizmo."

"Were you?" E was quiet for a moment, thinking. "Well, I accept your apology." She scowled at Carla. "For being late and nothing more. What happened to me wasn't your fault. I'm sure I did something stupid."

"Taking care of Gizmo is my responsibility. It's what you're paying me to do, and I blew it." Tears stung the back of her throat. "You fell because you had to do my job for me, because I wasn't there to do it. I'm so sorry."

"I fell because I'm a stubborn old woman with a soft spot for Gizmo's sad puppy eyes." Her own eyes welled now. "But for whatever part you think you played in my accident, I forgive you."

Carla took E's hand and raised it to her cheek for a moment. "Thank you," she whispered, relief washing over her. She had been so sure that E would be angry, that she would order her to leave. Instead, Carla was forgiven. Maybe now she could forgive herself.

"Just like you should forgive your mother." E smiled. "Thought you were off the hook, didn't you? Please. I want to hear the rest of your story."

She wasn't sure when E had lost consciousness after persuading Carla to talk about her past, the two of them lying on the wet walkway in the cold waiting for the ambulance. "How much do you remember?"

E squeezed her eyes shut for a moment. "Your mother was a teenager when you were born. Homeless." Carla nodded and E continued, her hand still in Carla's. "Addicted to something, I think. That's when I must have dozed off."

"Heroin," Carla said. "I was in foster care. When I was in sixth grade, she came back for me."

She could tell E about how happy she had been. Living with her mother wasn't perfect but she'd felt loved for the first time in her life. She could tell her about the awful day that changed everything, the day her mother threw it all away, threw her daughter away. It was stamped into Carla's memory, each excruciating detail still crystal clear. But if she told her what she had never told anyone, heard her own story of betrayal spoken aloud in her adult voice, would it sound pathetic? Would she sound like that awkward teenager, whining about her pitiful life and exaggerating some injustice done to her? Was that day as bad as she remembered it, or had she fed the memory until it grew into the monster that she carried with her? She could confide in E, exposing the wounded parts of her. Spilling all the ugliness might ease Carla's burden, but it would only add to E's, and doing that to a friend wasn't fair, especially one lying in a hospital bed. Being forgiven was enough. No, it was everything.

"That's the end of the story. She came back." E's eyes were closed, her jaw slack, and her narrow chest rose and fell with each peaceful breath. In a quiet voice Carla said, "But nothing good lasts forever."

She stood to leave, slowly sliding her hand out of E's.

"Nothing bad does either," E said, her voice far away and sleepy.

Chapter 21

Sunday, November 9, 1997

Carla raised her fist and held it poised to knock on Wallace's door. She'd made sure to arrive before noon. Wallace told her recently that his job as a computer operator meant he worked nights and had trained himself to sleep in the daytime, specifically from about one in the afternoon until eight. If there was a better solution to her problem, one that didn't involve asking her neighbor for another favor, she wouldn't be there, but this was for Gizmo. And she came bearing gifts.

The door opened to her knock, and Carla said, "I have pie." She held up a plate with a generous slice of Shaker Lemon under plastic wrap. E's well-stocked kitchen had everything she needed to bake it except the lemons. She only needed two and those she bought using a handful of coins left from E's twenty, mentally promising to pay her back.

"Come in! Come in!" Wallace was pleased to see her. Or maybe the smile had more to do with the pie.

"I can't. I need to be somewhere," she lied and handed him the plate.

"This looks delicious. Thank you. I'm glad you stopped by. I have your housekeys." He lumbered out of view for a moment. His apartment, which was neat and smelled clean, was identical to hers but with furniture.

"Your guest didn't stay long. Only one night?" He reached to put the key ring in her hand, and his pale wrist appeared beyond the cuff of his sweater. It was slender for such a big man, almost fragile. Something about it made Carla's heart ache.

"Long enough to cause trouble. As usual." She slid the keys into her pocket.

"Oh?" His pleasant face pulled into an expression of concern. The splinters of her past inched closer to the surface. After nearly opening up to E, it was getting more difficult to hold all the little fragments in. He was just being polite the way some people are. Or nosy.

"Any chance you could help out with Gizmo again? The dog?"

He looked confused. "I was under the impression you'd found his home."

"Yeah. But the lady's in the hospital, and I need to go to work tomorrow. I could leave him on his own, but—"

"I'd be glad to take care of him. Gizmo, is it? I must admit I enjoy the company of a pet, but something else I like is the clandestine nature of the situation." He rubbed thick palms together and smiled slyly. "Keeping his presence a secret from the management is half the fun. But I'm afraid tomorrow is the only day I can have him here. My mother is flying in Tuesday from Denver to stay with me for a few days, and she's allergic to dogs. Next week is wide open, though. If you need me then. I'm so sorry. Does this leave you in a bind?"

"No. No problem." Crap. She would have to work something out fast. E was counting on her, and she couldn't let her down again.

"Oh! And your car!" Wallace's big face brightened. "I spoke to my friend about picking it up, and he said as long as the day and time don't matter, they can squeeze you in soon. It could be as early as tomorrow, or it could be as long as a month. They get busy this time of year. People trying to hurry and make their charitable donations before the end of the tax year. Should I tell him it's a go?"

They worked out the details, and Carla turned over her car key.

"I was wrong about you," she said. "All these years we've been neighbors, and I had no idea you were so, you know, nice."

"Same here. I admit that I used to avoid you." His cheeks grew pink. "With my schedule it wasn't hard. That day your car broke down I was late getting home from work. All I wanted was to get in out of the cold and have a hot meal, put my feet up. But I remembered your roommate moved out and that you were alone. You looked like you needed a friend. Until that moment, I thought you were—well—a little scary." He laughed and the rubber ball of a belly under his sweater shook. "But I'm happy to say you proved me wrong. I think it was the way you looked after that stray dog. I'd hear you in the yard with him so early in the morning, talking to him. No one who was so gentle with an animal could be all bad." He laughed again.

At the curb, Carla paused and placed her hand on the roof of her old Datsun. The metal was cold and the surface rough where the paint had flaked away. She caught her reflection in the passenger window and gave herself a long hard look. Scary? Maybe she had been once, but now she looked ordinary. The difference was more than the missing slouchy hat and signature eyeliner. Something was different. Things were changing too fast.

"Bye, Dot." She gave the car a couple of light taps with her fingers and climbed into E's shiny cranberry-red Volvo.

Chapter 22

Monday, November 10, 1997

Carla dragged herself to work for her regular Monday shift, which was the obvious answer to the how to not get fired question. Libby was right about that. She'd been right about a lot of things. Like appreciating the good stuff in her life. Wallace for example, who was cheerful as ever when she dropped Gizmo off at his apartment early that morning. She owed him big time, especially since he arranged for the removal of her car too. Poor old Dot, off to the glue factory.

Central Kitsap school kids were given a long weekend for Veterans Day, so the town was crawling with families looking for something to do. What was more exciting than whale watching? Where was the best place to watch them on a cold, windy day? Through the big windows of the Coffee Spot.

Steam rose in clouds around her face as Carla emptied and reloaded the dishwasher for the hundredth time. How was it possible that she hated her job more than ever now? A few days away from this madhouse was all it took. Carla couldn't even listen to the music she liked. Her nerves jangled from the country music assaulting her ears. Sylvia had been shooting scowls like hot daggers at Carla all morning. No sense making things any more tense by switching stations.

The machine hummed to life, and she dried her hands. Time to finish the scones. The good thing about her job was the same thing that made it awful—the repetition. Blindfolded, she could turn out five kinds of muffins, three kinds of pie, coffee cake, pound cake, scones, biscuits, and cookies. Now on top of the usual stuff, she was churning out the new best seller: quiche lorraine. Great idea expanding the menu and adding to her workload. *Idiot.*

The repetition did leave her mind free to work through problems while her hands measured, mixed, filled, and frosted. Some of her best ideas came to her while she was up to her elbows in flour. Ever since that night in the library, the night of E's accident, Carla's thoughts had been dipping back into her research. Last night she read through her notes on the Barnes Lake rescue and on bridge design, studying the diagrams she had drawn of the two bridges spanning the Narrows. On a blank page she sketched a rough map of the area around Dyes Inlet adding roads and waterways—everything she could remember from the big library map.

Carla patted her dough to the perfect thickness and cut it into triangles with a heavy knife. Her ideas were all over the place today, unformed plans and what-ifs. She would talk to Nathan. She checked her watch. Another hour until closing. She hoped to catch him at the boat ramp to tell him what she learned at the library about bridges and oikomi pipes, and she was itching to see the whales. She slid the baking tray into the oven and set the timer for twelve minutes.

The noise level on the other side of the door told her that the dining room was still packed. Sylvia would slam in at any moment, demanding that Carla come and help. The truth was that pitching in to wait tables with Libby and Sylvia meant more of those generous whale-watcher tips. Now that Pee-wee was back from his big adventure and managing the shop again, she was back to her old hourly pay. That wouldn't cut it. And she could hardly ask E to pay her until she was home from the hospital. No way of knowing when that would be.

The door swung open. Libby hustled in with a full bus pan.

"Plenty of campers out there," she said, referring to customers who lingered too long after paying their bill. Trading dirty dishes for clean, she picked up a rack of glassware. Carla grabbed a tray of flatware and followed her into the dining room.

"Grab some bar rags!" Sylvia called, rushing toward them with a dripping pile of paper napkins in her outstretched hands. It didn't take a genius to see what happened. Three little kids—one wailing, two laughing—and their parents scrambling to mop up a spill. Milk filled a plate of brownies to the brim, pooled around a large red plastic cup on its side in the middle of the table, and dripped off the edge into a puddle on the floor.

Carla wiped up the mess. Sylvia reset the table with paper place-mats and flatware, and Libby replaced the soggy brownies with fresh ones from the bakery case, putting them on the table with a full glass of milk. The family settled again, red-faced. Behind the counter Carla dried her hands, keeping an eye on the oldest kid. He stuffed his mouth with two big brownies and guzzled the entire contents of the glass. And then he vomited.

"That's my cue," Carla said. She returned to the kitchen, hung her apron on a hook, and retrieved her things. The timer sounded, and as an afterthought, she pulled the tray out of the oven and filled a paper bag with piping hot scones before leaving through the back door.

For the first time in weeks, the sun was out. Carla claimed a spot not far from the boat ramp but away from the noisy crowd of whale watchers. Nathan wouldn't be looking for her until later. Walking out early meant she could have a long wait. She lit a cigarette and inhaled the first delicious lungful of smoke, feeling liberated like she was playing hooky from school. Even Gizmo's care was settled for now.

Using her hand as a visor, she scanned the inlet searching for a fin, thinking of the first time she did that three weeks before. She spotted one and felt the same electric thrill. The fin circled closer to the boat ramp, the sun gleaming off its wet skin, the tip hooking to the right. Faith! She drew hard on her cigarette to keep herself from shouting his name. The big whale rolled in the water, showing his pure white underside. Two females, his buddies Canuck and Lulu, surfaced nearby to exhale loudly from their blowholes. The mist hung in the air, catching sunlight and creating a rainbow.

Gradually the waves made by the passing whales became ripples, throwing glittering light into Carla eyes. She closed them and tipped her face toward the sun for a moment, gathering and storing its warmth. She didn't care that Sylvia was probably looking out the window, enraged and pointing at her, shouting something Carla was glad she couldn't hear.

What was it people said? The definition of crazy is doing the same thing over and over and expecting different results. That pretty much summed up the last few years of Carla's life. In the seconds that followed the kid upchucking all over himself, she saw the future. Her future. It was one of those fork-in-the-road moments: stay forever or walk out for good. In a strange way, she was grateful to the kid, as if he had come into the shop to nudge her along. And maybe she had come to work hoping some event would give her permission to burn that bridge.

⁓

"What'd you say we're looking for?" Carla called. Nathan skillfully maneuvered his boat away from the ramp. They were flying toward the

Narrows, and the wind whipped her words away. Boat traffic on the inlet was heavier than she'd ever seen it. From her seat in the bow, she looked back at the coffee shop, her smile grew as the restaurant shrank into the distance. The paper bag full of stolen treats sat on her lap.

At the mouth of the inlet Nathan cut the motor. Carla stood and took the binoculars he handed her over the console. She had no trouble keeping her balance in the boat now as it rocked over the small waves. Sea legs. She repeated her question.

"Signs the whales are dehydrated. Most obvious would be a collapsed dorsal fin. Orcas under stress can become dehydrated, like the ones in captivity. If you see an orca whose fin is leaning over to one side, it's a bad sign."

"Is Faith dehydrated?" The good news that big male was no longer missing was overshadowed by this new threat.

"Tip of his fin has always been that way. I'm talking about the whole dorsal." Nathan stretched his arm above his head. "Like this." He let the arm droop to one side.

Carla laughed and threw her own arm up, letting it flop from side to side.

"You're in a good mood," he said. "Thought you'd be concerned about the whales instead of clowning around. Something's different about you today." A beat. "You look nice."

Libby said the same thing, and so did Sylvia in her own thoughtless way. Something about how it was about time Carla tried a new look. Losing her beanie and running out of eyeliner forced her into this change in her appearance, but she didn't hate it.

Carla ignored the compliment. "I didn't know something living in water could get dehydrated."

"Orcas get most of the water they need from their food. They don't actually drink salt water. Not much anyway. So, if they run out of salmon, they'll die of thirst before they die of starvation."

Carla swallowed, her own mouth suddenly dry. She shaded her eyes with her hand against her brow, squinting at him in the bright sunshine. "Can't they eat other things? Like seals or whatever?"

"Transient whales do. They're a different ecotype that live in open water, hunting mammals like dolphins, harbor seals, sea lions. Even other whales. These orcas, the Southern Residents, eat only fish. Chinook salmon, mostly."

"So, we're looking for floppy fins?" She pressed the binoculars to her eyes.

"Tougher sign to spot is a slight depression behind the blowhole." He came and sat on the seat next to her and opened his camera case. "I want to take some pictures and compare with the ones I took when they first got here. It's the best way to notice changes." He loaded a roll of film into his camera as he talked. "After nineteen days they must be getting low on food."

There'd been an article in the newspaper about how local fishermen were complaining that they weren't catching many salmon since the whales arrived. "Can't they stop people from fishing here, to save the salmon for the whales?"

"Wouldn't do much good. Sport fishing hardly makes a dent in the salmon supply."

A canoe passed carrying a couple of middle-aged men. One gave a friendly wave. Carla waved back. At least these guys weren't assholes like the ones she met the day she capsized. All around them were smiling people bobbing in their boats.

She let the binoculars hang around her neck. "Could we feed them? Bring in a shitload of fish and dump it into the inlet?"

"That'd be a mistake. Ever feed a stray cat?"

Carla gave a short laugh. "A few."

"Well, if the whales can't find enough food here, it would be a reason for them to move on, find somewhere else to hunt."

Nathan fiddled with something on his camera. He attached a long lens onto it with the confidence of someone who had done it many times. It clicked into place. He lifted it to his eye and turned the rings to adjust the focus.

"They haven't been very active today," he said. "Trying to stay away from all these boats, if I had to guess. Must be at least five hundred out here."

It was true. The warm sunny weather brought people out in droves, but there wasn't a whale in sight. She scanned the surface of the water. "Where are they? Do you think they might've left?" Hope and disappointment fought for space in her heart.

"Nope. Saw them this morning around on the other side of Erlands Point in Chico Bay. Best guess is they're still there."

"Isn't Chico Creek where the salmon are coming from?"

"Yeah, but they weren't feeding. Saw them forming a tight group in the middle of the bay. Defensive behavior."

"What if..." Carla stopped, and Nathan rested his camera in his lap to look at her. The strong sun and his nearness made her uncomfortably warm. "What if the whales weren't chasing something into the inlet in the first place. What if something was chasing them? They're scared to leave because whatever's out there"—she gestured to the long channel—"is worse than whatever they are facing here." *Like me.*

Was she stuck in a life she didn't choose because of fear? Fear of failing in the wider world? This new thought rolled in her mind, gathering size and weight as it joined with other recent revelations. Never in her life had she been so aware of herself. Libby, holding up a mirror, showing Carla that her isolation was no one's fault but her own. Nathan pointing out the value of her skills. E, treating her with kindness and forgiveness, like Carla was someone who mattered.

Nathan's voice pulled her back to the present. "Chasing them? Unlikely. Orcas have no natural predators. Humans are the biggest threat. Fishing nets, pollution, boat traffic."

"But didn't you say the noise from the highway traffic on the bridge could be holding them back?" She peeled a large piece of black polish off her thumbnail with her teeth and spat it over the side of the boat.

"That's one theory. Could also be they're simply following the salmon around wherever they lead. The strongest argument in my opinion is they're avoiding contact with the boats in the Narrows. Look how jammed up they are." He pointed and shook his head. "All the noise from their motors is messing with their echolocation, confusing them."

If the loud motors were the problem, then instead of looking for a way to stop traffic on the bridge, she should figure out how to get the boats out of the inlet.

They were quiet for a moment, both looking out over the sparkling water. After days of rain and shivering under a plastic poncho, Carla relaxed in the warmth. She stripped off her flannel shirt and dropped it on top of the bullhorn at her feet. A T-shirt was enough. She tilted her face toward the sun, eyes closed.

"Minor Threat?" Nathan tapped the tattoo on her forearm.

"Hardcore punk band. You like music?"

"Lifelong Stones fan."

"Old-school rock and roll." Carla shook her head and blew air through her nose in a snort.

Nathan pushed his lips into the famous Mick Jagger pout and sang a few lines. Carla burst into laughter.

"You have a nice laugh. God, what am I? In junior high?" He chuckled. "It's just that you don't smile much. Or talk a lot about yourself. I mean, I don't even know your last name."

"Here's something about me. I quit my job at the Coffee Spot today." Saying the words aloud made it real. "And it's Peterson. My name."

Nathan stared at her with his mouth open. "Congratulations, Carla Peterson! Your true talents were wasted there."

"Something else about me? I'm a thief." This brought her mother to mind and the stolen bass. Would she ever see either of them again? Did she care anymore? Carla held up the paper bag. "My first offense."

Nathan reached into the bag and pulled out a scone. He turned it around, admiring it—the glistening cranberries, the golden crust, the sparkling sugar crystals on top—before he sank his teeth into it. A soft moan of pleasure. "You're a magician, Carla. Sure you want to quit? Because"—he took another bite—"wow."

She rolled the top of the bag closed. The rest would be a good start in paying Wallace back for all his help. He went above and beyond being neighborly. More like a friend.

"Hey," Nathan said, chewing. "I think there's an opening at the Whale Museum in Friday Harbor."

"You work at a museum?"

"No, my office is at the Center for Whale Research. Same town, different organization. Heard the Education Coordinator at the museum had a kid and quit."

Carla let out a laugh. "What makes you think I could do a job like that? I don't even know what that is. Education coordinator? You know my job skills. Dog walking, baking, pouring coffee, using a cash register. Hell, you had to teach me how to use that fucking bullhorn for Christ's sake." She nudged it with her foot.

"You're selling yourself short, Carla. You have an eye for detail, and a great memory. You're observant, intuitive, organized. And from what you've told me about the restaurant, you can handle a bit of pressure and can do some creative problem solving. On top of all that, you're crazy about orcas." He gave her a mock scowl. "But you might need to work on your people skills."

"What's wrong with my people skills?" She jabbed him in the ribs with her elbow.

Nathan put an arm around her shoulders and gave her a squeeze. "That's what I love about you, Carla. Sharp wit and sharper elbows."

She leaned into him, something fluttering in her belly. "So, what's the job like?"

Nathan finished off the scone and brushed crumbs from his fingers. "Nutshell? You'd be the contact person for schools wanting to visit the museum. You schedule tours, welcome the kids when they arrive. One of the educators will take over from there to show them the exhibits. At the end you thank them for coming, give the teachers a packet of activities to do back in their classrooms, and you're done."

"How do you know so much about it?"

"I worked at the museum for a couple months after college, before starting my master's at UW and landing this job. Doubt the job has changed much since then."

Carla's gaze drifted and so did her attention. The sky was a hard bright blue, and the water, dotted with white sails and boats of every size and color, danced and glittered in the sunlight. Gulls wheeled overhead, laughing and calling. She filled her lungs.

"I don't know. I mean, even if—a huge if—I got hired, I'd be stuck indoors all day. I'd rather be out here, doing this."

"Saved the best for last. June through August when schools are closed, you'd be helping with the Soundwatch program. Out on the RIB, the inflatable, in Haro Strait."

Carla's heart did a backflip. Out on the water. All summer with the whales.

"Happy to put you in touch with Janine, the director, if you're interested."

Getting her hopes up was dangerous. The way out of her dead-end job was always going to be through music. But being in a band, especially Gordon's band, was a dead dream. She didn't even have a bass anymore. A job in a museum?

"Nah," she said.

"Let me know if you change your mind. You're perfect for the job."

Carla sat up and leaned forward a little. Nathan's confidence in her gave her courage.

"Can I bounce something off you? An idea I had about helping the whales get out of here."

Chapter 23

Tuesday, November 11, 1997

The door opened, and Carla paused the story she was telling E about her time with Nathan and the whales that morning, including that she quit her job and that he gave her an idea for a new one. A man in a long apron stepped into the room to collect E's lunch tray. He picked it up but hesitated.

"Want me to come back for this later?" The food was untouched.

E was propped on pillows and still attached to an IV, but her eyes were alert, watching his movements. "No need. I'm finished. Thank you."

When the man was gone Carla said, "Is the food that terrible?"

"My appetite is a bit off. Nothing serious."

"Your housekeeper left some meals in the freezer yesterday. Want me to heat one and bring it later?"

Carla had snooped and found a meatless dish among the stews and casseroles. Eggplant Parmesan. Her stomach rumbled. The bran flakes she had for breakfast were a dim memory.

"Thank you, no. You enjoy them. It may be some time before they let me leave. Those people,"—E flapped a hand toward the door—"those...you know...those..." She pinched her lips together and tapped her forehead, searching for the missing word. "Bossy girls in uniforms. They're pushing me to go to some kind of long-term care place for a month or two, where they can keep an eye on me. It seems I can't be trusted to stay off the stairs." She frowned and pushed her glasses up further on her nose. "Let's talk about something more interesting."

Carla picked up the thread of her story about being on the inlet.

"It's crazy that no one is doing anything to help the whales leave. Nathan is trying to get a bunch of other people on board. He's meeting some wildlife biologists at UW this afternoon to make some kind of presentation about what we've been seeing, signs that the whales are in trouble. That's why I'm here and not out on the boat right now. He had to leave early."

Carla stood and looked out the window. After a moment, she said, "What I don't get is his attitude, though. I keep throwing ideas at him about ways to get them out, but he always says, 'I'm a whale researcher, Carla, not a whale rescuer. I'll lose my job if I cross that line.' Personally, I think he's pissed he can't do more." She paced across the small space in her heavy boots. "At least he told me my ideas are solid, even though I'm not the first person to come up with them. So why doesn't somebody do something?"

"Who?"

"That's the problem, E." She dropped into the chair next to E's bed. "People moan and groan about what's wrong in the world—poverty, crime pollution, and now global warming—but nothing changes because no one acts. Everyone's waiting for someone else to do it."

Carla told her about her research at the library, about Barnes Lake. "The whole community got together and rescued their orcas. Why can't we do that here? What did they have that we don't?"

"A leader."

"Exactly. Someone to organize and coordinate things, to get people excited about helping. Someone with good ideas."

"You!"

"No way. I wouldn't know where to start. And we don't have a kelp problem. We have hundreds of boats to deal with and a big-ass highway across the water keeping the pod stuck here. Somebody should figure out how to get cars off the bridge and boats off the water."

"It sounds like there's a lot to do and not much time." E sat straighter, like she was ready to hop out of bed and get to work.

"Who would be in charge of stuff like that anyway?"

E tapped her index finger against closed lips, thinking. "After the war, my father served on the board of commissioners for Central Kitsap County. He was a civil engineer in the Public Works Department. Sewers, flood control, road maintenance, that sort of thing. I think he had to close a few roads over the years. Why don't you start your search there?"

"Me? I'm a nobody." Nathan was the one who knew all the important people. They would pay attention to him. He was a scientist, for fuck's sake.

"Listen to me." E pointed a stern finger at Carla. "You're a tax-paying, law-abiding citizen of this town with something to say. That's all that's required. Show up and speak up." She slumped back into her pillows. Carla poured a cup of water and held it while she sipped through the straw.

"Thank you, Carla. I think the Public Works offices are still in Port Orchard."

The little town of Port Orchard was across from the shipyard, all the way around on the other side of Sinclair Inlet. A forty-mile round trip, at least. Not that she was planning to go, but the driving distance reminded Carla of the nearly empty gas tank.

"I hate to bring this up, E, but is there a way you could pay me? For walking Gizmo? It's just that—"

"Good heavens! I haven't paid you?" E's eyebrows shot up. "What's wrong with me? It's not like me to let something like this slide. I apologize, Carla. Of course you'll be paid immediately. Where's my purse?"

Carla found a drawstring plastic bag on the floor containing the clothes E had been wearing the night she fell, including a single shoe. Carla winced. A reminder of her own role in the accident. She pushed it aside and grabbed the leather handle of a small purse.

With a shaking hand, E wrote a check and carefully tore it from her checkbook. "I should also have told you I keep a bit of cash in the kitchen, in that blue tin. If you need groceries or dog food or gas, please help yourself."

Carla was about to say that the tin was empty but stopped. That wasn't something she should know. She took the check and read the amount. "No, this is too much, E." She tried to give it back.

"Nonsense. It's what I owe plus the next two weeks, assuming you'll continue on."

Carla's mouth hung open. "I—I don't know what to say." She stared at the slip of paper in her hand, the little scrap that could sustain her for a month. Maybe two. "Thank you."

E flapped her hand to wave away any gratitude. "Gizmo and I should be thanking you."

Carla shifted her feet on the floor and bumped into the paper bag she'd brought with her. "I almost forgot. I've got something for you. I figured you must be bored stiff by now, since you said reading and TV are out until your brain unscrambles." She held up her mini boombox. E's face brightened.

"I thought you might like to borrow this. I checked with the nurse. She said listening to calm music is fine if you keep the volume low. It's tuned to that classical station you like, and I put in a CD too." Carla found an outlet, set the small player on E's lap, and showed her how to work it.

"It's like a little robot!" E beamed and slid her fingers up the antenna. "How thoughtful." She pressed the Play button, and Al Jarreau's smooth voice oozed into the room.

Carla grimaced. "Not really my thing." Her mother loved his music and listened to it all the time when Carla was in middle school. She wasn't sure why she had kept the CD all these years.

E smiled and tapped her fingers to the beat. "It's not my usual, either, but I like it." She hummed along in a high, thin voice.

"It's the only CD I have that's mellow enough. The stuff I like would *give* you a concussion. My mom left it behind when she... Whatever." Carla reached into the bag again and pulled something out.

"What's that?" E craned her neck to see it.

On her way to the hospital, Carla had stopped at her apartment for the boom box that her mom must have decided was too crappy to steal. She looked around her empty living room wishing she had something cheerful like a plant or some flowers to give as a gift. Or something funny or whimsical. Zilch. She went into her bedroom, opened and closed her dresser drawers, finding only a single abandoned sock and a broken pair of sunglasses. Her mom was a thorough thief. On a shelf in the closet above the naked wire hangers was her child-size suitcase. The one her mother had given her on her eleventh birthday.

The scent when she opened it was no longer one of possibility and hope. The suitcase was musty, smelling only of lost dreams. Now it was full of odds and ends, and staring up at her was Gordon, posing with his van. She flipped the photo face down and sifted through her lucky charms and magic trinkets until she found what she hadn't known she was looking for.

"Here," Carla said now, placing the object in the palm of E's hand. A small plastic man in a green robe with an oversized gold medallion around his neck. "Saint Anthony. I figured you and old Arnold could use some company."

"Thank you, Carla. You are so good to me. Now,"—E squeezed Carla's hand—"go fight city hall."

Carla and Gizmo were having a noisy game of tug-of-war in the back-yard when Nathan called to her over the high fence. The sun had set, and the floodlights were on. She grabbed the dog by the collar and unlatched the front gate.

"Hey," she said. She had a lot to tell him. "How's the meeting?"

"Made some headway, but there's more work to do. They're on our side, at least." He held up a large envelope. "New batch of photos for the catalog."

Gizmo dropped his rope toy at Nathan's feet, panting. Carla grabbed it and ran with the dog on her heels, yelling, "Door's open. I'll be in in a sec."

"Impressive," Nathan said when she and Gizmo joined him in the kitchen. He sat at the table smiling, his clear gray eyes lit from within. In his hands was the stack of pictures Carla had finished labeling. "Not surprising, but impressive."

The job of comparing whale fins was a lot like those Spot the Dif-ference games on the puzzle page of the *Sun*. Crosswords made Carla feel stupid, but finding what was different in the two little drawings was a cinch.

"I just flick my eyes back and forth really fast a few times, and I can tell if they match. But you should check my work. There's probably tons of mistakes."

"Huh. That's the same technique astronomers use to find new objects in the night sky. They use something called a blink comparator, invented in 1904 by—"

Carla sat and dropped her face into her palm with a groan. "God, you know a lot of useless shit."

He laughed. "Sorry for nerding out. Bad habit."

"No big deal. But this"—she laid her notebook on the table between them—"*is* a big deal."

She gave him a summary of what she'd been doing after her visit with E. "I started out reading about echolocation at the library, because of what you said about how noise from boats could be messing the whales up. I read that whales make sounds and listen to the echoes to find food and stuff. But you know that already." Carla waved her hands, wiping away her words. "With so many boats around them all the time, it's no wonder the poor things are confused and can't find their way out.

"A while back," she continued, "there was a letter to editor asking why they couldn't close Dyes Inlet and the Narrows to boats, just until the whales got out. The next day I saw an article where some lawyer said the Coast Guard had the power to shut down a waterway even though it would violate something called"—she opened the notebook and flipped a few pages —"the right of navigation that legally protects boaters. I got my hopes up, but the end of the article really pissed me off. The lawyer said the Coast Guard would only do it for something extreme, like an oil spill, a situation dangerous to *humans*, and that protecting whales didn't come close!"

Nathan leaned back with his arms crossed over his chest, listening.

"So, if getting boats off the water is a lost cause," she said "I figured the next best thing was getting cars off the bridge. I learned more than I ever wanted to know about how city, county, and state government works. My brain is on overload. All I wanted to know was how to close a road for a few hours. Adelle, she's one of the librarians, got me a list of the main dudes and their phone numbers."

Carla flipped to the page where she had copied them all down. "This guy, guy by the name of Lyle Goronson. Central Kitsap Public Works Director," she read, pointing to the place on the paper. "His secretary gave me a lot of information. She said the first step is to apply for a road closure permit. Done. Cost me twenty bucks!"

"Quite an investment."

"For me, yeah." At least now she had money in the bank, thanks to E.

She told Nathan that once permission was granted to close a portion of Warren Avenue the real work would begin. The biggest hurdle was that seventy-five percent of the residents and business owners along the route had to agree to the closure. Getting that kind of cooperation would involve lots of legwork and knocking on doors.

"You could write a letter to editor," Nathan said. "Put pressure on those businesses. I wonder if the citizens of Bremerton would boycott any businesses that stand in the way. That would have a bigger impact on their bottom line than a couple of hours without traffic. How about I arrange an interview for you with a reporter at the *Sun*? An article in the paper would help get the word out, get people on board before you even knock on a single door."

"Interview me?"

"Why not? I can't get involved in a rescue, remember? Spoke to my boss more than once about it, but he won't budge. Unless he changes his mind, I have to stay out of it."

"Fine. I don't get it, but whatever. But I'm not doing an interview. Ask someone else." Carla pushed away from the table. "I'm starving." She opened a few cupboards and came back with a box of crackers.

"Even if I could get the road closed," she said with her mouth full, "how could I organize all the volunteers?"

"Volunteers?"

She swallowed. "We should talk about part two." She handed him a photocopy of the article from the *Daily Sitka Sentinel* about the rescue in Alaska. "Besides closing the bridge, there needs to be about a dozen volunteers with boats out there to herd the whales toward the bridge. I know you don't like the idea, but if they do it right—and you can explain exactly what they should and shouldn't do...." Carla trailed off. Nathan was shaking his head.

"Look," she started again, trying to keep her temper from flaring. Her frustration threatened to spill over, but she needed Nathan on her side, and biting his head off wouldn't help. She wiped perspiration from her hairline. "Stopping traffic on the bridge isn't enough. Giving the whales a chance to get out is only half the solution. Pushing them in the right direction at the right time is the other half."

They had been observing the whales' behavior for three weeks, and one thing was clear. There was no way to predict when they would approach the bridge. Some days they didn't go near it at all.

"You're talking about a lot of moving parts, Carla. A lot could go wrong."

"There *are* a lot of moving parts. And it all could go to shit. But it's the only choice. Please, Nathan." She leaned in. "I believe in this plan, and I need you to believe in it too. To believe in me."

Nathan picked up the *Sentinel* article, and Carla studied his expression as he read, her restless knees jiggling under the table. When he put the paper down, he looked into her eyes and held her gaze for a long moment.

Chapter 24

Wednesday, November 12, 1997

Carla's knees shook like a pair of maracas. The waiting room outside the office of the public works director was stark and cheerless. The carpet under her feet was threadbare, the upholstered chair she sat in smelled like dust, and the single window looked out into a slim, gloomy space between buildings. Her hands gripped a spiral notebook and a folder full of papers.

The drive to Port Orchard took longer than expected and figuring out which building was the right one delayed her even more. Now she was ten minutes late for her 5:00 appointment. It crossed her mind that she might have blown it already, that maybe Mr. Goronson left when she wasn't there on time. On the phone that morning, his secretary reluctantly added Carla to the end of the director's full schedule because Carla insisted it was urgent.

Most of the day she'd spent preparing for this meeting. She gave herself a series of pep talks and wished for courage on every lucky charm she owned, but now that she was here, all she wanted to do was run. No one was going to take her seriously, no matter what Nathan said. True, she had washed her hair and was wearing exactly two earrings, one in each earlobe, but she was still a punk.

She wiped her sweaty palms on her jeans. Her mom stole the few decent things she had. Even with the wide black belt cinched tight on her mom's skinny frame, Carla's best jeans would be hanging on her hipbones and the hems dragging under the heels of Carla's high-tops. Those black canvas knock-off Chucks were nothing like the yellow stilettos her mom wore when she showed up at the high school auditorium that day. The day her life went to shit.

Carla opened her notebook for the fourth time since she arrived, trying to chase away those memories and the sourness in her stomach. Her to-do list was even longer than before her conversation with Nathan. This would never work, especially with her leading the way. All her doubts and insecurities, the negative voices in her head—her mother, social workers, judges, foster parents—all the people who had rejected her or written her off, everything came crashing in. She snapped the notebook shut and stood.

At the elevator her finger stopped an inch away from the Down button. She heard other voices now, and they were growing louder. E's and Nathan's, saying she was a good person, that she had hidden talents, that they believed in her. And Libby's. What she said that day in the Coffee Spot, with her beautiful cards spread out on the counter. Something about Carla not letting fears from the past overshadow her future. "Whatever conflicts lie ahead, you *will* overcome them," Libby had said.

Carla's hand dropped to her side. *Get over yourself.* She walked quickly back past the main reception desk and down the hall toward the director's office. Before she could change her mind again, a woman in gray slacks and a red cardigan appeared in the doorway. "Ms. Peterson? He's ready for you now," she said and stepped aside for Carla to enter.

Mr. Goronson's office was no cozier than the waiting area. A cluttered desk, a bookcase full of binders against one wall, and three metal file cabinets hunched opposite, all made of the same institutional olive-green steel. This was a place where shit got done. A good sign.

"Have a seat," he said, standing briefly and motioning to a chair. He was tall with dark hair and a gaunt face. Deep creases ran in rows across his high forehead, made more noticeable by his receding hairline. Add a beard and a stovepipe hat, and he could pass for Abe Lincoln. Honest Abe. Another good sign.

She perched on the edge of the chair with his messy desk between them.

"Carla, isn't it?" He glanced at his appointment book. His smile was packed full of long teeth, possibly more than the usual human number.

"Thank you for seeing me." She had rehearsed this meeting in her head, her part anyway. She could play nice when she needed to.

"My assistant filled me in on your concerns about the visiting orcas and your proposal to close the Warren Avenue Bridge. Tell me your thinking behind this." He leaned back and crossed one foot over his knee, rocking slightly. His chair squeaked rhythmically.

"Over the last few weeks," she began, her quavering voice gradually finding its way, "me and Nathan noticed a couple of times that the whales would swim into Port Washington Narrows." She opened her notebook to a simple map she had drawn of the area around the inlet. She leaned across the desk, placing it in front of Honest Abe. With her index finger, she drew a line from the center of the inlet to the channel. "But when they get as far as the first bridge," she tapped a line representing the Warren Avenue Bridge, "they freak out, I guess, and turn back. The most logical reason is the noise. If we could keep cars and trucks off the bridge for a while, the whales would swim under and go back out to Puget Sound where they should be."

She sat back and inhaled. The man wrote some notes on a pad of yellow paper. Maybe she'd said something worthwhile after all.

"And Nathan is...?"

"That's Nathan Decoteau. A marine biologist." This guy was more likely to take the word of an expert over hers. Nathan should be here instead. Her confidence flagged. "He works at the Center for Whale Research in Friday Harbor on San Juan Island."

"I know of it, yes. Not far from the Whale Museum." The man wrote this information down and looked at Carla again. "And Mr. Decoteau agrees with you? About the noise from the traffic being the cause of the whales 'freaking out,' as you say?" Carla nodded. "Isn't it possible they're staying for some other reason? It's not as if they're trapped. I heard they followed a run of salmon into Dyes Inlet. Maybe they're just enjoying the buffet." He chuckled and rubbed his chin.

Carla told him how much a pod of orcas eats in a day and that after more than three weeks their food was running out. "Nathan says if they don't leave soon, they'll all die."

Honest Abe was quiet for a moment, considering this information. The creases around his mouth deepened. He stood and walked over to a large map of Kitsap Peninsula tacked to the wall and studied it for a moment. He rested his fists on his wide hips with his back to Carla. Her heart thumped watching him. He had heard her. He was thinking it through.

"If we close the bridge, how would drivers get across the Narrows?" he said and cocked his head. "The old Manette can't handle that much traffic. It would be backed up for miles, and we'd get nothing but complaints."

It was true that most people driving to and from Bremerton took the Warren Avenue Bridge, which was a four-lane highway built in the fifties to handle all the traffic when the population boomed. Not many people used the Manette Bridge anymore.

He placed his index finger on the map and drew it northward along Highway 303 saying, "The only other option would be to drive all the way through Meadowdale to Silverdale and down the other side of the inlet. It must be nearly twenty miles."

Carla deflated. "It would only be for a couple hours," she said, trying to keep the desperation out of her voice. "We could wait until after rush hour."

"Yes, but even so…" Mr. Goronson's voice trailed off as he continued to study the map on the wall. After a minute or two, he let out a long sigh and said, "I appreciate the seriousness of this situation, but I'm afraid I can't help you."

She stared at his back, this man who wielded so much power, and she felt the blood drain from her face. After everything she and Nathan had done, seeing their efforts come to nothing! She gripped the arms of her chair to stop herself from launching across Abe's desk to slug him in the kidneys. He was still talking, but Carla could no longer hear him over the roaring in her ears. She grabbed her things and fled.

Outside the courthouse, Carla sat in E's car under a streetlight. She hit the steering wheel with both palms, and a howl of rage tore from deep in her lungs. Goronson had led her on, made her think he would help her, only to pull the rug out from under her in the end. The whole system, bullshit elected idiots and useless pencil pushers, all worked together to get *nothing* done. Stalling, deflecting, postponing. How hard could it be to put up a couple of barricades?

Life had taught her to trust no one, especially people in authority—parents, social workers, judges, police. Now she could add county public works directors to that list. She let her hands drop into her lap and stared out onto the dark, empty street. She tipped her head back against the leather headrest and squeezed her eyes shut to stop herself from crying. No matter what she did or how hard she tried or how much she wished—even prayed—for something, no matter how close she got to her goal, she failed in the end. Whatever she touched turned to shit.

Chapter 25

Thursday, November 13, 1997

In the quiet of the hospital room, fluorescent lights buzzed, and Carla's head ached. E was sound asleep. Her fingers twitched, but she showed no signs of waking. Carla would have to wait for the big dose of empathy she needed. Nathan had listened to her vent over the phone the night before as she banged around in E's kitchen feeding Gizmo and heating the eggplant Parmesan for herself. He assured her there was still time to devise a new plan since the orcas' condition was stable. With the heavy fog keeping most boaters off the water that day, it had been quiet, he said, and the whales behaved normally.

By the time Carla got into bed, she was calm. Joan's voice in her head lulled her to sleep saying, "You tried your best. Tomorrow is another day."

What a bust that meeting with Goronson had been! She was no closer to a solution and another day had passed. How much longer could she believe her foster mom's words? How many more tomorrows did the whales have?

Restless, Carla reached for the *Sun* that was folded and unread on E's bedside table. On the front page she found an article about the dangers of crowding the orcas in the inlet. A special emergency meeting would take place tomorrow before the weekend boaters flocked to the water. Officials would discuss enacting a no-wake zone through the Narrows. The reporter said the city and county would be working together because the waterway fell within both the Bremerton city limits and greater Kitsap County. That was a positive step. Slowing boat traffic was good for the whales, even if it was only a reaction to complaints from the rich people about how big wakes were damaging their waterfront property.

Carla skimmed the names of the people who would attend the meeting. On the list were the mayor, the Kitsap County Sheriff, someone from the Bremerton City Council, and the Public Works Department Director, Lyle Goronson. Carla's jaw muscles flexed. Lyle—no longer Honest Abe—with his mouthful of crocodile teeth. She imagined herself storming into that meeting, demanding to be heard, insisting that they shut the bridge down. All those pasty-faced old white men staring in disbelief at this pissed-off punk. Her breath came faster, and her fingers tightened around the edges of the paper. *Bite me, Lyle.*

The door opened, and a young man entered carrying a covered dinner tray. Noise from the hallway followed him in and died away once the door closed. E stirred but settled back into sleep.

He put the tray softly on a table and wheeled it closer. "Meatloaf," he mouthed. Carla nodded her thanks. He waved a finger at the framed photo and the plastic statue next to the bed. "That's me," he whispered, and the pointed at his name badge. Carla read it: Jude.

He registered her confused expression and said quietly, "Saint Jude. Mom was a Beatles fan when I was born. You know, 'Hey, Jude'?"

Carla picked up the statue. She turned it around and over, searching for a clue to the little man's true identity.

"Patron saint of lost causes and desperate situations," he said. "I'll be back for this in about an hour." He gave the tray a little tap and left the room.

Saint Jude? She let this percolate. The social worker driving her back from seeing her mom had told Carla the figure was Saint Anthony and taught her the lines of that prayer. Had she been talking to the wrong saint all these years, asking the wrong guy for help finding lost things?

Carla looked at the figure in her hand. She didn't get the whole prayer thing anyway. Wasn't praying the same as making a wish? Wasn't believing in some magical power, whether it was a falling star or a saint or a god, just a way to pass the buck? A way of saying, *I don't have power to change anything on my own, so why even try?*

Saint Jude. Lost causes instead of lost items. It was fitting that the original statue was a gift from her mother, the queen of lost causes. There was no way she bought the statue, so someone must have given it to her, some holy roller she met during one of her many stints in rehab. "Here," they would have said. "You look like someone who needs all the help she can get." And then she re-gifted it to Carla because it was worthless. She couldn't pawn it or sell it, so she didn't want it. *Gee, thanks, Mom.* With a sneer and a little too much force, Carla set it back on the table next to the photo of Arnold. The sound woke E.

"Hello? Who's there?"

"Hey, it's me," Carla said, moving her face closer.

"My glasses. Where are my glasses?" E's hands fluttered over her blanket. Carla handed them to her.

"That's more like it," said E, adjusting the large frames over her ears and fussing with her hearing aid. "What's that awful smell?" She wrinkled her nose.

"Dinner." Carla rolled the table so it extended over the bed and helped E sit up. Carla lifted the stainless-steel cover, and they both stared at the plate. The meal was unappetizing, but Carla's empty stomach rumbled.

E pushed the gray slab of meat to one side with her fork and poked at the blob of mashed potatoes. "I can't possibly eat this. Would you like it, Carla?" Carla shook her head. "The dessert?" She held out a spoon.

Between grateful mouthfuls of butterscotch pudding, Carla told her about the wild-goose chase to Port Orchard.

"So that's how he left it? He can't help you? Infuriating!" E pulled her face into a frown. She was struggling to open a small cellophane packet of saltines. Carla opened it for her.

"Are you sure you don't you have any connections there because of your dad? Could you pull some strings?" Carla glanced at the statue again, *Hey, Jude. Can you help a girl out? I've got a desperate situation for you.*

E shook her head and nibbled on a cracker, crumbs falling onto the front of her hospital gown. "Even if I could, those officials need to do the right thing because it's the right thing, not because somebody throws their weight around." She looked at Carla, whose shoulders sagged. "You mustn't let that man discourage you. This fight is just beginning." Her eyes sparked with determination.

"But what can I do?" Carla hated how whiny her voice sounded. She scraped up the last of the pudding and licked the spoon.

"Go higher up the ladder! Don't stop until you get the answer you want."

It had taken all Carla's nerve to walk into Lyle the Crocodile's office. She couldn't go through that all over again with a different bureaucrat. Every cell in her body felt depleted.

She closed her eyes and pictured Faith breaching at the end of the pier the day she quit her job at the Coffee Spot. Seeing him again after fearing he was dead, she'd wanted to leap from the safety of the dock and join him in his wild game. His skin was pulled tight and smooth over his muscles, powerful muscles that allowed him to propel himself up and out of the water and hang suspended in midair before dropping like a fucking planet into the water below.

Carla looked at the little statue in the green robe. E was right. Carla didn't need a new plan. What she needed was the balls to see her original plan through. No, the fight wasn't over. She was just getting started.

Chapter 26

Friday, November 14, 1997

A couple of phone calls the next day was all it took for Carla to find out where and when the emergency meeting was taking place. She sat on a bench outside the Bremerton mayor's office. The topic being discussed was creating a no-wake zone in the Narrows. She'd been there for more than two hours staring at a large window and watching the light in the afternoon sky fade. Turns out, taking action meant a fuck-ton of waiting.

On the drive to E's from the hospital the night before, Carla began to see her way forward. Each step ahead formed an orderly sequence with a beginning and an end. This was step one: waiting there for as long as it took to catch the movers and shakers of city government after their meeting. This time she had no sweaty brow, no juddering knees, no dry mouth. Her hands lay loosely on top of the notes in her lap. This fight wasn't about her. It was about the orcas. She was their voice and nothing more. It didn't matter what she looked like or where she came from. It didn't matter how many times she had failed. She was no good at a lot of things, but she knew a thing or two about survival.

The voices inside the conference room grew louder and someone laughed. They were moving around, pushing in chairs. Finally. She stood and faced the door, feet planted.

"Excuse me," she said when the four men emerged. "I need a minute of your time." They exchanged glances.

Mr. Goronson spoke. "Hello, again. Good to see you. Carla, right?" He smiled his crocodile smile. The others continued toward the elevator.

"Wait!" Carla called. The knot of men turned, their conversation stopped.

"I'll catch up with you," Goronson said, waving them on. "I can take care of this."

"No, you can't!" Carla raised her voice, addressing him. "You can't help me. Isn't that what you said yesterday?"

"You left in such a hurry I didn't have time to explain," Goronson said.

A big bald man broke away from the others as the elevator door slid open. He took long strides toward Carla with his hand extended. "Mayor Philips." He gave her a firm handshake. "City of Bremerton. How can we help?"

She looked him in the eyes. "It's a matter of life and death."

A moment later the three were seated at one end of a long conference table. The mayor invited her to fill him in on the main points she'd laid out for the public works director the day before. He leaned in, and Lyle nodded along.

"Here's the thing, Carla," Lyle said when she'd finished. "It's not every day I'm asked to close a road, so I wasn't one hundred percent sure how to proceed in your case. When you came to my office, it occurred to me that I have no jurisdiction to close the Warren Avenue Bridge, but I was sure I could find someone who does. You were just barking up the wrong tree."

"But you're in charge of roads!" Carla was sure E had said to go to the public works department.

"Roads *are* my responsibility. Road maintenance, anyway. But it's complicated, the way these things get divvied up. Warren Avenue is a State Highway, so after you left, I called my buddy at the Washington Department of Transportation. He told me Kitsap County is responsible for bridges, so the ball was back in my court. Long story short, I got the runaround, but in the end, I found out it's the city of Bremerton that controls *traffic* on the two bridges, so the person you need to talk to is Mayor Philips." He pointed at the other man.

"You're barking up the right tree now. I'm so glad you persisted," the mayor said.

Carla looked at Lyle's lined face. Honest Abe once again. She shrank a little at the names she called him after leaving his office.

"Let's get down to business," the mayor said. "If I'm getting this right, we stop traffic on the bridge, the orcas swim under it and back out to the Sound. Not a bad plan, but I see two problems with it."

Carla bristled, ready to argue.

He continued. "First, the whales might not be in the right place at the right time, shall we say. Meaning once the traffic on the bridge is stopped, who's to say the whales will decide to make a run for it? What if they're hanging out in the inlet and don't even know the coast is clear? You said yourself they've gone as far as the bridge only a few times."

"More than a few," Carla said. "But I get your point, which is why—"

"And second," he took a breath, but barreled on, "if drivers pile onto the Manette instead, jamming it with noisy vehicles, who's to say the whales won't do the same thing when they reach the Manette Bridge? Turn around and swim back to Dyes Inlet."

Carla opened her notebook and flipped the pages, hunting for the map she had drawn. She had to make this guy understand.

"True," Lyle said. "There's no guarantee that once past the first bridge the whales would continue under the second." He shook his head and sighed. "And don't even ask to close both bridges at the same time."

Carla stood and placed her open notebook on the table. She pushed it across so that her sketch of Dyes Inlet lay in front of the two men. She was prepared for this battle.

"Nathan Decoteau—the guy I told you about from the Center for Whale Research—can have volunteers with their boats here"—she pointed to the north end of the inlet—"and here." She tapped the mouth of the Narrows in the south. Nathan hadn't agreed to help her yet, but how could his boss refuse to let him do this once she managed to get the city officials on board?

She explained how the first group of volunteers would close in on the whales slowly, banging on metal pipes held underwater, to move the pod from the inlet to the Narrows. There the second group would join in and together they would herd the whales into the channel and block them from swimming back into Dyes Inlet. "That's when we would stop traffic on the bridge." She removed her copy of the *Sitka Sentinel* article from her folder. "It worked in 1993." She dropped the pages in front of the mayor.

"And the second thing you said was a problem," she continued, "that the orcas might turn back because of noise on the Manette." Reading a couple of articles in the library about bridge design hardly made her an expert. Her facts were shaky—or possibly nonexistent—but her passion might be enough to convince them. "The two bridges are different. The way they are built." Carla flipped to the page in her notebook where she had sketched several types of bridges.

"The Manette Bridge is fifteen hundred feet long. It's two lanes wide and has steel trusses like these." She leaned forward, talking fast, and tapped one of the rough drawings. "And four piers supporting it." What she lacked in understanding, she hoped to conceal with speed and a barrage of information. "And the Warren Avenue, four lanes wide, is over seventeen hundred feet long. It has girders and seven massive pairs of concrete piers holding it up." She pointed to another picture. "When traffic passes over them, you can hear sounds underwater."

"How do you know this?" asked Lyle.

"We listen to the whales sometimes from Nathan's boat with his hydrophone, and we also pick up vibrations near the bridges. Humans can't hear much difference, but Nathan said whales' hearing is more sensitive than people's. So, what they can hear under the Warren Avenue Bridge would be different from under the Manette."

"I can't say I know anything about what a whale can hear, but it stands to reason that structures of different sizes, materials, and designs would react differently to heavy traffic," said Lyle.

"Is that so?" The mayor rubbed one hand over his bald head.

"It really is a matter of life and death. Nathan says they're in trouble. They're dehydrated and running low on food. The sooner you agree to help the better, because I still need to work on raising money for the fees and getting business owners to go along with the plan." Steps two and three of her carefully thought-out plan.

The men were quiet for a moment. Lyle scratched his cheek, and the mayor drummed his fingers softly on the arm of his chair. She had pushed too hard, been too demanding. Expected too much. Perspiration prickled her upper lip.

Then the mayor spoke. "These orcas have captured the hearts of the people of Bremerton. And beyond. As a show of support and good faith, we'll waive any fees and dispense with the need for signatures to expedite things. It wouldn't be a good look if we let red tape get in the way of saving the whales now, would it?" He and Lyle exchanged a glance.

This was more than Carla could have hoped for. She thanked them both, shaking their hands in turn with her clammy one.

"Well," said the mayor, glancing at his watch, "it's past five on a Friday. I'll arrange another emergency meeting for Monday. City council will want to weigh in on this. If they go against me, I can use the power of my office to override them, but I hope it doesn't come to that. Best case scenario, they'll see things our way, and we can move forward immediately. Can I make copies of your notes? I want to be sure I don't miss anything important when I present your ideas."

Carla collected her notebook and papers and tucked them under her arm, feeling stronger than she'd ever felt. She had persuaded the mayor, so why not take it to the next level? "Can I do it? Present my ideas to the council?"

Chapter 27

Saturday, November 15, 1997

Carla spotted the bright orange sign from the parking lot at Lions Park early the next morning. She walked to the boat ramp for a closer look. The sign announced the no-wake zone in the Narrows, enforced by the Kitsap County sheriff's department. Effective immediately. Lyle had told Carla about the ordinance as they rode the elevator down to the Government Center lobby the day before. It would expire on December fifteenth. He said they could extend it if the whales needed more time.

"They won't," Carla had said.

"I admire your confidence," he'd said.

Leaning against the edge of a picnic table near the ramp, fear pricked the back of her neck. She wasn't feeling confident. If her plan failed, the no-wake ordinance wouldn't need to be extended. The whales wouldn't need protection a month from now because if they didn't leave soon, they'd all be dead.

Over the still channel, mist filtered the first weak rays of sunlight. She checked her watch. Nathan would be there in a few minutes. They still had work to do. His newest photographs revealed that four adults were seriously dehydrated. He wanted to monitor them today and to check on the youngest calves who were especially vulnerable to dehydration.

Beneath her fears about the whales, a selfish panic was building. The more she thought about standing before the council on Monday, the more she wished she hadn't been so quick to volunteer to do it. Why did she have to open her big mouth? What was she thinking?

Thanks to Mayor Philips, at least she wouldn't have to come up with money for the road closure fee or collect a single signature. The council meeting was only two days away, and this one would be make or break. No pressure. Carla pulled out and lit a cigarette. How could she make those men take her seriously? Her notes were a jumble of scribbles, and the maps and sketches she'd made were a mess. Worse, she was a mess. She surveyed her appearance, taking in her scuffed boots with their broken, mismatched laces, her torn jeans that could use a wash, the faded plaid flannel shirt. This shouldn't be about how she looked, but it was, at least a little bit. A trip to Goodwill would be a start. She could find something decent and cheap. A skirt, something like the ones Libby wore. *When was the last time I wore a skirt?*

An image of Libby floated up, laughing and smoking on the steps of the Coffee Spot. It had been almost a week since Carla walked out of the restaurant for the last time. She had no regrets about quitting, but she missed Libby and felt bad about leaving her to deal with the vomit alone. Prissy Sylvia wouldn't have touched it with a ten-foot pole. Libby had looked exhausted that day, but as soon as the whales were free, she would be free too. She could go back to her quiet life.

Maybe there was a chance Carla could stay friends with her. For now, at least, she knew where Libby worked. But once the coffee-swilling whale watchers all crawled back into the woodwork and Libby's help was no longer needed, how would Carla find her? Her fingers found her worry stone in her pocket.

She had no less uncertainty about her future, but she was learning to believe she could make a difference in the world. This was a new kind of faith. Not like pinning her hopes on magic charms and magic words, horoscopes or tarot cards. Making the choices that would steer her in a new direction was up to her. This was faith in herself.

She walked a few steps to the water's edge, scanning the surface for a fin, anticipating the moment one appeared. She took a final drag before crushing the cigarette under the heel of her boot. She bent to pick it up and paused. All around her feet were stones—black, gray, brown, white—all smooth, worn down by the little waves lapping over them day after day, year after year. Thousands of stones on the beach. Thousands of beaches on the planet.

She chose one and examined it, feeling the texture and the weight of it. It was larger than her worry stone, which she held out in her other hand, and darker in color. Sugary sand clung to its wet surface. But the only real difference between the two was her belief that one had magical powers. Her believing was what made them different.

She dropped the wet stone onto the ground at her feet. It made a musical clink when it landed among the others. Then she drew her arm back and threw her worry stone as far over the Narrows as she could and smiled at the soft *plunk* it made.

She took a deep breath. The scent of salt and pine refreshed her senses, and the twitter of sparrows and finches joined the gentle rhythm of the waves making sweet music. Cool mist settled on her skin and held her in its soft embrace. One fin poked up and then another. "Hello," Carla said, smiling. There was nowhere she'd rather be at that moment than exactly where she was, in the company of whales.

Chapter 28

Sunday, November 16, 1997

Carla cleared her throat. Her voice was hoarse from calling through the bullhorn for two days straight. "How do I look?" She fiddled with the collar of Libby's white blouse and smoothed the dark paisley skirt over her hips with her sweaty palms.

Nathan smiled from the sofa in E's living room. "Perfect."

She felt ridiculous standing there in her stocking feet and borrowed clothes, but he was right. Well, at least the clothes were right.

"Should I do a ponytail?" She pulled her coarse, salty hair back. Maybe she should have accepted Sylvia's offer to style it for her.

All weekend she and Nathan had been on the inlet monitoring the health of the whales. At least they had help controlling the boaters. Two scientists from the Center for Whale Research were out on the Soundwatch RIB, along with boats carrying officers from the Coast Guard, Marine Fisheries, and Fish and Wildlife. The sheriff had boats in the Narrows to enforce the no-wake zone.

Saturday afternoon Carla had waited outside the Coffee Spot until Libby emerged after closing. Her face lit up when she spotted Carla skulking at the edge of the parking lot. In a rush, Carla told her what she needed and why, and Libby promised to meet her after work the next day with some clothes to try on.

"I like this skirt better than the first one." Carla turned side to side, catching her reflection in the living room window.

"Both are nice," Nathan said.

Everything was ready. Carla had redrawn her sketches of the two types of bridges, taking care to make them neat. She'd labeled the girders and trusses above the water and the piers and footings below. Nathan had made photocopies at the library.

"Can you listen to my speech?" Without waiting for an answer, she ran back to her room and hung Libby's clothes in the closet. Her Doc Martens were in the corner where she had kicked them. Carla's big feet didn't fit into the ballet flats Libby brought. Maybe no one would look at her feet.

In her jeans and T-shirt again, she sat cross-legged on the oriental rug next to Gizmo, clutching a stack of index cards. She had written out her speech, point by point, as she learned to do in high school. She read each one aloud for Nathan.

"I suck at this. I sound like an idiot." She tossed her cards across the room.

"You're doing great, Carla," Nathan said, sending a familiar shiver up her bare arms at the sound of her name. "Relax. Try it again, and practice making eye contact this time."

"How the hell can I make eye contact when I'm reading? And I don't want to see all those people staring at me like I'm a train wreck about to happen. I hate this. You should be doing it instead of me."

"You can do this." Nathan knelt and placed his hand lightly on her shoulder. She let it stay there, enjoying its warmth. "You're going to knock their socks off."

She slipped her hand into her pocket for her worry stone, for its reassuring familiar shape. Her heart sank remembering the little splash. She was going to fall on her face. Her fears—of screwing up, of not being good enough or smart enough, of being laughed at—bubbled into rage, ugly and raw, and she threw it at Nathan with all her might.

"Why am *I* doing everything?" she shouted, jerking out from under his hand. Gizmo whimpered and sat up. "Isn't this *your* job?" She pointed her finger at him, rigid and shaking, but stopped short of jabbing him in the middle of his chest. "I'm sweating my balls off, doing all this for free, while you collect your paycheck for sitting there doing fuck all!"

"Hold on a minute." Nathan raised his hands in surrender. "I came here to study and protect the whales, and that's what I've been doing. You wanted to come along and help me, which I totally appreciate, and you got wrapped up in trying to get them out."

"And what are *you* doing about that? Huh? I'm trying to do the right thing, helping the whales get out because you won't."

"I want them to leave as much as you do. I'm not acting on my own out there. Not everyone is a freewheeling rebel like you with no one to answer to. I'm helping you—and the orcas—as much as I can. I promised you I'd talk to my boss first thing tomorrow, didn't I? If he gives me the go-ahead, then we're on. If he doesn't, my hands are tied."

Carla glared at him. "You'd rather follow the rules and let the whales die here?"

His face fell. "The thing is, I screwed up at my last job. Really screwed up. If I had done what I was supposed to do…" he trailed off. "My mistake cost me my job. I have to do things by the book, or I could get fired."

"So what?" Carla threw her arms out, fingers splayed. "Get another job. Smart guy with a couple of degrees. You can have any job you want."

"Wasn't just a job I lost. My pigheadedness cost the lives of two juvenile orcas."

Carla let this information sit for a moment. Just because it happened once didn't mean it would happen again. When Nathan opened his mouth to speak, she cut him off. "I must have my head up my ass. One minute I'm arranging shitty muffins on a plate, and the next I'm dressing up like some kind of fuck-nugget to go talk to the mayor and a bunch of suits." Carla's head swam and the room tilted. "I think I'm g—" Carla's hand flew up to cover her mouth, and she tore from the room making it to the toilet just in time.

She ran cold water in the sink, splashing some on her face and into her mouth.

"Carla?" A soft knock on the bathroom door. "You okay? Can I come in?"

She opened it and brushed past Nathan, bumping her shoulder into him, hard. Still queasy she headed for the kitchen and grabbed a can of E's ginger ale from the fridge.

Nathan leaned against the doorframe and watched her take small sips while she glowered at him over the top of the can.

"Where's all this anger coming from?" he asked, his eyebrows pinching together. "Nerves? You don't strike me as the stage-fright type."

"No?" Carla stepped forward until she stood in front of him, her wild, unbroken gaze fixed on him. "So what type am I, since you think you know me so well?" He didn't answer. "I thought so. You don't know me at all."

"And whose fault is that?" Nathan raised his voice. Then, more softly, "I've been trying to get to know you, but"—he lifted his hand to caress her cheek, and she slapped it away—"you don't make it easy."

All her life people had said she was hard to like. Hard to love. Social workers, teachers, foster parents, coworkers—they all told her the same thing. Her own mother. Carla pushed past Nathan into the living room.

He followed her, saying, "Help me understand why the meeting tomorrow has you so worked up."

"You wanna know why?" She spun to face him. "Because I know how it feels to be humiliated in front of a roomful of people, that's why, and I can't go through that again!" she hollered. "I can't."

"What've you got to lose?"

"Everything!" she shouted. "My self-respect, my safety, my*self*! It's all I have."

"You're not going to mess up and embarrass yourself tomorrow just because it happened in the past. I mean, hasn't everyone had a moment like that? Last week I—"

"I'm not talking about being embarrassed, getting teased about a bad haircut or peeing your pants on the fucking playground. I'm talking the kind of humiliation that makes you feel less than worthless." Carla's voice caught. She turned and faced the window overlooking the front yard. "The kind that cuts you off at the knees."

Her thoughts and emotions were jumbled. She was saying too much. The tiny scraps about her past she shared with Elizabeth and Libby left her feeling exposed. Breaking open that little bit loosened the bands that held her together, released something that made her feel clumsy and wobbly, a colt taking its first steps on new spindly legs. Now she was letting Nathan get too close. Darkness pressed against the windowpane. Her quick, shallow breaths kept pace with the ticking clock on the mantel.

Tsk, tsk, tsk, the clock scolded.

"The kind of humiliation that never leaves you." She should quit talking. Now. Before she said another word about the day she stopped trusting that the world would ever do right by her, the day her heart turned to ice because her survival depended on it. She swore she would never let anyone close enough to hear the story. *Stop talking.* "The kind of humiliation that shines a spotlight on all your secrets, showing the world how fucked up your life is."

"Who did that to you? Who hurt you?" Nathan clenched his fists.

"My mother." Carla's eyes burned and tears spilled over her cheeks. Nathan brushed them away with his thumbs, but they kept coming. She pressed the heels of her hands into her eye sockets to hold back the flood. After a moment, he took her hands and guided her to the sofa. He didn't let go.

"We're rehearsing for the spring concert." Why did good memories blur while terrible ones stayed in sharp focus? Bringing that day to mind caused the emotions to snap back into place. "It's my junior year. Everyone's in the auditorium. The band, the orchestra, choir, pop group. A hundred people at least."

Her friends and Mr. Pitman, the band director, were there. Singers were setting up mics on the stage, warming up their voices. People were talking, tuning instruments, clowning around. Carla was sitting in the front row between Julie and Gordon, and they were giving this other kid good-natured shit about messing up his solo.

"Over the racket, I hear my mom's voice. 'Cargo!' she's yelling from the back of the auditorium. 'Where's my baby girl?'"

Carla could still hear the snickers, see people swiveling for a look at the small woman standing in the doorway. Carla didn't need to look. She slid down in her seat, wishing she could disappear.

"Her speech is slurred. Drunk. I'm thinking, what the hell? My heart is pounding, and I'm wondering what my friends are thinking."

During the years Carla lived with her, her mom was sober—mostly. The times she fell off the wagon were their little secret. Alcohol became her weakness, and as far as Carla knew, her heroin addiction was in the past. Handled. The social worker had cautioned her mom that she would lose custody if she ever used again. She talked about it a lot in those days. How she had to stay clean because of Carla, because she wanted her daughter in her life.

But there was something in her voice that day that Carla didn't recognize. The pitch was off when she called her name again, closer this time. Carla heard her mother's shoes clacking down the center aisle. And then her mom fell. Mr. Pitman rushed forward and helped her up. She was swearing and laughing, lurching awkwardly on one bare foot and one bright yellow stiletto. Mr. Pitman guided her to a seat and retrieved her missing shoe.

"The doors at the back of the auditorium open again and suddenly the police are there." Carla gripped Nathan's hands, her knuckles white. "They handcuff her, my mother, right there in my high school auditorium, in front of all the people I care about—people who knew nothing about my past, nothing about the years in foster care, nothing about my mom's addictions."

Nathan inhaled sharply.

"They lead her out, she's still screaming my name, and I think the worst is over." Gizmo approached cautiously and rested his chin on Carla's knee. "One officer stays behind. She speaks to Mr. Pitman, and he points me out. She crouches in front of me. 'We're going to take good care of your mom,' she says. 'She'll be charged with possession and distribution of heroin. But don't worry. We're going to take care of you too.' She keeps saying she's gonna take me to a safe place, but I tell her I'm safe where I am. I tell her I need to stay for band practice, that the concert is in less than a week, but she isn't listening."

The officer took Carla's arms and got her to her feet. Carla dug in and wouldn't take a step. The officer pulled, and Carla resisted, twisting her face to keep from crying. She was strong, but the cop was stronger. Mr. Pitman backed up slowly. Julie sobbed. Gordon looked like someone had slapped him.

"I look around. Everyone is staring, mouths hanging open. No one says a word except me and the officer. I'm shouting. Growling like a wild animal. She's telling me it'll be okay." Carla stopped talking and dragged her sleeve over her eyes. "No one can do anything to help me. I'm on my own." She heard the raw tenderness in her own voice, the pain of telling this truth.

The tears came again, but from a deeper place this time, a cave buried and hidden away. Nathan's steady gaze, his complete attention, gave Carla the sense that he could see inside her to the marrow of her bones.

"That's so unfair," he said quietly. "What happened after that?"

The memory was crystal clear. Carla had stopped struggling. The auditorium was quiet except for the sound of the officer's boots on the concrete floor as she led Carla up the aisle toward the exit. Her classmates sat mute, feeling the way anyone would after a spectacle like that—shocked, but also secretly thrilled that they had witnessed something so horrific.

Carla shrugged. "I left with the officer. I was powerless."

And just like that, seventeen years old, she was back in foster care. They took her to a group home with other teens, all of them too close to aging out of the system to bother placing in a family. No friends. New school. She never got to perform in that concert.

Carla sniffed and blotted her nose on her shirt sleeve. "The only person who didn't write me off was my boyfriend, Gordon."

He was the only constant that spring and the next school year, their senior year, driving across town most weekends to see her. She turned eighteen a few weeks after graduation and was no longer a ward of the state. She had nowhere to go until Gordon's parents agreed to let her live in their house. Carla and Gordon formed the Gutter Rats with their friends Sully and Leon and practiced in the basement all summer.

Then they drove out to Seattle. She swallowed hard, remembering how excited she was, how full of hope.

"But he took off a couple of years later, and I ended up here."

Nathan wrapped his arms around her and held her, murmuring, "Oh, Carla. Carla."

Shivering, limp, like she had been pulled from icy water, she slumped into him, inhaling the faint scent of his clothing, his skin, his breath. The heat of his body seeped into hers. Safe. Rescued. Nathan kissed her forehead, pressing his warm lips there for a long time.

Chapter 29

Monday, November 17, 1997

Half-awake in bed that morning, Carla had drifted away from her familiar self like a bit of fluff, loose and light. Telling Nathan about the moment everything changed—losing her mother, her friends, her home, and her safety all at once—had left her hollowed out.

Now her heavy boots—clean and sporting new laces—anchored her to the polished marble floor of City Hall. Or maybe determination was what grounded her. Her hands with their pale unpolished nails gripped her notes. Libby's skirt was too long and brushed the tops of her boots as she followed Mayor Philips down a long hallway a few minutes before the meeting at four. The pep talk from E that afternoon had quieted her jittering nerves. Mostly.

At a pair of double doors, the mayor stopped. Muffled voices hummed on the other side. This wasn't the conference room. Carla's heart hammered under her ribcage. At E's the night before, with Gizmo snoring nearby, Carla visualized this meeting. She'd conjured an image of a handful of dudes in suits sitting around that table where she sat with Lyle and the mayor last Friday. Manageable. Terrifying, but manageable. This was a different room. Her upper lip prickled with sweat.

"Are you familiar with how this works?" the mayor asked, reaching for the door handles. She shook her head. Words refused to form in her mouth.

"The council is seated and ready for you. We'll do a bit of housekeeping first, calling the meeting to order and such. You can have the floor for as long as you need. Ready?"

She shook her head again and took a step back.

"Butterflies, that's all." His smile was warm. "I can see how much these whales mean to you. It shows in all you've done to prepare."

No lie, this was the hardest she had ever worked for free. She was grateful to the mayor for making it easier and speeding up the process. It would have taken days or weeks to mess with all the red tape and paperwork that he waived.

She took a shaky breath, and Mayor Philips pulled the doors open. The room was huge and full of people with chairs in rows on either side of a center aisle like a wedding. Or a...funeral. *My funeral.* Carla swallowed.

A podium stood in the middle of the aisle. Beyond it half a dozen people sat behind microphones at a long table. The council members. Voices swirled, making Carla dizzy. Her knees turned to rubber as she stepped into the room. A guy turned in his seat. Noah? What the fuck was he doing there? He touched the brim of his cap in greeting.

The man next to him also looked back. "Attagirl, Carla," Delbert called with a wink. "Give 'em hell."

More people turned. Carla froze and her gaze flicked from face to face. Libby. Mr. Wilson. Sylvia. Wallace. Stewart leaning against the back wall.

"Here, I saved a seat for you up front." Nathan touched her elbow and guided her forward. She dropped the folder she'd been carrying, and the papers slipped out all over the floor.

"Great news," Nathan said, gathering the papers. "Boss gave us the go-ahead to use boats and pipes."

Carla nodded, but his words barely registered. She slid into the vacant seat next to Libby.

"Why are all these people here?" Carla whispered.

"It's a public meeting. They always are. But I bet they don't usually draw such a big crowd," Libby said. She gave Carla a huge grin. "I'm so proud of you, honey. You look cute, by the way. Kind of a gypsy-goes-to-Washington vibe. Oh, this here is Kevin, my better half." She patted the knee of a stout man seated next to her.

"But..." Carla swiveled to look behind her over her left shoulder and then her right. "What the fuck is going on?"

"I spread the word around the Coffee Spot about what you're doing, that's all. We're your cheering section, you might say. I thought you'd feel less nervous with some friendly faces in the room. Even your nice neighbor Wally's here." Libby gave him a wave. "He came in and bought a dozen muffins yesterday. Mine aren't half as good as yours, but I'm improving!"

Carla could hardly breathe. Her fears about failing and looking like a fool in front of a handful of officials exploded. She was going to fail and look like a fool in front of people she knew, people she cared about. Libby meant well, she'd but made things worse. Carla's knees bounced, causing the silky fabric of the skirt to move in little ripples. She tried to swallow but her tongue had adhered itself to the roof of her mouth. In her lap, her hands twisted into pretzels.

Nathan sat beside her and held out the folder. She pushed it back. "You do it. You won't get fired now, right?"

"My job is safe, yes. But it's your speech."

"I can't."

Nathan laid the folder on her lap. "This is your big moment, everything you worked so hard for."

"But...what if—"

Nathan took her clammy hands into his warm ones and held them tight. "I believe in you."

An amplified voice made Carla jump.

"I call the Monday, November 17, 1997, Bremerton City Council special meeting to order," said the mayor into a mic at the center of the long table. Voices quieted. "There's only one item on the agenda for this meeting, called solely for this purpose, as the issue is a time-sensitive matter." He cleared his throat. "Ms. Carla Peterson, welcome. You have our undivided attention." He smiled and gestured toward the podium.

Nathan released her hands. The blood drained from her head as she stood and walked to the podium. Council members were seated in a row like judges or a jury in front of her. Except for the mayor, no one smiled. Off to the side was a second table where Lyle Goronson and a man in a brown sheriff's uniform sat along with two men in polo shirts bearing the Washington Fish and Wildlife Department logo. Behind her was her community. Her friends.

She laid her folder on the podium and rested her fingertips on top, drawing strength from the smooth manila cardstock full of photocopies, as if office supplies could make her feel like she belonged in this world of powerful people. She removed her papers from the folder and squared the corners, buying time to gather her courage.

"Um. Hi. Hello." Her voice sounded small. Nathan hurried over and repositioned the microphone.

She slipped a stack of index cards out of her skirt pocket and began to read.

"On October twenty-first a pod of orcas lost their way and swam into Dyes Inlet. This pod is made up of three generations of four related families, nineteen whales in all." She moved the first card to the bottom of the stack. *Relax. Make eye contact.*

"Marine biologists," she continued reading, "have studied and tracked the members of this pod, called the L pod, along with two other pods in the Southern Resident population, the J- and K-pods. Each whale is given a number and a name. For over ten years, scientists from the Center for Whale Research have documented and recorded the births and deaths of these orcas, keeping track of their migration along the coast, from San Francisco to Juneau, Alaska. They watch for effects of pollution and global warning." *Shit. Duh.* "Warming."

Carla put her notes on the podium and held up the family tree she had drawn with Nathan's help. "This is a chart showing the names, ages, and family relationships of the nineteen whales, who at this moment are in danger of dying on our watch."

There were murmurs as Nathan distributed copies to the council and the men at the side table.

"As you can see," Carla went on, reading from the next card, slightly less terrified, "the oldest whale is number L-21. Her name is Ankh. She's fifty-seven years old. The youngest, L-96, is only one year old. He doesn't have a name yet. I suggested Johhny Rotten—" a smattering of laughter. "Some Sex Pistols fans here, I see." She smiled over her shoulder at the audience behind her. "But it's probably going to be Bernardo." More chuckles.

"These beautiful animals," she continued, "have been here twenty-eight days, which is twenty-seven days longer than anyone thought they'd stay. For almost a month, people have flocked here from all over Washington, all over the United States, all over the world. They came to witness something that might never happen again. From the shore and from boats, we watched them dive and breach, photographed them, filmed them, and marveled at their size and speed." She smiled inwardly. Nathan wrote that part. "This community has profited from the visitors who filled hotel rooms and restaurants and bought mugs and T-shirts to commemorate their time here. But now the whales are under stress, and they're running out of food." She paused for effect and then punched the last sentence. "They are running out of time, and they need our help."

Nathan appeared at her side with a cup of water. She took a long drink, draining it.

"What can we do?" came a woman's voice from the back of the room.

A man with a beard seated next to the mayor spoke into his mic. "There will be an opportunity for questions after the presentation, ma'am. Please continue, Ms. Peterson."

"I have a plan that might—that *must*—work." Carla placed her palms flat on the podium and leaned toward the microphone. "That's why I'm here."

Nathan handed out copies of a map showing an enlargement of the area around Dyes Inlet. Carla put her note cards back in her pocket and laid out her plan, step by step. When she was finished, Beard said, "Thank you, Ms. Peterson. Before the vote, does any member of the public wish to comment?"

Carla took her seat. Her armpits were soaked. Nathan beamed and Libby whispered, "Way to go, hon."

"What if there's a fire or an accident? Lives could be lost if help can't get across the bridge," said an old man sitting off to Carla's right.

"Not to worry," the sheriff said. "Even while the barricades are up, there will be room for emergency vehicles to pass."

"You said herding is dangerous. Who's gonna keep boaters safe while the volunteers try to drive the whales out?" someone asked from the back.

One of the Fish and Wildlife guys assured him they would have official boats in the inlet to keep an eye on things.

A man stood and crossed big hairy arms over his chest. "I work at the shipyard. How am I supposed to get to work if the bridge is shut down?"

The sheriff adjusted his mic. "Detour signs would be posted and traffic directed south to the Manette. It might take a little longer, so we'd all have to practice patience. Both bridges will remain open until after morning rush hour."

"Couldn't you close the bridge at night or on the weekend? Save a lot of headaches for people trying to get to work," Hairy said.

Nathan approached the podium, introduced himself, and explained that while orcas actively forage, travel, and socialize at any time of day or night, midmorning would be the best time to stop traffic. "That way, we'll be able to see if the plan is having the desired effect, and we'll have plenty of daylight hours. As far as waiting until the weekend," he shook his head, "I'm afraid that would be too late."

A woman joined Nathan, and he introduced her as Sarah Curtis, UW Professor of Wildlife Conservation in the School of Marine Biology. The two experts fielded dozens of questions from the audience and members of the council. Once everyone had been heard, the room grew quiet.

"So the day of," Nathan said, "I'll be on the water to direct my volunteers with the oikomi pipes, and Carla will assist me with the recording equipment. Sheriff, can you have someone stand watch on the bridge?"

He nodded and said, "We can outfit you with radios so you can keep us in the loop. I'll have men posted at the barricades in black-and-whites, lights on, and a couple in the middle of the bridge to watch from above."

At the end of the meeting, the council members voted. Unanimous in favor.

The mayor addressed the group. "Thank you, everyone. And special thanks to Ms. Peterson for bringing the urgent plight of the whales to our attention and for pulling this mission together. By this time on Wednesday, I hope we'll be celebrating and patting Carla here on the back for her perseverance and her passion." Applause. Delbert let out a whoop, and Carla's cheeks warmed.

"Tomorrow morning signs will go up along Warren from 11th Street to the bridge," Mayor Philips said, tapping the map on the table in front of him, "and on the other side from Sheridan to the bridge, warning motorists of the impending closure on Wednesday."

The sheriff folded his arms on the table. "You want the barricades up by when? Ten a.m.?" The mayor gave a thumbs-up, and the sheriff scribbled something on the paper in front of him.

The mayor scanned the audience. "We have members of the press here today, reporters from the *Sun,* the *North Kitsap Herald,* and KOMO-TV, so the community will be aware of the situation in advance of the closure. I'm sure they'll want to ask you a few questions, Carla, so stick around if you can."

Carla's head was floating. It was happening! They heard her. Saw her. Believed in her. She couldn't wait to tell E, the only friend who wasn't in the room to see it for herself. She stood, and Nathan pulled her into a hug, his eyes brimming.

Chapter 30

Carla waited at the boat ramp. A chorus of Pacific tree frogs accompanied the hushed rhythmic sound of ripples lapping the shore. She pulled the hood of her plastic poncho snug around her face and peered across the inlet. Lights from a passing car on the opposite shore flickered through the trees and the steady rain. The smell of rotting seaweed told her the tide was out. Not the best news for the orcas.

She glanced over her shoulder at the lighted window of the Coffee Spot. Libby waved and held something up over her head.

Seeing the whole coffee shop crew at the meeting Monday afternoon had surprised and terrified Carla. Surprised that they all cared enough to show up and terrified at the prospect of so many people witnessing what she'd been sure would be a cluster fuck. And it had been Libby, with her won't-take-no-for-an-answer attitude, who got everyone on board. They were all there. They all came. For her.

The sound of quick footsteps made Carla turn. Libby approached, a bright pink umbrella bobbing over her head.

"Hey, girl," Libby said. "This is it!"

"Yup." It was now or never.

"Those whales are lucky to have you in their corner. Here." Libby handed her a paper bag and a thermos. "Blueberry muffins. I'm following in your footsteps as much as possible, but we all miss you, hon. Not just your *phenomenal* baking," she said, doing a fair imitation of Mr. Wilson, "but mostly you. I miss you."

"Thanks." Carla tucked the bag under her poncho to keep it dry. "I miss you too."

Libby stood next to her with the umbrella over both their heads, and together they watched for Nathan's boat.

Libby nudged Carla's ribs and said, "I saw you and Nathan outside City Hall last night. That was some kiss. Hot stuff!" She fanned her face and laughed. "I thought you said he had a girlfriend."

"Not anymore." Carla couldn't hide her smile.

After the meeting, Nathan waited while she answered reporters' questions. They photographed her alone and in a group shot with Nathan, Professor Curtis, and the mayor. To celebrate her success, Nathan treated her to pizza and ice cream at the Silverdale Mall food court. The two strolled through the shopping center holding hands like teenagers. He didn't seem sad at all when he told her about his breakup. "We weren't right for each other," he'd said.

Lights appeared around Windy Point, and the faint sound of a motor rolled over the water. Nathan. Something flapped its tiny wings deep in Carla's belly. Not far behind him were other boats, the volunteers, following in a line like baby ducks. They broke off and formed a wide semicircle near the center of the inlet, ready to close ranks and herd the whales toward the channel.

A few minutes later, Carla was settled in the stern, hugging the still-warm bag of muffins, as Nathan drove slowly toward the Narrows. Libby's pink umbrella bobbed back toward the coffee shop, and Carla felt a tug of emotion. Part of her wished she was in the kitchen, radio blasting, cutting biscuits and shooting the shit with Delbert. A small part.

They passed the second group of volunteers who waited where the inlet met the Narrows, armed with long metal pipes and hammers, their bright anchor lights shining over the water in all directions. Except for an occasional fin, the whales kept out of sight. Nathan killed the motor in the channel, midway between the mouth of the inlet and the Warren Avenue Bridge, taking a position where they could see both.

Carla raised the thermos of coffee, offering it to Nathan. He shook his head. Judging by the clenched muscles in his jaw, he was nervous too. Carla's insides lurched and swam. She didn't feel like eating or drinking either.

Nathan communicated with his team on the water and the officers on the bridge while Carla took charge of the hydrophone. She tried to hear any change in the whales' clicks and squeaks over the faint metallic ringing of hammers banging on oikomi pipes in the inlet. The first group of volunteers was slowly closing in.

The barricades wouldn't be in place until ten o'clock, so traffic continued to cross the bridge overhead. Heading to the shipyard or the ferry dock, the morning commuters were unaware of the tension building below among the volunteers.

Boat traffic was light. Carla was grateful for the rain that was keeping most whale watchers off the water. The *Emerald Star*, a tour boat from Port Orchard, came slowly up the Narrows. No passengers were outside on the deck, but a few faces peered through the rain-spattered windows, hoping for a look at what they had paid to see: the orcas. It passed and chugged out into Dyes Inlet. Its gentle wake dissipated, and all was quiet again.

Then one whale appeared, swimming back and forth across the mouth of the channel. Carla tried to get a good look at the fin through the curtain of rain. The fin was tall and straight, so it was a male. The tip didn't hook to the right, so it wasn't Faith. It was either Cetus,

Hugo, or Raina. After a few minutes, a second whale joined the first. A young female. Moonlight.

Carla checked her watch. Past ten. From their position in the Narrows, the old Manette Bridge was too far away to see well. It would be jammed now that traffic on the Warren Avenue Bridge had slowed to a trickle. Two men in billowing black rain capes stood against the railing in the center of the bridge. Police officers. One gave a wave, and Carla waved back.

She turned her attention to the sounds coming through the headset from the hydrophone. The ringing from the pipes was so loud now she had to concentrate to hear the orcas. They sang in full voice. Were they scared?

Nathan stood, binoculars pressed to his eyes. "Here they come!"

A group of fins cut the water, creating white ruffles of foam as the whales sped down the waterway in their direction. Behind them, the volunteers moved in to form a line of boats stretching across the channel, cutting off the whales' route back to the inlet. The ringing of their pipes was deafening as they continued forward, closing the gap between their boats and Nathan's. Carla pulled off the headphones and stood too.

Several whales split from the rest, racing ahead of the others toward the bridge. Carla squinted to make out the markings. "Ankh's out front." The rest of the whales followed behind her. They were so close as they passed that spray from their sleek bodies hit her face. The group continued moving toward the bridge, but their fins slipped below the surface.

A moment later, Nathan shouted, "Dammit! They're coming back!" He handed the binoculars off to Carla. "I'm going to try to block them."

One hundred thousand pounds of frightened predator barreled toward them. Nathan steered his boat back and forth across the Narrows as fast as it would go, zigzagging from one side to the other. Carla's heart thundered in her chest.

But it was useless. They swam past, heading straight for the little boats blocking the way out. If the whales surfaced among them, they could be tossed or crushed. There was nothing Carla could do, and she couldn't look away.

Then the whales disappeared one by one as they slipped below the surface.

Nathan cut the engine. It was eerily quiet. No boat motors, no ringing pipes, no traffic noises from the bridge. Even the crows paused, perched in the evergreens that rose on both sides of the channel like church spires. Besides the muffled static from the walkie-talkie, the only sound was rain smacking Carla's plastic poncho.

A long moment later the whales emerged in the inlet beyond the boats. Crisis avoided.

Relief passed over Nathan's face followed by despair. The volunteers were unharmed, but the whales had missed their chance to free themselves.

Carla squeezed her eyes shut. Would a silent prayer to Saint Jude help? This was a lost cause on a huge scale. But no one was out there to hear it. No lucky charm or wish or incantation could guide the orcas out. She'd done everything she could do. It was up to the whales now.

"Look!" Nathan shouted.

The whales were coming into the Narrows again. The flotilla of volunteers closed the mouth of the waterway for a second time, and the sound of fierce, incessant banging on pipes carried over the water and vibrated through every bone in Carla's body.

This time, instead of gliding silently toward Nathan's boat, the whales formed a tight circle nearby, splashing in a flurry of pec-slapping. Carla reached over the side of the boat and joined in, slapping her hands on the surface of the water. Nathan grabbed his empty camera case and slapped it on the water too.

"I think they're paying attention to us!" Nathan shouted, his face pulling into a grin. "I wish I knew what message we're sending."

The whales came nearer, swimming slowly in a tight group. This time Ankh and the other females fell back, and Faith took the lead. They passed Nathan's boat. Keeping a few hundred feet behind the pod, Nathan followed the whales ever closer to the bridge.

Faith arched out of the water into a deep dive, his gleaming tail sweeping in an arc, beads of sparkling water flying. He was out of sight. And then it happened. He launched himself into the air on the far side of the bridge and came down with a mighty splash.

Carla's heart nearly burst. On the bridge above their heads, policemen pumped their fists in the air. Nathan threw an arm over her shoulders and pulled her close. Together they watched a second whale imitate Faith, diving deep into the water under the bridge and popping up like a cork on the other side. One after the other, the orcas passed Nathan's boat on their way to freedom.

The radio in Nathan's hand crackled to life, and an officer's voice declared, "Mission accomplished."

Nathan started his motor, and they made their way slowly under the bridge, unwilling to stay back and watch this triumph from a distance. Carla counted the whales as they regrouped and moved toward the Manette Bridge and the open water beyond.

"Sixteen. Or could be seventeen," Carla called. The whales churned the water in the channel into a froth with their wild dance. Pec slapping and breaching, they were a happy tangle of fins and tails.

She began her count again, and Canuck lifted her massive head out of the water, gazing back toward the bridge and the inlet she had just left.

"What's she looking at?" Carla raised the binoculars. She scanned the surface of the water on the wrong side of the bridge. At first there was nothing, but then a single fin emerged. "It's Ophelia! What's she doing? Why won't she join the others?"

Carla's question was answered when the small face of Ophelia's two-year-old daughter Nerka poked upward near her mother. The little one opened and closed her mouth before submerging again.

"Something's wrong!" Nathan shouted. "Why are they hanging back? The pod's already heading for the Manette. They're going to be left behind!"

Carla turned. It was true. The pod was making a beeline for the second bridge. *Wait!* she wanted to yell. But before she could open her mouth something stopped her.

"What the hell! Here comes Canuck!" she yelled. "She's coming back."

Then another whale broke away from the group and followed Canuck. *Shit.* This couldn't be happening. They were turning back. Nathan and Carla exchanged glances, unable to speak. The pair of whales passed their boat and approached the Warren Avenue Bridge again, heading for Dyes Inlet. Carla recognized the second whale. It was Cetus, Nerka's older brother.

The other whales continued toward open water, the dorsal fins getting smaller as they swam away. Carla should be happy that fifteen whales would soon be free, but the thought of the ones left behind made her heart ache. Mother and daughter were near the bridge but on the wrong side, while on the right side, Canuck and Cetus swam in tight circles near Nathan's boat.

Cetus breached as if trying to urge his mother and sister on. His body hit the water alongside their boat. Water poured in over the side, soaking Carla's feet with icy water. A moment later, all four whales disappeared, diving deep into the channel.

Carla threw her hood back to have an unobstructed view, barely aware of the soaking rain, and stared at the place where the whales had gone under. They waited, the people on the bridge above waited, and the whole world seemed to hold its breath. Which side of the bridge would they choose?

A quick glance back toward the Manette Bridge in the distance. Not a fin in sight. The L pod was gone, swimming back to the Sound. Carla's heart dropped. This was not the ending she'd hoped for.

Above them on the bridge, there was a sudden commotion as the police officers and handful of onlookers who had braved the weather waved and pointed, their voices faint but full of joy. They had seen something from high on the bridge that Carla could not. Her head whipped from left to right, searching for a fin or a splash anywhere. What was happening? And where?

"Look!" Nathan yelled. He pulled her shoulders around. A tremendous cheer burst from her own throat when she saw what he and the people on the bridge were pointing to. Four dorsal fins emerged in the distance and sliced through the water beneath the Manette bridge to catch up with the others and begin their long journey back to Puget Sound.

Chapter 31

Thursday, December 18, 1997

One Month Later

Carla stood in the doorway of the tiny, windowless office. She flipped the light switch, and a single fluorescent tube hummed to life overhead. Bathed in the cool glow was a desk, half of which was bare, showing plenty of nicks and scratches. The other half was cluttered with papers and office supplies. In the middle of the mess were a plastic pot containing a dead African violet and a stained mug. Someone else's stuff had been shoved aside to make room for the new girl. The new girl was Carla.

She sat in the chair behind the desk and smoothed her skirt over her knees. She swiveled this way and that, pushing with the toes of her new high-tops—*real* Chucks this time!—and grinning like a kid. Seldom-used muscles ached from smiling so long and so hard. She still could hardly believe this was where she'd be working now. The Whale Museum. Education Director. Fancy title and everything.

"Hey." A voice startled her. Nathan stepped in carrying a folder and a wrapped gift. "First day jitters?"

"It's been a long time since my *last* first day at a new job."

Nathan put the gift on the corner of her desk. Carla was eager to open it, but he presented her with the folder.

"This will give you an overview of everything here," he said, pulling a chair next to hers. She inhaled his clean scent—soap and toothpaste. Lifebuoy and Colgate. His ponytail curled tenderly against the nape of his neck, and she fought the urge to touch it. The new job wasn't the only big change in Carla's life. The day the whales left marked the beginning of a promising fresh start for Carla.

On the front of the slick folder, overlayed with the words *Whale Museum,* was a photograph of an orca and her calf. It reminded Carla of Ophelia and Nerka on the day she and Nathan escorted the whales out.

"That was something else, wasn't it? How everything worked out?" Carla said and rested her fingertip on the image of the little whale, thinking of how she and Nathan followed the last four orcas through the Narrows to Sinclair Inlet where the rest of the orcas had gathered. "I still can't believe they all made it."

Carla and Nathan had counted them a second time and a third. All nineteen were accounted for. Seagulls hovered above while the whales rolled and splashed below. They were feeding, Nathan had said. A feeding frenzy. A sure sign the whales had been starving in Dyes Inlet.

"You amaze me, Carla. What you did? Nothing short of heroic. When they headed into Rich Passage..." Nathan shook his head. "I nearly cried."

Carla nudged her shoulder against his and laughed. "Nearly? You were bawling like a baby. And then when Faith hung back like that, I lost it too."

The last whale to leave, Faith lingered, performing for the watchers along the shore who braved the stormy weather to see them one more time. Nathan kept his boat at a distance, and he and Carla looked on, she through binoculars and he through his camera, both of their faces wet with rain and tears of joy, witnessing this final encore.

Faith pushed his huge head up, straight up, higher and higher, turning like a corkscrew. The shutter of Nathan's camera clicked and clicked as he captured this last spy-hop, and when Faith paused at the top of his spiral, Carla caught a glimpse of the giant creature's liquid eye. Her lips moved silently. *Goodbye.*

With the whales safely on their way to Puget Sound, she had prepared herself for another goodbye. Nathan would return to his research job on San Juan Island. Their brief infatuation wouldn't survive a long-distance relationship.

At the Tracyton boat launch that day, Nathan piled his equipment into the bed of his truck, winched the boat out of the water, and secured it to his trailer for the long trip back to Friday Harbor. Carla watched, swallowing hard to ease the pinched feeling in her throat. When he opened his arms, inviting a hug, Carla fell into them. The cold and the wet forgotten, they embraced for a long time.

Before he pulled out of town, Nathan wrote a name and phone number on the back of Carla's hand. The Whale Museum director.

In all her dreams of a better life away from the Coffee Spot, Carla couldn't have imagined this.

"New place okay?"

"Perfect," she said.

The rental she'd found was a short drive from the museum and from Nathan's office. Turned out everything was a short drive in the town of Friday Harbor. Even his house on the southern tip of the island was only fifteen minutes away. Her new place was a duplex, comfortably furnished. Poppy lived in the other half. The two women shared the fenced back yard. Poppy and her basset hound, Thunder, welcomed Gizmo as their new best pal. Until E was strong enough to leave the senior rehab center, Gizmo would live with Carla, who promised to visit at least once a month, making the four-hour trek with Gizmo to Silverdale in the red Volvo, now her own.

"This brochure tells about the exhibits and the hours of operation." Nathan slipped it out of the folder and set it on the desk in front of Carla. "And this one"—he placed a second brochure on top of the first—"has a bit of the museum's history." But you can read all that later. Today you'll want to spend some time getting familiar with student programs."

Carla took the typed pages he held out to her. "Thanks, but Janine already went over these with me." She set them aside and gave them a little pat.

"Great. In the summer when schools are closed, you'll be on the water with the Soundwatch team. Someone will train you, don't worry."

"I'm not worried. Relax." Under the desk, Carla gave his knee a little squeeze. "I've got this."

"Sorry for the overkill. I know you can handle everything," Nathan said.

Not that long ago her life was spinning out of control. Carla's conviction that she was powerless almost landed her on the street. True, there would always be things she couldn't control, like when—or if—her mother would pop up again. After telling Nathan about her mother being arrested in the auditorium, it didn't matter so much anymore. If her mom showed up again, she might give her cash or a place to stay, or she might not. Her mom no longer had the same power over her.

"Did Janine tell you about these?" Nathan stood and lifted down a black cardboard box, one of about a dozen on the bookshelf behind her desk, each labeled with a range of dates. The box he held was the most recent one. *July 1997 to...* blank.

"Not yet. She said they could wait until I got my bearings. What are they?"

"Part of the museum's archive." He lifted the lid. "Here's where you'll keep any important documents related to the education programs." Inside were photographs, newspaper clippings, and a thank-you card in a child's handwriting, all of them mounted neatly in protective plastic sleeves.

Nathan pulled out a photo of a colorful mural painted by kids on the wall of a school hallway. All kinds of ocean life with an orca center stage. He tapped a white sticker near the bottom edge. "Each item will need a label like this one. The date and where it came from along with a catalog number."

Carla picked up a newspaper clipping, mounted like the rest. It was taken from the *Sun*, dated October 22, 1997. She touched the headline: WHALE OF A SIGHT. She had pinned this article to the bulletin board in the coffee shop the day after the orcas arrived.

"Since winter vacation for the schools starts next week, there won't be any tours until the new year. How would you feel about working on the archive stuff today?"

That was the best news Carla had heard all morning. "Works for me."

He plopped a stack of recent newspapers on the desk. Carla let out a long, happy sigh.

"You can begin by clipping stories related to the L pod's visit last month." He leaned closer and said proudly, "There's a couple about you in there."

Reporters from the *Sun*, the *North Kitsap Herald*, and the *Seattle Post-Intelligencer* had interviewed Carla. When the stories and photos of her at the council meeting appeared in print, Carla had seen herself as others had that day. The difference was more than the borrowed clothes, the subtle makeup, and pared-down jewelry. Confidence radiated from her smile, her posture, the angle of her chin, and the fire in her eyes. The woman in those photos believed in herself and in what she was doing.

"I almost forgot." He reached for the gift.

Carla tore away the colorful paper to reveal a simple black frame holding a photo taken at the Coffee Spot. Delbert, Noah, Stewart, Sylvia, Mr. Wilson, and Libby all posed for the camera. In the center Carla and E sat side by side, both beaming, with Gizmo between them. A paper *Congratulations* banner hung over the lunch counter, and on the table in the foreground was a cake. All Libby's doing, of course. She threw the party to celebrate Carla's success and decorated the cake with waves of blue frosting. Eighteen tiny plastic orcas swam around the edge and in the middle was one big one beneath the words: Never Lose Faith.

She set the little frame on her desk. "It's...oh—" She couldn't finish.

Her success with the whales, her new job, having a place to live and money in her bank account. Wishing didn't make any of it happen. Neither did praying to Saint Jude or Saint Anthony or rubbing her worry stone or crossing her fingers. Guidance didn't come from tarot cards or her horoscope. Those things could never show her what she needed to see—that she mattered, that she could change her small corner of the world. *She* made it happen. She, Carla Peterson, with the help and encouragement of her friends and her community, made it happen.

Nathan looked at his watch. "Gotta run. I have a meeting in a bit, but I'll pick you up at five." He glanced at the door to be sure no one was close enough to see, then kissed her tenderly. He brushed her cheek with his warm fingers and tucked a bit of hair behind her ear, gently freeing the strands from a dangling silver skull earring. "We can get takeout."

When he was gone, Carla dug through the pile of newspapers until she found what she was looking for. The *Sun* from November 20, the day after the whales left. Pride in the part she played in freeing them was tempered by the knowledge that they might have left eventually without any help. She could live with not knowing.

The headline read: WHALES TURN TAIL. She smiled and read the first sentence of the article: *Shattering all fears for their well-being, 19 killer whales chose a stormy day to say goodbye to Dyes Inlet and head for the open waters of Puget Sound.* This was one for the archives. Carla found a pair of scissors in the desk drawer.

Kathleen from the gift shop popped her head in. "Sorry about the mess. I'll help you clear out this stuff later. We're glad you're here. This is for you." She set an African violet on the desk. Her eyes darted to the dead plant nearly buried in the clutter, and she laughed. "I'm not very original in my choice of welcome gifts."

"Thanks," Carla said, admiring the velvety leaves and ruffled purple petals. "It's beautiful." She would take it home and put it near a window. She could buy a snake plant or a spider plant for her office, something that didn't need much light.

"Got everything you need?" Kathleen asked.

Carla looked around the room, taking it all in. "It's a lot. I'm not sure where to start."

"I always start with coffee." Kathleen held out a steaming mug.

"Thanks." Carla took it and smiled at the spouting orca on one side of the cup under the words *Mornings blow.* She picked up her scissors and got to work.

Author's Note

A movie that begins with the phrase "based on a true story" always gets my attention. As I watch, I wonder what parts are true, what was omitted, and how much was invented. *In the Company of Whales* is based on actual events. For readers curious about what really happened, here you go.

On October 21, 1997, a pod of nineteen orcas was spotted in Dyes Inlet, located near the Kitsap Peninsula of Washington State. None had been seen there for over forty years, and never more than a few at a time. To reach the inlet, they had come through Puget Sound and up the Port Washington Narrows, passing under two high bridges. The whales left together a month later. No one knows why they stayed so long, and no one knows why they left.

The local newspaper, *The Sun*, renamed *Kitsap Sun* in 2005, ran daily stories about the whales. Television news crews and reporters from the Seattle papers covered the story too. Word spread nationally. Over the thirty-day period, tens of thousands of people came to see the pod for themselves, overwhelming the town of Bremerton which at that time had a population of 37,000.

Letters to the editor revealed community members' opposing views about the whales' presence. The influx of visitors created heavy traffic resulting in some minor accidents but also increased business for hotels, restaurants, and gas stations. Tour companies packed their boats with whale watchers. Outdoor outfitters rented their full inventory of kayaks and canoes. Entrepreneurial residents sold cold drinks out of ice chests, charged fees to park on their property, and sold commemorative T-shirts Others complained about cars blocking their driveways, people urinating in their yards, and the disruption to their quiet way of life.

Among the visitors were scientists taking advantage of the unique opportunity to study orcas up close. One group of marine biologists arrived by boat from the Center for Whale Research (CWR) on San Juan Island, about fifty nautical miles away. For years, they had been tracking, photographing, and recording the larger group of whales called the Southern Residents that includes this pod.

Weeks passed and the scientists, who were on the water almost daily, began to see troubling signs. The orcas were likely running low on salmon, their preferred food, and were behaving in ways that indicated stress, possibly caused by heavy boat traffic. One Sunday in early November, an estimated 500 boats were in the inlet, more than four times the previous record.

Debates began to surface among the experts: Was an intervention needed or was it best to continue observing the whales, hoping they would resolve the situation on their own? Theories also emerged regarding the whales' observed reluctance to cross under the Warren Avenue Bridge, the four-lane highway that stretched across the Narrows connecting East Bremerton to Bremerton. Each time an orca approached the bridge, it turned back, rejoining the others in an inlet that couldn't support the pod's needs. Some believed the bridge created a psychological barrier caused by the vibrations from heavier than normal traffic.

On November 19, a cold and rainy day, one boat carrying several CWR researchers and a second with scientists from the National Marine Fisheries were near the Warren Avenue Bridge. They witnessed events unfold. Faith, a big male, and Ankh, the matriarch, dove under the water and surfaced on the other side of the bridge. The others followed except for two—Ophelia and her calf, Nerka. Canuck, an older female, seemed to wait for them as the rest of the pod continued toward open water. Then Cetus, Nerka's older brother, swam back. Together, the four remaining whales made a dive that lasted for two very long minutes. They finally surfaced a mile away near the Manette Bridge.

The biologists followed the pod, watching as one by one the orcas moved closer to Rich Passage leading to Puget Sound. The two researchers from the CWR recounted the most memorable moment—Faith emerging from the water and swimming slowly alongside their boat, only ten feet away. He then turned on his side and looked directly at them as he passed.

The rest of the novel was a product of my imagination. A pretty yellow house sits where I built the fictional Coffee Spot. There is no pier or dock there, only a concrete boat ramp. And, most importantly, the orcas left on their own. Quietly. With no human intervention.

Where are they now, those nineteen orcas? I am happy to report that as of this writing, twenty-eight years after the events described above, five are still alive. That's the good news. The bad news: the Southern Resident orcas are critically endangered. Several organizations are conducting ongoing research and working diligently to reverse this.

To learn more about the orcas of the Pacific Northwest, visit:

The Center for Whale Research https://www.whaleresearch.com/

Orca Lab https://orcalab.org/orcas/

Orca Conservancy https://www.orcaconservancy.org/

Acknowledgments

It's a myth that writers work alone. True, banging away at my keyboard or staring into space and muttering happens mostly in solitude, but this book would not be in your hands today without the assistance of many. The challenge is to remember everyone, and I'll undoubtedly leave someone out. Apologies if that's you.

I am grateful to my editor, Alison Imbriaco, for her thorough reading, careful attention to punctuation (oh, those darn dashes!), and for catching Carla in the act of preparing blueberry muffins on the wrong day. It's always maple-pecan on Thursdays, girl! Also, much appreciation to SusansArt@99D for designing a beautiful cover. Looking at it and knowing my story is inside makes me feel like I've won a prize.

A huge thank you to Xiao Chen for creating the whimsical map of my fictionalized version of the Kitsap Peninsula, complete with the web of waterways that a pod of whales meandered through to end up stuck in Dyes Inlet. She is also responsible for the Loon City Press logo. Much gratitude to Molly Clark for the brainstorming sessions about promoting and marketing my book.

Thank you to Marylee MacDonald, my mentor, friend, and wizard of all things related to writing and publishing. Twenty years ago, I joined a writing group in Tempe, Arizona with Marylee at the helm. There I exposed my first imperfect stories to the light of day. I learned as much from that group of gifted writers as I could have in any MFA program. Their feedback—meaningful and specific—was always delivered with love.

Two of the original members of that Tempe group have joined forces with me to form our own spin-off, a sisterhood of support. A million thanks to Bridget O'Gara and Polly Baughman, who write with me almost daily through the magic of video chat now that I live sixteen hundred miles away. Their humor, sound advice, and inexhaustible willingness to celebrate my successes and to prop me up when I fall flat on my face keep me sane. They have read and reread early versions of this novel and offered thoughtful comments that helped give shape to my story. Bridget, with your ear for language and meticulous editing skills, you could polish a lump of coal until it gleams like a diamond. And the hours you spent when my cover design deadline was looming! I am in your debt. Polly, your ability to see the big picture and distill my sprawling writing into golden nuggets when I need a pitch, a blurb, a synopsis, or to brainstorm ideas for a title is invaluable. And you give me so many reasons to laugh. My love for you both is fierce.

Before this novel was ready for the wider world, it was read by people in my writing community and beyond who offered honest opinions of my work. Marylee, Polly, Bridget, and Curt. Thank you all for being instructive and gentle. Also—and especially—boundless gratitude to my tireless beta readers, Donna Barten and Sharon Wishnow. I met these accomplished and generous friends through the Women's Fiction Writers Association, a diverse and inclusive community. Page by page and chapter by chapter, these two heroes checked for plot holes, inconsistencies in character, unrealistic dialogue, and implausible situations. But they also shined a light on what was good, giving me the courage to revise—and revise again. Working with you both made what I feared would be a tedious process into something truly magical.

A special thank you to my grandson, Lucas, who snuggled next to me as I revised a chapter on my laptop, and read some of it aloud to me in a voice that gave the scene on the page so much sweetness.

Writing a novel requires research to get the details right. Katie Walters, Kitsap County Commissioner, District 3, put me in touch with Anne Presson, Kitsap Board of County Commissioners, who answered my general questions about road closures. At Ms. Presson's suggestion, I spoke to Glenn Akramoff, Public Works Operations Manager for the City of Bremerton. It was Mr. Akramoff who patiently explained the steps a member of his community would need to take to stop traffic on a road or bridge. My heartfelt thanks to them all for taking time to help me in my quest for accuracy.

Living in Port Orchard, Washington in 1997 when the orcas made their unexpected visit to Dyes Inlet, I was in awe of their beauty and size, their playfulness, and their curiosity, but beyond that I knew very little about them. Most of what I learned about orcas over the course of writing this book came from the Center for Whale Research, the Orca Conservancy, and other groups devoted to protecting orcas through research and education. The newspaper archives of the *Kitsap Sun* and the *Seattle Post-Intelligencer* gave me a first-hand look at articles, photographs, and letters to the editor published during the whales' monthlong stay and beyond. I appreciate the work these organizations do and the passionate people who keep them running.

Besides not knowing enough about local government and orcas to write this book, I also lacked knowledge about other topics needed to round out the narrative. Thank you, Miki Taylor, for recommending some less well-known punk bands of the time. I have listened to more grunge, punk, ska, and alternative rock in the last couple of years than I ever have. Someday I might even answer a music trivia question correctly.

Thanks to Marshall Schlink for educating me about methods—both simple and high-tech—of tuning a guitar. Thanks also for sharing some warm-up exercises a bass player might use for practice. For details about working for the US Postal Service, I turned to my brother Jim, who delivered mail for thirty-six years. I am grateful for the work he did, slogging through all kinds of weather in St. Paul, Minnesota, and for tales of the daily life of a mail carrier.

I would be remiss if I failed to thank my parents, Irene and Romeyn, my first teachers. I miss them every day. Mom was a voracious reader, rarely without a library book or a New Yorker in her hand, and a prolific writer of short fiction, modeling for me the perseverance and dedication it takes to begin a writing career later in life. Dad, a self-proclaimed news junkie, subscribed to multiple newspapers and newsletters that he managed to keep up with while doing the work of a history professor and helping to raise five children. My parents taught me the importance of paying attention to the world around me and caring for the planet. They recycled, turned down the heat, and rode the bus before it was cool. They stood up for civil rights, women's rights, human rights, and for peace and justice. I think they would be proud of the book I have written and of the person I have become.

I owe deep gratitude to my family for their support and encouragement, not only in pursuing my dream of publishing but through all the ups and downs of life. Your love means the world to me. My siblings, Sally, Jim, Amy, and Dan, my children and their partners, Miki and Breida, Ben and Xiao, stepchildren, Kyle, Rob, and Caitlyn, and my tremendous extended family, including two of the youngest members, Lucas and Louisa, whose delight in books and reading warms my heart. Thanks, Alfie, for keeping my feet warm and for just being a dog.

Finally, and most importantly, I thank my husband, Curt McLelland, who provides endless love, tempting snacks delivered to my desk at regular intervals, and reminders to come up for air. Thank you for cheerfully taking on the mundane tasks of the household so my writing wouldn't be interrupted. Our love story is my favorite story of all.

About the Author

Born and raised in Minneapolis, Judy M. Taylor taught English in Arizona and Washington State before returning to her Minnesota roots where she now devotes herself to writing full time. Her teaching career offered opportunities to explore stories with hundreds of teenagers and to be inspired by their creativity. Her short fiction has appeared in literary journals and an anthology. For more information, visit judymtaylor.com.